# A SINGLE STEP

ISBN: 978-0-9813895-3-0

e-book ISBN: 978-0-9813895-4-7



Printed in the USA and the UK.

Cover design by Sam Oliver © 2011. www.samoliver.biz

Cover photo by Mary Pitchford © 2011



3rd Age World Publishing. Vancouver and London.

www.3rdageworld.com
2011

# A SINGLE STEP

BY

TERRY OLIVER

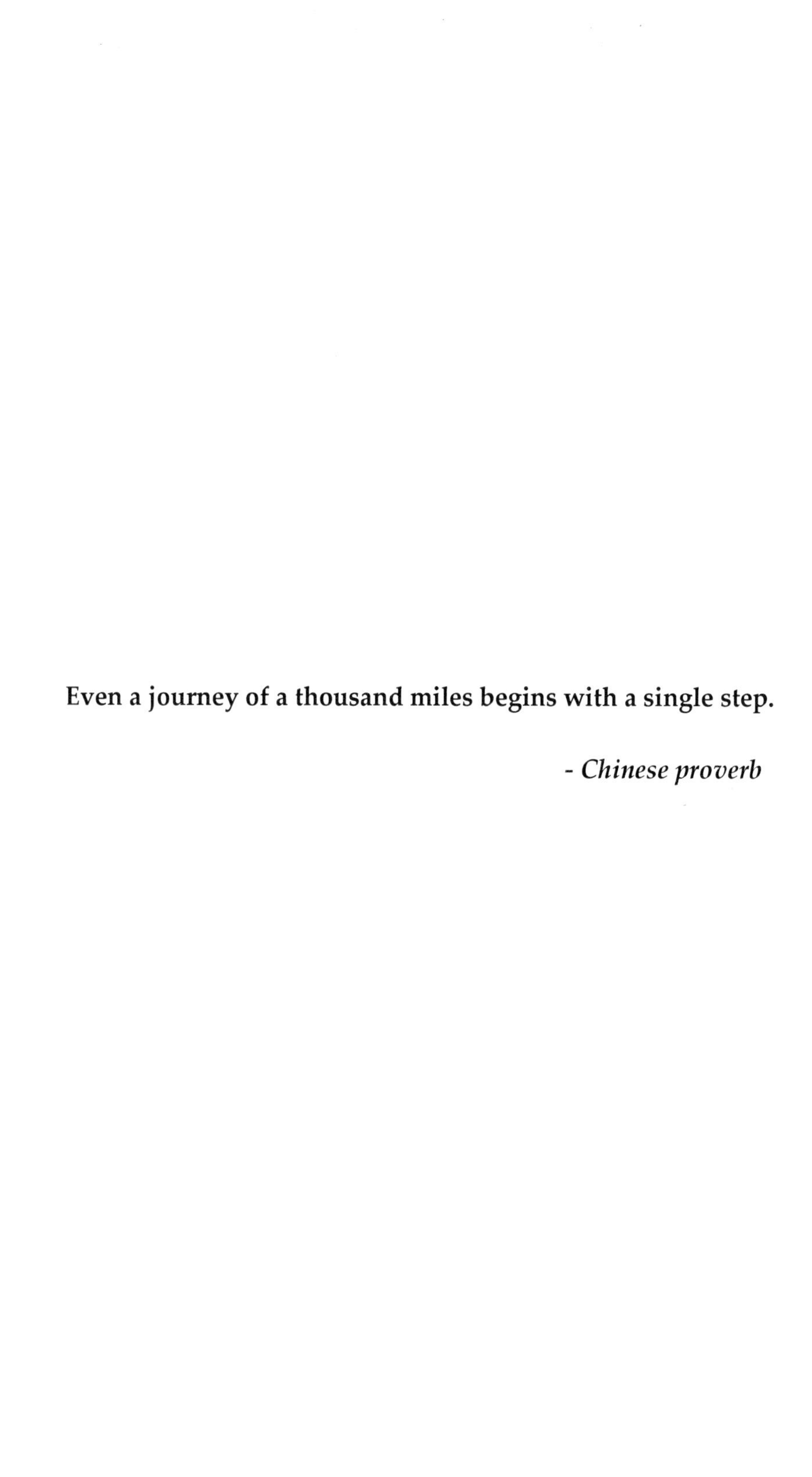

Even a journey of a thousand miles begins with a single step.

- *Chinese proverb*

# Dedication

*To the memory of my mother and father*

# CHAPTER 1

Barney Roper knew the rules. Keep your mouth shut. 'Smile and smile and be a villain.' Trust the 2nd law of thermodynamics – the inevitability of things to break down. In divorce, this was the only way forward, he believed.

He also believed that things happened in threes. So when he saw the flames from his canal boat he was not too surprised. Because in the space of a few hours, his on-going argument with his wife Alice, over her continued refusal to divorce, first led to him losing his temper and secondly to drinking too much in the Bridge Inn this evening – both things he vowed, at the age of 72, he would not do. And now this.

As he stood on the canal lock gates at King's Cross basin in central London, looking down towards his boat on the darkened towpath, he thought the flickering lights were coming from a neighbouring boat.

His mind, dulled by the unaccustomed drinks he'd had at the pub after the argument, took its time reacting. It was only as he got nearer that he realised the boat was his own, the *Iron Sea Horse* and that the flickering lights were flames. By the time he arrived at the side of his old steel-hulled canal boat, the fire was already spreading throughout its 40-foot length and the pine-panelled interior had ignited.

He clambered aboard the front deck and felt in the usual place for the magnetised door key under the metal seat locker – gone. He wasted precious minutes on his hands and knees fumbling in the dark for the missing key before his muddled brain abandoned the search and changed tack.

Water. The surface of the canal lay three feet below him and he hunted about on the front deck for a bucket. Nothing. He climbed back over the side to the canal bank and ran to the stern. He tried the rear hatch but knew it too would be locked. Through the brass porthole he peered inside, seeing only a wall of flame as the wood panelled interior fed the fire. The back deck was bare – no bucket, only a deck mop. He hopped off onto the towpath and stumbled towards the neighbouring narrowboat. If only Alf were aboard. He banged hard on the roof and shouted. A dim light flicked on.

"Alf – Alf! It's me, Barney – quick – my boat's on fire –"

Alf's bald head poked out through the front entrance of the old wooden butty boat to stare at the flames creeping out through the roof ventilators of the *Iron Sea Horse.*

"I can't find my bucket – where's yours?" shouted Barney.

The old man ducked back inside and reappeared at the rear of his boat holding a plastic pail on the end of a short rope. He handed it to Barney and they scooped water from the canal in turns to throw onto the roof of the steel-hulled narrowboat.

"This is no good, Barney. We need a hose to shove in the roof vent," puffed Alf.

"What if I smash a port-hole and pour it in that way?" said Barney, looking about for a rock or tree branch.

Alf shook his head. "Christ, no – that'll make it worse, just feeding in more air. Look, I'll grab my bike and ride down to the pub to call the fire department."

"Okay, but hurry – this is getting out of control," said Barney, flinging more water through the small roof ventilator. Alf re-emerged out of the darkness with an ancient pushbike and stopped beside Barney.

"I don't think this was kids – I've seen somebody goin' in and out here the last few days – thought it was a friend of yours. He had a key." He wobbled off down the canal towpath and Barney bailed more water from the canal – still thinking about smashing a window but frightened of causing a real inferno... He could see that his efforts were ineffectual and paused, gasping from his futile bailing with the heavy buckets of water. His mind raced from one idea to the next, still muddled from the unaccustomed drinking.

If he got up on the roof of the boat, he'd be able to pour water straight down the brass vent. He heaved a full bucket of water from the canal up onto the roof and hurried to the rear to climb up the folding stirrup steps on to the top of the narrowboat. His heart thumped from the exertion and he told himself to be careful. In the clutter of boathooks, flowerboxes and odd bits of loose timber, he could easily trip and end up in the canal – or worse, on the concrete towpath.

He reached the middle of the roof and watched the flames licking round the brass dome covering the vent. Without thinking, he started to unscrew the brass cover. With a yelp he snatched his hand away from the hot metal, the tips of his fingers scorched. He swore and plunged his hand into the bucket of water, then poured some of it on to the metal until it stopped sizzling even though flames still darted out around the brass dome. With his other hand, he felt the metal gingerly, then unscrewed it by spinning the dome off with quick flicks of his unburned left hand. The dome spun off and rolled down the roof into the canal. At the same time, a jet of flames spurted up into his face from the small opening. He grabbed the bucket and threw the remains of the water down the four-inch hole.

The rope was just long enough to reach the canal surface and he hauled the heavy bucket up onto the roof and poured it into the opening repeatedly. Sometimes the fire seemed to abate, only to flare up again and shoot out the vent even higher. His heart hammered against his chest wall and the arthritis in his hands made them ache from his exertions with the heavy water bucket. The steel roof began to heat up and he could feel it through the thin soles of his shoes.

With a last glance at the fire pouring out of all three brass roof vents now, he turned and fumbled his way back to the stern. Something Alf had said stuck in his mind and distracted his attention. As he reached the edge of the roof, his foot caught the sliding hatch cover and he pitched forward in the blackness onto the steel rear deck, four feet below.

# CHAPTER 2

Alice woke with a jolt, her eyes wide, staring up into the dark canopy of the four-poster bed. The faint flash of light was not enough to illuminate the bedroom and she lay watching it flick on and off, sometimes with a hint of blue. Was it the dream that had wakened her, with the same heavy feeling of dread she remembered from that night in the other four-poster in Rome? She tried to shut it out by closing her eyes and then heard again the faint knocking sound and sat upright in bed, listening hard. The pulsing light was definitely blue, then white. Police. She held her breath, waiting for the sound again.

Her first thought was Cassie – oh God, it's finally happened. The free-floating anxiety about the fate of her youngest child, away in Africa, that never left her but lurked in the crevices of her daytime mind and only came to the fore at night, flooded her consciousness. Don't let it be Cassie was all she could repeat to herself.

Beside her, the big four-poster lay empty. Heck had not returned yet – what time was it, anyway? She peered at the old alarm clock and made out the hands in the pulses of blue light – 3:29 am. He should have been home ages ago – maybe it's Heck, he's been caught again with those crazy anarchist students, spraying slogans on 4x4s. No, he promised her – swore that he would never go out with them again. It would be insane. It had already cost him his career as professor of archaeology at St Anne's College in East London. His attempt at helping student activists protest against huge gas-guzzling Hummers had backfired and landed him in court, just as Alice had warned. If he were caught a second time the magistrate wouldn't let him off with community service work. He'd surely go to jail.

The thought made Alice clutch compulsively at her chest, at her missing breast and she felt a choking sob rise in her. She made herself breathe deeply while she counted to five. The familiar framework of the Rome dream rose in her mind as clear as if it had happened yesterday. Heck's big bony fingers fondling her breasts – then stopping, probing, withdrawing. She gulped hard, swallowing the rising fear, her hand moving again to the reassuring shape of her other breast.

If only Netta were here. Why hadn't she agreed to let her stay when she offered to keep her company until Heck's night duty sentence at the Mile End hospital finished next week? But Alice had said no, she'd be fine. The recurring nightmares were diminishing and her daughter should concentrate on her own treatment. She and Philip still had several more sessions with the fertility clinic to complete. Had Alice been just a little selfish in refusing Netta's offer, knowing how churned up she felt to see her eldest daughter keep the hurt of her infertility bottled up inside?

The knocking became louder, insistent. Someone banging at the front door. Alice grabbed her dressing gown and switched on the upstairs hall light. As she descended the curving elm staircase, she could make out two shadows through the glass door panels and beyond them the flashing blue and white lights of a police cruiser. She opened the door on the safety chain.

"Mrs Roper – Mrs Barney Roper?" A plain-clothes policewoman held out her ID photo while the uniformed policeman stood beside her. Alice nodded.

"We're trying to locate your husband, Mrs Roper. Is he at home?"

"No, he left this afternoon. What's happened – is he in trouble?"

"We don't know for sure, Mrs Roper," said the policewoman. "I know it's late but we need to ask you some questions. May we come in for a minute?"

Alice unfastened the chain, opened the door and switched on a light. The two police officers followed her into the living room. She stood there waiting.

"Please sit down, Mrs Roper. Now, do you know where your husband went?" said the policewoman.

"Not exactly. He mentioned that he might go to his boat. It's at King's Cross canal basin."

"And did he say when he would be back?"

"No. We had an argument. He just took a bag and said he would sleep on the boat."

"Is the boat called the *Iron Horse*?"

"The *Iron Sea Horse* – yes. Has it been stolen or something? What is it?" asked Alice, perching on the arm of the sofa.

"There's been an accident, Mrs Roper – a fire. The firemen rescued a man from the canal boat and took him to St Pancras hospital. We don't know who he is. His clothing was too badly burned. No ID they could find."

"Oh my god – and you think it's Barney – my husband?"

"That's why we're here, Mrs Roper," said the policewoman. "We got his name and details from the Waterways Board computer system as the owner. And a man on a nearby canal boat said he spoke to him earlier at the fire."

Alice stood up. "And he's in the hospital now. Is he badly burned?"

The woman nodded, "I'm afraid he is, Mrs Roper. And he inhaled a lot of smoke. Can't speak, his lungs may be damaged. We don't know how long he was in the fire before they got him out."

"But you still don't know if it's Barney or not? Oh God, I wish Heck was here."

"Your son?"

"No, my partner. My husband and I are divorcing. That's what we were arguing about when he left. Can I see him – at the hospital?"

The policewoman nodded again. "Yes, we'd like you to come to St Pancras with us and try to make a positive identification, if you will."

Alice was already starting back up the curving elm staircase. "Just give me two minutes to get dressed –"

Detective Sergeant Esther Parry led Alice through the A&E department and up to the intensive care floor of St Pancras hospital.

"They brought him here because they have a Special Burns Unit, Mrs Roper," she said. She stopped before they approached the nursing island. "The doctors said to warn you that he has extensive burns and is heavily bandaged. You can't see his face. They wanted to know if he has any identifying body marks – tattoos, scars, birthmarks, earring. Anything."

Alice stared at the detective, her mind a blank. "He had a scar on the back of his hand. His left hand from when he was a boy."

The detective nodded and spoke with one of the intensive care nurses. The nurse shook her head and the detective turned and came back to Alice.

"His hands are completely bandaged she says. Was there anything else – anything at all, Mrs Roper?"

"Well, he had several moles on his back and chest," she said. "He's seventy two," she explained. "Can I see him, now?"

The detective glanced at the nurse, who raised her eyebrows but said nothing. "I'm not sure we can identify him, but…." She gave the nurse a nod and they all three entered the dimly lit room. Alice stared at the body in the bed, uncomprehending. The head and upper torso, both arms and hands were completely swathed in bandages. Only a slit for the eyes and nostrils was uncovered. The eyes were closed. Alice turned to the detective who motioned her closer to the bedside. She stepped cautiously nearer and peered at the closed eyes, the only thing visible, then turned a questioning look at the nurse and the policewoman. They conferred in whispers then beckoned Alice to them.

"The nurse said would you recognise his feet?" asked the detective in a low voice.

"His feet? I don't know. Why his feet?"

"He was wearing leather boots and they protected his feet. They're not burned, at least not badly."

Alice stared at the pile of bedding and bandages, trying to feel some sense of Barney from the heap of white cloth and shook her head. She turned away and the nurse opened the door as they all tiptoed out. Halfway to the dim-lit nursing island, Alice stopped.

"His birthmark. It's on the sole of his foot. A cherry birthmark, beneath his little toe."

"You sure?" said the policewoman. "Which foot – left or right?"

Alice shook her head. "I can't remember."

The intensive care nurse turned and led them back into the room. They stood at the end of the bed while the nurse carefully undid the sheets at the bottom end and lifted them up to expose first one foot and then the other, looking back at Alice.

For a minute, Alice stared unbelieving at the mahogany skin and pale yellow soles confronting her. She looked at the two other women and said in a puzzled voice, "My husband is not black."

# CHAPTER 3

The taxi pulled up in front of the old Georgian semi-detached in London's East End. Barney climbed stiffly out and let himself into the house by the side door. He went into the kitchen and opened the fridge to remove a loaf of bread and a package of Polish salami he had bought the previous morning from the corner shop. He looked at the old pendulum wall clock. 7am. Almost twenty-four hours since he had been standing in this same spot, putting the salami in the fridge.

He moved silently about the old-fashioned kitchen, making himself a sandwich and a pot of green tea, not wanting to wake Alice and Heck upstairs. He perched on a stool to eat, wondering how he would explain his reappearance to Alice after he had stalked off so dramatically yesterday. He still felt shaky from the accident on his boat last night and he hoped the green tea would calm his jittery stomach, unused to the amount he had drunk in the pub.

The fall from the roof of his canal boat had stunned him – he must have banged his head on the metal locker. He could feel a large tender swelling through the thin hair on his scalp. But the hospital x-ray at Mile End had revealed no concussion and the young doctor in the casualty department told him he was lucky not to have any broken bones when he told him what happened. As it was, he felt like a bus had run over him and all he wanted now was to crawl into bed and sleep.

He knew he should go back and check out his narrowboat but couldn't face what he was sure would be a total ruin. Maybe later, he could persuade Heck to drive him down to King's Cross canal basin to survey the damage. He sipped the hot pale green tea and munched glumly on his sandwich. What a mess – not only did he have to confront a hostile Alice, at some point he would have to get in touch with Russell and tell him that his half share in the *Iron Sea Horse* had gone up in flames. And could he even stay here any longer – the situation with Heck and Alice had become intolerable, largely due to his own ineptitude. If he hadn't been so insistent in forcing his wife to begin the divorce when she clearly didn't want to....

The sound of a key in the side door lock made Barney look up to see the big lanky frame of Heck filling the doorway, holding a bulky bag of produce.

"Barney – what are you doing here? Alice told me you cleared off yesterday afternoon." He deposited the bag on the long wooden harvest table and some apples rolled out the top. He picked them up then stared at Barney, seeing the bandage on his head. "What happened to you – forget to duck your head going down the hatch? Alice said you went to the boat."

Barney looked sheepish. "Not quite. I fell off the roof in the dark –"

"What the hell were you doing up on that slippery metal roof in the middle of the night? You're getting too old to be doing stuff like that – you're just asking for an accident." Heck fetched another cup and sat down at the table, helping himself to some tea. He peered closer at Barney through his bifocals. "You look like hell."

"I feel like it, too," said Barney and gave Heck a brief account of the fire and his fall. "I managed to call the fire brigade before I went to Mile End Hospital but I doubt they could do much – it was too far gone by then. I didn't want to go back – thought for sure I'd smashed my elbow – all I wanted to do was come back here and sleep. Maybe later today after you get up we could go down together?"

The big man rose and started putting the fruit and veggies in the cool pantry. "Sure, but first I need some sleep – my relief didn't show up until 5am and I had to do a double shift. Is Alice awake yet?"

"Haven't heard her. I've been tiptoeing around down here not to wake her. I couldn't face another row with her now. She isn't going to be exactly pleased to see me back here after what I said yesterday."

Heck surveyed him through the top of his spectacles. "You've put me in an awkward spot, Barney. I'm beholden to you for what you've done for us but I'm angry that you felt you had to upset Alice when she's still recovering. You know how this operation has undermined her self-confidence. It's a good thing you weren't here when she told me what happened or I might have helped you out the door. I'm not sure you should stay here any longer."

Barney nodded agreement. "I'm sorry too, Heck. Believe me, I didn't intend it to happen – but you know how she can wind me up. I thought I was past all that...." He gave his head a shake. "Anyway, as soon as I get some sleep and can think straight, I'll pack all my stuff and clear off – maybe go down to stay in Gloucestershire with Russell."

"Okay – we can talk later – for now let's get to bed. I think I'll sleep in the spare room. I'm bound to wake Alice if I go into our room and she'll get all upset if she knows you're here and the boat's been destroyed. Take your shoes off, will you?"

The two men removed their shoes and headed up the curving staircase in the old Georgian house. They had almost reached the first landing when the heavy oak front door opened behind them and Alice stepped into the hall. She watched a police car pull away before she turned towards them. Barney stood on the step below Heck and saw her first.

"Alice! I thought –"

She peered up the staircase at him for a full two seconds before letting out a strangled shriek.

# CHAPTER 4

In the living room of the old house, Heck sat with his arm round Alice on the rosewood sofa. In the kitchen, Barney poured boiling water into the teapot to make fresh tea. He appeared with a cup for her and she held it with both hands to sip it.

"I should call Detective Parry right away, Heck. She has police hunting for Barney all around King's Cross –"

"Later, Alice, later. Let's get some sleep first; we've been up all night. Just drink your tea and then we can go to bed."

"But they're talking about dragging the canal," she insisted.

"For me?" said Barney. "Do you have her number? Maybe I should call her and tell them I'm okay."

Alice handed her cup to Heck and fumbled in her jacket pockets, pulling out a crumpled card and handing it to Barney. "It's more than that. They think the fire was deliberate and you're a suspect –"

"Me? Why would I burn my own boat?"

She shrugged. "I'm just telling you what I heard. Maybe because you were seen at the fire by Alf and then disappeared."

"But I told you I went to call 911. Then some young guy in the pub drove me to the hospital – my head was bleeding."

"And you have no idea who this black man they found is?" asked Heck.

"Only what Alf mentioned. He didn't think it was vandals or kids set the fire because he saw this man going on and off the *Iron Sea Horse* a few times –"

"Maybe he was homeless and just broke in?" said Alice.

"Or found my key under the seat locker," said Barney. "It was gone when I looked for it."

"Too bad he found it," said Heck.

"The poor man. When I saw him, he was covered in bandages. All I saw were his eyes – and his feet. He must be in agony from all those burns." Alice shuddered at the memory of her visit.

Heck tried to reassure her. "They'll keep him all doped up with morphine and stuff. He won't be feeling anything."

"All the same, it's horrible. I don't want to think about it too much," she said.

Barney studied the card Alice had handed him. "I think I'd better call this Detective Parry now. Why don't you two go up and get some sleep? We can talk later." He went into the kitchen to use the phone. The policewoman was out so he left a message saying he would call again. By the time he returned to the living room Heck and Alice had gone upstairs and he followed them to collapse onto the antique brass bed in the guest room.

But his brain refused to let him sleep. It buzzed with images and questions. If someone had been inside the boat all the time he was trying to put out the fire, why hadn't he seen him? Why didn't he try to get out? There were exits front and rear. Had he been trapped somehow? And who was he anyway?

Barney had only ever been in a fire once before, years ago when he first started working as a teenager in a warehouse. He still had a vivid image of those huge leaping flames as he fled the building. He tried not to think of the mystery man trapped inside his old narrowboat and scrubbed his eyes with his fists. If he had gone straight to the boat instead of spending half the evening in the pub, it might never have happened. He thought again of the series of three events – the argument, the drinking and the fire. Even while they happened, he knew he was in the wrong, could feel the wrongness but still kept on. And now a man lay badly burned, maybe dying, because of him. But that's crazy. It was the guy's own fault for breaking into the *Iron Sea Horse*.

Barney tossed about on the big old bed with its lumpy mattress. He was so tired, why couldn't he sleep? These last two or three years he never seemed to sleep right through the night anymore. His once-proud boast that he could fall asleep the instant his head hit the pillow could no longer be repeated. At 72, he seldom slept more than three or four hours at a time – dozing seemed a better description of his broken nights.

Before he and Alice finally broke up, she had long since abandoned sharing a bed with him and relegated him to his son Hunter's old room. He couldn't blame her; he knew he snored and tossed about, going to the loo at least once, sometimes twice a night. But he did blame her for their lost intimacy. He knew it was unfair but he still felt that if only they had continued sleeping together things might have worked out. His childlike faith in sex as the great healer and solver of all their problems had been shattered by their symbolic, to him, separate beds and led to their eventual separation.

But not divorce. Over two years now and Alice refused to agree, kept saying she wasn't ready even though she and Heck lived together almost from the beginning of the break-up. When Barney left home to go off on his 3rd Age explorations as he referred to them, Alice had returned to university to study her first love, archaeology. Heck was her professor and tutor and they had fallen quickly into a relationship that they had to keep secret from everyone because of ethical student/teacher rules.

They had even left Oxford for the anonymity of London to avoid discovery, only for Heck to become embroiled in some student activist schemes for tackling climate change. When Heck had been caught by the police, spraying slogans on big 4x4s, they had fled to Rome, hoping it would all blow over. It was there Alice, or rather Heck had discovered her breast cancer and her life had begun to unravel. Barney knew it had something to do with her mastectomy and her fear of losing Heck, which made her cling to both men.

And now here he was, sleeping or trying to, in the guest bedroom while Alice and Heck lay in the master bedroom next door. An arrangement that had been going on for nearly two months since he had flown home from his travels in Nepal – flown, against all his green principles when Heck implored him to come back to Alice's hospital bedside.

He grimaced and stared at the elaborate plaster ceiling rose with its cupid cherubs cavorting above his head. The expression 'a spare prick at a wedding' crossed his mind as he thought of the two of them in the big four-poster in the next bedroom. Heck was right – he couldn't stay here any longer.

The problem was he had no place to call his own anymore, since his canal boat burned. His decision to cut all his ties to his old life with Alice and their three grown children meant he was homeless. At the time, this suited him. He determined to become a free agent – to follow T.S. Eliot's advice that 'old men should be explorers'. This combined with his fascination for the Indian idea of the four ages of a man, had been enough to set him off in search of the way to live this third age of his life – he would become a 3rd Age explorer.

As he stared at the ceiling, unable to sleep, his mind roved over all his searching. First, back home to Canada to find his roots after living and teaching for over 30 years in England. Then to explore the Far East – India, China, Tibet and Nepal, in search of the elusive wisdom of the Buddha. The Buddhist philosophy of non-attachment held great appeal for Barney as he advanced into his seventies.

But non-attachment was easier said than done, he found. He'd been forced to abandon his search twice. First, from Vancouver, to rescue his son, Hunter from jail in London, after a custody battle ended in a charge of attempted kidnapping. Then called back from Asia by a desperate Heck when Alice got breast cancer.

This was the reason he lay here in the spare bedroom of Heck's crumbling Georgian semi in East London while his wife slept next door with her new partner. He tossed fitfully on the antique brass bed with the faint musty smell from its old unsprung mattress. Perhaps he should reconsider his approach to 3rd age exploring. Try something closer to home for a while. Instead of his fruitless attempts at non-attachment, why not practice the reverse – engaged Buddhism, like the Vietnamese monk, Tich Nhat Han?

He thought of Russell's organic smallholding in the Golden Valley, near Wales. He could go there, get away from London. He would call Russell when he got up. Shit. He'd have to tell Russell about the fire. It was his boat too. He'd bought a half share from Barney when Alice said she didn't want to go cruising with him anymore. Not that Russell used it much except as a place to stay when he came to London for an art show – or more often for a new woman. And sometimes he lent it to friends. Maybe the mystery man was a friend of Russell's. He should get up, call him straight away, but he didn't move.

Even thinking about Russell made him tired. The man was a dynamo; nothing tired him. He could work all morning on his organic market garden, spend the afternoon in his sculpture workshop welding lumps of metal together, then go out half the night chasing some woman he'd met in the local pub. And the next day start all over again. Russell was younger than Barney, of course. Seventy, to be exact. Barney still remembered the marathon birthday bash Russell had thrown to commemorate his three-score and ten. He closed his eyes. Time enough to call Russell later.

# CHAPTER 5

The waiting room of the Burns Unit at St Pancras Hospital looked like the aftermath of a train wreck. People sat or stood in clusters with various limbs, torsos and heads wrapped in bandages, expressionless faces turning to stare at Barney and the detective as they approached the reception desk. The police officer showed her ID to the girl behind the counter who picked up a phone and made a call. She told them to take a seat for ten minutes as the doctors were with the 'mystery man,' as Barney referred to him. There were no seats left in the crowded waiting room so they stood by the coffee machine out in the corridor.

"What I still don't understand is why you never waited for the firemen, Mr Roper. It seems odd that you wouldn't want to see if they saved your boat or not," said Detective Parry. She fed coins into the machine and turned to Barney. "Black or white?"

"None for me thanks," he said.

"Don't blame you, this machine stuff is revolting." She removed her steaming cup and crossed to the windows looking out on the hospital garden. "Do you mind if we go outside? I can have a cigarette and we can talk privately." She led the way and sat down on a wooden garden bench. "So – could you just clarify why you left?"

"Well, I was stunned by the fall off the boat roof. I guess I knocked myself out when I hit my head on the metal seat locker – anyway when I came to, blood was dripping down my face. So by the time I got back to the canal pub I must have looked kinda scary. They wanted to take me to Casualty right away but I said I had to call 911 first. After that, this young guy insisted on driving me to Mile End Hospital, near where I'm living."

"So they kept you in overnight for observation?"

"No. They stitched my scalp up and sent me for an x-ray. The doctor said I was doubly lucky – no concussion or broken bones so I could go home – besides they had no empty beds to keep me in."

"And your boat?"

"By the time I left the hospital I knew it would be all over – it could wait till the morning – and the doc said I should get some rest first."

"You know that the man they rescued is severely burned, Mr Roper. His right hand may have to be amputated. It got trapped and crushed in the fire as well as badly burned."

"Alice told me he's in a bad way. I've been worrying about him ever since. I feel sort of responsible – I mean, on my boat and all…."

"I'm sorry we upset your wife by bringing her down here in the middle of the night but we were led to believe it was you. I hope she's feeling better today – I understand she recently came out of hospital herself."

Barney looked at the policewoman. In her forties, he guessed, rather plump and full-breasted. "Did she tell you why?"

Detective Parry nodded. "Mastectomy."

"She hasn't really come to terms with it yet – has bad dreams."

"Every woman's nightmare, Mr Roper," she gave a slight flinch to her shoulders, gazed at her cigarette a moment before stubbing it out. "I really am sorry – we won't bother her again."

"This man," asked Barney, "have you identified him yet?"

"All his clothing was just cinders. We're relying on your friend Russell Kline to recognise him."

"How? Alice said all she could see were his eyes and feet."

"I'm not sure, exactly. We may have to wait a few days for a positive ID but at least Mr Kline can fill in some of the blanks – describe him enough for the other boat owner to confirm if it's his friend."

"Russell sounded fairly sure it would be. He wanted to come down straight away but I said he'd better wait until I spoke to you," said Barney.

"I've asked him to meet us here this morning. His train should have arrived half an hour ago – we're only a ten minute cab ride from Paddington." She checked her watch.

"Russell won't take a cab. He insists on using public transport, even out in the Golden Valley where he lives. You miss a bus there and you wait an hour and a half for the next one – if you're lucky."

"All the same, I think we'd better go back inside. I don't want to miss him. What's he look like anyway?" she asked.

"Russell? Stocky, pot belly like me but shorter. Better looking, or at least women seem to think so. Lots of hair too," said Barney, running his hand over his thinning hair and lightly touching the bandage on his scalp.

The detective smiled. "A ladies' man, eh? Will I like him?"

"Bit old for you. He's an artist – a sculptor. A lot of women find that appealing."

He followed her back into the waiting room and spotted Russell almost immediately, chatting to one of the nurses. The policewoman saw him at the same time and raised an eyebrow to Barney. He nodded and they threaded their way across the crowded waiting room.

"You picked him out straight away," said Barney over her shoulder. "Good detective work or my good description?"

"Neither, really," she said. "He's the only person in here not bandaged up." She stopped behind Russell. "Mr Kline? I'm Detective Parry."

Russell turned from the nurse to take the police officer's hand, flashing his warm smile. He was about to speak when he saw Barney standing behind her.

"Barney – god, I hope this isn't going to be what I think." The two men hugged. "Jesus. Good to see you. How long has it been? A year? I thought you were still in Tibet or somewhere, till you phoned."

"I came back sooner than I planned, Russell – because of Alice…."

"Yeah, I heard. Christ, poor Alice. I wanted to phone her but didn't have her new number. The 3rd Age, eh? It's all to come, Barney." He turned back to the policewoman. "Some inside information for you, Detective Parry. Reliable source. Don't grow old – I can't recommend it."

"Thanks for coming so swiftly, Mr Kline," she smiled. "I'm hoping you can help us. Follow me." She led the way down the passage to the nursing station and spoke to the nurse at the desk who rose and nodded for them to accompany her. At the door, she stood aside to let them enter, then crossed to put on a low light by the bedside.

Russell stood with Barney at the foot of the bed until the police officer beckoned them to go closer. For a few moments, the two men stared at the closed eyes in the slit among the bandages, then at each other. Russell shook his head and shrugged, stepping away from the bed. Barney studied the narrow eye slit and let his gaze go down the bed, trying to discern an outline. The body didn't seem that big under the covers, smaller than himself, he judged. He too, joined the detective waiting at the door with the nurse.

Russell spoke first. "It could be Landon – he looks about the right size, but...." He looked from the detective to the nurse. "And he's definitely black, you say?"

The nurse nodded and held the door open as they all filed out of the room.

Detective Parry took as full a description of Landon Freers as Russell could recall and said she would be in touch with them after she spoke to Alf on the neighbouring boat. She thanked Russell for coming down and said there was nothing more she needed him for, if he wanted to catch a later train back to Gloucester. If he thought of anything else which might help identify the black man in the hospital bed he could phone her and she handed him her card and drove off.

He watched her go then turned to Barney. "We've got some catching up to do, Barney. Where shall we go?"

"You hungry? We could go to the Lock Inn at Camden Town – I need a walk and we can go along the towpath."

The two men threaded their way through the back streets behind the hospital and went down some steps at a small bridge which led on to the towpath. They turned westward along the Regent's Canal, following its leafy course through north London to Camden Lock.

"That copper told me you were a possible suspect because you left the fire before the firemen arrived," said Russell. "I told her she was bonkers – Landon's an alcoholic and probably set the boat on fire himself."

"If it is him and not some homeless vagrant. If he's such an old friend how come I never heard you mention him before?" asked Barney.

"Long story. I didn't want to get into it with that detective unless I had to."

"Well, you better tell me. Seeing as my narrowboat's a write-off, I think you owe me an explanation."

"Yeah, you're right," nodded Russell, sitting down on a stone wall beside the canal. "The reason you never heard me speak of Landon is because he's not really a friend. I only met him this past year. It's his wife I know. We had an affair a few months back and she left him. He's a musician – tenor sax, plays all up and down the country with this trad jazz group. He's never home and when he is, he's on the booze so she finally decided to leave him when she met me."

Barney sat beside him, listening to this familiar story from his old friend. Russell moved from one woman to the next with a predictable regularity.

"Do I know her?"

"No, I don't think so. She's a palliative care nurse. Works at the Golden Valley hospice. I met her at one of their fund-raising evenings that I donated a small sculpture for. We hit it off straight away so she started living with me at the farm, helping out when she wasn't nursing."

"What's her name?"

"Tash – Natasha."

"And her husband found out obviously –"

Russell ran his hands through his thick grey hair. "Yeah, that's when it all got messy. He went on a huge bender – kept coming out to the farm in a taxi and banging on the door, pleading with her to come back."

"Did he threaten you or anything?" asked Barney, recalling previous angry partners' reactions to Russell's affairs.

"No – just the opposite. Tried to get me to persuade Tash to come back to him."

"I still don't see how he ended up on my boat," said Barney. "If she's living with you, he's got their place, hasn't he?"

"She's not with me anymore. It only lasted a month – you know what nurses are like, obsessed with order and cleanliness. The constant mess and chaos at my place drove her mad. But she wouldn't go back to him. She said she'd had enough of his drinking and absences for weeks at a time, so she rented a little place at Gloucester docks. In one of those old warehouses they've done up into posh flats. I helped her move in."

"You've lost me," said Barney. "Are you saying you and he became pals then?"

Russell grimaced and began pacing up and down, unable to sit still any longer. "I told you it's complicated. What happened was Landon just stayed permanently on the booze, quit working even. Became obsessed with getting her back, pestered her constantly till she got a court order restraining him. So then he started coming out to me, drunk and asking me to help."

"Christ, Russell. Why do you do this screwing around with married women? There's dozens of unattached women out there our age."

"I thought she was unattached – at least separated. Turns out it only looked that way because he spent so much time away. He goes to Amsterdam and Hamburg a lot. There's loads of jazz venues over there. Anyway, I tried to help but he couldn't get off the booze. Wanted to move to London, said he had an old pal who'd give him a job playing in his pub but he needed somewhere to stay.

In the end I told him if he could get his drinking under control, prove he could stay on the wagon for two months I'd let him use the boat to live on for awhile. He stayed here at the farm where I could keep an eye on him. Helped out a bit once he sobered up and in the evenings he started playing his sax again. He hadn't touched it the whole time since Tash left him."

"Is he any good?" asked Barney as they continued along the canal towpath.

"If you like trad jazz – yeah, he's good. Been playing since he dropped out of school and he's about my age. He could be doing well if it weren't for the booze."

"I suppose it goes with the job," said Barney, "– working in pubs and clubs."

"Not anymore," said Russell. "not according to Karla at the hospital."

"Who's Karla?"

"That intensive care nurse I chatted to in the Burns Unit when I was waiting for you and the policewoman."

"Jesus, Russell, don't you ever give it a rest?" said Barney, shaking his head in disbelief.

Russell grinned, "What's wrong? – she's unattached. She told me she had a lousy social life working in intensive care. 'Unsociable hours' she said."

"And did she also tell you she's young enough to be your daughter?"

"It didn't come up – we got talking about Landon. When I said I was his closest friend she told me what the doctors are saying. It's bad news for Landon."

"His hands are too badly burned to play again?"

Russell stopped and stared into the murky brown water in the canal then turned to Barney. "Worse than that."

"What?"

"His right hand? They have to amputate."

# CHAPTER 6

Alice, Heck and Russell sat in the garden of the old Georgian house drinking wine from Heck's stock while Barney finished cooking pasta in the kitchen.

"You've got your work cut out for you with this old garden, Heck," said Russell. "Those old espaliered fruit trees will all have to be cut right back to the rootstock and even then I doubt if they'll produce. If it was me, I'd grub the whole lot out and start again."

"The outside is Alice's domain, Russell. She makes the decisions out here. I'm just the jobbing gardener."

"Well I don't want it looking like a commercial production setup. That's okay for you, Russell, down on the farm. We're not trying to make money out of it," said Alice.

The old Georgian semi-detached had been discovered by Alice and Heck when they abandoned Oxford for London. Mrs Hollis, the elderly widow who owned it, had taken an instant liking to them and they had struck a deal to restore the house for her in return for a chance to buy it. The nursing home where she now lived would remain her home – she was too frail to move but her house was stuffed with antiques which Heck and Alice promised to help her dispose of.

"Alice dreams of having a *'hortus conclusus'* – something out of a John Donne poem," said Barney, helping himself to the heaping bowl of pasta and passing it round.

"That's a new one on me, Alice. What's a *'hortus conclusus'*?" asked Russell.

"An enclosed, walled garden – sort of a 17th century romantic notion of recreating a Garden of Eden."

"Nice idea," said Russell gazing around. "You've got a way to go yet, though. What you need is a couple of my sculptures to set around. Put one over there by the orangerie."

"I thought you were a farmer, Russell," said Heck. "I didn't know you were a sculptor, too."

"Market gardener – not farmer. It subsidises the sculpture. In a philistine culture like ours, no one can make a living as an artist."

"Unless they happen to have talent," said Alice. "Just because he took a course at the agricultural college in blacksmithing, Russell thinks welding bits of junk together makes him a sculptor."

"Lots of people like them enough to buy them, all the same," said Russell to Heck. "Alice just doesn't happen to be one of them."

"I'd like to see them sometime," said Heck.

"Don't go dragging them back here. This is going to be a Georgian garden, not a junkyard," said Alice.

"You see what I mean about philistinism, Heck," Russell smiled.

"Just don't give up the day job, Russell," said Alice, pulling the bowl of pasta away from Barney and passing it round again.

"You'll be pleased to hear I'll soon be off your hands, Alice. Russell needs extra help since his last lady friend left and has offered me bed and board for awhile," said Barney.

"Have you ever thought of hiring someone, instead of luring in unsuspecting women on the pretext of romance, Russell?" said Alice. She had a low opinion of Russell for the way he treated his female friends, many of whom she knew and had tried to warn off him. But he had a way of charming them into living with him in the cluttered muddle he called his organic smallholding and they all ignored her warnings, preferring to find out for themselves.

Russell turned to Heck, grinning. "If Alice sounds a little bitter it's because she turned down my offer for her to come and live on the farm after Barney took off and she's probably regretted it ever since."

"Lucky for me," said Heck. "I caught her on the rebound from you and Barney."

"The two of them deserve each other, Heck. It'll be a reprieve for the local women in the Golden Valley. Much as I hate to see you both go, when are you leaving?"

"I have to sort out my freighter passage back to Canada next week but Russell has to get back tonight," said Barney.

"But I couldn't leave without seeing you again, Alice. I know how secretly fond of me you are," said Russell, rising and giving her a squeeze.

"I'm probably one of the few women who managed to resist your charms," she smiled and hugged him back. "Thanks for giving me one more chance though, Russell. It's good to see you again. Look after Barney and keep him out of trouble."

"What kind of trouble could I get into down in the Golden Valley on an organic market garden with Russell as overseer?" asked Barney.

"I shudder to think," she said.

"What's going to happen to your friend in hospital, Russell?" asked Heck. "Do you know how long they'll keep him there?"

"No idea. They still haven't identified him positively and they won't amputate until they get permission from a family member, so I guess it will be awhile yet."

"Won't Detective Parry contact his wife and ask her?" said Alice.

"Not until she's had the full report on the fire and spoken to all the witnesses. It may not be Landon, so they're trying to trace his whereabouts but so far, nothing."

"If he's gone missing doesn't that suggest it must have been him on your boat?" asked Heck.

"It does to me and Barney but not to her – she wants proof positive. Meantime, I've got seedlings dying off in my greenhouse, waiting to be set out. I have to get back today."

# CHAPTER 7

A week later, Barney was sitting in the Burns Unit of St Pancras hospital by the bedside of the mystery man, reading aloud. The man had been moved out of intensive care into a room off the main ward. He was still swathed in bandages and tubes and drips were plugged into him.

A soft rap on the door made Barney look up as an older woman dressed in street clothes entered. She stopped when she saw him beside the bed.

"Oh. I didn't expect anyone to be here. Are you a friend?" she nodded, indicating the bed.

"My name's Barney Roper. It's my narrowboat that caught fire. Do you know who he is?"

The woman approached the bed and studied the white figure. "Maybe if I could see his eyes –" She glanced at the various drips and machines hooked up to him. "It looks like they're keeping him permanently sedated for the present. Has he opened his eyes while you've been here?"

Barney shook his head. "I've come in most days since they transferred him from intensive care and he's always asleep. I tried reading to him a couple of times but he never reacts – never opens his eyes. How did you know he was here?"

"The police telephoned me, asked me to come in. I'm supposed to meet Detective Parry here but I'm a bit early. "I'm Natasha Freers," she held out her hand.

Barney shook it then offered her his chair and pulled up another from against the wall. "This must be a shock for you, Mrs Freers. Did the police say they knew it was your husband?"

"No, but Detective Parry said they found something on the boat that might be proof if I looked at it. I went to the police lab before I came here but she had to see someone else first."

"They told me his wallet and his clothes were too badly burnt for any identification. Did they find something else?"

She nodded. "At first, they didn't connect it with him. Thought it belonged to the owner of the boat. But when Russell told them he was a jazz musician, that's when they called me. It was a saxophone."

"Russell mentioned he knew you," said Barney tactfully. "And could you identify it – the sax?"

"Yes. It's all twisted and warped with the heat but it had a special little thumb grip that Landon had made for it that I recognised right away. But it looks too badly damaged to be repaired." She paused and looked at the bed. "I guess he won't be playing it again anyway."

"They told you about his hand?"

"Yes. Poor Landon. Playing that old tenor sax is all he cares about."

"Will you sign the permission papers?"

She shook her head. "I couldn't possibly – he'd never forgive me when he found out."

"Are you his only next of kin or does he have children?"

"No children – he didn't want any, so we never had them. Maybe if we had.... He has a widowed sister in West Africa – Sierra Leone, but he's not much of a letter writer."

"I'm very sorry about your husband, Mrs Freers. It looks like it's definitely him from what you say. What will you do now – stay here in London?"

"I can't. I have to get back to the hospice. They gave me a few days off to sort things out but that's all."

"Do you have a place to stay here?" said Barney.

"Not yet. I'll find a B&B later."

"I'm sure my wife would be pleased to have you. She's got a big old house in Mile End and she knows about your husband – she's even been here to see him. The police thought it was me the firemen rescued."

"If you're sure it's okay. I am a little overstretched for money. I've just moved and the expenses were more than I'd expected."

"I'll call her and confirm it now if you like," said Barney rising. "I won't be long."

When he returned from telephoning Alice, Detective Parry sat next to Natasha Freers at the bedside.

"Mr Roper – Mrs Freers tells me you've been visiting here most days since they moved him from intensive care. Any response from him at all?"

"Not a thing. I've tried reading aloud from the newspaper a few times. Mrs Freers thinks he's too heavily sedated to react."

"I've just been asking her if she will sign the papers for the amputation."

"Does that mean you're convinced it's her husband?" asked Barney.

The detective grimaced. "I think so. The positive identification of his saxophone seems to clinch it. In a court of law that would be enough to convince a judge, probably."

Natasha Freers rose to gaze at the bandaged figure in the bed again. "I'm sorry, Ms Parry but I just don't get any feeling that this is Landon. It could be anyone lying here. Perhaps if he opened his eyes –"

"I don't blame you for not wanting to sign. What if he turns out to be a stranger?" said Barney.

The detective stood up and picked up her briefcase. "I'll ask the doctors when they expect to reduce his sedation enough to recognise us," she said. "It may be a few more days yet. Will you stay in London, Mrs Freers?"

"I told you before, detective, my husband and I are no longer a couple. I'm just waiting for the divorce. I have no intention of getting involved again and let him think we might get back together. I'm sorry this has happened if it actually is him and I will try to be of assistance to you in his identification but beyond that…." She stopped and turned to Barney. "I left my overnight bag at the nurses' desk. I don't think there's any more I can do here."

The detective shook her hand. "You've already done a lot by identifying the saxophone. I appreciate this is an awkward situation for you. I'll phone you if I get any definite answer from the doctors and arrange for you to come back again, Mrs Freers."

"She'll be staying at my wife's house tonight if you hear anything," said Barney as the detective followed them out of the burns ward.

*******************************************

Alice, Heck and Barney were giving Natasha an inspection tour of the vegetable garden at Tiberius Road with drinks in their hands.

"This is like an old country house garden, Alice. Mixing in the flowers and vegetables together – it looks lovely," said Natasha.

"It's called companion planting," said Alice. "The idea is supposed to be that certain flowers attract beneficial insects and others deter the pests."

"That's the theory," said Heck, picking off a slug from a young lettuce. "In practice I'm not so convinced."

"It seems to work okay for Russell. He swears by it," said Barney. "He says you have to allow the bugs a certain portion of the crop and not get too obsessive about not losing a single plant."

"Russell's method is far more disorganised. He used to drive me wild with the way he worked," said Natasha.

"I gathered you had a different approach, from what he told me," said Barney.

"That's putting it mildly. We were total opposites in every way. I can't imagine why I thought it would work," said Natasha, bending down to pick one of the ripe strawberries from the circular bed surrounded by herbs. "I put it down to being determined to get away from Landon at any cost."

She and Alice worked round the circular bed, filling the bowl Alice held with the large, succulent red fruit. Heck and Barney left them to it and went off to check on the espaliered fruit trees that they'd been pruning hard under Russell's advice.

"She doesn't look like the wife of a jazz musician, Barney. I was expecting somebody more…." Heck waggled his hand.

"I know what you mean – more arty-looking. Blowsy. Not so neat and tidy. Maybe that's what appealed to Russell, eh?" said Barney.

"And she is a nurse. I suppose most men are attracted to nurses."

"Surrogate mothers," said Barney. "I guess Russell was too anarchic for her to bring under control."

"I'd still like to see his place all the same," said Heck. "He invited me down anytime for a weekend."

"If you don't mind being put to work. Nobody gets a free ride at Russell's place, but I enjoy it. He's good company despite what Alice says."

"So what will happen with Natasha's husband now?" asked Heck. "She sounds adamant she's not having him back from what she said."

"At the moment she doesn't even know if it's him or not. Perhaps if it really is Landon, she'll change her mind. After all, she is a nurse –"

The two women moved to the wooden Victorian garden swing Heck and Barney had restored. They sat hulling the strawberries and eating the irresistible ones.

"I don't usually approve of eating unwashed fruit," said Natasha, "but this looks safe enough with no insecticides and it tastes gorgeous."

"I promise you it's organic. If you see any holes they're made by blackbirds, not bugs," said Alice. "Even Russell approved of them and you know how fanatical he is about organic growing."

"He said I'm obsessive about things but he's just as bad – worse, in some ways."

"Oh, Russell's a hopeless case," said Alice. "There's only one way of doing things and that's his way. His arrogance is unbelievable."

"I suppose I knew what to expect after 27 years with Landon. These creative types are so self-centred nobody else's ideas matter."

"What do you think Landon will do when they tell him they want to amputate his hand?"

"He'll never agree – it means the end of his playing career. I think he'd sooner give up a leg than a hand," said Natasha.

"I feel sorry for him when he wakes up," said Alice. "It's a horrible decision to have to face."

"Barney told me about your mastectomy, Alice. I can't really imagine how you feel, but I can guess."

"Yes. I know it's not as critical as losing your right hand, although it feels like it sometimes."

Natasha nodded. "I meet a lot of women in the hospice who've lost a breast and each one is devastated at the time. Some of them never get over it."

"I'm not so sure whether I will either. But whenever I start feeling too pathetic I think of my younger daughter Cassie in Africa. She works in an orphanage with amputee children. It makes me realise I don't begin to know what suffering is like."

The phone rang in the old house and Barney went in to answer it. He returned two minutes later.

"Detective Parry," he said. "She spoke to the doctors and they've agreed to reduce his sedation long enough to try to make a positive identification."

"How will they do that?" asked Alice. "His whole head's covered including his mouth."

"That's what I said but she says he can blink his eyes for yes and no questions," said Barney.

Natasha nodded, "Yes, we use eye contact all the time at the hospice for people who are too ill to speak."

"Anyway, they'll take him off the morphine tonight and want Natasha and me to come in at eight tomorrow morning. They're keen to get him to agree to the amputation."

# CHAPTER 8

Promptly at eight the following morning, Barney and Natasha stood by the bedside in the hospital burns unit. A nurse leaned over the bed and spoke in a raised voice. "Mr Freers. Landon. Can you hear me?"

The mystery man's eyes flickered open and closed again. The nurse nodded to Natasha. "Your wife is here, Landon. Can you open your eyes now?" The eyes flickered again.

Natasha bent closer to him. "Landon – is that you? It's Tash." His eyes stayed open this time. "Can you hear me, Landon? Blink if you can." The eyes closed, then opened again. "Landon, blink twice if it's you." The eyes slowly shut and opened two times. She turned to the other nurse and nodded to her, stepping back out of the way. The nurse leaned in again and spoke again in her raised voice.

"That's good – very good. We need to ask you some questions. So blink once for no and twice for yes. Now. Is your name Landon Freers?" His eyes stared at her then blinked twice and remained open.

"Your wife is here, Mr Freers. Is her name Natasha?" The eyes opened wider then blinked twice. "She wants to speak to you, now."

"Landon, do you know what happened to you?" asked Natasha. He blinked once. "You were in a fire on Russell's canal boat. You're in hospital, do you understand?" Once again he blinked twice, then squeezed his eyes shut. "I think he's in pain."

"Tell him about his hand," said the detective, moving closer.

"Landon, you're badly burned – very badly. Your hands especially." His eyes opened again to focus on Natasha.

"Go on," urged the policewoman. "You have to tell him."

Natasha looked at Barney and the other nurse who nodded encouragingly. She bent over him again. "Landon – your right hand. It has gangrene and it's spreading. The doctors want to amputate." The eyes bored into hers and she looked away, then back. "They want me to sign for you – to give them permission." The eyes closed tight. "Landon. Do you agree? Shall I sign?"

His eyes remained closed. Then slowly opened to look fully at Natasha.

He blinked. Once.

# CHAPTER 9

In the bright morning sunshine, Barney and Russell pricked out trays of rocket salad greens at Russell's organic smallholding in the Golden Valley. Natasha entered the polytunnel with a tray of mugs and large gooey Chelsea buns.

"Where did these come from?" asked Russell wiping the compost off his fingers onto his jeans and picking up one of the sticky buns. Natasha opened her mouth, then closed it again, biting her lip.

"I brought them," said Barney, "from the bus station coffee stall." He rinsed his hands in a watering can on the potting bench then took a bun and a mug of coffee.

"Let's sit outside," said Natasha, picking up a coffee but leaving the last bun untouched.

They sat in the dappled shade of a gnarled pear tree on three garden chairs made from old horseshoes welded together.

"When did you make these, Russell?" asked Barney, testing one.

"Last winter. I got the cast-off horseshoes from the College of Farriery in Hereford before the scrap man did. Not bad eh?" He sat and drank coffee, licking his sticky fingers. Natasha looked away.

"I'm glad you're here, Tash. We're swamped with work. How long can you stay?" asked Russell.

"I didn't come here to work for you, Russell. I came to talk about Landon. What are we going to do?"

"He still won't agree to them removing his hand?" asked Russell. She shook her head.

"Can't say I blame him. I wouldn't fancy losing my right hand. Left either, come to that." Russell held up his grubby hand, then licked the icing off his thumb.

"Maybe he needs more time to come to terms with it," said Barney. "It's only been a few days since you told him."

"The doctors say they won't be responsible for what happens if I don't sign soon."

"It's your decision, Tash," shrugged Russell.

"Legally maybe," she said, "but you're involved too. You're the one who let him use that boat."

"I was only trying to help since you refused to have anything to do with him. Don't try to blame me. You might as well say it's Barney's fault too. It's his boat."

"Don't be ridiculous – Barney doesn't even know him," she said.

"All the same, I do feel responsible in a way," said Barney. "When are you going to see him again, Natasha?"

"I promised the hospital I'd go down again tomorrow. He's had a few days to think about it and I'll tell him what the doctors say if he doesn't agree."

"And if he still refuses? Then what?" asked Russell.

"That's why I came to talk to you," she said. "If I can offer him something after the operation, maybe he'll agree."

"Like what?" said Russell. "Take him back?"

She shook her head. “Not a chance. I told you I’m through with him. It’s over.”

“Do you have something in mind, something we can help with?” asked Barney.

Natasha took a long swallow of her coffee, then looked at Barney. “I’ve been talking to the doctors about what happens when he’s released. They said if he could have a nurse visit him daily to change his dressings, he could become an outpatient at Gloucester hospital. They know I’m a nurse and assume I’d be looking after him.”

“But you just said you’ve washed your hands of him,” said Russell. “And now you’re saying you’ll take him back?”

She shook her head. “I didn’t say anything of the sort. I said they assumed I would. I was only asking what would happen to him next.”

“And you think Landon would agree to the amputation if he thought you’d look after him?” asked Barney.

She nodded. Russell studied her for a minute. “I don’t get it, Tash. You’re going to trick him into thinking you’ll have him back if he agrees?”

“Don’t be daft, Russell. Of course not.”

“But you do have something in mind?” said Barney.

“That’s why I’m here – to check it out with Russell first,” she said.

“Well, go on then. Let’s hear it. If you’re not here to help, I’ve got work to do. We’ll be up to midnight setting out those seedlings.”

She glanced at Barney for support. “Okay. Here’s what I was thinking. If you let Landon come back here to recover after the amputation – I’ll agree to nurse him and change his dressings, before I go to the hospice.”

"You mean you'll move in here again till he recuperates?" asked Russell.

"No, definitely not. I said I'll visit daily – do what's necessary, then go to work. I'm not giving up my hospice position – or my new flat," she said.

"So who looks after him when you're not here, Tash? Not me. I'm already sinking under the workload here without taking on a bed-ridden suicidal invalid."

She looked at Barney again, waiting for his reaction.

"If you think it might work, Natasha, I'm willing to give it a try – under instruction, of course. It's been a long time since I looked after my own kids when they got sick."

"Thanks Barney." She turned to Russell. "Well?"

"What about the out-patient clinic – have you thought about that? I can hardly take him to Gloucester in the back of my old delivery van. Besides, I can't spare a day a week to drive in there and hang around for him."

"You won't have to. The hospital will send an ambulance to collect him and bring him back," she said.

"I can get his meals, Russell. We have to cook anyway," said Barney.

"There's something you seem to have forgotten, Tash. Remember why you left? Said this place was unfit for human habitation? And now you want to bring an invalid in here –"

Natasha stood up, collecting the coffee mugs onto the tray. "You let me worry about the hygiene, Russell. I'll soon get a sterile room ready. That so-called den off the living room you never use will be perfect, once I clear out all that junk you've dumped in there."

"Wait a minute, I haven't agreed to anything yet. I need to think about it first," said Russell.

"What's to think about, Russell?" asked Barney. "I'll help Natasha clear the room and look after him. We owe him that much surely."

Russell frowned, stalling. "I thought you came down here to help me – not play nursemaid."

"Well think about it this way," said Natasha. "In a few weeks you'll have Landon working for you – for free. You'll like that, won't you Russell?" She winked at Barney and took the tray into the kitchen.

# CHAPTER 10

Mrs Oswold ran the Golden Valley Hospice day centre. Her iron-grey hair pulled into a bun gave her a severe look but she sounded friendly enough when she spoke to Barney.

"Mrs Freers persuaded you to join us after all, Mr Roper. She mentioned you a couple of weeks ago as a possible volunteer but when you didn't show up, I thought you'd got cold feet. Many people do."

Barney looked around at the day centre patients grouped in small clusters with staff and volunteers laughing and chatting. "I admit it's not quite what I expected a hospice to be like. Everybody seems to be very friendly – hugging each other," he said.

Mrs Oswold laughed. "Oh, you'll get used to that. We're into hugging in a big way here."

"I told Barney he'd be surprised," said Natasha. "Everybody thinks hospices are gloomy places full of po-faced people speaking in hushed tones."

"The day centre can get quite noisy sometimes. We have to keep the doors closed so we don't disturb the patients in the wards," said Mrs Oswold. "Some of the activities get rather boisterous."

"Barney's a man of many parts, Alma. I told him he'll fit right in," said Natasha.

"Excellent. I'm a champion at exploiting volunteers, Mr Roper. When would you like to start?"

"Right away, if you can use me. I've worked with disabled groups before when I was still employed, so I know how to manage wheel chairs on and off minibuses. I've been tested to drive them and I've still got my police check clearance for working with vulnerable people." He produced an envelope holding the documents and handed it to Mrs Oswold who skimmed through them.

"I like to arrange outings each week but we've been short of drivers so you're going to be very useful. Anything else you'd like to do? We're always open to new ideas for our patients and most of them are willing to try anything on offer." She stood up. "Would you like to meet some of the regulars – patients and volunteers?"

He followed her out of the office and she led him around the large open plan day centre, introducing him to staff members working with the patients. A volunteer offered him a coffee and a plate of biscuits.

"New blood, Alma?" said the woman, smiling at him. She looked Barney's age or older.

"Mr Roper has offered to drive the minibus so we can get our outings going more regularly, Dolores."

"Good. You can start by taking us up to Bluebell Wood – perfect timing. They're all out I noticed the other day, Mr Roper," she said shaking his hand.

"Barney, please," he said. "Name the day, Dolores. I'm your man."

Mrs Oswold continued her tour, stopping at a small group near the patio windows. "Usually they like to paint outside on the terrace but it's a little cool this morning so they're using the window to frame the view, I think. Have I got that right, Harry? This is Barney Roper, everybody. A new volunteer driver." She introduced him to the half dozen patients balancing their sketchpads on their laps.

"Do you paint, Barney?" asked a tall thin woman wearing a crimson turban. "Harry could use some male support here. We outnumber him five to one."

"Haven't touched watercolours since high school. But I've done a bit of illuminated lettering using acrylics and gold leaf," he said. "Calligraphy is something I've been interested in for years."

Mrs Oswold pounced. "Calligraphy – wonderful. I know lots of people who'd love to do that. Would you take a group if I arranged it, Barney?"

"Just as long as they realise I'm still learning myself."

"Put me down as your first student," said Maddy, the woman with the turban. "I know exactly what quotation I want to write – it's my favourite."

"Who's it from?" asked Barney. "Wordsworth?"

She shook her turbaned head. "No, it's Shakespeare. One of the sonnets."

"Go on then, tell us Maddy," said Mrs Oswold.

"'*Like as the waves make towards the pebbl'd shore,*

*So do our minutes hasten to their end,*'" recited Maddy.

"Good choice," agreed Barney

As Mrs Oswold led him away to meet more of the patients, Maddy watched him go. Barney felt he had found an ally, someone he might talk to about living in the here and now.

He figured the turban indicated she had lost all her hair in chemotherapy so that probably meant she had some sort of cancer. Maybe she could help him understand why Alice was behaving so strangely since her mastectomy.

Back at the smallholding, Barney and Natasha hauled clutter from the den out to the garden shed where Russell said they could store his stuff. He left them to it, saying he had too much to do to help. He'd been outmanoeuvred and didn't like it. He stomped off to the polytunnel.

Barney piled up the odds and ends of materials that Russell claimed were his raw materials for his sculptures. They looked like broken bits of junk to Barney but he stowed them all away in the shed as Russell didn't want them left outside to rust.

Natasha swept, dusted and scrubbed the floor and sash windows while Barney dismantled a single bed from upstairs. He reassembled it near the window for her to make up with clean bedding she had brought with her that morning. He watched fascinated as she spread the sheets drum tight and folded perfect hospital corners over the mattress.

"We need more pillows," she said, surveying the bed. "I'll bring some next time I come. I can borrow a few from the hospice stores."

Barney sat down to rest in a wicker armchair he rescued from the clutter. "When do you think they'll let him out, Natasha?"

"Not until they remove the stitches from his stump. Maybe another week or so," she said. "I want to have this all ready before then. I'm going to ask Russell if I can repaint these walls white – it's so dark in here like this."

"How did Landon seem when you saw him?"

"About what you'd expect. Feeling depressed and sorry for himself," she said. "I don't think it's fully hit him yet. When it does, I don't like to think how he'll react."

"Have you talked to him about an artificial hand?"

She nodded. "He just closed his eyes – like he didn't want to hear."

Barney studied her face. "This must be tough on you, being back with him just when you felt you'd made a total break."

"You do what you have to do. It's not my choice but there's nobody else. No family, except his widowed sister in Africa. And he's still my husband."

"Is that why you're doing it – because you're legally still his wife? I often wondered if anything happened to me, if Alice would feel obligated. We're not divorced yet, either. As it turns out, she's the one who got ill, but she had Heck to look after her," he said.

Natasha was silent for a minute, then she said, "She told me you came all the way home from Asia when you heard she had cancer. I guess you must understand a little of how I feel."

Barney nodded, "There's a lot of shared history you can't just turn your back on."

"Do you still love her?" she asked.

"In some way, I guess. Do you still love Landon?"

"It's complicated," she said. "I can't imagine ever not feeling a fondness and attachment to him. It's all mixed up with a sense of loyalty and duty – but love? I'm not sure. I don't think so – more like responsible in some way I can't define."

"For me, my feelings for Alice are tied up with her being the mother of my children. I'm grateful to her and that's why I feel responsible. But if it was only the two of us, would I still think the same way? Maybe – maybe not."

Natasha adjusted the blankets on the bed, smoothing them with her strong ringless hands. She stopped and held up her right one to look at it, turning it back and forth and flexing her fingers. "I can't imagine what Landon must be feeling – it must be so weird to lose a hand, especially for him – playing is his whole life. I think he'll end up hating me for what I did."

"For leaving him or because you signed the permission papers?"

"Both. The one led to the other," she said.

"I don't believe that victim stuff. We're not children, we have to take responsibility for our own lives," said Barney.

"So why are you getting involved at the hospice?" she asked. "Misplaced guilt about Alice's cancer? Are you doing penance, Barney?"

"No. More like facing up to my own fears about dying. I want to see how other people deal with it."

"Pick up some tips?" Natasha smiled.

"Something like that," he said, rising and looking out the window towards the polytunnel. "Speaking of penance, I think I'd better give Russell some help. He's feeling put upon."

"He thinks we ganged up on him," she said, "and he doesn't like not getting his own way."

"I envy people like Russell and Landon," said Barney. "If you're artistic, life is much more straightforward, you just follow your talent. Not like the rest of us who agonise about how to live our lives."

"Well I've had more than my share of self-centred people, artists or not. I'm not getting hooked by Russell again. And I'm not going to be derailed by Landon either." She picked up her handbag. "I'll help him get back on his feet – what he does after that is his concern."

Barney grinned, "You talk tough but you don't act it, Natasha. I'll bet Landon and Russell will both try to win you back if you're not careful."

She gave him a hug. "Why didn't I meet you first, Barney? You're much nicer than either of them."

"We all know what happens to nice guys, Natasha," he said, heading for the polytunnel. "See you at the hospice."

# CHAPTER 11

In the darkened old Georgian semi-detached house, Alice lay moaning and rolling her head from side to side until Heck awoke. He shook her shoulder gently. "Alice, what's wrong?"

She jerked awake, then clutched at his hand on her shoulder, crying and burying her face in the pillow.

"Is it that same dream again?" he asked, putting his arms around her. She nodded, pulling away from him and sitting up. "Why can't you tell me about it, Alice?"

She tried to get up but he drew her back down and she lay stiff and unresponding beside him. "I don't like sleeping in this bed, Heck. I want to go in the other room by myself."

"Why are you pushing me away, Alice? I need to know what you're thinking. Please talk to me – let me help."

"It's no use Heck. It's not going to work. I've known all along it wouldn't." She attempted to get up again but he held her down with one arm across her chest, cradling her remaining breast. She pried his fingers off and he slipped his hand down around her waist instead.

"You still think I care about your missing breast," he said, accusing. "Even though I've told you a hundred times it doesn't matter."

"It does to me," she said, not moving.

"You know what I mean, Alice. If you'd only explain what's going on in your mind. It's crazy letting a bad dream come between us." He tried once again to draw her to him but she resisted, lying firmly on her back, staring up at the canopy of the old bed.

"It's nothing to do with the dream, Heck. It's us. Why can't you understand plain English? I've told you enough times. Now let me up." She removed his arm and this time he didn't try to resist. She swung her legs over the edge of the bed and stood up.

"Where are you going?" he said, turning on the bedside lamp. "I thought you said you wanted to go in the other room?"

She was fumbling in the closet, grabbing handfuls of clothes and stuffing them in a case. She pulled on her skirt and jumper which lay on the chair where she had discarded them the night before. When she scrabbled under the bed for her shoes, Heck sat up alarmed.

"What are you doing? It's the middle of the night. Alice – wait." He threw the covers off and got up as she headed out the bedroom door with the bag. He heard her going down the curving elm staircase as he snatched his dressing gown off the back of the door and covered his naked torso. She was nearly at the front door before he could stop her. "Alice!" He blocked her path and she turned to go into the kitchen, heading for the side door. He grasped her arm as she went down the two steps to the landing.

"Let me go. I'm leaving," she said, not looking at him. "This time I mean it." She pulled her arm away and opened the side door.

"But you can't wander off at this time of night – where will you go?"

"Netta's," she said. "I'll find a cab. Don't try to stop me, Heck. I must go now before it's too late."

"Too late for what, Alice?"

"Cassie. I've got to find her." She pushed the door wide and stepped onto the lawn, refusing to look back.

Outside her elder daughter's flat, Alice stood pressing on the door buzzer until a light came on inside.

"Mother!"

Alice took a step forward into the flat and dropped her bag to embrace her daughter. "Thank God you're home, Netta."

"It's 4 am, Mother. Where else would I be? What is it? Has something happened?" She led her mother into the living room and sat beside her on the battered sofa, dislodging Beowulf, her battle-scarred old tomcat.

"I'm sorry, Netta but I had to come – I knew I couldn't wait another night."

"What are you talking about, Mother – couldn't wait for what?" She looked at her mother's dishevelled hair and clothes. "Are you alright? – where's Heck?"

"I've left him," said Alice, smoothing her skirt.

"In the middle of the night? – Did you have a fight?" she asked, noticing Alice's bag by the front door.

Alice shook her head. "I can't make him understand. Is Philip asleep?" She peered over Netta's shoulder.

"He's in Bournemouth. At an Anglo-Saxon symposium for the weekend."

"Can I stay here for tonight? – just till the morning, then I'll get a hotel," said Alice. "I can sleep here on the couch."

Netta took her mother's coat and stood up. "You're not going anywhere until you tell me what this is all about." She scanned Alice's uncombed hair and sleep-smeared appearance. "He didn't hit you or anything, Mother?" she said in disbelief, trying to imagine Heck doing such a thing, knowing how he treated Alice like eggshell china since her mastectomy.

"Of course not. Why would you say that? You don't understand either. Cassie's the only one who really knows me and she won't answer my emails. I've got to find her, Netta. Will you help me?" She grasped her daughter's hand and stood up, too.

Netta released her hand and crossed to the tiny kitchen alcove to open a cupboard and take out a bottle. "First, I'm pouring you a brandy and then you tell me what this is all about." She handed Alice a stiff drink and sat beside her while her mother alternately sipped and shuddered, then sipped again. She watched as Alice began to relax and lean back against the tattered sofa cushions.

"He thinks it's because I keep having this same dream about him discovering my breast lump when we went to Rome," Alice began. "We had a big old four-poster bed there, too. He says it makes no difference to him, he appreciates my one breast even more." She tried to take another swallow of the brandy and started to cry silently. Netta took the glass from her and put her arms round her mother, rocking her like a child, letting her cry.

After a minute, Alice continued. "He makes such a fuss over my other breast, says how beautiful it is – how sexy I look with just one." Her hand rubbed her chest as she spoke, more tears running down her sagging cheeks.

"Oh Mother," said Netta, enfolding her again. "Is that why you left – in the middle of the night?"

Alice nodded. "I told him I hate that bed now and I don't want to sleep with him. I'm frightened."

"And did you tell him why?" said Netta, continuing to hold her mother.

"I tried. But I'm too frightened," she spoke, almost to herself.

"Frightened he'll leave," said Netta. "So you left him first."

Alice nodded and held out her hand for the glass. Netta passed her the brandy.

"And is that your dream, Mother – that Heck's leaving you?"

Alice drank off the last dregs of the brandy and set the glass on the floor by her feet. "No," she said, straightening up, wiping her wet cheeks with the heel of her hand.

Netta waited for nearly a minute, then took both of Alice's hands in hers before she spoke. "You can tell me, Mother. It's alright."

"It's always the same dream. We start to make love and he fondles my breast – my remaining breast and stops. Then he starts again only he's not caressing it – he's probing it with his long bony fingers until he finds it. Finds the lump."

# CHAPTER 12

Outside the Golden Valley Hospice, two nurses wheeled patients to the specially adapted minibus and Barney loaded them in through the lift by the rear doors.

Maddy, wearing an emerald green turban stood waiting with another younger woman much shorter than herself. The younger woman puffed hard on a cigarette as they watched the loading process. Natasha helped to settle everyone in the seats while Barney dealt with the two wheelchairs – all the minibus could handle without removing another row of seats.

Mrs Oswold came out and saw the two women standing together, Maddy tall and regal in her turban and long skirt, the younger woman short and slight in a multi-coloured tracksuit. "Elinor, you're not thinking of going out today, I hope? I'm sure Dr. Nichols wouldn't advise it. Maybe next time when they aren't going so far."

"Maddy said I could go if I wanted to," said Elinor, puffing faster on her cigarette and clutching Maddy's arm for support."

"But you've only finished your treatment at Gloucester yesterday. I can't think Dr. Nichols agreed to an outing so soon," said Mrs Oswold, taking her by the other arm but Elinor pulled away.

"Well he did. Better than sitting around chain-smoking, he told me," said Maddy, patting her friend's arm.

Mrs Oswold frowned, then turned to Barney as he emerged from the rear of the minibus and fastened the wheelchair hoist in position. "If anyone starts feeling unwell," she said, looking at Elinor, "make sure you come directly back. They can visit the farm another day, Barney."

"I'll keep an eye on her," said Maddy, taking the cigarette stub from Elinor and grinding it out on the path. "Come on, Elinor. Natasha's saved us the front seats." She steered the smaller woman to the front door and Barney passed her up to Natasha inside.

Mrs Oswold watched them settling the frail young woman in the front seat. "I'm going to have a word with Dr. Nichols before you leave," she said to Barney and turned to go back through the sliding glass entrance doors.

Maddy stuck her head out the minibus door. "I'm sure I saw him leave for the hospital twenty minutes ago, Alma." Mrs Oswold hesitated then continued on into the hospice. "Come on, Barney," said Maddy, "get us out of here before she finds him."

Barney shot a glance at Natasha who nodded back. He started the minibus and pulled carefully around the turning loop and over the speed bump. Mrs Oswold and Dr. Nichols appeared in his rear-view mirror as he turned out onto the main road. Maddy and Elinor raised their clasped hands in the air and cheered, "Go Barney, go!"

In the sorting shed at the organic smallholding, piles of fresh vegetables and boxes spilled onto the wooden floor from the counters. Russell stood trimming leeks as the minibus pulled into the farmyard. Barney honked the horn until he appeared, to shoo away the two geese cackling and hissing, their necks outstretched.

"It's okay, they're harmless," he called above the din. "See?" He made a dive towards the gander and the two geese fled back behind the shed. The minibus door opened and Natasha stepped out.

"We brought you some visitors, Russell. Customers maybe," she said, helping the walking patients out of the minibus while Barney opened the rear doors to release the two wheelchairs.

"I've got too many customers already," said Russell. "What I need are workers."

Elinor poked her head in the sorting shed. "I used to prepare veggies for Tesco's. I'll give you a hand. Do you want to help, Maddy?"

Maddy lifted her long skirt and tucked the hem into her waistband. "If you show me how. I haven't got a clue."

"Right this way, ladies. I even have aprons for you," said Russell, holding out a couple of grubby white smocks for them to put on. "Do you know how to trim leeks?" he asked Elinor. For answer, she picked up a knife from the counter, topped and tailed a large leek and held it up for inspection. "Not bad," he nodded with approval. "Leave a bit more of the top greens though." He demonstrated and compared the two leeks.

"This is how Markies liked them," said Elinor. "Yours is more Tesco style."

Maddy watched, puzzled. "What are you talking about?"

"We had to grade everything into four groups for the supermarkets," explained Elinor. "Marks and Spencer's got the best quality and well-trimmed. Sainsbury's was next best, then Safeway's and last of all was Tesco's." She held up Russell's leek.

"Everybody gets the same quality from me," he said. "Only my customers like to see lots of green, so don't trim them too hard."

"Makes them feel virtuous," said Barney, pushing one of the wheelchairs. "Closer to the land, eh Harry?" The gnarled old man leaned forward in the chair to pick up an untrimmed leek.

"Them's how I like 'em. Still with the dirt on so's I can see what the soil was like they grew in," he said. "I trim my own veggies – no waste that way. Look at all them good tops you're chuckin' away," he pointed to the pile of trimmings on the ground by the bench.

"Don't worry, nothing's wasted here. The chickens and geese get all this stuff," said Russell.

"Okay, I get the picture," said Maddy. "People pay a premium for organic vegetables and they want to see the difference. Let me try now."

"Why don't you give them the grand tour, Russell, before you press-gang them?" said Natasha, shepherding a small group down the crowded aisle.

Russell grinned at her. "They asked me first. How could I refuse?" He tucked Maddy's arm in his and showed them all how the vegetables moved from the deep beds and the polytunnels to the sorting shed to be prepared, weighed and boxed for delivery once a week in his ancient electric delivery van – a former milkman's float.

"So where is everybody?" said Elinor. "How come you're on your own with all this stuff to get out?"

Russell pointed at Natasha and Barney. "There's my help. Abandoned me to go and work with you lot at the hospice. I offered them good organic food and a roof over their head." He winked at Elinor, "Even prepared to share my bed. There's no pleasing some people, though." Several of them turned to look at Natasha who flushed under their scrutiny.

"Wouldn't have to ask me twice," said Elinor. "Or Maddy either, I bet."

"I like the sound of the good food," agreed Maddy. "Not so sure about the bed sharing. I'd have to talk to Natasha first."

"How about a trial, Russell?" asked Elinor. "See what we can do. I'm free most days 'cept when I get my treatment."

Harry touched Barney's sleeve. "If we was all to pitch in now, I figure we could fill most of these orders before you take us back to the hospice."

Barney looked dubious. "I'm not sure what Mrs Oswold would have to say about that, Harry. What do you think, Natasha?"

"I suppose if anyone wants to help for awhile before we leave," she said.

Maddy picked up a trimming knife. "Alma will tell us off anyway – might as well give her something else to complain about."

"Stay as long as you like," Russell smiled. "Barney will even make you some tea."

Two hours later all the patients sat on the patio watching Barney and Russell load the last orders of veggies, packed and labelled, on the milk float. Natasha sat with them, checking her charges as they drank mugs of tea. "I hope Russell didn't wear you out, Elinor? Harry, how about you?"

"I could do it all over again tomorrow, Tash," said Elinor, puffing on a cigarette away from the others.

"Too bad there's no cake for the workers," said Harry.

Russell came over to his wheelchair with a large box of fresh vegetables. "There will be next time, Harry. You'll have to settle for these for today."

"I'm not sure there'll be a next time if Mrs Oswold gets wind of this," said Natasha. "Come on, Barney, We'd better get everyone back to the hospice."

"Can't we come back again in your car, Maddy? She doesn't need to know," said Elinor. Her cheeks were flushed a high colour and she smoked with short pulls on her glowing cigarette.

"If Barney's willing to use my car. I'm not supposed to drive anymore. You sure you want us back, Russell?"

"Move in tomorrow, Maddy," he said, helping her into the minibus. He leaned across to Elinor. "How about a kiss goodbye, Elinor?"

She put her arms round his neck and they all cheered. "We'll be back," she said, kissing him. Her thin face glowed with high patches of red.

Natasha watched, shaking her head as Russell winked at her and waved them off. Barney swerved to miss Percy and his consort, hissing round the corner of the barn, necks stretched, screeching at full pitch.

# CHAPTER 13

Netta stood in her grandmother's kitchen in the old mansion flat in Highgate, North London.

"Where did you get this list from, Gran? It's three pages long," said Netta, flipping through it.

Martha brought another sheaf of papers from the big Welsh dresser in her kitchen where they sat round the table. "That's the short list – this is the original my friend Elsie emailed me. Took George twenty minutes to print it all off."

"By the time we've contacted all these, we'll have enough books to fill a ship, not just a crate," said Netta. "Do you know any of these school librarians, Gran?"

Martha shook her head. "No, but Elsie knows most of them. She used to be the London school library liaison before she retired and she still keeps in touch."

Alice paged through the stapled wad of paper then pushed it aside. "I'm not convinced this is the right way to do this. We haven't heard from Cassie for over two months. How do we know she's even at the refugee camp anymore?"

"Because I've spoken to Marcel at the *Amis du CFA* office in Paris and he promised to let me know if he hears of any changes," said Netta. "They have a courier going out to Guinea this month and he'll report back when he gets there. Marcel says it's not unusual for them to be out of contact, Mother.

Even when they do get to a town or city there's often no power for any internet connection."

Martha poured Alice more coffee. "At least we know Cassie wants these books. She was the one who suggested I approach the local schools. She knows George has been on the school board for years." She patted her daughter's hand. "You surely don't want to go out there empty-handed, Alice?"

"I don't give a damn about the books. It's Cassie I'm worried about."

"And I've told you, nobody's going anywhere until we hear from her," said Netta. "So in the meantime we might as well do something she wants us to do."

"It was only a suggestion, Alice," said Martha. "I thought you'd approve. Think how much Adina loves the books you send her." She rose and crossed to remove a small photo of a nine-year-old African girl from under a fridge magnet and brought it back to the table. The child, dressed in a blue and white school uniform and wearing steel-rimmed round glasses, held up a book to the camera. "Remember choosing this one for her?"

Netta took the photo and peered at it. "What is it, Mother? I can't make it out."

"'*Shirley Sharp-Eyes*,'" said her grandmother. "We knew how much you loved it when you had to have glasses."

"God, I hated wearing those glasses," said Netta. "Pretty crude psychology, but it worked. I decided that they gave me special vision, like Shirley Sharp-Eyes. I hope she has the same effect on Adina." She handed the photo to her mother.

Alice looked at the solemn little girl. "Glasses are the least of her problems. What good are books to a child with one leg?"

"We're not doctors, Alice. We can only send what Cassie asks for. She's the one out there working with them. If she thinks books are important for these children, then so do I," said Martha.

"And if she's not there anymore, then what?" said Alice.

"We don't know that, Mother. We have to wait and see. Marcel's courier will be there soon. Meantime, why not do what Gran suggests instead of sitting here wringing our hands." Netta held up the short-list. "She's already done the spadework. I can tackle some of these libraries near me. They're constantly weeding out their stock."

Alice turned to face her. "You promised you'd help me find her, Netta. If we don't hear soon, I'm going to ask Hunter instead...."

Martha began clearing the table. "Let's make a start, shall we? I always feel better when I'm doing something rather than just talking about it."

# CHAPTER 14

As Barney and Russell waited for the ambulance to arrive, Russell talked it in on his mobile phone. They stood outside the stone farmhouse, looking up the long lane towards the road. Russell spoke into the mobile, making swooping gestures with his free hand. "You go down a steep dip then sharp left at the top of the hill for about a half a mile. Turn right just after a red brick bungalow. You'll see the sign at the top of the lane. 'Golden Valley Organics'. We're right at the bottom."

"Do you think you'll recognise Landon with the bandages off?" asked Barney. "Natasha says he's going to be seriously disfigured until they can do some skin grafting later."

"I imagine it's the loss of his hand that will be the worst for him," said Russell.

"When I made the insurance claim for the *Iron Sea Horse* they showed me his old saxophone," said Barney. "I took it into Boosey & Hawkes at St Giles Circus in London, to see if they could fix it but they said it wasn't worth it. The insurance adjuster asked if I wanted to claim for a new one and I didn't know what to say."

"Let's not even mention it until he asks. He's never going to play again with one hand." Russell looked up the lane. "Here they come."

As the ambulance came slowly down the lane, Percy and Lucy set up a screeching racket until Russell chased them back around behind the shed. By the time he returned the ambulance had pulled up by the side of the farmhouse. A young paramedic hopped out and opened the rear doors. Natasha appeared first and then the driver came round to help get the stretcher out the back.

Barney stood at the house door, holding it open. Russell approached the ambulance. He stared down at the man lying on the stretcher, reached out a hand, then pulled it back before he touched him.

"Hello, Landon. It's me, Russell."

The man turned his head a fraction to look at him but said nothing. Natasha walked beside him, steering the paramedics into the house past Barney. She smiled at him, not speaking and he got his first impression of the 'mystery man' since his facial bandages were removed. What he saw unnerved him. The man's mouth was contorted into a leering grin and he had no eyebrows or hair, only pink splotches of new skin on his black face and scalp. Barney tried to smile at him as he went past but the man was watching Natasha who held onto the side of the stretcher.

Russell and Barney followed them into the house and into the empty room with its white-painted walls and fresh-curtained windows. They watched from the doorway as Natasha turned down the sheets and the paramedics eased Landon onto the bed with practised movements.

"Okay, Mr Freers, you're in good hands now. Natasha will look after you," said the driver, an overweight middle-aged man with a sweating bald head.

"We'll be back every week to take you to the clinic in Gloucester," added the younger man. "If she gives you any trouble you just let us know." He smiled at Natasha. "Will you be here to accompany him?" She nodded and the two men folded the stretcher and squeezed past Russell and Barney by the door.

Natasha bent over the bed. "I'll be here for awhile before I go to the hospice, Landon. Are you hungry, yet?" When he shook his head, she said, "I'll make you a drink then. This is Barney. He's going to help look after you when I'm not here."

Barney moved closer to the bed. "Hello, Landon. I found an old cowbell in Russell's junk pile and he brazed a handle on it. See? You just ring this any time you need me. We tried it out and we can hear it in the sorting shed." He set the brass bell down on the bedside table. "I'll put it here where you can reach it."

Landon followed him with his eyes. Too late, Barney realised he'd put the bell down beside the man's amputated right hand.

# CHAPTER 15

Maddy helped Barney and Elinor lay out the calligraphy boards in the hospice day centre. Elinor distributed the felt-tipped calligraphy pens in handfuls around the two tables to the waiting patients. Harry watched from his wheelchair, his gnarled fingers bunched in his lap.

"You want to have another go today, Harry?" she asked, holding out a pen to him but the old farmer only smiled and shook his bald head, covered in large brown melanoma patches.

"I'll just keep an eye on you lot; see you don't nick any of Barney's kit. I can manage them paintbrushes okay but these here calligraphy pens is too small to get my old mitts around." He held up one twisted hand to Elinor.

"We still want to include your quote in our collection, Harry. Have you chosen one yet?" asked Barney as he set up the flip chart with its pre-ruled paper and sample half-uncial alphabet.

"Got it right here. My grandson copied it out for me from Old Moore's Almanac." He pulled a folded page from a school notebook out of his shirt pocket and handed it to Elinor to read.

"Maybe you better read it, Maddy. I'm not too good at reading out loud. My boys used to read faster'n me when they were little."

"You do just fine when you're reading my stars to me from those magazines, Elinor," said Maddy. "Go ahead; let's hear what Harry's found. If it's a good one, maybe we can write it out for him."

"Okay." Elinor stood up and put on her glasses. "It says, 'Whatsoever thy hand findeth to do, do it with thy might, For the night cometh wherein no man shall work.'" She paused, "I can't make out the last word – looks foreign to me."

"Ecclesiastes," said Barney. "He's full of good quotes."

"I reckon that's spot on for an old farmer like me," said Harry, folding up the paper again.

"Anybody else choose something from Ecclesiastes?" Barney looked round the faces at the table. Louisa, a quiet wispy-haired woman he had only met once before caught his eye. "Louisa?"

"My mother's favourite was; 'To everything there is a season and a time for everything under the sun'," she said.

"Do you know anymore of it?" asked Barney.

"A time to work and a time to play," said Louisa.

"A time to sow and a time to reap," added Harry.

Other hands went up round the tables as old memories triggered thoughts in the country people, who made up the bulk of the hospice patients.

"A time to laugh and a time to cry," some one said.

"A time to live and a time to die," this from Maddy as she looked at Barney, her eyes as steely blue as her turban. The tables fell silent as each one absorbed the ancient aphorisms.

Elinor broke the silence humming a tune and nodding her head. "I know that song. It's The Byrds – 'To everything, turn, turn, turn,'" she sang, "There is a season, turn, turn, turn." The others joined in humming as she sang in a shaky treble. "A time to laugh – a time to cry. A time to live – a time to die...." She stopped and turned to Maddy. "It's a great song, but that's the only bit I remember. Hey, Barney. I want to choose that one for my calligraphy piece."

"It's up to Louisa – she mentioned it first," said Barney, looking down the table at the small farm woman.

"Elinor can have it," she said. "I was only remembering it, is all."

"What are we going to call our collection, Barney?" asked Maddy. "We ought to have a name."

"I'm having trouble with that," he said. "Originally I thought of it as a sort of medieval Book of Hours with illuminated lettering, that sort of thing. With a quotation for each day."

"Teach Yourself Dying," said Elinor.

"Or The Beginner's Guide to Dying," said Maddy. "Seeing as we're all new at this." Some of the others smiled and nodded.

"You gonna scare folks off with a title like that," said Harry. "We want them to look at it first, don't we?"

Barney watched the faces of the patients round the tables. "You can see why I've been having difficulty choosing. I thought of A Bedside Book of Dying but Harry's right. It may be too gloomy and off-putting. Anyway, we don't need a title today; we're a long way from being ready for the front cover."

"We could have a contest – ask everyone in the hospice to suggest a good name and give the winner a prize," said Elinor. "A bottle of vodka."

"Or a free copy of the book," said Barney.

"A free copy of the book – *and* a bottle of vodka," said Maddy.

# CHAPTER 16

Landon lay propped up in bed staring at the TV they had wheeled in from the farm kitchen, where it usually lived. Russell filed a piece of metal to a sharp point and Barney read emails on his laptop on the other side of Landon's bed. A pile of plates and bowls half-covered the raised adjustable table Natasha had borrowed from the hospice storeroom.

"We gonna watch this DVD or not?" asked Russell. "There's nothing on the box I want to see. You want to look at anything, Landon?" Landon shook his head.

"Okay, I'll put it on after the news. Clive says it's only half an hour. I haven't watched it yet but he says it's good," said Barney, taking the disc out of the padded delivery envelope. "Shall I read you what it says on the sleeve, Landon?" He looked up to see his reaction. So far, they had only been able to get nods or shakes of his head from him.

Natasha said the doctors told her his lungs weren't permanently damaged so he probably just didn't want to talk. They had evolved a sort of *modus vivendi* since he arrived, of eating evening meals with him and spending time in his room after dinner, including him in the conversation. That mainly meant reading to him, asking yes or no questions and just watching the News At Ten. Often, Russell went out to the pub and left Barney and Landon to listen to an audiobook or see a film on TV.

Barney read from the DVD back cover. "'*A fascinating documentary account of the re-enactment of the journey of the Amistad, the slave ship made famous for its mutiny by the slaves aboard and how they sailed back to Africa. As part of the voyage, the crew, made up entirely of volunteers, plans to spend several months sailing down the West African coast visiting each of the old slave ports along the way.*'"

Russell held up his piece of work for Landon's inspection. Landon nodded. A long heron's beak was beginning to take shape. "And he wants you to go with him to make the same journey on his boat. Why?"

"Oh, every year or so, Clive gets restless staying around Vancouver. He likes to do extended cruises somewhere different. Alaska, the Baja, Hawaii."

"So you're going all the way back to Vancouver and then turn around and sail back to West Africa?" Russell laid down the bird beak on the raised table and spoke to Landon. "And he says I'm the weird one. You're mad, Barney. Barking." A ghost of a smile moved over Landon's distorted lips.

"I haven't agreed yet. We're still discussing it. That's why he sent me this DVD – to convince me. It's one way for me to get to see Cassie in Guinea."

"Helluva roundabout way to go."

"I'm in no hurry. Besides, be nice to spend some time again with Clive. He's into meditation too but he prefers to do it at sea, on his boat."

"How long have you been messing about with this Buddhist stuff, Barney? Must be ten years or more, isn't it?" said Russell.

"About that, off and on."

"I thought this last trip to China and Tibet would have got it out of your system. Didn't you tell me it was all a load of empty rituals now?"

"Not all of it," said Barney. "Anyway, who am I to judge someone else's cultural beliefs? I just meant it didn't work for me."

"So now what – you giving up on this 3rd age experiment of yours or you got something else in mind?"

"Trial and error, Russell. It's all I know. Keep on looking, exploring, trying things out – see where they lead."

"You're 72, Barney. At this rate you're gonna run out of life before you find any answers. What kind of example are you setting your kids?"

Barney laughed. "You can talk. You don't even know where your kids are."

"They know where I am if they need me," said Russell. "More than you can say."

Barney appealed to Landon. "He's always been such a smug bastard just because he happens to be talented. What about the rest of us who aren't artists, what are we supposed to do with the rest of our lives? Russell can go on fiddling with his sculptures – welding bits of junk together until he drops."

"You're starting to sound like Alice, Barney. What about my organic market garden, is that just playing too? Alice likes to pretend I'm just an arrogant womaniser."

"She's got a point there, Russell. I've lost track of how many women have passed through your artistic little fingers."

"I like women – women like me. What's wrong with that?"

"Ask Landon."

The black man stared at Russell and his lips twitched. They both waited to see if he would speak but he only continued to stare.

"Landon knows it was all over with Tash before I came on the scene. Isn't that right, Landon?" The black man shook his head and turned away. Russell moved nearer the bed. "I suppose you want to blame me for what happened to your hand, too?"

"Take it easy, Russell. The man can't defend himself," said Barney, but Russell was wound up now.

"I'm tired of you all saying what a shit I am – you, Tash, Alice – Landon. But I'm the one who took him in after Tash dumped him. Let him stay on the boat. Then when he tries to commit suicide, I take him in here." He turned to Landon who hadn't taken his eyes off Russell the whole time. "Isn't that right, Landon?"

His voice when he spoke had a rough, scratchy tone. "It was an accident."

For a minute they both stood mute. Then Barney picked up the drink from the raised bed table with the glass straw and offered it to him. "Here, this will help your throat."

The black man sucked awkwardly at the straw before he spoke again. They had to lean forward to hear him.

"She tried to steal my sax," he rasped.

"What?" asked Barney. "Who?"

"I dunno."

"What d'ya mean you don't know?" demanded Russell.

"Some woman from the jazz club. She came back to the boat with me. I don't remember her name. We had a few drinks. I wanted her to stay but she wouldn't – said I was too drunk."

"I can believe that," said Russell.

"All she wanted was my money only I didn't have none left."

Barney nodded, "So she tried to steal your sax."

"She was half way up the steps with it when I grabbed it. She kicked me in the chest but I hung on, so she let go an' ran off. I fell back down the steps, holdin' on to my old sax. Pulled the cupboard over and it fell on top of me. Must of knocked over the lamp on the table when my head hit it, I guess. I don't remember anymore…."

All three men sat staring at each other, trying to picture the scene.

Russell turned to Barney. "You think we should tell that police detective?"

"Would you recognise her again, Landon?" asked Barney.

Landon shook his head. "Not her fault – my fault."

"And meantime my boat's destroyed," said Russell.

"It was my boat, too," said Barney. "Not that it matters now. It was an accident. The important thing is you're alive, Landon."

"Well, when he's better he can damn well work here until he's paid me back," said Russell.

"Don't worry, you'll get your money's worth. I can do more with one hand than you can with two."

"Okay, okay," soothed Barney. "So what's our story to Detective Parry?"

Landon shrugged. Russell grabbed his coat. "You two figure it out. I'm going to the pub."

Landon closed his eyes and slumped down on the bed. "Just an accident."

# CHAPTER 17

Under Vancouver's Art Deco Burrard Bridge, the *Sea Mist* lay tied to Fisherman's Wharf. Barney had bought it under the guidance of his sailing friend Clive and he and his son Hunter had been converting it to a live-aboard before Barney left for China. Since then, Hunter lived on it with his Czech girlfriend, Lottie, while his father was travelling.

In the main cabin below deck, Hunter and Clive hunched over Lottie's shoulder reading an email.

*Dear Hunter,*

*I know that Netta is writing to you but I want to ask you myself whether you have heard from Cassie recently. Netta spoke to the man in the Paris office of Les Amis du CFA but they have no news until their courier goes out to Guinea again. The address I have for Zinadine just returns my emails undelivered.*

*The last time I heard from Cassie she told me she had asked if you would come and make a video of her refugee children's camp. She said that you needed a project to complete your film course in Vancouver and you agreed to go. But when will you be ready? If you need some money for the trip, I'll pay for your fare.*

*I wanted to go myself to see her but my doctor says I need to finish my course of cancer treatment first and that my immune system is too weak to risk travel in West Africa. I know that sounds pathetic but the truth is this whole business with my mastectomy has wrecked my self-confidence. So when Netta suggested you'd be more likely to find Cassie than me, I decided to ask you.*

*Martha and Netta have convinced me I can do more for Cassie here in London than by getting lost in West Africa. I had to agree; in my present feeble state they're probably right. Martha and George are organising a collection of children's library books and school texts to ship to her war orphans.*

*Most of the kids are from Sierra Leone so they learn in English. I don't know how we're going to get the books to Kissidougou from Freetown but maybe you can help. It will take two or three months for the ship to arrive there.*

*Please let me know soon what your plans are and if you hear anything at all from Cassie. I hope you and Lottie are still coping with living on Barney's boat. Please do be careful. There was a horrible fire on our old canal boat and a man nearly died in it.*

*Much love,*

*Alice.*

Lottie finished reading the email aloud and swung her long tanned legs around in Barney's old wooden swivel chair to face Hunter and Clive.

"So 'Untair, do you want to reply right now?" she asked, taking his hand in her large expressive one. "I see Alice is quite worried about Cassie and this is not a good thing when she is so ill. You must reassure her, yes?" She spoke English with a strange mix of Czech and French accents.

Hunter nodded and put his arm round Lottie. He knew how close she and his half-sister Cassie had become since their student days at the Sorbonne.

"Alice has always worried about Cassie since the day she first left home to go and study in Paris. But ever since she and

Zinadine went to Africa, Alice has tried to persuade her to come home. And the more she tries the more Cassie resists. I'm sure that's why she doesn't write that often."

Lottie nodded, her ash-blonde hair spilling out of the loose coil piled up on her head. Although almost six feet tall, she made no attempt to disguise her height. Rather, she exaggerated it with tall hairdos, high-heeled sling back shoes and short shorts exposing her impressively long legs.

Now she turned to Clive who had brought them a printout of Alice's email as Hunter had no computer on the Sea *Mist*.

"How soon will you be leaving on *The Betsy*, Clive?"

"Not for awhile. Hunter's promised to help me fit some new stays to the mast and I haven't worked out my provisioning yet." Clive's weatherworn face with its bushy white beard looked tired. He'd been working hard on his old Dutch sailboat, readying it for his proposed epic journey and was still absorbing his setback. Barney's email saying he wouldn't now be able to join him for the trip had unsettled him more than he cared to admit. He smiled at the two of them now.

"Unless of course, you can spare Hunter for a couple of months, Lottie?" he said.

"But 'Untair has not sailed further than Salt Spring Island. Also, he must finish his film course," she said, sitting on Hunter's lap and wrapping her arms round his neck. "And I could not trust him with you." A foolish grin spread over Hunter's face.

"I know I haven't got your experience, Lottie. But Clive could teach me."

"Teach you what, though? You think I do not know how sailors behave when they are in a foreign port?" She waggled her long fingers at Clive and clutched Hunter closer.

Clive grinned at her. "I thought you were worried I might drown him, not lead him astray."

She pursed her lips as though considering this choice for a moment, pretending to study Hunter's face. "It is true I would be very sad if you drowned him, Clive. But if I had to choose there would be no doubt in my mind which it would be."

Clive laughed and Hunter protested, dumping her off his lap onto the bunk. She sprawled, draping her hand dramatically across her forehead, her long tanned legs propped up on his lap. He shrugged his shoulders at Clive and stroked her bare feet.

"I can see you two need to discuss this matter privately," said Clive, rising. "Let me know what you decide at lunchtime. I'm grilling some spot prawns, if you want to join me after you've worked up an appetite." He climbed up the four steps to the deck and slid the hatch closed behind him. Lottie raised an eyebrow at Hunter, then shifted over on the wide bunk as he rolled in beside her.

"You wish to continue this discussion now or later?" she asked, wrapping her long legs round him.

"First things first," he said.

Clive's boat, *The Betsy* lay moored next to the *Sea Mist.* The three of them sat beneath a navy blue canvas awning, eating local BC spot prawns, grilled on the tiny barbeque strapped to the stanchion railing. They drank cold, duty-free Czech beer, courtesy of an endless supply from Lottie's diplomat father, currently stationed in Vancouver's Coal Harbour.

"What does Trish think of your '*Amistad*' adventure, Clive?" asked Lottie, peeling prawns with the tips of her manicured fingers and feeding them to Hunter who lolled back in his deck chair in a post-coital inertia.

"She says if I go, she's going back to Scotland – for good, this time," he said. Trish and Clive's relationship was marked with stormy partings and clashes of stubborn wills but so far they had managed to weather them. He was philosophic about this threatened rupture, too. "We'll have to see."

"I'd planned on going by train to Lakehead and catching a Dutch freighter from Thunder Bay to Rotterdam," said Hunter. "Dad told me he found an Italian line that stops all along the West African coast. But it takes a long time."

"You could save a lot of money by coming with me," said Clive. "And it might even be shorter if we're lucky with the weather."

Lottie tipped up a Czech blond lager to her mouth, drinking from the bottle. "It would be even faster if you took me along. I could show you a few tricks I learned on the Vendée Globe race."

"I'll bet you could," grinned Clive, ducking as she threw a chunk of bread roll at him.

"Pay no attention to him, Lottie. He's just a dirty old man," said Hunter. "You can teach those tricks to me instead."

She ignored him, addressing Clive again. "I mean it. If 'Untair insists he won't fly, why not take advantage of my experience?"

"I already am, Lottie", said Hunter.

"Be serious for a minute, 'Untair. Think about Cassie's war orphans. Wouldn't it make more sense to get there as quick as possible? And as long as you're documenting the refugee camp you might as well film Clive's re-enactment trip, too."

"Mmmnn, what do you think, Clive?" asked Hunter.

Clive stroked his white moustache. "I don't know. I'm as superstitious as the next sailor about having a woman on board, I guess."

"Just think of me as an extra pair of hands. Experienced hands," said Lottie.

He gazed at her slender Slavic figure sitting on the deck of his sailboat and smiled.

"Tall order," he said.

"And while you're thinking of that, think about taking something with you, like Alice and Netta are – toys or sports equipment," she said. "It would make a good theme for 'Untair's documentary. Might even raise some money for Cassie."

"It's not a bad idea," Clive conceded. "And it ties in with my *Amistad* theme, too."

"I like the documentary link," said Hunter. "Not so sure about the sports equipment though. Sounds a bit cruel giving that stuff to kids with no hands or legs."

"Well, think of something else they need then," said Lottie. "We can ask Cassie."

Hunter opened another beer. "That's just it. We can't. None of us has heard from her for ages."

"Maybe Barney has," said Clive. "I'll email him and ask."

# CHAPTER 18

Maddy appeared in the doorway of Russell's vegetable sorting shed wearing a new pale green turban on her head. She was alone.

"Where's Elinor?" asked Barney. "She usually likes coming on delivery day."

"She's had a relapse. They had to take her into Gloucester Hospital last night. I've just come from her flat to make sure her boys are okay. That's why I'm late." She slipped on a coverall over her spotless cream dress.

"You didn't need to come, Maddy," said Russell, "but I'm glad you did. We're way behind as usual."

"We've even pressed Landon into service," said Barney, pushing the wheelchair closer to the counter so Landon could work the calculator with his good hand. The bandages were now off his hands and he held the calculator down with his stump.

"I wanted to come," said Maddy. "The hospital won't let me visit Elinor until this evening anyway."

"How serious is it this time?" asked Russell. He brought a fresh load of his mixed salad greens and set it in front of Maddy, to sort into bundles for the row of boxes being filled by Barney and Natasha.

Maddy began to sniffle and took out a tissue to blow her nose. It was obvious she had been crying. "Mason, her 13 year old asked me if he could come with me to visit her tonight. I didn't know what to say." She fumbled with a package of ties for the greens.

Natasha stopped her packing and came to put an arm round her.

"I'll find out how she is when I go in this morning, Maddy. They may have to keep her in for a few days to stabilise her. Perhaps I shouldn't have agreed she could help out here." She turned to Russell. "You weren't letting her lift any of these boxes, I hope?"

Russell shook his head. "I told her to take it easy, Tash. But she's a demon when she gets going. Barney's been keeping an eye on her."

"Yeah, I told her I'd tie her to that stool if I caught her shifting any of these completed orders," said Barney. "Landon's been watching her when I'm out in the polytunnel."

"She can't help herself," agreed Landon. "Fills these orders faster'n any of you."

Maddy nodded, "Elinor loves it here, Natasha. I thought it was doing her good or I wouldn't have brought her out so often."

"It's not your fault, Maddy. It's Russell who should know better," said Natasha. "I told him how ill she was."

"So now I'm going to be blamed for Elinor as well as Landon?" said Russell. "Why not? I suppose Maddy'll be next to add to my list, Tash."

"You can't help yourself, can you? The moment anyone offers to help, you work them into the ground." She removed her coverall. "You've even got me back in here, when I swore I wouldn't. Well, from now on I mean it."

"What about Landon? You abandoning him too?"

"I might if he keeps acting so stubborn about his hand," said Natasha.

"She's tryin' to turn me into Captain Hook. Well, I don't want any steel claw." He pinned the calculator down with his stump while punching in numbers with his left hand.

"Nobody's talking about hooks or claws, Landon. You know fine how much better prostheses are today. You've seen the demo at the Gloucester clinic," she said.

"How come lots of people don't use them, then?" he said.

"Maybe they just like being dependent," she said. "Is that what you're thinking, Landon? As long as you don't have a right hand, I'll stick around and look after you?"

"No!" He punched the calculator hard with his stump and it flew off the counter onto the ground. He whirled the wheelchair round to glare at Natasha. "I never asked any of you to do anythin'," he waved his stump around at the others who had stopped work to stare at him. "If you think I need you, Tash, you're mistaken. You can take your guilt feelin's and clear off, for all I care."

"I stopped feeling guilty about you a long time ago," she said. "I'm here because the law says you're still my husband and I'm responsible for you, that's all. You just sign those divorce papers and see how fast I disappear." She stooped to pick up the calculator and put it down on the counter with her smock.

"Now I see why you're so keen to get me a new right hand," said Landon.

Barney moved between them. "Russell and I had to do some hard talking to persuade Natasha to agree to this arrangement, Landon. She didn't want to do it, at first."

"Yeah. Don't be such a fucking ingrate. If it wasn't for Tash you'd be stuck in some dreary geriatric day centre," said Russell. "In fact, if you don't like the arrangement here, just say. We can damn soon change it."

"Well look at you two, stickin' up for poor little Tash. She's set you both up, gettin' you to agree to look after me so she can disappear. You heard her," he said, his dark eyes bulging beneath the hairless eyebrows.

"You're wrong, Landon," said Maddy. "Natasha is doing this for the same reason as Russell and Barney. The same reason you watch out for Elinor."

"Elinor's different. She's dyin'."

Maddy sat down on a stool beside his wheelchair so she could be at his eye-level. "What do you think she'd say if she was here now, Landon?"

"I know whose side she'd be on, anyway. Elinor likes me. We understand each other," he said.

"And you think we don't? Don't understand?"

"Elinor's young – she's got two young boys to worry about. She's not old like us. It doesn't matter what happens to us – we've had our lives." He stared down at his stump, covering it with his left hand. Maddy reached out to put her hand on top of his.

"It matters to me, Landon. Nobody cares more about Elinor than me. I love her like a daughter. But I care about my own life too. All of it, not just the good bits. And it's not over till it's over." She reached up to remove the pale green turban from her pale bald head. "I used to have the most beautiful red hair once. I was so vain. I thought I'd rather lose my right arm than lose my hair. And now it's all gone. And it's not coming back – not unless I stop the chemo. And if I stop that, I stop living." She turned to look at the others, then picked up her green turban and pulled it back over her naked head. "So now I have coloured turbans instead. This one is called '*eau de Nile*'. I even have a red one to remind me of my hair. It's not the same but my life's not the same now either. It's different, but it's still my life."

# CHAPTER 19

The calligraphy group at the Golden Valley Hospice day centre were bent over their work, laboriously shaping the unfamiliar letters the way Barney had showed them. He had taught them four or five of the basic scripts, some easy and some more difficult.

Elinor favoured the Italic alphabet for her collection of quotes because she could work faster. She had already compiled several completed ones while the others were still only partly finished. She offered to do one for Harry but he had settled on the Gothic lettering which she found tedious.

"It's too hard to read, Harry. Makes me go all cross-eyed when I look at it too long." She held up one of her pieces for him to compare. "See how nice and easy this is to read, next to all these Gothic squiggles?"

Harry picked up the sheet and read aloud. "'*You are the bows from which your children as living arrows are sent forth. – Khalil Gibran*'. Where did you find this, Elinor?"

"In Barney's slush pile. He's got masses of them. D'you like it?"

Harry considered it. "Yeah. I don't see the connection to dying, though. Aren't we supposed to be choosing stuff that fits our title now we've settled on it?"

She appealed to Barney. "Harry says I shouldn't have chosen this."

"It's your choice, Elinor. Not Harry's. Does it have a connection for you?"

She nodded. "I like it. And so does Maddy. She helped me choose it."

"Guess you're outnumbered, Harry," said Barney.

"Never said I didn't like it," protested Harry. "I just don't see what it has to do with a booklet that's gonna be called '*The Beginner's Guide to Dying Well*'."

Maddy flipped through the accumulating pile of calligraphy pages the group had written so far. "Let's not get started on that again, Harry. We're not changing the title after all the arguments we went through choosing it. Nobody's objecting to your pieces," she said, going through the pile in front of him. "Although I'm surprised Alma didn't say something about this one." She held up a single sheet in Gothic script.

"Let me see it, Maddy," said Elinor peering over her shoulder. "Oh, it's in that damn German script. You read it to us."

The rest of the group stopped what they were working on to hear what she'd found. "It says: '*On the whole, I'd rather be in Philadelphia*'."

"I don't get it," said Elinor.

"It's off a tombstone," said Harry. "W.C. Fields."

"It's a joke, Elinor," said Barney. "A running joke. He always pretended to dislike Philadelphia."

"I still don't get it," she said.

"How be we let Harry keep his W.C. Fields quote if Elinor keeps hers?" said Maddy, holding up the two sheets to the group.

"A Solomon in our midst," said Barney. Maddy stuck out her tongue at him.

Mrs Oswold left her office clutching a sheaf of paper and approached the group. "Barney, I've just had a disturbing report from the Gloucester Clinic. They claim it appears Elinor's relapse was due in part to physical over-exertion. She told them she was working on a farm. Do you know about this?" she demanded, holding out the report to him.

He skimmed the pages before looking up at her standing over him. He nodded slowly. "She has been helping occasionally at the organic market garden on delivery days." The others at the tables turned to look at Mrs Oswold.

"We thought it would do her good to get out in the countryside, Alma," said Maddy. "I know it's helped me feel better."

Mrs Oswold looked from Barney to her. "And who exactly is 'we'?"

Maddy opened her mouth to reply, then closed it, saying nothing.

"It was my idea," said Elinor. "I wanted to help. I used to work on a produce farm. That's what I told the doctor at the hospital."

"Who else has been working at this farm, Barney?" asked Mrs Oswold.

He looked uncomfortably round the group. "Different people at different times," he said. "Depends on who came on the minibus."

"And you allowed this to happen, Natasha – people like Elinor whose condition you knew?"

"I made sure they didn't overdo it, Alma. They were enjoying the experience," she said.

"Do you realise how bad this looks, if the board or the public hears of it," said Mrs Oswold. "Allowing a private business to exploit hospice patients for free labour?"

"Nobody's been exploited, Alma. You've got an over-active imagination," said Maddy. "We're all adults and we did it because we wanted to. No other reason."

Mrs Oswold took the report from Barney and waved it at her. "This is not imaginary, Maddy. And it will be seen by the hospice doctors who report to the board."

"It was my suggestion which started these outings to Russell's farm," said Barney. "If you're worried this will reflect badly on you, I take full responsibility, Mrs Oswold."

She flushed and turned on him. "I have only one concern, Barney and that is the well-being of our patients."

"Calm down, Alma," said Maddy. "Nobody's accusing you of neglect. We all know we're dying and we're entitled to enjoy what's left of our lives as we see fit. I'm sorry Elinor overdid it but I doubt she blames us, or you."

"It's my own fault," said Elinor. "I didn't know that doctor was going to write it in a report. I just thought he was interested, is all." She began to cry. "And now I've spoiled it for everybody. Alma won't let us go anymore."

Harry pushed his wheelchair over towards Mrs Oswold. "If you're looking for a scapegoat, Alma, I'm the one who said we should help Russell with his orders. Don't blame Barney or Natasha – they just drove us there for an outing."

The others all muttered in agreement. Mrs Oswold looked round the group, then shook her head at them. "It's not that simple, Harry. The local newspapers are bound to hear about this –" she held up the report, "I can see the headlines already." She turned back to her office.

# CHAPTER 20

In the old mansion flat in Highgate, North London, Martha, Alice and Netta sorted through boxes of books on the dining room table which was pulled out to its furthest extent.

"Where's Granddad?" asked Netta. "I need more of those empty boxes made up."

"I sent him into the bedroom to lie down," said her grandmother. "He's been working like a Trojan all morning."

Alice piled more picture books onto the growing heap in front of her. "Do you really think Cassie needs so many of this kind of storybook, Netta? Most of her orphans must be too old for these." She flipped through an illustrated hardback before adding it to the pile.

"You read the email from the courier, Mother. She says they love looking at the pictures because most of them can't read yet."

"I didn't pay all that much attention to the report," said Alice. "I just wanted to hear how Cassie was and whether she's still safe. And there wasn't a word about it from her."

Martha patted her shoulder. "No news is good news, dear. I'm sure she's well or she would have mentioned it to the CFA agent."

"The best thing we can do for the present is have this load of books ready for Hunter when he gets to Dakar," said Netta. "He and Lottie will be leaving soon and we've barely started cataloguing. Have you seen inside the garage lately?"

"George just leaves the car outside now. It's full of books from the school libraries and more keep coming every week," said Martha.

"Do you think Heck would help us, Mother? I'm worried about Granddad lifting all those heavy boxes of books," said Netta, glancing at Alice to see how she would take this mention of her split with Heck.

Alice gnawed her bottom lip. So far, she had refused to discuss Heck at all or allow him to visit her and when he phoned, she wouldn't take his calls. "I don't want to see him," she said. "I'm not ready yet."

"Aren't you being too hard on him, dear?" said Martha. "And we could use the help – he's such a big man."

"Too big," said Alice. "He intimidates me with those big hands of his."

"Mother, that's not fair. Heck wouldn't lay a finger on you and you know it."

"I know it was those bony fingers of his that started all my trouble –"

"But Mother –" Netta was about to continue but caught her grandmother's frown and stopped.

"Anyway, he's not here. He's gone to Rome," said Alice.

"What?" said Netta. "When?"

"A week ago. He sent me an email."

"Oh Alice," said her mother. "You were going to go together – you had it all worked out. What a shame."

"You could still go, Mother. Meet him there," said Netta. "Think how much you've wanted to spend time in Rome – you working on your doctoral research and Heck writing his new centurion novel. Your dream scenario, you called it."

Alice shook her head. "No. It's too late. I don't want to. I'm going to get in touch with Barney again," she said. "I know I said I wouldn't after our last row but he promised he'd go out to visit Cassie sometime, so why not now. At least we know she's still there. I expect Russell's fed up with him hanging around waiting for some freighter. It's so frustrating when he insists on going overland or by boat everywhere – and now he's talked Hunter into not flying, too."

"If you start attacking him about that, you'll just have another row," said Netta. She could not get used to her mother's changed attitude. She seemed determined to alienate Heck and even Barney had stomped off to the country when she refused to discuss the divorce. From the moment Alice showed up on her doorstep in the middle of the night, she had become a changed person – a stranger to her daughter who previously felt she knew all her mother's moods. Not looking at her grandmother, she determined to return to the attack.

"This is crazy, Mother. Why are you being so stubborn? You're just driving everyone away – first Barney over this divorce nonsense and now blaming Heck for discovering your breast cancer."

"Netta –" warned her grandmother.

"I don't care. It's childish."

Alice put down the picture book she was holding and faced her mother and daughter. "You haven't understood anything I've said. I thought you might be able to appreciate my situation, Netta. It's not so unlike your own with Philip," she said.

"At least Philip and I are dealing with it like adults. You and Heck are behaving like children, if you ask me."

"Nobody's asking you to interfere. I'm not a child. I'm 62 years old. I don't need your advice on how to conduct my life, Netta."

"Could've fooled me, Mother. Some role model you are for me and Cassie."

"I'm here, aren't I? Working on this book project you and your grandmother seem to feel is so important to Cassie."

"I'm quite aware you think it's a waste of time, Mother. Cassie and Gran and I don't happen to think so," said Netta. She rammed an armful of books into an empty box. "Until you come up with a better idea, I intend to continue with it."

George appeared in the kitchen doorway. "What's all the shouting about, Martha?" He beckoned to Alice. "I've just had an email you need to read," he said, going back towards his den. "It's from Heck. He says to tell you Mrs Hollis is in hospital. A stroke they think."

# CHAPTER 21

In the geriatric ward of the Mile End Hospital, Alice sat by the bedside of the sleeping old lady, holding her hand.

"Mrs Hollis? It's Alice – can you hear me?" She looked at the old woman she had come to regard as her confidante. Her visits to the nursing home, which started as a duty, had become as enjoyable to her as they so obviously were to Mrs Hollis. After the first few times when she went with Heck, Alice began going on her own. The old lady loved using the digital photos of her old Georgian house that Alice showed her, as a springboard into her past. She told Alice the background of each piece of furniture and bric-a-brac Heck was cataloguing so meticulously for her.

Alice studied the old face lying on the pillow with its translucent skin and wispy hair brushed back by the nurses from off her forehead. Mrs Hollis' hairline was receding just like an old man's, she thought. Would she ever recover enough to deal with the sale of her house and possessions? Looking at how frail the old woman seemed, made Alice realise her own parents, George and Martha would soon be this vulnerable. They were only a few years younger than Mrs Hollis. As an only child, she would have the old rambling Highgate mansion flat to dispose of, too.

Thinking of all her parents possessions and the accumulated history of her childhood so lovingly preserved by them, gave her a new feeling of empathy with this old woman lying here, her features almost as white as the hospital sheets she lay between. Mrs Hollis opened her pale violet eyes, at first not focusing on Alice but taking in the room.

"Mrs Hollis – can you hear me?" Alice repeated.

The eyelids flickered then opened a bit more and her gaze settled on Alice.

"Hello dear," she said, slurring the words. "Is Heck with you?"

"No, he's in Rome," said Alice, stroking the veined skin on the back of Mrs Hollis' hand.

"But I asked for you both to come." Her head rolled back and forth in agitation. "I wanted to tell you together."

"He'll come and see you as soon as he comes back," said Alice. "You mustn't worry about the house. He finished all the cataloguing before he left."

"But that's what I wanted to see you about, dear. I have a new proposal to make and you should both be here to agree to it." The old lady fluttered her hands in frustration.

Alice tried to calm her, taking her frail hands, little more than skin and bone now, in her own. "We'll have plenty of time to talk over any new plans when you're better and back with Mrs. Morton at the nursing home. Heck will be back from Rome by then, I'm sure."

The old woman gazed into Alice's face. "You don't have to pretend any more, Alice. We both know I'm not leaving here.

It's only a matter of time before I have a second stroke that will finish me. That new young doctor told me as much."

"Why, what did she say?"

"She told me that it would be advisable to sort out any personal business while I still had the strength to do so. That's why I asked the nurse to phone you – only you weren't there. Neither of you. So she sent you an email instead. Where were you, dear? The nurse said she called several times and left messages – has something happened?"

Alice looked at her worried face as she formulated her reply. "Heck wanted to go to Rome to work on his book, Mrs Hollis, now that everything is completed at your house and ready for the sale. The auctioneers said people love to go to house sales rather than auction rooms so we arranged all your possessions on display. I didn't like to disturb things once it was ready so I've been staying up in Highgate at my mother's. She and Netta and I are organising a shipment of school books for Cassie's refugee camp that I told you about."

The old woman nodded, "I remember, Alice and that's part of what I have to say. I've been lying here thinking about it ever since I spoke to that young doctor. I've decided to give the proceeds of the sale to Cassie's orphans."

"But we already agreed that money was for you to live on and pay your expenses at the nursing home, Mrs Hollis," protested Alice. "Besides, you don't even know Cassie."

"I feel as if I do," said Mrs Hollis, smiling at her. "Martha and I have talked about her quite a lot on her weekly visits. She's very proud of her youngest granddaughter. We both admire her courage. I wish I'd had the nerve to do what she's doing when I was a young woman. Martha showed me some of the pictures Cassie sent of the children." Tears clouded the old lady's eyes. "I would have been useless, of course, blubbing away at the sight of those little hands and feet chopped off. How can people be so barbarous, Alice?"

"Please, Mrs Hollis, don't upset yourself," she said and gave her a tissue to wipe her eyes.

"I'm sorry, dear. But you see what I mean – just the thought of them makes me cry. Anyway, I've decided that if I can't be of any use at least my money can. I've been thinking how much Arthur would've approved of spending it on these children – he wanted so much to have children of our own but we could never..." she faltered, pressing the tissue to her mouth, biting on it.

Alice stood and put her arms around the old woman, holding her slight frame gently. "It's a wonderful, generous thought, Mrs Hollis. I'm sure Arthur would have agreed. Perhaps your solicitor could arrange for a donation after the sale. Cassie will be thrilled."

"I'm not talking about a donation, Alice. I want it all to go to the war orphans." She folded her hands. "My solicitor has already made the arrangements for the full proceeds of the sale to go to Cassie's refugee camp. He even suggested setting up a fund for them with Cassie as the administrator – how does that sound, dear?"

"You amaze me, Mrs Hollis. Your ability to make decisions and then carry them out. All these months with the mountains of Arthur's antiques to be evaluated and disposed of, I worried about you exhausting yourself. Instead you sailed through it while I dithered about, running to you with every little detail."

Mrs Hollis smiled. "You know how to flatter an old lady, dear. But I did do all the books for Arthur when he was alive.

He was such a pack rat I had to learn to be ruthless about what to keep and what to sell."

"You've just provided me with fresh ammunition to bring Cassie home, you realise," said Alice. "She'll want to meet her new benefactor and tell you all about her orphans in person. When can I tell her, Mrs Hollis?"

"As soon as you agree to the rest of my news, dear. I've only told you half of it," she said, taking Alice's hand again. "The reason I wanted you and Heck to both be here is to make an announcement. My Tiberius Road home is now officially yours. Once the sale of all my stuff is over and cleared out, you and Heck can take final possession."

"You know it's what we've hoped you'd agree to, Mrs Hollis. But things have changed, I'm afraid," said Alice.

"You mean you don't want it after all? Oh dear, I thought –"

"It's not that. It's only..." she hesitated. "I don't know quite where to begin."

The old woman squeezed her hand and waited.

"You've been so good to us, Mrs Hollis – so kind. I feel horrible having to say this..."

"Just say it, dear – don't worry. You won't upset me; I'm a tough old bird. If you and Heck have had second thoughts, I understand." It was her turn to pat Alice's hand in reassurance.

"I've left Heck, Mrs Hollis, that's why he's in Rome. Alone. I'm sorry to tell you like this. I didn't mean to – not till you came out of hospital."

Mrs Hollis dismissed this with a wave of her hand. "Never mind that, Alice. Tell me what happened. Is it serious? You're a bit too old for a lovers' tiff, surely?"

"I don't think I can explain it to you," said Alice. "I haven't been able to make my mother or my daughter realise what happened, either."

"Try me, dear. I might be just old enough to understand."

Alice stood up and walked about the small hospital room. She fiddled with a bunch of gladioli she had brought, rearranging the bright blooms in the vase. "I doubt if you will. You and Arthur seemed to have had the perfect marriage."

The old woman shook her head. "You know that's not true, Alice. Oh, we loved each other right to the end but there was always that gulf of sadness between us, not having children. It's why I'm trying to bridge it now with Cassie's orphans."

Alice's hand strayed to her chest. "When I said I left Heck I lied to you, Mrs Hollis. He was planning to leave me, so I simply left first."

"Go on, Alice. I'm listening."

Alice stared out the hospital window, unseeing. "He doesn't want me anymore," she said.

"How do you know, dear – has he told you that?"

"He doesn't need to. I know. Ever since my breast was removed, he barely touched me." She spoke in a dull monotone, not looking at the old woman. "I don't know what to do, Mrs Hollis. Nobody seems to understand what I'm feeling. The only person who might is Cassie and she's so far away."

"Come here, Alice. Sit down and look at me," said Mrs Hollis. "I know that empty feeling too well. I want to ask you something. A favour."

Alice nodded and sat beside the bed.

"I need to see Heck – would you ask him to come and visit me?" said Mrs Hollis.

"After what I said I don't think he'd answer my email."

"But if you spoke to him, not just wrote, Alice?"

She shook her head. "I don't even know where he's staying. I haven't got a phone number."

"You could find him, dear," she said clutching Alice's hand, "if you went there."

Alice felt the old woman's steady gaze on her.

"I need you to go to Rome and bring Heck back. Will you do that, Alice? I want to see him before I die."

# CHAPTER 22

At *The Builders Arms* pub in the Golden Valley, Maddy, Elinor and Barney sat in the beer garden so Elinor could smoke. Barney and Maddy drank beer at a cast iron table in the shade. Elinor sat with her chair turned away from them, sipping her vodka and tonic between nervous puffs on her cigarette.

Maddy began, "The reason we asked you to come here Barney, is Elinor wanted me to ask you something." She looked from one to the other. Elinor took long drags on her cigarette, waving the smoke away from them. "It's about her boys."

Barney smiled, "Sure – anything I can do." He liked Elinor's two sons, Mason and Gareth. Chalk and cheese he had told her. Gareth at fifteen was outgoing and full of a young teenager's breezy confidence but Mason at thirteen had withdrawn as his mother's illness progressed. Once or twice, Barney had brought them out to the farm and they both fought over who would feed the animals. Russell gave them each some chores and they raced through them, asking for more.

"Elinor's worried about them," Maddy continued. "Since she's been sick these last two years they're too much for her to cope with. She feels they need a man's hand." She paused, glancing at Elinor who had finished her vodka and fiddled with the remaining ice but kept her gaze averted. "Anyway, she wants to know if you would speak to Russell – about them moving to the farm," she finished.

Elinor looked up now to see his reaction. Barney felt the two women watching him, waiting.

"Moving to the farm," he repeated. "You mean to live?"

Elinor nodded. "They both love it. Always asking when can they go again."

Maddy adjusted her steel blue turban. "The doctors have told Elinor she is in the last stages of her cancer, Barney. She's on palliative care from now on."

"I'm sorry, Elinor," he said. "You seem so much better since you came out of hospital this last time."

"It's only my boys I worry about – what will happen when I'm gone. My mother's too old to care for them. She's in a home herself," said Elinor.

"And their father – does he know that you're –"

"He's in Iraq somewhere," she said. "A mercenary with some American company since he got kicked out of the SAS. He's a drunk. I divorced him long ago and I don't want him anywhere near them."

"I could help for awhile if Russell agrees," said Maddy. "But I don't want the boys to get too attached to me. I might have a year – might not."

Barney looked at the two women. In the few short weeks he had known them, they had become close friends. It was hard for him to accept that they would soon be dead and he could live for another ten years. Five anyway. Elinor at 43. Maddy at 66. And him – 72 now and who knows – maybe 80?

"Russell likes your boys, Elinor. He told me so. But you know Landon's living there now. And me for awhile. I'm not sure what he'd say. Natasha and I had to twist his arm to take Landon."

"It might not be immediately," said Maddy.

"Will you ask him for me, Barney?" Elinor gripped his arm. "Please?"

"Let me speak to Natasha. She can still persuade Russell to do most things. See what she suggests."

Elinor hugged him and said she wanted to buy him a drink. They watched her walk unsteadily into the pub bar. Maddy looked at him.

"That meant a lot to her, Barney. She's made herself even sicker if that's possible, worrying over who will care for her boys. She knows she doesn't have much time left."

"I'm not too sure Russell will even consider it, Maddy. He's used to having his freedom. Being responsible for two teenagers is asking a lot of him."

"Is there anything I could do to make him consider it? I have some money. What if I paid for a housekeeper – do you think he'd agree to that?"

"It's possible. But I don't want to get Elinor's hopes up too soon." He rose to take the tray Elinor had returned with and set it down on the table. She put vodka and tonics down for Maddy and herself and a whisky sour in front of him. She raised her glass.

"To Barney and Russell."

"To Mason and Gareth," said Maddy.

"To both of you," said Barney. He took a folded piece of paper from his pocket. "I got this email last night from my son Hunter in Vancouver and I wanted to tell you about it. He has a Czech girlfriend called Lottie and the two of them are living on my old fishing boat there. Lottie's dad is somebody at the Czech consulate – cultural attaché or something like that and he's always going to charity events and invites them along for the free food and drinks. Anyway, listen to this:

*Hi Dad,*

*Nearly finished my film course and ready to go to make Cassie's documentary on her refugee camp. Alice offered to pay my expenses if I'll promise to go soon. She's worried something will happen to Cassie and wanted to go out to look for her herself when she didn't hear anything for a long time. Netta persuaded her not to and to ask me instead as she knew I'd promised Cassie ages ago I'd come when my course ended.*

*I've been helping Clive get the 'Betsy' ready for his 'Amistad' voyage – we've renewed the sails and fitted a furling jib and new heavy-duty stainless steel shrouds on the mainmast. He was pretty choked when you told him you wouldn't be joining him after all. I take it Alice has been putting the pressure on you as well, to go to Guinea. Clive's talked Lottie and me into crewing for him instead. She's done a lot of ocean racing in the past – even crewed on the all-women boat in the Vendee Globe race last year. All I've done is sail round a few of the Lower Gulf Islands with Clive.*

*Anyway, Lottie convinced Clive he should take some stuff for Cassie's war orphans and I could make a documentary of his Amistad trip and maybe link it to the refugee camp to raise some money for them. Only we didn't know what to take. Alice and Netta have got a ton of books so we didn't want to do more of that. We asked Cassie's organisation, Les Amis du CFA and they said they're desperate for artificial hands and feet but they cost thousands new. They said hospitals and rehab clinics have lots of used ones they give away to third world countries. So Lottie's been doing some digging while I was helping Clive. Last week we were at one of her dad's charity events and she met a man who organises a Limbs For Life charity that recycles prosthetic limbs. He's promised her as many used ones as me and Clive can pack in the 'Betsy'.*

*I haven't told Cassie yet until we see what Lottie brings in. I may have to sacrifice a bit of space I'd earmarked for all the free Czech beer her dad gives us. Me and Clive have been studying the charts and he reckons we could be in Dakar in about two months with any luck. Lottie told him with her at the helm she'd cut that down to six weeks but Clive says 'The Betsy's' no ocean racer.*

*We thought if you went overland via Gibraltar, we could meet up in Dakar and go to Guinea together. What do you think? Maybe buy an old truck there cheap.*

*Let me know soon before we leave.*

*Love, Hunter.xxxxxxx the kisses are from Lottie.*

"What did he mean by Alice putting pressure on you, Barney?" asked Maddy.

"That's what I wanted to talk to you about," he said. "She's been emailing me to get me to change my plans and go to Africa first. I hoped to find a freighter to Montreal and then take the train to Vancouver. I've had this project in mind for a long time to build a retreat centre on a plot of land I own on Vosges Island. Clive was going to help me, then he changed his mind and wants to organise this 'Amistad' trip first and tried to get me to go with him."

"Why can't you just fly there?" asked Elinor. "Save all the bother."

"If I thought there was any real danger, I would," he said. "But otherwise, I'm determined not to fly anymore."

"Why not? I used to love flying to Ibiza," said Elinor. "It's so cheap."

"I just don't feel right about it. I'd rather not go if I have to fly."

Maddy smiled. "It's his green credentials, Elinor. Flying is taboo."

"That's right," he grinned. "Be drummed out of the Green Party if they found out. I'd more or less agreed to put my project on hold and go with Clive to Africa but now Alice is badgering me to go direct to Guinea and make sure Cassie is okay.

She keeps reading these internet news items about the youth gangs roaming around remote parts of Sierra Leone, Cote d'Ivoire and Guinea, raping and terrorising villagers. She's convinced Cassie is in constant danger. I've told Alice Zinadine will make sure Cassie's safe but she doesn't believe me. He keeps leaving her to go off on other projects, Alice says."

"Is Zinadine her boss?" asked Elinor, lighting a new cigarette from the butt of her last one.

"He's her boyfriend," said Barney. "The real reason she went to Africa in the first place. Alice doesn't trust him."

"Because he's a black man? Landon's from Africa too but I'd trust him," said Elinor. "He tells me lots of stuff about Sierra Leone and the civil war. Is Cassie near there?"

"Guinea sort of surrounds it," he said, making a crescent shape in the air with his fingers. "Her children's refugee camp is near the border. That's why Alice is so nervous."

Maddy looked at him. "Aren't you worried, Barney? I don't blame her. I would be too."

"I trust Zinadine. Anyway, Cassie's got enough sense to know when she's in any danger. She told me they'll move the camp if there's any risk. The civil war's over. It's only pockets of thugs still hiding out in the bush to avoid the army patrols."

"Sounds scary to me," said Elinor. "I hope this boyfriend of hers looks after her. I wouldn't want my boys in that kind of place."

"I'm in a bit of a quandary, since I got this email from Hunter," said Barney. "Now that I've told Clive I won't be doing his *'Amistad'* trip there's no sense in waiting for a freighter to Montreal. Once Alice and Netta have their crates of books ready to ship to Senegal, I can go overland to meet the boat in Dakar when it docks."

"You've told Alice you'll do that?" asked Maddy. "I thought she wasn't talking to you?"

"We're not talking – we're emailing. Keeps the arguments to a minimum that way. You have time to think about your reply," he smiled.

"So what's the problem?"

"Timing. I've promised Russell I'll stay for the summer to help him through the busy season. But if Hunter's going to be in Dakar in two months, I'll have to allow three weeks to get to Senegal to meet him and find an old truck to buy. Russell's counting on my help. I know he's got Landon now that he doesn't need his wheelchair but he can't lift boxes with only one hand."

"Natasha and I are working on him," said Maddy. "I think he's coming round to the idea of a prosthesis but he's a proud man."

"You know what he told me the other day?" said Elinor. "He said what's the point – whoever heard of a one-handed sax player?"

"I hope you didn't agree with him, Elinor," said Maddy.

"I just told him I'd change places with him any day of the week."

Maddy stood up. "Finish your drink, Elinor. Barney can drive us back to the hospice in time to catch Natasha before she leaves. See what she says about asking Russell if your boys can move to the farm."

"I'd better hold off telling him my bad news until we hear what he says," said Barney.

# CHAPTER 23

The little Fiat *cinquecento* bumped over the chariot ruts of the Via Appia Antica. Giorgio drove with one hand and gesticulated with the other, occasionally changing hands on the wheel as he pointed out sights on either side of Rome's oldest thoroughfare. Alice sat beside him, gripping the door handle, too nervous to do more than glance at the places he indicated.

"Is it much further, Giorgio?"

"Only a few minutes now," he said. "Don't worry, I am almost positive Hec-tor will be there." He smiled to reassure her, misinterpreting her nervousness. He spoke, putting the emphasis on the second syllable of Heck's name. When Alice had turned up at Giorgio's apartment after an early flight from London, asking if he knew where Heck was, he agreed at once to bring her out to the site.

"Do you know where he's staying if he isn't here?" she asked.

Giorgio shook his head. "Some cheap little *pensione* near here. I tried to persuade him to use my place but he said he likes to walk back and forth to the site and explore the area for background details. I am too far away, he says. I have the phone number but I am sure he will be here." He studied

Alice's face, not looking at the road. "Will you be staying long, Alice? You and Hec-tor can use my apartment and I will go to my sister's – she is only two streets away."

Alice clamped her hands together to keep from grabbing the steering wheel, willing him to watch the road as a taxi approached. "Thank you, Giorgio. I don't want to impose on you. I wouldn't have bothered you but I didn't have Heck's address..." she stopped.

Giorgio nodded and returned his eyes to the Via Appia, manoeuvring around the taxi with one hand. A short slight man, still with thick black hair but streaked now with grey, she guessed him to be a year or two older than Heck. She had seen old photos of the two friends on archaeological digs, Heck towering over him, his big arm on the little man's shoulder. He spoke now, not looking at her.

"Hec-tor told me you had left, Alice. I am sorry. He was very upset and didn't want to talk to me." He gestured eloquently with both hands off the wheel. "I think that is why he wouldn't stay with me – not the distance." He pointed ahead. "There it is – *Capo di Roma.*"

Giorgio wheeled the tiny car through the old gates and parked in the empty parking area. He jumped out and came round to open Alice's door before indicating a lone figure through the trees. She saw at once the unmistakable bulky shape of Heck, kneeling down scraping soil off the broken tiles on the floor of what must have been a very large room. He looked up at their approach.

"Alice!" he said, scrambling to his feet. He took a step then stopped, uncertain.

"Hello, Heck. Giorgio said we'd find you here." She saw the small man watching them and moved to greet Heck with an offered cheek then stepped back before he could respond.

Giorgio smiled at them. "Why don't you show Alice the whole site, Hec-tor?" He looked at the large gold watch on his narrow wrist. "I can come back around one and we can all have lunch to celebrate. I want to hear more about this project of your daughter's, Alice." He hugged both of them in turn then walked back to the little Fiat.

They watched him leave before facing each other. She spoke first.

"I guess you're surprised to see me here, Heck, after the way I behaved."

"Why didn't you let me know, I could have met you – saved Giorgio a trip away out here."

"I wanted to take a taxi, but he insisted. He said he's worried about you." She put a hand on his arm. "I'm sorry, Heck. I really am."

He covered her hand with his large one. "Would you like to see the site – now that you're here?" She nodded and he led her over the uneven ground, explaining the layout, taking her elbow to steer her from room to room or rather from space to space. Only a few low walls remained but the tiled floors delineated the outlines of the villa quite clearly. "I'm only here unofficially, courtesy of Giorgio's boss," he said. "They let me poke about in the off-limits areas as long as I don't disturb anything."

"Are you finding what you're looking for?" she asked and he glanced up quickly to read her face but she only stared at the ground.

"Do you really want to know?"

"Oh Heck, you didn't think I meant any of those snide remarks? I was only lashing out because you packed in your career – everything you've worked for and built up over the years. You have this fine reputation as an archaeologist and you just threw it away. For this." She gestured vaguely round her at the partly excavated Roman villa.

He crouched down to examine a shard of pottery, careful not to disturb its location as they were in the off-limits area.

"I know you feel what I'm doing is frivolous, Alice but for the first time in years I'm enjoying myself. It had all become so arid and academic and then along you came and shook me up."

"Swept you off your feet." She gave him a small smile.

"Besides, the dean told me they wouldn't consider renewing my contract. After my venture into green activism. Blotted my copybook, he said."

"How long do you think you can support yourself writing Roman thrillers? You said yourself your last one barely made back the publisher's advance."

"I thought I'd solve that problem by marrying one of my ambitious students," he said.

"But she let you down by getting sick."

"...And leaving me on some trumped-up excuse. So here I am scrabbling about on my hands and knees, trying to scrape a living as an ageing historical novelist."

She held out her hand to help him to his feet. He hung on and pulled her to him and they kissed properly for the first time.

"You could always get work as a jobbing gardener, I suppose," she said, wiping her lipstick off his mouth. "I could give you a reference."

"My prospects are improving already. See what good luck you bring me, Alice?" He slipped his arm around her, careful not to touch her breast and they strolled along the paths marked out with rope and stakes.

"You don't know the half of it, Heck. Shall I tell you why I'm here?"

"You mean you didn't come here to plead with me to take you back?"

"Partly, I suppose," she said. "I've been getting a lot of flak at home from my mother and daughter for my idiotic behaviour, as they see it."

"Couldn't agree with them more," he said, squeezing her arm. "Just confirms my opinion that I was marrying into a whole clan of smart women. How are they all?"

"Beavering away on a mental health project for me, but ostensibly for Cassie."

"Sounds intriguing. Tell me more."

"Later. First, I want to explain this sudden appearance. It's not what you think, Heck. I haven't really changed my mind." She led him to a bench shaded by the olive trees bordering the site. "It's Mrs Hollis," she said.

"Is she still in hospital or back at the nursing home?"

"She won't be going home, Heck. She's putting her house in order. Literally. That's why I'm here. She asked me to come."

"For me? I got the impression from that nurse's email I forwarded, it was you she wanted to see," he said.

"Both of us. She said she wanted to see you before she dies."

Heck rubbed his tanned face with both hands and looked at her. "Is it that bad?"

Alice nodded. "She knows. But she's hanging on till I bring you back so she can tell us both together."

"Is it about the house, Alice?"

"Yes. Her solicitor has drawn up the papers ready for us to sign."

He stared at his bare feet in their dusty leather sandals. "Did you tell her we can't afford it now? That I don't have a proper job."

"I told her everything, Heck. That I'd left you and the house was finished and ready for auction. At first I said you had come to Rome to do some research but then I just blurted it out, when she started to talk about us having Villa Tiberius."

"Villa Tiberius – our little joke that back-fired on us," he said. "I'm sorry, Alice. It was so close until I screwed things up with my 'juvenile pranks' as you so rightly called them. Poor Mrs Hollis. She can't even die in peace with her house in order. Was she very upset when you told her?"

"I haven't told you the strangest part yet. When I said you'd catalogued all her houseful of antiques for the auction, she showed me this." Alice opened her handbag and took out an envelope. She handed it to him. "Read it – it's from her solicitor."

Heck unfolded the letter and scanned the legal document. "The entire contents are for Cassie's refugees? They're worth a fortune, Alice – the Meissen china collection alone." He shook his head in amazement, re-reading the folded sheets. "Why?"

She explained the old woman's interest in Cassie's war orphans and related how her mother's visits had influenced her decision. "She has no one else to leave it to, except us, she says and we were supposed to have the house, but…"

"...But we blew it," he said. "I quit Queen Mary's and you left. He looked at her with a rueful grimace. "I'm surprised she still wants to see us – together."

"When she asked me to bring you back, I couldn't refuse. Not after what she's doing for Cassie."

"I suppose Mrs Hollis just wants to hear it from me, before she makes alternative arrangements," he said. "Maybe Kew Gardens will be the lucky recipients – she loved to visit there with old Arthur, didn't she?"

"You still don't get it, do you? Mrs Hollis is giving it to us – not selling it to us. That's why I'm here, Heck. What are we going to do now?"

# CHAPTER 24

Landon and Barney worked together, separating the root-bound herbs from the plug trays and potting them on into individual 3-inch containers for the Farmer's Market in Gloucester the next day.

"So what made you change your mind?" asked Barney.

"Elinor," said Landon. "For someone who never made it past junior school, she's one powerful little woman."

"You and she been talking things over, eh?"

The black man stopped to wipe his brow with the stump of his right arm. It was only mid-morning but already the humidity inside the polytunnel made both men perspire freely. "This place reminds me of home," he said. "Elinor likes to hear me tell stories of Freetown in Sierra Leone. Do you know that girl has never been further than Bristol? To her sister's house."

Barney put a tray of the re-potted herbs on the battered metal trolley Russell had devised. He brushed his hand over the tops of the bright green bush basil. The powerful fragrance filled the warm air of the polytunnel. "I don't suppose she'll make it much beyond that now, Landon."

"I told her about my family's piece of land by the ocean outside Freetown that belongs to me. I said one day I plan to go back and live there – maybe grow some organic vegetables just like Russell here. My sister's a widow since the civil war. She could live with me."

"She have any children?"

"Three grandchildren. Her daughter's with an NGO upcountry somewhere and her son is dead. Shot by the army when his child was a baby. My sister looks after them all."

"I'm sorry, Landon. She must have a difficult life on her own there," said Barney.

"I always sent her money – up till now. Tash says I thought more about them than I did about her, but it's not that simple."

"Nothing ever is. So what was it Elinor said?" asked Barney.

"She said if I were to have a new hand I could start a new life raising my great nephew and nieces. Teach them to swim in the Atlantic Ocean and grow veggies for them to eat. She said she wished she were me…" he stopped and rubbed his left hand over his stump.

"Elinor doesn't have your choices, I guess," said Barney. "No new life for her and no one to raise her boys. She's pinning all her hopes on Russell and I still haven't spoken to him about it."

"She told me she was going to ask you," said Landon. "She thinks Russell listens to you."

"If only she knew, eh? Russell listens to Russell. Always has," said Barney.

"Tash said you persuaded him to take me on, though."

"That was a joint effort. It was her idea, I only backed her up. Anyway, you and Russell were mates long before I showed up."

They finished loading the basil herbs onto the trays and went into the kitchen to make some coffee. Last night's dirty dishes lay heaped in the sink, a pile of washing overflowed a basket on the floor and the counter held a collection of vegetables from the garden, waiting to be cleaned and cooked. Barney rinsed out two mugs and filled them from the coffee maker, still one-third full from breakfast. He paused to take in the shambles in the kitchen and grinned at Landon.

"This is going to be a tougher sell than you were, Landon. Got any ideas?"

"Maddy said she'd pay for a housekeeper to help look after the boys," said Landon. "And she's offering to come here herself for as long as she can."

"Gonna be pretty crowded here with all us lot in on top of old Russell," said Barney. "Can't see him agreeing, myself. It's a big commitment and he likes his freedom."

"The boys are pretty handy even though they're only teenagers. And they love coming out here to help –" The frantic honking of Percy and Lucy signalled the arrival of Russell's old electric milk float. Landon looked at Barney. "You gonna ask him now? I'll back you up."

They went outside to meet him.

## CHAPTER 25

The calligraphy group were assembling the booklets in the hospice day centre, collating the pages of quotes into various sections. They punched holes in the covers, ready for the spiral binding machine Maddy had borrowed from the Art College in Gloucester. Barney appeared in the doorway and she looked over at him.

"Alma's after you again, Barney."

"What'd I do this time?"

"She's been reading the minibus logbook and wants to know why there's so many trips to the farm."

"I'll hide out here with you lot for awhile," said Barney. "Try to think of a good reason for her. Ever since that newspaper story about you all working at Russell's, I've been in her bad books."

"How many of these are we going to make?" asked Harry, unpacking a box full of the plastic binding coils.

"I persuaded my old boss at the Art College to print five hundred covers for us," said Maddy.

"Five hundred!" said Elinor. "There's only nine of us in the Calligraphy group, Maddy. How'll we sell that many?"

"We don't have to sell them all at once," said Barney. "It's because the printer said 500 is the minimum run worth doing. Mrs Oswold said we can store them here and bring some out for all their fund-raisers for the hospice."

"But we want to give the money to Cassie's refugee children. We all decided," she said, looking round the group at the table.

Maddy nodded, "I know. And we will. Whatever we can sell now goes to them. What's left over we store here for the future."

"The future – huh," said Harry. "Alma said that, did she?"

"That's what she decided," said Maddy.

"Suppose there's none left over, then what will she do?" asked Elinor.

Barney laughed, "First you're worried about how we can shift 500 and now you're talking about running out. We can always print more, we've got the originals."

"Put me down for ten copies," said Harry. "One for each of my grandchildren."

"Your grandchildren aren't going to be interested in dying lessons, Harry," said Elinor."

"One day they will," he said. "It'll be my legacy."

"I'm going to the smoking room for a fag," said Elinor. "I'll keep an eye out for Alma for you, Barney. You can duck out the back way and wait in Maddy's car."

# CHAPTER 26

At the Fisherman's Dock beneath Burrard Bridge in Vancouver, Hunter and Lottie were helping Clive prepare *The Betsy* for its voyage to West Africa. Clive rearranged the layout of the boat's interior, removing as many of the non-essential items as he could. He passed them to Hunter and Lottie to store on Barney's motor sailor, the *Sea Mist*.

"You and Lottie can use the forward cabin and I'll sleep in the lounge," said Clive. "That way we can store all the artificial limbs in the main cabin and close it up for the trip."

"Can't we use the main cabin and store the limbs forward? It's only got bunks up there."

"Improvise. I'm sure you'll think of something. Besides the main cabin is bigger," said Clive.

"What about all the stores?" asked Hunter. "We've got a mountain of stuff here already. Are you sure we need this much, Lottie?"

"You will be glad of it in the middle of the Atlantic Ocean, 'Untair. Two months is a long time," she said.

"He thinks you can live on love, Lottie," said Clive. "My experience is it makes me ravenous."

"Perhaps we must go on short rations then, 'Untair, if Clive is right," she said, stopping to give Hunter a squeeze.

"Maybe that's why he's putting us in the bunkroom, Lottie. So we can practice abstinence."

"What is this 'abstinence' – will I like it?" she asked, looking from one to the other.

Clive grinned. "Try it and see. 'Abstinence makes the heart grow fonder.'"

"This is an old saying, Clive?"

"No, it's a new one, Lottie and I don't like the sound of it," said Hunter. "Don't listen to him."

"You must teach me about abstinence then and I will teach you how to stow supplies the way I learned on the Vendée Globe race."

*The Betsy* settled lower in the water as Lottie and Clive distributed the stores around the lockers and under bunks. Lottie had given the 'Limbs For Life' man a list of the children and their ages and whether they needed hands or feet, legs or arms, right or left.

"What happens when they get bigger?" asked Hunter. "How long do these things last?"

"Mr McWilliams says they do not wear out, they just outgrow them so he is putting in lots of different sizes," said Lottie. She held up a small child's leg for Hunter to film with his video camera.

"I thought the guerrillas only chopped off hands or feet," he said. "That's a whole leg."

"A land mine, Cassie said," explained Lottie, handing the little limb to Clive who was packing them in odd corners of the main cabin.

"God, Lottie. I'm not sure I'm gonna cope with filming these kids," said Hunter. "Even shooting these artificial legs makes me feel strange." He switched off his camera and went on deck to walk around. Lottie followed him.

On the front deck he turned to face her and tried to blink back tears as she put her arms round him and pulled him down to sit on a hatch cover.

"I didn't realise some of these kids would be so young – Christ!" He pushed his face into her long blonde hair. "How does Cassie do it, Lottie?"

She stroked his back, comforting him. "She has Zinadine and you 'ave me, 'Untair. We will be fine when we get used to it. It is just the shock of seeing so many artificial hands and feet all at once. To us, they represent horror but to the children they mean hope, you will see."

Hunter sat up to blow his nose and look at her. "Are you sure you want to go through with this, Lottie? Clive and I could probably manage and Dad will meet us in Dakar, I hope."

"Cassie is your sister, 'Untair. But she is my best friend. I want to go as much as you do." She kissed his face. "Besides, you need me to teach you how to sail and I need you to teach me abstinence – so you will grow fonder, yes?"

He watched her smile spread over her generous mouth as she brushed her long blond hair off her cheek. He pressed her to him hard.

# CHAPTER 27

In Highgate, North London, Heck and George too, were clearing a space. They stood in the former maid's room in the old mansion flat, where George and Barney had long ago set up Hunter's elaborate train set.

"I told Martha we can't get anymore books in the garage, Heck, so she said I have to use this room. I hate to dismantle all this. Barney and I spent days in here setting it all up and adding stuff to it. I think we used to get more fun out of it than Hunter," said George.

"It's a fantastic setup, George. All this detail." Heck crouched down to read a tiny station signboard.

"Martha says I should pack it up and get rid of it. It's been years since Hunter and Netta used to play in here. She's right, of course, wasting a whole room with all this stuff that nobody ever looks at. And we do need the space for storing Cassie's books." George stood gazing round the maze of tracks and tunnels, signal boxes and stations, passenger locomotives and freight trains loaded with miniature logs and cattle.

Much of it he had saved from when Alice was a child and he had bought a whole train set for her, out of a misguided notion that girls loved trains as much as boys. He and Martha prided themselves on their feminist principles but his daughter had shown no interest, preferring her doll's house, which he built for her as a consolation. When Alice and Barney joined ranks, his granddaughter and Hunter loved the old toy train set and spent entire days playing in this room together.

These past few days he had been turning an idea over in his head and wanted to check it out with Heck, whom Netta persuaded to help with clearing the room.

"It seems a shame to chuck all this stuff, Heck. I was wondering – do you think African kids would like this if I boxed it up with all the books?"

"I bet they'd love it more than the books," he said. "Only thing is, it's pretty complicated, George. They'd need an adult to help set it up. I don't imagine Cassie would have any time – unless she could persuade Zinadine to do it."

"I thought Barney and Hunter might like to show them how. Alice has persuaded them to go to Cassie's refugee camp together."

"Let's do it, George. I'll make up some boxes and you start dismantling – you know how it all went together." Heck began assembling the flat-pack storage boxes. "We'd better mark them fragile so they don't pile heavy boxes of books on top of them."

"Don't tell Martha about this, Heck. She just thinks I should get rid of it. Not take up space for her precious books." He started uncoupling the passenger cars and wrapping each one in newspaper before handing them to Heck.

By the time they were finished breaking it all down they had filled over a dozen boxes. Heck marked each with a code number in black pen and sealed them up with duct tape.

"I'll give these code numbers to Barney for when they unpack, George."

George watched him stack the boxes in one corner of the room. "I've half a mind to go out there and help them set it all up again. Martha would never agree, though. She says I've been overdoing it. That's why Netta roped you in to do the heavy lifting, Heck."

"I don't mind, George. I'm not going back to Rome for a while until after I've seen Mrs Hollis. Alice and I should have gone in to the hospital yesterday but she's had another setback."

"Martha says the old lady's on her way out," said George. "What did she want to see you for?"

Heck shrugged. "Alice thinks she's going to give us her old Georgian house on Tiberius Road and wants us both there together. But now she knows we've separated, I don't know…"

"Is Alice still adamant she's not going back, Heck?" asked George. "I thought that maybe when she went to find you in Rome –"

"Me too. God knows I tried my damnedest. But she said she only came because the old lady asked her to and she couldn't refuse, after all she's doing for Cassie's war orphans."

"Alice can't think of anything else, these days. She's convinced if she can get Cassie whatever she needs for those poor kids, then she'll come home. Netta says her mother's obsessed with the notion Cassie's in constant danger." George chewed his bottom lip. "Four women's too many for one old man like me to have in his life."

"I don't know how you do it, George. I can't even handle one."

"Two," said George. "Mrs Hollis isn't finished yet."

# CHAPTER 28

Mrs Hollis lay propped up on her bed in the Mile End Hospital Stroke Unit, holding Alice's hand. Heck sat on the opposite side of her.

"You must think I'm being very self-indulgent, dragging you back from Rome, Heck, but I have a very good reason," she said.

"I thought it was Alice you wanted to see or I would have come back sooner," he said. "However, I have to say you look suspiciously well – you sure you're not just shamming to get attention? I know what you women can be like."

The old lady smiled at Alice. "Perhaps it's just as well I lured him back from Rome. Those Italian women would soon succumb to all this flirting."

"He can't help himself, Mrs Hollis. Charm is his fatal flaw."

"You don't have to practise on me, Heck. I'm already a convert," said Mrs Hollis. "What I needed to see you and Alice together for, is so I can make an announcement and a request."

"If it's about Tiberius Road, Alice has already told me of your proposal to sign it over to us," said Heck. "But she may not have explained our changed situation. I've been sacked by the university so I can't afford now to buy your house, much as I would love to."

The old woman brushed this aside with a wave of her hand but he continued.

"More importantly, Alice and I have separated, Mrs Hollis. Without her, I have no wish to own it even if I could afford to. I'm sorry to disappoint you like this when you're not well, but I had to tell you the truth."

"Alice has already explained all this to me before she went to Rome. It doesn't change my mind. The house is now yours – both of you. The papers are all drawn up by my solicitor. I want you to accept it as a gift, not buy it. What you decide to do with it is between you. My only request is that you keep it until I'm gone – that won't be long now, my doctor says."

Alice hitched her chair closer to the bed. "Would you like to come back to Tiberius Road, Mrs Hollis? I spoke to your doctor earlier and she said it's your decision how you spend this time."

The old woman glanced at Heck. "You mean with both of you, Alice?"

Alice nodded without looking at him. "It would be our way of repaying you for all your kindness to us and to Cassie, Mrs Hollis."

The old woman looked doubtful.

"But how would you manage, dear?"

"Heck could put up a bed for you downstairs and I will arrange for a nurse to come in each day. In fact, we know the perfect one. She's even been to your house and loved it."

"D'you mean Natasha, Alice?" asked Heck.

She nodded. "Landon doesn't need her anymore and she's only working as a casual at the hospice. I'm positive we could persuade her to come and stay at Tiberius Road. She's an expert in palliative care, Mrs Hollis – you'll like her, I know."

"Is it a deal, Mrs Hollis – will you come if we can get Natasha?" asked Heck.

"Well, it would be lovely to see the old place again. And the doctor did say I could pop off any day," said the old lady, smiling.

Alice rose to embrace her, "We'll take that as a yes, then. I'll start to make the arrangements right away."

Mrs Hollis put a restraining hand on her arm. "I still have something else to ask Heck. It concerns my husband, Arthur."

"Shall I leave you two to discuss this, while I make arrangements with the doctor?" said Alice.

"Alright, dear. This is just some unfinished business I'd like to ask Heck to deal with."

Alice left them to it and went off to find the duty nurse. Heck watched the old woman and waited for her to begin.

"Are you familiar with the railway arches behind King's Cross station?"

"The old warehouses under the tracks," he nodded.

"Arthur rented one of them for storing big awkward things he couldn't bring home, or I refused to let him. Goodness knows what he stashed away in there over the years that he didn't tell me about."

"Definite packrat, your Arthur. What sort of things are you referring to, Mrs Hollis?"

"At one period, he had a very lucrative contract with a chain of pubs supplying them with bric-a-brac. There was a craze to fill them with old memorabilia – junk if you ask me."

"I remember," said Heck. "Trying to pretend the pubs were older than they were, by stuffing them with period antiques mounted on the walls and hanging from the ceilings."

She nodded. "Ludicrous idea but hugely popular at the time. Arthur said they always wanted themes for them and he was forever on the lookout for job lots of similar things. Once he bought a whole brass band – all the instruments, I mean. Another time he found a garage full of old enamel painted advertising signs – they were always in demand."

"I loved those myself," said Heck. "Instant nostalgia."

"Another time, he went to a country auction and bought a complete restored old steam engine – not a railway engine, more a threshing machine one," she said. "But it was too big even for outside a pub, so he never sold it."

"And you want me to get rid of it, Mrs Hollis. How?"

She shook her head. "I haven't told you the worst, yet. Arthur heard about a circus that went bankrupt and he decided it would make a great pub theme –"

"So he bought a whole circus?"

"Not quite, Heck. But he did buy a complete working calliope and carousel."

"A merry-go-round?"

"That's right. An enormous Victorian thing. Gallopers, we used to call them when I was a child. He knew he couldn't sell it complete so he planned to dismantle it and just sell the painted horses individually."

"My god, is it still sitting in there under the railway arches?"

"Along with lord knows what else he never told me about," she said. "And now comes the best bit."

"You mean there's more stuff stashed away somewhere?" asked Heck.

"No. At least not that I know of. What I need your help with is this; the railway is re-developing the whole area around King's Cross and St Pancras because of the Eurostar terminal and they want all that warehousing back."

Heck nodded. "I've seen some of it already – lots of posh cafés and boutiques. Maybe you could sell Arthur's stuff to them, Mrs Hollis."

"Not quite their style, I'm afraid. Even my solicitor is stumped for any ideas, so he suggested asking you. I'm sorry, Heck but it's been preying on my mind for months and meanwhile I'm running out of time – in more ways than one."

"I could go and have a look at it, Mrs Hollis. See what we're up against."

"Thank you, Heck. And please don't worry Alice with this, will you?"

"I'll just tell her it's full of junk and I'm emptying it for you."

She held out her arms to him and he hugged her very carefully. She handed him a large padlock key.

"Now I can feel I've done my best for Arthur." She closed her eyes and he left the room to look for Alice.

# CHAPTER 29

In Russell's sculpture workshop in the barn behind the vegetable sorting shed, Barney and Landon, Maddy and Natasha, were all helping Russell to load his metal sculptures into the old trailer he used to take vegetables to the Farmers' Market. Landon wore his new prosthetic hand fitted with a leather glove to protect it. He had been off the booze ever since the fire and was regaining his old strength and dexterity. He no longer needed the wheelchair. The skin grafts on his face and body were gradually healing.

"The South Docks Gallery is quite a coup for you, Russell," said Barney. "How did Natasha swing it?"

"She met the owner's father when he was a patient in the hospice. She has a standing invite to all the gallery openings," said Russell. The two men lifted the latest bird sculpture onto the trailer for Landon to wrap in padded horse blankets for the trip. The long heron's beak and the spiky beard had been swaddled in bubble wrap to protect them from damage.

"Be careful of 'Mrs Oswold', Landon," said Barney, who had nicknamed the bird sculpture, after Russell offered to donate it to the fund raising event Maddy and Elinor had organised. Half the money would go to the hospice and the other half to Cassie's refugee camp. Russell had won over Mrs

Oswold with a combination of charm and bribery. As a result, the gallery opening could be guaranteed a big hospice-supporter crowd for the launch of the hospice calligraphy booklet and Russell's first major show of his work.

Natasha showed Maddy how to swathe the more fragile parts of the metal sculptures in bubble wrap and masking tape.

"This is like bandaging up Landon, Natasha," said Maddy, passing the long strips to her.

"Yes, I'm getting out of practice now he doesn't need me anymore."

"Will Elinor be well enough to come to the opening, do you think?" asked Barney.

Natasha nodded. "Fingers crossed. She wanted to come and help here today but I told her to save her strength for the main event."

"She's so excited," said Maddy. "Her first time to a gallery art show. I don't know what she's expecting. I hope she's not disappointed."

"I told her an art auction is a little different from a normal one," said Barney. "I think she imagines it will be like the cattle market auction sales in Hereford."

"Elinor asked me if I'd bring her boys to see it," said Russell. "She says Gareth likes taking things to pieces and maybe I could show him how to put them together. I said that's how I got started in sculpture."

Landon finished lashing the last piece onto the trailer. "It's funny how she can talk you into doing things. I doubt if I'd have been in touch with my band if it hadn't been for Elinor. She asked me if she could phone them, to see if they'd play at the opening."

"What did they say?" asked Barney.

"They told her they didn't have a tenor sax player. So she said maybe I could sing instead."

"Why not? That's what Louis Armstrong did when he couldn't play his trumpet anymore," said Barney.

Landon shook his head. "Not me. I'd frighten people away with my voice."

Natasha said, "Elinor told me if you'd sing, the band would all come and play, so they're not that worried about your voice."

"Russell said you used to sing when you stayed here before," said Maddy.

"I haven't had much to sing about lately," said Landon. "Besides, we're musicians, not vocalists. Just let them play without me."

"No deal," said Natasha. "They told her that was their condition for playing."

"I'd have to talk to them first," he said. "See what they had in mind."

"Good," said Russell. "I'll drop you off in Gloucester after you help me unload this stuff and you can meet up with them for a rehearsal. You coming, Barney?"

"No, I promised Elinor I'd take Gareth and Mason out to see her at the hospice in Maddy's car. Mrs Oswold has banned me from driving the minibus except on official outings approved by her," he said.

"Before you all leave, I want to tell you something," said Natasha. "Alice has offered me a job in London, looking after Mrs Hollis who owns their house. The old lady's been allowed home from the hospital as she hasn't long to live. And as Landon doesn't need me now, I'll be going right after the opening."

"I still need you here, Tash," said Russell. "There's plenty of work to last till autumn."

"I've already said yes to Alice, Russell. I told you I was only staying till Landon was discharged from the outpatient's clinic."

Russell shrugged and climbed into the old electric van. "Oh well. At least I've got Barney and Landon."

"And me," said Maddy. "Don't I count? Or have you written me off already?"

"Sorry, Maddy. I just thought if Elinor couldn't come, you'd change your mind," he said.

"I guess I'd better tell you now that I'm leaving too, Russell. Alice has convinced me to meet Hunter when he and Clive get to Dakar –"

"Jesus Christ, Barney. I can't run this place on my own with only Landon. I thought you promised to stay until after the summer? I'm helping you and Alice with Cassie's amputees –"

"I know. I'm not leaving immediately – I just wanted to give you time to plan. Clive's only got to the Caribbean, so I can stay for another month."

Landon sat beside Russell in the old van. "I suppose I should give notice too, as long as everyone's announcing plans. Elinor's got me thinking of going back to my sister's in Freetown."

"Looks like you're stuck with me, Russell," said Maddy. "At least for awhile."

# CHAPTER 30

Outside Elinor's council flat, Barney and Maddy sat waiting in her car for Elinor's sons to return from school. Maddy fiddled with her steel-blue turban, adjusting it in the rear-view mirror.

"God, this thing itches like hell some days," she said. "Makes me want to sling it out the window."

"Why don't you take it off?" asked Barney.

"I might frighten the boys. Gareth and Mason have never seen me without it."

"Intrigue maybe – not frighten," he said. "Bald heads are not that unusual, Maddy."

"On men, no. I'm not quite ready for people staring at me in the streets."

"You could get a wig instead. A nice flaming red one. It would make a sensation at the art show."

"I appreciate your concern, Barney. But I'll just stick to my turbans." She turned to look at him. "Why didn't you say anything to Russell? We had him all set up – first Natasha, then you, then Landon. I even gave you a lead – twice."

He grimaced. "I know. I was all ready to – but he just kind of deflated when we told him all at once. Especially Landon."

"But I thought that was the idea – throw him a lifeline. You're all leaving and along comes Maddy with the two boys to the rescue."

"I couldn't do it – lost my nerve. I thought what if he says no, then what do I tell Elinor?"

"You've got to tell her something, Barney. She's sitting there in the hospice waiting for us to turn up with Gareth and Mason, so she can make the announcement to them. What are you going to say?"

"Christ knows, Maddy. I don't know which is worse – asking Russell or telling Elinor he says no. I wish I'd never allowed her to get her hopes up."

"I'm at least partly to blame. I put her up to it in the first place. I hated watching her make herself sick with worry," said Maddy.

"Seeing her so happy these last few weeks, working on the calligraphy project and then the art show," he said, "really put the pressure on me to deliver for her. I don't think I can face her if Russell says he won't take them."

Maddy stared out the car window, looking for the boys. "There's always Social Services. I suppose Alma can help arrange a foster home. Unless…."

"What?"

"Unless you could delay your trip a while longer, Barney. I think Russell would consider having them if he had you and me for backup."

"Has she told the boys how ill she really is, Maddy?"

"They're not stupid; they know their mother's dying. Haven't you seen their faces lately?"

"You don't think she's told them about the farm, do you?"

"She may have hinted – but she wanted to make it an announcement today when we bring them to her. With all of us there," said Maddy.

"Christ! What a mess. I can't hold off more than a month. Hunter and Clive might even arrive earlier if Lottie's as good a sailor as Hunter says she is."

"Shall we ask Alma to talk to her?" said Maddy. "It's supposed to be part of her job."

"You know Elinor doesn't trust her," he said. "It would be just passing the buck. And we don't know yet what Russell will say. We're just assuming he'll say no."

"Well we'd better think of something," she pointed. "Here comes Gareth and Mason."

# CHAPTER 31

While George helped Heck re-assemble the bed in what was the morning/breakfast room of the Georgian semi-detached in Tiberius Road, Mrs Hollis, from her wheelchair supervised the position for the best view of the garden. Natasha unpacked the old woman's suitcase. In the kitchen the three women, Netta, Martha and Alice prepared lunch for everyone.

"The house must seem bare to you since the last time you were here, Mrs Hollis," said Heck. "The auction sale cleared it right out and what didn't sell we sent to the sale rooms."

"Yes, I'd forgotten what lovely proportions these old houses have. You and Alice have done a fine job restoring all the original features. I love the wainscoting in this breakfast room. Arthur and I sat here every morning plotting what to do next in the garden."

"In that case I'll be in for my daily instructions from you," said Heck. "You can't be any more of a slave-driver than Alice."

"You might have them both ganging up on you, Heck," said George.

"I can always make the excuse that you and I are clearing out the railway warehouse if it gets too much here."

"You don't know how relieved I am that you agreed to do it," said Mrs Hollis. "Are you making any impression on all that stuff in there?"

"We've shifted tons of moth-eaten stags' heads and old bicycles and ex-army uniforms, Edith. Still haven't made enough space to work on the calliope," said George.

"What's a calliope?" asked Natasha, making drum-tight hospital corners on the old brass bed.

"It's a millstone that I've put round Heck's neck," said the old lady.

"A merry-go-round," said George. "A beautiful old Victorian one from what I've seen so far."

"Can you keep a secret, Natasha?" asked Heck.

"Part of my job description. What is it?"

"George suggested it and Mrs Hollis agreed. If we can get it re-assembled in the warehouse and working again, we'll ship it out to Sierra Leone for Cassie's orphanage."

"But you'll have to take it all apart again," said Natasha.

George nodded. "That's right. But they did it all the time for the old fairgrounds. They're specially built for it. Took them apart and put them back together for each new town."

"I think it's a wonderful idea but we don't want to tell Alice about it until we're sure it works," said Mrs Hollis. "She's already stressed enough with the book project."

"If Martha got wind of it, she'd ban me from helping Heck," said George. "She already thinks I'm overdoing the book project."

"Once the deadline for sending off the container's passed we'll have plenty of time – only a few more days, then we can crack on with 'Operation Gallopers,'" said Heck.

"Can I come and see it, sometime?" asked Natasha.

"Depends if you don't mind getting filthy, eh George?"

"That's right. You'll need some old clothes. The dirt is caked on everything. But we could use some help."

"Russell had me doing all kinds of mucky jobs on the farm so I expect this won't be any worse," she said.

Netta appeared in the doorway to announce that lunch was on the table. She pushed the old woman's wheelchair into the kitchen and up to a place at the long pine harvest table.

"Do I recognise these greens, Martha?" asked Heck, poking his long fingers into the wooden salad bowl.

"You should, they're from your own garden," she said. "You haven't been thinning them recently and the rocket is bolting."

"Maybe you and Netta can pick some later to take home. Since we've been in Rome the garden has got out of control."

"Cassie's library books have had us working all hours," said Alice. "I'm afraid I've neglected the garden rather badly, Mrs Hollis. But I did rescue these flowers from the weeds for you."

"They're lovely, dear," said the old lady. "Gladioli were Arthur's favourite because they lasted so long, all the way up the stem. I remember we had the same problems, keeping on top of the glut of veggies this time of year."

"Only three more days till the container leaves," said Netta. "Then Granddad can relax and just sit in the garden."

"You should know your grandfather by now, Netta. He can't sit still for ten minutes before he's on to the next thing," said Martha. "I expect he's already got another project in mind."

"Well I like to keep busy so I don't seize up," said George.

"There's plenty to do here, Dad, if you run out of ideas," said Alice.

"Oh, Edith's already beat you to it. She's put Heck and me to work on her own project for Cassie."

"Yes, I overheard them just now," said Netta. "They were plotting in the other room with Natasha."

"Why what's going on, Natasha?" asked Alice.

"My lips are sealed," she said. "Sworn to secrecy."

"Edith – what are you up to with my husband?" said Martha.

Heck intervened. "I've already explained to Alice. George and I are clearing out some old junk of Arthur's from that railway arch storage down at King's Cross."

"And what's that got to do with Cassie?" persisted Martha. "George, you promised me –"

"Well, Heck uncovered something that the children might like, so we're just cleaning it up to have a look, that's all," he said.

"What have you found, Heck – why all the secrecy?" asked Alice.

"I told you – old junk mostly – toys and stuff."

"Toys? To sell?"

"We don't know yet," he said. "First we have to renovate them."

"I still don't see what the secrecy is about, Dad."

"It's a surprise, Alice. You'll have to wait and see," said George.

"And you and Heck and Natasha and Mrs Hollis know what it is," said Alice.

"We just didn't want to burden you with anything more, dear, that's all," said Mrs Hollis.

Netta leaned over to George. "You can tell me, Granddad. Just whisper it in my ear."

"If I tell you, I'll have to tell your grandmother and she'll have to tell your mother. No, you'll have to wait and see."

"We'll see about that," said Martha. "George talks in his sleep, you know."

Since returning from Rome, Alice had slept in one of the spare bedrooms, refusing to go back to their four-poster despite Heck's pleading. Natasha was now using the main bedroom. The only other spare room had no bed because Heck and George moved it downstairs for Mrs Hollis. The big brass double bed that Alice had been sleeping in, had a sagging spring and rolled them to the middle.

"I don't think this is going to work, Heck. As soon as you get that couch set up in the spare room I want you to move in there."

"Tomorrow, Alice. That's a promise. I was just too tired to do it today." He climbed into the old bed wearing only his boxer shorts and waited for her to join him. She left for the bathroom across the hall and came back wearing a nightgown with a high neck. She got into bed on her side and clung to the side of the bed to keep from sliding to the centre.

"Please don't make me go downstairs and sleep on the couch, Heck. Just stay on your side of the bed."

"We have to work something out for living together now that Mrs Hollis is here. Can't we start again, Alice?"

"I don't know. Perhaps I made a mistake inviting her to come back to live here but..."

"She's come back to die, not live – in her own home. You didn't make a mistake; she's going to die happy. And Natasha will look after her until she does. Meantime, we have to get on with our own lives."

"Everything is happening at once and I can't seem to handle it," said Alice. "Some days I feel like I'm out of control. If it wasn't for Mother and Netta I'd probably curl up in the foetal position and stay there."

"But they are there. And so am I, Alice. Right here." He slid his arm round her shoulders but she stiffened and after a minute he removed it. "Don't you want me in your life anymore, is that it?"

"I can't make any decisions for myself. I've told you that already. All my clever plans for completing my PhD in villa life have collapsed – like me," she said. "That's what no one understands. I've collapsed. Nothing makes sense for me these days. I cling to Cassie as the one thing in my life I still care about."

"And us – don't you care about us?"

"I thought I did – before. But now…"

"Would it help if I left for awhile – went back to Rome, Alice? Give you space to sort out what you want to do."

"But what about Mrs Hollis? She dotes on you," she said.

"I'll come back and forth. Rome's only a day and a half away on Eurostar. I could leave as soon as the book container is shipped."

She sat up on the edge of the bed. "It's your decision, Heck. Don't ask me to make it, I can't." She stood up. "I'm going downstairs. I can sleep on the sofa."

He reached out his hand to stop her. "We have to decide what happens with this house when the old lady dies, Alice. Will you think about that while I'm away?"

"I already have, Heck. When she's gone, I want to sell it."

"Why? We've only just got it into shape. Think of all that work – and the garden. What you've always dreamed of, Barney said."

She shrugged. "Dreams are about the future. I'm like Mrs Hollis, I have no future. I have to think about the present. Do what I can for my children before it's too late."

"You're being melodramatic, Alice. People live for years after a mastectomy."

"Some people maybe. I don't feel like I'm one of them," she said.

"It sounds as though you're giving up. That's not like you."

"I don't know what I'm like. I only thought I did," said Alice. She walked to the door and opened it, peering into the blackness of the darkened old house.

# CHAPTER 32

Landon's former jazz group played a Scott Joplin rag, as a good-sized crowd circulated among Russell's sculptures in the Gloucester South Docks gallery. Elinor, arm-in-arm with her two sons Gareth and Mason, appeared frail but happy as she approached Barney.

"Did you hear how much that man bid for the calligraphy book, Barney?" asked Elinor. Barney shook his head. "Tell him, Mason."

"Two hundred pounds," said Mason, grinning in disbelief, "for a book."

"It's an original work of art, Mason," said Barney. "Bet you didn't realise your mum was such an important artist."

"She's only got three pieces in it," said Gareth, refusing to be impressed.

"That's three more than most people ever do. Are you going to buy a souvenir copy to show your teacher?" said Barney.

"I've already bought each of them one," Elinor said.

"And she bought a whole stack to give away as well," said Mason.

"Me too," said Barney. "It's for a good cause, don't you think, boys?"

"You mean the hospice or the African kids?" asked Gareth.

"Both. Do you like Russell's sculptures, Mason?"

Mason nodded. "Some of them are kinda funny – he uses all those broken bits of other things to make something completely different." He pointed at a nearby animal figure. "Like that deer made out of old bicycle parts. Its horns are made out of handlebars."

"I hope he makes more for his heron piece than we got for the book," said Elinor. "It's worth it. Maddy says she's going to run the price up when they auction it off at the end."

"Where is she?" asked Barney, looking around at the crowd.

"Right over there talking to Russell," Gareth pointed at a bright scarlet turban above the heads of the viewers. "He said he'd show me how to use his welding kit, if I wanted to make something out at the farm."

"Your mum says you're good at taking things apart. Maybe Russell can teach you how to stick them together, too," said Barney. "I'm going to talk to Maddy. Be sure to get your mother a glass of that free champagne before it's all gone."

"She's had two glasses already," said Mason.

Barney edged his way through the big crowd of hospice supporters who had been mustered by Mrs Oswold and her volunteers, keeping his eye on the bobbing red turban.

"How's the book sales, Maddy?" he asked, looking at the piles on the table where she and Russell stood.

"Better than my sculptures, Barney. I can't compete with these calligraphy artists."

"He's had plenty of compliments though and a few nibbles," said Maddy.

"No offers yet?"

"Mostly tire kickers so far," said Russell.

"Landon's band sounds great," said Barney. "Have they persuaded him to sing yet?"

"Not yet. It looks like he's been getting some Dutch courage at the bar," said Maddy.

"I thought that might happen," said Russell. "He's been on the wagon ever since the fire. And there's Elinor with him. Not sure if she's encouraging him or trying to stop him."

"Russell, I guess Maddy's told you that Elinor's only on palliative care now."

"Yeah, she said, so I don't suppose a few drinks will matter one way or the other."

"The thing is," persisted Barney, "she wanted me to ask you if you'd consider having Gareth and Mason out at the farm. She can't look after them anymore. Otherwise it's Social Services…"

"Jesus – I've just got Landon off my hands and now you want me to take on two teenagers. Why me?"

"Because they like you, Russell and they love your farm," said Maddy.

"And with me and Landon gone, you'll need some help for the rest of the season," said Barney.

"What happens after the season's over –who looks after them then?"

"I've already offered to help you, Russell. And I could hire a housekeeper too," said Maddy.

"Will you think about it, Russell – you're Elinor's last hope," said Barney.

Russell drained his glass of wine. "They're teenagers – and I'm 71. It's crazy to even suggest it. Not a chance." He shook his head and turned to go to get another drink from the bar where Elinor and Landon stood watching them.

Elinor took his arm as he approached. She handed him a fresh glass of wine from the bar. "So have you been talking to Barney and Maddy, Russell?"

He nodded. "Yep. And I told them it's not on, Elinor. Sorry, but I'm too old to take on your boys. I shouldn't have let Barney talk me into letting Landon stay, either."

Elinor said nothing but the smile faded from her face and tears spilled over onto her cheeks as she turned and moved away unsteadily from the bar. Landon went to follow her, then stopped in front of Russell. He poked his finger in Russell's chest.

"You are one selfish bastard. After all the help she's given you and you treat her like that," said Landon. "If I didn't think I'd break it, I'd punch your head in with this - " He brandished his artificial hand in Russell's face.

"You're drunk," said Russell. "The very first time you get a chance to prove yourself and you fall off the wagon. I'll bet your band is proud of you tonight."

Landon grabbed him by the lapel of his jacket and pushed him hard against the drinks table. Russell flung out his arm to stop his fall and knocked over several bottles and glasses.

With the crash of glass and Russell's fall, the jazz band's playing came to a ragged stop. The whole crowd turned towards the bar and fell quiet as Barney pushed through them to reach Landon. He stood over Russell, lying half under the drinks table nursing the elbow he'd thrust out to break his fall.

"I hope you broke your bloody arm, you fucking hypocrite," shouted Landon. His eyes bulged in his scarred face and his chest heaved. Barney moved between them and Landon tried to push him out of the way. Russell made no move to get up, too stunned from the surprise attack. "I'm sick of your patronisin' ways, pretendin' to do everyone favours and the whole goddam time you're busy usin' us all. Well no more. I'm finished bein' grateful."

Russell glared at him. "Good. Clear off – and don't bother coming back to the farm either – you make me puke, wallowing in your self-pity. Tash is well rid of you – and so am I."

The three band members had surrounded Landon and led him outside while Barney helped Russell to his feet.

"You okay, Russell? I've never seen Landon like that before."

Russell flexed his arm gingerly. "You've never seen him drunk before – I have – too many times. Now you know why Tash left him. There's only so much of that shit anyone can take." He allowed Barney to help him to the men's washroom at the back of the gallery, leaving Maddy and Elinor to clear up the mess around the bar. In the washroom, Barney turned to Russell who stood at the sink peering at his face in the mirror.

"Look, Russell, I think I'd better get him home and let him sleep it off. He'll apologise in the morning, I'm sure. You said yourself it's just the booze talking."

Russell shook his head hard. "No way. I want him off my place for good – you and Tash can deal with him from now on. If he's still there in the morning, I call the cops."

"Come on, Russell – where am I going to take him this time of night?"

"I don't give a shit – he's your problem now. Just keep him away from me." He shouldered his way past Barney and back into the gallery. Barney went outside to talk to the band members. He persuaded the drummer to take Landon home with him until he could figure out what to do next.

Back inside, he found Maddy standing beside Elinor who sat on a chair clutching Mason's hand. Gareth stood behind her, white-faced. He looked up as Barney approached.

"Elinor's not feeling well," said Maddy. "I think we'd better get her and the boys home."

Barney drove Maddy's car and dropped them off, then took Maddy home. She asked him in for a coffee and they sat glumly drinking it in her spacious flat.

"Well I couldn't have made a bigger hash of that if I tried," he said. "Elinor took it badly, didn't she? I knew it was a mistake to let her even hope he might consider having Mason and Gareth."

"You did your best, Barney. If Landon hadn't lost his temper, Russell might have been talked around but now…"

"My little experiment in 'committed Buddhism' has done the opposite of what I intended, Maddy."

"You couldn't have known it would end like this," she said. "Your intentions were good."

"We all know what the road to hell is paved with, don't we. The idea was to relieve suffering, not create it." He drained his cup. "Any more of this, Maddy? I don't fancy facing Russell in the mood he's in tonight."

She rose, poured him another cup and patted his shoulder. "Stay here tonight, Barney. Let him cool down by himself. I'll make you up a bed on the sofa."

"Thanks Maddy, I'll talk to him in the morning – see what we can salvage. It's Elinor I'm most worried about, not Landon and Russell."

"Me too," she said. "She's going to go into a downward spiral now that her last hope for the boys is gone."

"I think the best thing I can do now is back off and not make things worse," he said.

"Will you stay on at the farm still, if Landon leaves?"

"Until I go to Africa. I promised Russell I would. It won't be long now."

"What will happen to Landon? He can't stay with you. You heard Russell."

"I expect one of his band members will put him up for awhile until he decides what to do. I'll talk to him tomorrow when he's sobered up," said Barney.

Maddy carried in some sheets and a pillow and blanket for him and he helped her make up a bed on the sofa.

"We can't do any more damage tonight. Might as well try to get some sleep. Goodnight, Barney."

Around 3 a.m., the phone rang and he heard Maddy answer it in her bedroom. A few moments later she appeared by his side. "That was Gareth. Elinor's worse. They called 911 and an ambulance took her to Gloucester hospital. I have to go over and look after the boys, Barney. Will you drive me?" She disappeared back into the bedroom and he scrambled into his clothes.

After he dropped her at Elinor's flat, he went on out to the farm, unable to sleep. He checked his laptop and found an email from Hunter.

*Dear Dad,*

*We're in Bridgetown, Barbados ready to make the big crossing tomorrow to the Cape Verde Islands. Sure glad we have Lottie along. We ran into a Force 10 gale in the Caribbean and she and Clive had to do everything. I was laid out on the cabin sole for three days, too sick to move. They just stepped over me whenever they came below for a rest. The Betsy rolls around like a drunk in this weather but Clive maintains she's unsinkable.*

*Lottie reckons we'll reach the Cape Verdes in three weeks at the rate we're going. She loves being at the helm but when it's my watch I just hook up the autopilot – it steers a better course than I can.*

*Have you heard anymore from Cassie? I thought there might be an email when we arrived here in Bridgetown but I haven't heard anything since we left Vancouver. She knows we have the prostheses with us anyway, and I told her we'd be meeting you in Dakar.*

*Hope you have a good trip overland to Senegal – at least you won't get seasick. Clive reckons I should have my sea-legs by now and should be fine for the crossing. That's what he said about the Caribbean too.*

*I'll check in at an internet café in the Cape Verdes when we arrive. Wish me luck.*

*Hunter, plus more kisses from Lottie. Clive says hello and if you beat us, you can look for a good 4x4 while you're waiting.*

Russell had still not showed up, so he went to bed. He lay awake for a long time, thinking of Elinor's dilemma. He had not anticipated becoming so fond of her and Maddy and the thought of having to leave, when they were both so vulnerable troubled him. But there seemed no way out of this impasse – Elinor could die anytime according to Natasha and Maddy was too ill herself to help with the boys. It had been unrealistic to expect Russell to take on such a commitment and Barney felt he should have said so immediately to Elinor and not allowed her to build up her hopes.

Maybe Mrs Oswold could use her connections with Social Services to help find some foster parents. Or Natasha. Yes, he would phone her tomorrow. He felt more comfortable asking her to help than Mrs Oswold. After this evening's fiasco, he didn't think Mrs Oswold would want to hear any more of Barney's proposals.

As he tossed fretfully, he tried to assess the likelihood of his trip to Africa proving any more fruitful than his hospice experiment. So far, his attempts at committed Buddhism were no more successful than his previous searches for Buddhist enlightenment in China and Tibet had been. At least he could do something useful for his youngest daughter, as she conducted her own experiment in the refugee camps of West Africa.

# CHAPTER 33

The Blue Note café bar in Gloucester held only a scattering of patrons at midday. Barney had agreed to meet Landon here and was relieved to see him drinking only an espresso. This was the first time they'd seen each other since the art show the previous week. Russell remained adamant he wouldn't have Landon back and Landon had no wish to return. The bitterness between the two men had deepened over the incident and neither could be persuaded to reconsider.

For his part, Barney had given up the role of mediator and settled for listening to each man poor-mouth the other, without taking sides with either one. He spent his time between helping Russell on the farm and visiting Elinor at the hospice, where she had been removed to the intensive palliative care ward. He shuttled Maddy and the two boys back and forth to visit her.

"Thanks for coming, Barney," said Landon. "I know you're busy but I wanted to ask you something. I've made up my mind what I'm going to do."

"Sorry I haven't been before, Landon. What with my own preparations for Africa – getting all my jabs done and packing up all your stuff. Anyway, it's all out in Maddy's car so we can drop it off at your mate's flat after. You still staying at the drummer's?"

Landon nodded. "For the time bein'. That's what I need to talk to you about. I'm goin' to live with my sister in Freetown. I'm takin' Elinor's advice – help my sister raise her grandchildren and build a house for them all, on my piece of land there."

"Well, I think it's a good move for you, Landon. You've been talking about going there as long as I've known you."

"Yeah but what I want to ask is, if I can travel out there with you when you go."

"It means a long trip overland, Landon. I gave up flying except for emergencies."

"I want to see the country too but my French is a bit shaky – in fact, it's almost non-existent, so I'd need your help with all the formalities," said Landon.

"What about the booze – are you back on it again after the art show? I don't think I want to be responsible for you, if you get legless every night."

"That was a fluke, Barney. I lost my nerve when the band asked me to sing – I couldn't face an audience sober. But in the end I didn't face them at all," he said. "I realised I could never go back to that life as a hanger-on, pretendin' to be a musician. Have people starin' at my burned-off face and feelin' sorry for me. I swore off that way of life and the booze at the same time. That's when I decided to go back to Africa."

"You haven't made things any easier by antagonising Russell that way. Maddy and I hoped we might convince him to give the boys a try – see how it worked out."

"Yeah, I know. I just lost it when I heard the way he dismissed Elinor – he didn't even attempt to soften the blow.

Punched her straight in the stomach," said Landon, "so I punched him back."

"You didn't do her any favours, Landon, and you've put the rest of us in a bind. I have to leave to meet my son in Dakar and Maddy is looking after two teenagers, when she should be looking after herself."

"Russell would never have agreed to have them, that's the thing. I knew it, you knew it and so did Maddy. Only Elinor believed he would – until he slapped her in the face. I'm not sorry I shook him up. He deserved it. And more."

"Settling old scores, eh? Getting in a few kicks for Natasha, as well as Elinor?"

Landon grinned, his lop-sided mouth twisting into a smile. "I guess I'd been waitin' a long time for that chance."

"Was it worth putting Elinor in hospital and destroying her sons' future?" asked Barney.

"Elinor's a good friend. I would never do anythin' to hurt her."

"You just did, Landon and now we're all in a mess. You got any ideas for sorting it out, before we both clear off to Africa and let two dying women deal with what we're leaving behind?"

"Well we sure can't take the boys with us, Barney. Maybe when we get to Freetown I could offer to have them there – they could help me get my own place goin'."

"You just saying that, Landon or do you mean it? Elinor couldn't handle another disappointment like that."

"Yeah, why not? If you help me get there, Barney, I'll offer to have her boys. Tash and I never managed it ourselves so this could be my chance."

"Even if it were only for a short while, it might work, I guess. Will you go out to the hospice and tell her yourself, Landon? I'll drive you there, after we dump your stuff off here at your mate's flat."

Landon rose to his feet and held out his artificial right hand for Barney to grasp. "You've got yourself a deal."

"Well it would be good to have you with me, Landon. I could use your help when we get to Dakar and start looking for a 4x4. Hunter's expecting me to have one ready when they arrive. Do you know anything about trucks?"

"The band always put me in charge of the minibus when we toured, so I got to know my way around a diesel engine over the years. Not repairs but basic maintenance and stuff."

"That's more than I know," said Barney. "I imagine it'll be tough finding a good cheap truck that's not going to let us down in the bush. From what I understand, Dakar is where everybody brings cars and trucks from Europe to sell. I'd like to have a week or so to check out the market before I buy anything."

"Nothin' I like better than kickin' tires, Barney. I've bought and sold my share of old bangers over the years."

"Okay Landon, we've got ten days before we need to leave. Let's get started. I want to see Elinor's face when you tell her."

# CHAPTER 34

In the old walled garden at Tiberius Road, Barney was weeding in the vegetable patch. Alice emerged from the side door of the house carrying a tray of tea and biscuits.

"Mrs Hollis sent me out, Barney. She says you look as if you need a break. She's been keeping an eye on you." Alice nodded her head in the direction of the house and he waved to the old woman propped up in her bed by the window. She fluttered her hand at him. Alice set the tray down on a round garden table made from old horseshoes – a present from Russell to her and Heck. He unfolded two canvas chairs and they sat facing the old walled garden with the espaliered fruit trees.

"This place is getting away from you, Alice. When's Heck coming back again?"

She shrugged. "Not for a while. He's staying at Giorgio's for the summer, I think."

"Don't you keep in touch – phone or anything?" asked Barney.

"He calls Mrs Hollis regularly." She poured the tea, avoiding his glance.

"You want to tell me what's going on, Alice? I figured maybe once I got out of your way and went down to Russell's, things would get better between you two…"

"I told you before you left you weren't the problem, Barney."

"So what is – Mrs Hollis?"

She shook her head. "No. She's providing us with a breathing space. I'm glad she's here. It would be impossible on my own. And Natasha makes it all go smoothly."

"What then? I never believed all that stuff Netta told me about you and Cassie," he said.

"Why, what did she say?"

"Oh, that you were convinced she's in constant danger and Zinadine left her on her own all the time."

"Well he does. She told me once, he goes away for a month or more."

"Anyway what's that got to do with you and Heck? I thought you two had it made – this place," he gestured towards the house. "Is it true the old lady has signed the house over to you?"

Alice nodded, glancing back at the window where Mrs Hollis' bed stood. "To both of us – wouldn't accept a penny. That's why I suggested she come and spend her remaining time here."

"And after – what then?"

"I told Heck I want to sell it. I can't stay here any longer."

"Where will you go?"

"I haven't mentioned it to them yet but I thought I'd go back to Highgate and live with George and Martha. They're going to need looking after soon."

Barney laughed. "I'd like to be there when you tell them that. Those two are as active now as when I first met them."

"Mother maybe, but Dad's slowing down. He's worn himself out with this book project. I'm glad it's over at last."

"They'll be more likely to look after you, than the other way around."

"Maybe they will," she said. She fiddled with her teacup, twirling it round and round on the saucer.

Barney reached over and covered her hand to stop her. "Alice, look at me. I know there's something you're not telling me. Have you had some news about your cancer – is that it?"

"No – not news." She tried to withdraw her hand but he hung on to it.

"I want you to tell me. Whatever it is, get it – out."

She made a wry grin. "You were going to say 'get it off your chest.'"

"You always knew what I was going to say before I said it. So go on, Alice. Get it off your chest."

"If I tell you, you must promise not to repeat it. To anyone." She extricated her hand from his and waited.

"I promise."

"Not to anyone. Ever."

"I promise, Alice." He pulled his chair closer and held out his hand again but she ignored it. She rose and bent down by the circular herb bed and pinched out the tips of some bush basil.

"When I first went in hospital they did a whole battery of tests on me," she said. "You were still in Nepal somewhere when I got the results, so I had no one to tell." She looked up at him accusingly.

"You had Heck, for god's sake."

She tossed her head. "He's the last one I could tell."

"I came back as soon as he contacted me, Alice."

"Yes. You did. But by then I'd made up my mind." She continued dead-heading the herbs.

"That you were going to leave Heck?" he asked, puzzled.

She shook her head. "Just let me tell it in my own way, Barney. Don't ask me any questions, okay?"

He held up his hands. "Go on. I'm listening."

"One of the tests was called the BRCA1," she said. "It's for the breast cancer gene. It was positive."

"Positive," he repeated.

"That means I've got it – the gene." Her hands moved over the basil bushes releasing the pungent aroma into the warm afternoon air.

He said nothing and waited for her to continue, knowing there was more.

"It's only a matter of time until it returns and then..."

"Alice, I'm sorry – you never said anything before –"

She clutched a handful of the crushed herbs, pressing her nose in them. "I tried to tell you – remember, in the hospital?"

He frowned in concentration. "You mean the pre-emptive strike? I thought you were only joking."

"I know you did. That's why I couldn't tell you about the test. You thought it was just my other breast."

"Has it spread, Alice? Is that what you've been hiding from everyone?" He knelt down beside her, his arm round her shoulder.

Tears coursed down her face now but she kept on methodically pinching out the tips of the herbs with both hands. He waited for her to speak, joining her in topping the other mixed herbs of oregano and sage.

Finally, she spoke again. "It's genetic, Barney. Genetic. Don't you understand what that means? I've passed it on to Netta and Cassie." She slumped down into the herb bed, crushing them so they released a powerful scent of oils around the two of them as he hunched over her, stroking her back, listening to her sob.

"You don't know that for sure, Alice. They might not have it – isn't that possible?" he asked, in an attempt to convince himself as much as her.

"It would mean taking the test," she hauled herself up into a sitting position, her face streaked with dirt where she had rubbed her eyes. "That's the only way we'd know – they'd know. Unless they waited till the same thing happens to them as me."

He sat beside her trying to absorb what she said. "There must be some kind of drug – something they can do."

She nodded, "Yes there is. Pre-emptive surgery."

"That's crazy, Alice – nobody would agree to – to…"

"- To have both breasts removed?" she said. "It's already happening. Women are doing it now. Not just old women like me. Young women."

"Jesus – doctors are doing this? Mutilating young women deliberately?"

"What's the alternative – let them die? Is that what you want for our daughters, Barney?" She sat in the middle of the herb bed with her bare legs stuck out in front of her like a child and stared at him, waiting for his reply.

"I don't know. But we can't play God, Alice."

"Is that what you think I've been doing all this time? Playing God with my own children?"

"What do you think they would do if you – if we told them?" He helped her up, unable to bear seeing her so vulnerable, sprawled on the ground.

"They might do what I'm going to do," she said. "Have surgery."

"Will you tell them first? Before you do it?"

"I'll have to. But both girls together. I need to tell them together, Barney. I couldn't bear to do it twice. That's why you have to bring Cassie home."

He nodded, his voice abandoning him.

Barney and Alice sat late into the night, talking. Her confession had released a dammed up blockage and she poured out a stream of memories of their children she demanded he relive with her. It was almost as if they were gone already, Barney thought, as he listened to her recalling their past life from early childhood.

He didn't try to stop her, although he felt uncomfortable with all this past tense discussion. Maybe she could haul herself out of the miasma she had been sunk in since her first mastectomy. He marvelled that she could even contemplate a second one but felt too unsure of discussing it with her.

Perhaps if he could persuade Cassie to return, if only for a brief visit, Alice might get her life back into perspective. He knew the likelihood of Cassie leaving Zinadine for long would be slight and her commitment to the war orphans in her refugee camp would not let her stay away for long. If Alice wanted to spend time with her youngest child, she would have to go out to Guinea herself. In her present weakened condition, she could not consider it, she said. She needed Barney and

Hunter to go in her place and had harassed them non-stop until they both agreed.

So the whole family had been mobilised in the cause of repatriating Cassie. A lost cause, he was convinced, from his sporadic email correspondence with her. She longed to see them all but wanted them to come out to visit her and try to understand her work. Only Barney and Hunter encouraged her to stay. The women were united in their determination to bring her home – with or without Zinadine. They supported her from a distance by fostering her orphans – Martha, Alice and Netta each had one. And they mobilised a crew of volunteers to make the book project a reality. But these were unspoken bribes to persuade her to come back.

Barney could only persuade Alice to go to sleep by promising he would leave for Africa as soon as possible. He stumbled up the curved staircase to the old army cot Heck had put in the third bedroom and sank into a deep sleep.

Some time later, Natasha shook him awake. He sat up, dazed and punch-drunk for lack of sleep.

"Barney – Maddy just phoned," she said. "It's Elinor. She's gone."

"What? Gone where?"

"She died two hours ago."

# CHAPTER 35

Barney propelled himself out of London on a wave of guilt for having abandoned so many people whom he felt he had let down – Maddy and Elinor's two boys, Mason and Gareth; Alice and her harrowing secret and Russell, inundated with orders and gluts of vegetables.

Landon he had also abandoned, still awaiting his passport and a final series of inoculations for rabies and yellow fever. He took the Eurostar to Paris and at the Gare du Nord transferred to the Gare d'Austerlitz for the trip south to Spain and Gibraltar

As the overnight train to Madrid dragged itself over the Pyrenees and down the Mediterranean coast to Algeciras, he had plenty of opportunity to ponder this next move in his five-year plan. Although he had now been separated from Alice for almost three years, she still dragged her heels about the divorce. He had filed the papers for it at the end of the second year of separation but discovered in the small print that unless both parties agreed, it could not happen automatically. That required five years – two more to go and then the divorce would go through on the nod, regardless of which one objected.

He had no heart for a hostile court battle and hoped that in another two years Alice would have recovered her old self sufficiently to acquiesce in a mutually agreed finish to their 30 year-long marriage. Although she and Heck were estranged now, he felt optimistic about them resolving their differences. From what he knew of Heck, he would not let her just slip out of his life without a fight. And Barney knew, or thought he did, that Alice loved Heck much more than she ever had him. Was it just her wounded pride that made her push Heck away? Barney wasn't sure but from what he observed, this seemed the most likely explanation for her alienating of Heck.

He supposed the refusal to contemplate the divorce was part of the reason – an excuse to put Heck off. But her confession of her secret fear about herself and their two daughters, was probably the main cause of her obstinate clinging to their dead marriage. It provided her with some semblance, however unreal, that her former family life still existed. Barney could not bring himself to badger her further over the divorce in her present fragile condition.

So the five-year plan it would have to be. That would make him 75 years old. The three-quarter century mark. Only two years away and yet it sounded like the age of a building or a tree or an elephant – not him.

He peered at his face in the reflection of the window, as the train streaked on through the night. The shape disconcerted him with its familiarity. He felt it should appear different to match his changed mental picture of himself but there it was, same as ever. At other times, he saw it as that of a stranger. Those times generally were at home when he looked at the individual features with a more critical eye, noting wrinkles, bags, and pouches of skin.

Here on the train in a foreign country, what he looked for was reassurance, he supposed. Are you still in there? And who are you? Do I know you, you 73 year old shape? Short sideways glances could provide momentary reassurance. It was the long close perusals that unsettled him.

# CHAPTER 36

Africa! The ferry from Algeciras bore him across the Straits of Gibraltar to the shores of Arab Africa. Barney moved through the wide avenues of Tangier to the train station and continued south to Marrakech, where he drifted about for a day in the Arab souk before catching a long distance bus to Agadir.

It pulled into the huge echoing new bus station just before midnight. Nothing was open inside it but outside he found a street stall, where he bought sweet mint tea and a doughy pastry. Back inside the grandiose station, he found a wooden bench to lie down on, to wait for his connection south through the Western Sahara to the end of the line at Dakhla. He settled his pack beneath his head, pulled his jacket over him to keep out the chill and tried to sleep. He awoke to a uniformed guard shaking him roughly.

"*Pas dormir* – no sleeping here," he said and waited until Barney sat up groggily, before moving on to roust up the other illegally dozing travellers.

The contrast between the sleek air-conditioned bus and the desert landscape continually startled Barney with unexpected sights. The road followed the Atlantic coastline closely with only sporadic signs of life. Herds of wild camels wandered unconcernedly across their path munching at tufts of small thorn bushes. The bus stopped at an abandoned gas station where he saw several hundred goats lying about between the rusting pumps.

Once the driver stopped in the middle of the road and got out without a word. Barney watched as the Arab went round the rear of the bus and off into the sand dunes at one side. He took off his shoes, spread out his prayer mat, kneeled down and proceeded to perform his afternoon obeisance to Allah. That done, he rose, rolled up his mat, started up the bus and drove on through the scrubby desert.

At Dakhla bus station, Barney collected his pack and spoke to the Moslem driver.

"*Pardon, monsieur,* is there a bus to Mauritania from here?"

The man pointed to a battered old Mercedes diesel cargo van across the street, "*le voilà,*" he said, indicating a young bearded Arab arguing with a man and his wife beside the van.

Barney took his turn waiting to negotiate a price to the disputed border. To his surprise, the young man spoke English and quoted Barney a reasonable price. For reassurance, Barney asked the Arab couple in front if they agreed and when they nodded and smiled, he handed over the fare to the bearded driver. The young man tapped his watch.

"In one hour only, we go, *m'sieur.*" He heaved Barney's rucksack into the back of the van which was heaped high with bundles and jerry cans. Carpets covered the floor, along with a few greasy cushions and several people stood about, in no hurry to climb into the windowless van. Barney wandered around the empty streets, not venturing far from the truck.

When he returned, everyone had already climbed in but they made a space for him on the carpets and motioned to him to pull over a bundle to prop himself up. A square opening covered with a wire grille facing the driver's cab allowed the soupy warm air to circulate once they reached the main highway south.

From here on, public transportation no longer existed, the guidebook said and Barney would have to bargain for rides in bush taxis through West Africa. The bearded driver dumped him with his rucksack at the military post, that marked the edge of no-man's land between the two countries.

"How will I get to the border?" asked Barney.

The young man shrugged. "Ask one of these cars. It is not far."

"Can I walk, then?

"No, no – that is not permitted. Mines are everywhere from here on," said his driver, reversing his beaten-up old Mercedes van off the road to head back to Dakhla.

Barney tried to find a lift through the heavily mined area to the Mauritanian checkpoint but nothing was available. After eating a goat stew in one of the funnel-shaped Arab pottery *tagines* at the lone border café, he discovered a large Bedouin tent in the rear courtyard filled with mattresses. For five euros, he spent a night wondering if he would be stranded again the following day.

In the morning, a Frenchman in a touring campervan offered to give him a lift through the border strip. They followed a caravan of trucks over the rutted unmarked tracks, half expecting to see one of them get blown up when it veered off and took a slightly different route to the checkpoint. Inside the tin customs shack, he paid ten euros to have a transit visa stamped in his passport. He left the Frenchman who was heading inland to Atar while Barney followed the new main road to the capital, Nouakchott.

From the flyblown coastal town of Nouadhibou, it took him awhile to find a *sept-place* estate car going to the capital. He travelled through the night, jammed with eight others into an old Mercedes that deposited him and another young Moslem Arab at the garage park in Nouakchott around three in the morning. The young man spoke French and asked Barney where he was staying.

*"Je ne sais pas,"* said Barney. "I will look for a hostel somewhere." He rooted around in his pack for his copy of The Lonely Planet and held it up for Abdul, the young Arab to see.

Abdul shook his head. "It is late *monsieur,* not safe to walk about here. Please come with me," he said. "You are welcome to share my *apartement.*"

They walked through unlit lanes of soft sand into a warren of concrete blockhouse apartments, lugging their bags, with Barney shifting his from arm to arm to ease the weight. Abdul stopped in front of a building.

"Is this yours?" asked Barney.

He shook his head. "No, it is still another two kilometres. Please wait here a few minutes." He disappeared into the gloom of the stairwell and Barney sank down on the sand beside his rucksack. A dog howled further down the street and he remembered the warnings about rabid street dogs in Africa. After a short wait, Abdul appeared holding up a set of keys.

"Come," he said, helping Barney to his feet and hoisting the heavy rucksack for him. "I have a ride for us." He went around the back of the building and down a narrow darkened lane. Barney followed, wondering what he had let himself in for. Abdul stopped by a shed and unlocked it with one of the keys. In the gloom, he found an old 125cc motorbike and wheeled it back down the lane and out onto the sandy road before starting it.

"My friend has loaned this to us," he explained, helping Barney onto the bike with his rucksack in between them. They set off in the dim light from the old bike's headlamp and swerved along between ruts in the soft sand. Balancing himself with one hand, Barney clutched his heavy rucksack with the other as Abdul navigated the unmarked lanes.

He turned into a wider more deeply rutted street and revved the motor to pull out of a rough section of road. The little motorbike slewed sideways and Barney lost his grip, as he tried to hang onto his rucksack. He toppled backwards off the bike and flung out his arm to break his fall. He landed in the hard sand with the full weight of his pack on top of him and let out a yelp, as he felt a sharp pain in his left wrist.

Abdul righted the bike and helped Barney to his feet, picking up the rucksack.

"Sorry," said Barney, massaging his wrist. "I lost my balance." He tried to take his pack from Abdul but couldn't hold it with one hand and hang on with his left hand.

Abdul wedged the pack in front of himself between the handlebars. "We are almost *chez moi*," he said, pointing ahead of them at another cluster of concrete blockhouses.

Abdul's flat was one cement-walled room with a steel door, a single bare light bulb and a small window high up on the wall. Beneath it lay his narrow kapok mattress on the floor, which he insisted Barney must have. He explained that he would sleep next door with a friend and said he would be back shortly. Barney only protested feebly as his wrist now throbbed with pain. Abdul showed him where the communal toilet and tap for water was on the landing and loaned him a flashlight as there was no light in the hall. Barney let the trickle of cool water run over his wrist as he filled an empty bucket for flushing the stand-up toilet.

Half an hour later Abdul returned with a Styrofoam tray of rice and grilled meat, that he had brought from some nearby café. He handed it to Barney and found a spoon on the table for him.

"But aren't you going to have some too?" asked Barney. "Please – how much do I owe you?" he said, fumbling in his pocket for some Mauritanian *ouguiyas*.

Abdul shook his head, refusing the money. "I have already eaten at the café," he said, motioning for Barney to eat while he prepared mint tea over a single burner mounted on a gas cylinder. He laid out several small grubby glasses on a tray with chunks of coarse grey sugar and a large bunch of fresh mint that he proceeded to stuff into a metal teapot.

A knock on the steel door signalled the arrival of two of his friends. Saleem and Arif sat round on cushions on the floor, watching Abdul pour tea from an arm's length height into a tiny glass. He poured it back and forth between the glasses until the desired strength and consistency was achieved before handing Barney a glass. The three men watched him take a sip and then raised their glasses to salute him. They looked in their mid-30s and told Barney they taught French in an EFL school in Nouakchott, to local Arab businessmen.

"You are all from Nouakchott?" asked Barney, sipping the powerful mint tea.

Saleem shook his head. "*Mais non*, we are from Senegal."

"*Oui,*" said Arif. "We are here on a work visa, *seulement.*"

Abdul stuffed more fresh mint into the long-spouted metal teapot and boiled more water on the gas burner. "Tomorrow, I am going back to my village in Senegal to see my wife. I will go with you to the border."

The teachers all roomed nearby and shared one common desire – to get a visa for Europe, preferably France but anywhere that would take them out of Mauritania and their subsistence lives here.

"In Canada, everyone speaks *francais et anglais, n'est ce pas?*" asked Saleem.

Barney shook his head and smiled. "In theory, yes but in practice, mainly in Quebec. Otherwise only a little, *comme moi-meme.*"

"Your arm is still sore?" asked Abdul, noticing Barney nursing it against his chest.

Barney nodded, gingerly wiggling it in circles and wincing. "I don't think it is broken – only sprained. But it hurts like hell."

The three young men spoke rapidly together, then Arif stood up and left the room.

"He is getting something to…" said Saleem making wrapping motions round his arm.

Barney tried to protest but Abdul shook his head. "He lives in this building – he will be back in a moment."

A few minutes later, Arif returned with a length of cotton cloth and a tube of salve. Expertly, he massaged the salve into Barney's wrist and wound the bandage tightly round it, pinning it with a tiny safety pin Abdul found on his cluttered table.

"*Alors,*" announced Arif, "Tomorrow it will feel much better." He patted Barney on the back and Abdul poured more of the aromatic mint infusion for him. As he sipped it, Barney began to relax, grinning and nodding at his new Arab friends.

Saleem returned to the questioning. "We have a friend in Montreal. Perhaps you could help us get a work visa for Canada when you return home?"

Barney looked at the three expectant faces and didn't have the heart to tell them how unlikely their wish to emigrate could be realised. "If you write down your names and addresses and your friend's in Montreal, I will try," he said.

Smiles broke out all round and they quickly wrote down their details for him. Fired up by this new fantasy, they talked on and on into the night about the hopelessness of their situation until Barney begged off to get a few hours sleep before heading on to the Senegal border.

As he tossed about in the blackness of Abdul's room, trying to ease the pain in his wrist, he wondered whether it had been fair to raise hopes that he felt sure he could not fulfil. He thought of the mess he had made of Elinor and Maddy's lives back in the UK. His dilemma over committed Buddhism left him feeling very uneasy about what lay ahead over the border in black Africa.

# CHAPTER 37

The town of Rossi, on the Senegal River, infamous in the guidebooks for its corrupt officials, marked the border crossing between Mauritania and Senegal; between Arab and black Africa. The huge Arab customs officer towered over Barney, the three shiny brass pips on his shoulder glittering in the African sun. He reminded Barney of the Iraqi dictator Saddam Hussein. Perhaps people in Mauritania got promoted based on their size, he thought, as the other officers of lower rank were much smaller. The big man barely deigned to listen to Barney, who struggled in his rusty French to ask why he was being refused the stamp in his passport that should have been automatic.

He knew why, of course, because several eager young men touting for business told him – the customs men wanted a bribe and Barney refused to give one. He told the glowering giant standing in front of him that he would take everyone's name in the run-down office and report them to the Tourism Department. The big man looked at him pityingly. Barney was ten yards from the ferry, crossing the Senegal River into black Africa. It was an empty threat. The names of the customs officers on their official badges were in Arabic script for a start, so Barney couldn't write them down, although he brandished a pen and notebook in front of the big man's face. And secondly, how would he report them when he was crossing into a non-Arab country? The official had him in a bind and they both knew it.

The huge officer brushed past him with a dismissive gesture, leaving Barney to stew over his next move in the steamy humidity of the late African afternoon. He stared at the open-decked ferry as it filled with a colourful mixture of Arabs, Africans and a handful of Westerners in Land Rovers. They were all jumbled together with nomadic herdsmen, who shouted and whacked at a herd of camels that stubbornly refused to board the ferry.

"May I assist you?" Barney turned to see his young friend Abdul, who stood to one side during his conversation with the large customs official.

Barney and Abdul had ridden from Nouakchott in the battered *sept-place* bush taxi to this border crossing at Rossi, notorious for its hassles. He explained the problem with his passport and the young Arab spoke to one of the customs officials.

"They won't release it until you pay the fee," he relayed to Barney and the customs official nodded vigorous affirmation.

"But there is no fee – the Lonely Planet says it's a scam – a bribe."

Abdul shrugged and Barney heard for the first time the phrase he would hear repeatedly in the following weeks.

"This is Africa," Abdul smiled. "For ten euros you can get your passport back and be on that ferry with me. It is only a small bribe," he said, by way of encouragement. It was true that the big customs officer had at first demanded 50 euros but by degrees had climbed down to this mere pittance, just to save face amongst his lower ranks.

Barney conceded that he would have to pay the large man his bribe, or he would hold him here all day until he wore him down. Frowning his displeasure, he paid the ten Euros from his dwindling supply that had shrunk at an alarming rate.

The big officer took his money and beamed goodwill as he gestured to one of his clerks to stamp the passport, which he then signed with a flourish. "Is not a bribe, m'sieur, *je jure* – I swear, it is a fee." He presented the passport to him, all smiles and Barney grinned back despite himself, shaking his head in defeat.

Abdul stood waiting for him and they ran the twenty yards to the ferry, where pandemonium had broken out. The herd of over fifty camels that refused to go up the ramp over the few feet of water onto the ferry, bunched into an ever-tightening clump, with the rear ones thrusting against the front row. The pressure from the camel-drivers behind, shouting and whacking with sticks, drove the lead camels to stumble. The others broke ranks and surged up the ramp into the open deck area, towards a single rope separating them from the passengers.

Barney and Abdul, seeing the camels pouring towards them, scrambled behind the rope strung across the deck. The panicked animals charged forward as if the rope didn't exist and Barney fell back into the crowd, as a camel shoved its head right at his face. He dropped his rucksack in fright and it disappeared under the splayed hooves of the leading camels.

Now the camel drivers forced a passage down the side of the herd to the front of them and flailed at their heads, beating them back from the cowering passengers. Barney plucked the sleeve of one of the nomadic herdsmen and pointed to his rucksack. The man plunged into the melee of churning legs. He rescued the trampled backpack from under one camel, which had entangled itself in the shoulder straps. He hoisted the bag over his shoulder and glided out under the animals' bellies to present Barney with his battered rucksack. The man stood smiling and nodding at him, until Abdul offered him a small coin and the camel-driver turned back to whacking his animals.

The Senegal River was crowded with long wooden pirogue-style boats, powered and un-powered and the ferry drove straight through them, scattering any in its path. When they landed in Senegal, the passengers were let off before the camels. Barney felt for the first time, he had finally arrived in the real Africa. He said goodbye to Abdul, who left for his village in the opposite direction of Dakar.

Barney felt suddenly bereft at the loss of his new Arab friend, alone on the edge of black Africa. For a few minutes, he watched the herdsmen struggling to unload the camels, that were as reluctant to leave the ferry as they had been to board it. He followed behind the great lumbering beasts with the camel-drivers whacking and shouting their strange cries – oaths, he imagined but could make out nothing of the Arabic dialect they spoke.

A skinny young black man tried to take Barney's pack from him but he clung to it, shaking his head. The man pulled his arm, pointing at a wooden booth with a crowd from the ferry gathered round it.

*"Passeport,"* he said, beckoning for Barney to give it to him. *"Allemande? Americain? Anglais?"*

"English… *Canadien,"* he replied, refusing to hand over his passport, after the recent hassle on the other side of the river.

"*Bon,* I help you get customs stamp – just give me money and I do it for you. Then we find good hotel. You have euros or *cefas*? Twenty euros for the stamp," he said, holding out his hand.

"No thanks, I don't want any help," said Barney joining the crowd at the shabby customs booth.

"Okay. After, I take you to change money – I know best rates here. You like to eat before we go to get a hotel?" the man persisted.

Barney only shook his head and waved him away. At the booth, he handed over his passport, prepared for another battle but the official barely glanced at him before stamping it and handing it back. Surprised, he waited for the demand for money but the customs man turned to the next person elbowing his way to the counter and Barney stepped back onto the street.

The skinny young man reappeared from the crowd and once again tried to take Barney's rucksack. "Okay father, now we change your money. Come this way," and he led off down a narrow lane.

Barney stopped and looked round. "No. I want to find a bank."

The young man nodded impatiently. "Yes, yes. Bank is this way,"

Barney turned back to the crowded market area they had just left and looked about for a *bureau de change* but saw nothing. Instead, men with rolls of money sat outside ramshackle tea stalls, beckoning him over. He approached one and took out his remaining Mauritanian *ouguiyas.* The moneychanger did a rapid calculation and wrote a figure on his pad, holding it up to Barney.

Without agreeing, Barney stepped back to check in his guidebook for the official exchange rate and did his own calculation. The skinny young man looked over his shoulder.

"I told you – you come with me. This rate is no good. I get you much better rate," he urged, tugging at his rucksack.

Barney ignored him and tried two more moneychangers, each one offering slightly different rates. He settled for the second one, stuffed the reduced handful of *cefas* into his side pocket and buttoned it. The young black man renewed his urging.

"Okay father, now we find you a hotel. I have friends here with good rooms. Let's go. Not far. I'll carry your bag," and once again he tried to wrest Barney's rucksack from his grip but Barney clung to it, shaking his head.

"No, I don't want a hotel. I'm going to Dakar. Where is the bush taxi garage?"

"No problem, father, I take you there in taxi. Too far to walk. But first we go to a restaurant for food, okay?"

For once, Barney agreed as he had eaten nothing except two bananas since leaving Nouakchott. They headed down an alley of low concrete-block shops with open fronts. The skinny young man entered a room with two or three men sitting on benches at a long trestle table. They ate large mounds of rice and some stewed meat – goat or chicken, perhaps.

"So, what you like, father?" asked the grinning young man, sitting down. He beckoned to a woman who sat in a cramped adjoining room on a low stool, tending a large pot on a gas ring.

Barney pointed to what the other men were eating and nodded.

"Okay, good," said the young man. "You want coke or beer?"

"Beer, I guess."

The man snapped his fingers at the woman and she came over to the table. He ordered two dinners and two beers in a pidgin French. Barney could only partially make it out and the woman disappeared back into the kitchen area. She reappeared with two bottles of the local beer and they sipped them, waiting for the food. This too, appeared almost immediately, as Barney watched her scoop large mounds of rice topped with a single ladle of the meat stew on top. The meat was fiery and chewy but unidentifiable to him and he ate mostly the rice with some of the sauce on it. The young man devoured his in enormous spoonfuls then sat back to finish off his beer.

"Now I take you to the bush taxi garage, father," he said, calling the cook over once again. He spoke quickly to her and she replied without looking at Barney.

"How much is it?" asked Barney and the young man mentioned a figure which struck Barney as far too much. "Is that for both meals?"

The grinning young man nodded, "*Oui,* both."

"Why should I pay for your meal?" demanded Barney. "I don't owe you anything."

"But you said you wanted to eat, so I brought you here to my friend's restaurant."

"And I told you I don't need any help. I can find a café on my own," said Barney.

"And the bush taxi garage – you know where that is too?" the young man demanded, pretending to be offended. "Look, I offer to help you – keep you from being cheated by some of these people. I have to eat too, father."

Barney gave the woman half the money he had been asked for. "There's my share, okay?" He pointed first at his plate and then himself and she nodded. He turned to the skinny young man, who had stopped grinning by now. "I told you I don't want any help – goodbye," and picking up his rucksack left the open shop. He heard the woman shouting at the young man and smiled to himself as he walked back down the lane to the main street. There were no taxis in sight but several two-wheeled donkey carts, with an old car seat for the driver and passenger and a small space behind for bundles.

"Hey, father," shouted the young black man running up to join him. "We go to the bush taxi garage now, okay? You want a car or horse? Horse is cheaper." He ran up the street without waiting for an answer and jumped on to an empty donkey taxi, pointing to Barney. The driver pulled up in front of him and the young man climbed down and tried again to relieve Barney of his rucksack to load it. Barney stood his ground, holding on to his bag.

"How much to the bush taxi garage?" he said to the driver but the young man replied first.

"Only 200 *cefa*." He tried again to take the bag but Barney shook his head and walked back towards the other donkey carts and drivers. "Father, wait. I can get it cheaper." Barney kept on walking and approached the drivers.

"Dakar bush taxi garage? *Combien*?" he asked the first man.

"150 cefa."

"100 cefa," said another driver. Barney was about to climb on his cart but instead, stopped a woman coming out of a shop.

"*Excusez moi, madame*. How much is it to the bush taxi garage?" He pointed at the donkey drivers.

"*Vingt-cinq* cefa," she said. He thanked her and turned back as the young man appeared at his elbow.

"Come on, father. I will find a cheaper taxi for us. Don't listen to these people," he indicated the woman with a jerk of his head. "They don't know anything."

"She knows the fare is only 25 cefas, anyway," said Barney. He took out some money and counted out 25 cefa, showing it to the driver who had said 100 cefa. "Dakar garage?" The man shook his head.

"See, father?" said the skinny young man grinning again. "I told you. This woman ignorant – she don't know how much is right." He spoke rapidly in his pidgin French to the driver. "This man say he take us for 50 cefa, okay?"

Barney paused and they all watched him. Then he nodded and the young man seized his rucksack and heaved it up on the back of the donkey cart. He boosted Barney up onto the car seat beside the driver before climbing on himself. The donkey trotted off and the driver and the young man began an animated conversation across him.

"He say the Dakar bush taxi leaving soon," reported the young man. "Next one not till tonight, maybe. You want him to catch this one?"

"Yes, can he go a bit faster?"

"For ten more cefa he promise to catch this one," grinned the young man. Barney agreed and the driver at once whipped the donkey into a gallop down the sandy street, shouting at everyone in his path. He tried to pass another donkey taxi ahead but the other driver refused to budge. The skinny young man shouted and gestured at him but he only whipped his donkey faster and the two carts careened along the street with children and dogs leaping out of the way.

A clear space appeared ahead and Barney's driver stood up to urge his donkey past the other cart. The two drivers lashed their donkeys towards what looked like a dead end, both standing by now and glancing across at each other. The skinny young man shouted oaths while Barney clung to the back of the old car seat for support. The street ahead had a road leading off to the left and Barney's donkey had the inside lane.

Neck and neck, they slewed round the corner, both drivers standing like Ben Hur charioteers. He felt the cart tipping but the young man reached over to the other one only inches away and gave a shove, which righted them. His driver pulled ahead just in time to avoid an approaching car.

Barney looked back at the other driver who waved his whip at them. The skinny young man laughed with glee, punching their driver on the arm and shouting back at the other man behind. Barney's driver sat down, hauling on the reins to slow the donkey. They trotted along at a sedate pace in the narrow dirt lane, occasionally shouting a casual oath at the driver behind them.

The driver pulled in to the bush taxi garage, a large sprawling sandy lot half full of beaten-up old minibuses, fitted with wooden bench seats. Rows of even more-battered *sept-place* Peugeot seven-seater cars stood nearby, in which the drivers packed a minimum of ten people, plus small children. The skinny young man leapt down from the cart and ran off to talk to a group of men selling spaces to passengers looking for rides.

Barney knew what his skinny guide was up to and made his own enquiries amongst the waiting passengers, to determine the fare to Dakar. It was cheaper in the minibuses on the small hard bench seats, he discovered but he decided to choose a *sept-place*. When the black youth came back, he was ready for him.

"Okay, father, I save a front seat for you in very good car but you need to pay now to keep your place. Only 450 cefa." He held out his hand. "You give me money and I pay the driver. Come," and he began the tussle to commandeer the rucksack.

Barney held him off, smiling. "No thanks. I'll find my own car – much cheaper. Only 190 cefas."

The grinning face scowled, then recovered. "Oh, those are very old cars. Always breaking down on the road. This is very good one." He urged Barney by the sleeve towards a half-empty Peugeot.

"When is he leaving?" asked Barney.

"Soon – soon," the young man assured him. "Only need one or two more people."

Barney spoke to the seat seller who had joined them. "Dakar?" The man nodded.

"190 cefas, okay?" said Barney. The man held up four fingers.

"*Quat' cent*," he said. "Four hundred."

Barney shook his head and started to walk away. The man grabbed his arm. "Okay, 300."

"190 cefas," said Barney, holding up the money. The man looked at it.

"250 cefa," he said, reaching for the money but again Barney shook his head.

"What time are you leaving?"

The man shrugged. "When the car full – two, maybe three hours."

The young black guide came forward. "You want me to look for another Dakar car nearly full? Come on," he darted off amongst the old vehicles loaded with bundles and plastic 5-gallon drums of palm oil on the roof racks.

"Here is a car – not so good but ready to go – only one more passenger. You want it?"

Barney stared at the decrepit vehicle stuffed with people and the roof rack heaped with bundles. "But it's full," he objected.

"No, not full. One more seat, here in front." The young man pointed at a large African woman overflowing the seat by the driver. She looked at Barney, expressionless.

"There's no room," Barney said again.

"Yes, yes. This seat is for two people. You get in on driver's side and sit in the middle." The young man gestured at the driver who stepped out and the young man climbed in to demonstrate. "See? Plenty room." He got out again.

Barney looked again at the poker-faced large woman who had not budged.

"How much did she pay for that seat?"

"She pay for two seats – double. Your seat is only 250 cefa," he grinned at Barney, sniffing victory.

Barney looked at the seat-seller. "190 cefas – okay?" The man nodded agreement and his apprentice swung Barney's pack up onto the over-laden roof to be lashed down. He waited to see it was secure, then clambered into the space between the two front seats where the driver had stuffed a greasy cushion on top of the raised driveshaft compartment.

"Hey, father – what about my money?" said the young man, poking his head in the door.

"What money?" asked Barney. "What for?"

The skinny young man looked outraged. "For all my help and my time. You must pay me, father."

Barney laughed and took ten cefas from his pocket. "Here. That's for nothing."

The young man snorted in disgust. "This is no good. I want fifty cefa."

"Okay, give me that back," said Barney leaning across to take the coin but the young man snatched his hand away. The driver, who had been watching all this, shouldered him roughly out of the way and climbed in beside Barney. As he drove out through the crowded parking area, the young black man jogged alongside, demanding more money in a louder aggressive tone, the grin replaced with an angry frown. He shouted one last curse as the old Peugeot shuddered up the slope onto the road to Dakar. Barney slumped back against the bundles rammed in behind him in the gap.

## CHAPTER 38

The Lonely Planet guidebook had only one or two cheap hotel options and they were both far from the centre of Dakar in an area called *Les Mamelles.* An old wooden lighthouse stood high on a cliff overlooking the Atlantic Ocean. He had arrived at nine o'clock at night and shared a cab from the bush taxi garage on the outskirts to a dirt road near Hotel Mamelle. His room on the top floor was right on the roof with an outdoor shower stall. This was the first proper hotel room he'd had since Morocco. He emptied his rucksack of dirty tee shirts, socks and underwear, to wash them by hand in the laundry area by the shower stall.

The single room had been added almost as an afterthought on the otherwise bare roof and it felt like a penthouse to Barney. He dragged a plastic deck chair out of the room to sit and drink the cold beer he'd bought from the cooler at the hotel front desk. The full moon lit the coastline and the old lighthouse opposite his hotel would be an easy landmark to orientate himself to the sprawling city of Dakar.

The warm African night air made the tepid shower, lit only by moonlight, enjoyable as he washed first himself then his dirty clothes and hung them on a rack he found leaning against the side of his room. He wandered around wearing only a towel while he sorted out his belongings and studied the map of the city to find where he was in relation to the port.

Where were Hunter and Clive and Lottie? They still had another week before he expected them to arrive but Landon should be here by now. He would find out in the morning when he located an internet café but he was too tired to look for one tonight. Landon would have to fend for himself if he was already here. The thought crossed his mind that the lure of Dakar's fabled nightlife with all its clubs and music venues might prove irresistible to Landon and he could end up drinking again. He shrugged and put the thought out of his mind. I'm not his keeper, he told himself.

Tomorrow he needed to start his hunt for a reliable used 4x4 truck to get everything for Cassie's orphans loaded on to it. He should really go out now and see if she had sent him any email while he was travelling. He rolled over on his back and closed his eyes to conjure up a mental picture of his youngest child and fell asleep.

# CHAPTER 39

Maurice Valois, in his late sixties, owned a curious mixture of a French café bar and an African open air restaurant. It had a roof shaped like a thatched conical hut with sidewalls open to the elements except for the street-side which was solid adobe. Inside the café, the large open space full of wicker armchairs was divided by a series of glass display cases filled with crude-looking models of wood and metal cars and motorcycles.

The short dapper Frenchman lived here with a Senegalese woman named Lisette. He had a wife back in France, somewhere in Brittany, whom he visited each year as she refused to live in Africa. The arrangement suited them both, or so he said and he told Barney he had no plans to change it. Always curious as to how people ordered this third stage of life, Barney quizzed him on his way of living here.

They sat drinking strong French coffee and eating fresh rolls baked by Lisette. Barney commented on how good they were but Maurice made a deprecating gesture.

"Lisette cannot make proper croissants – they are horrible tough things, so I tell her to stick to what she knows. This is the result. I eat real croissants when I visit my wife. It is what you

English call a trade-off, a small price to pay to live here. After 28 years I am used to it – almost."

"These model cars and motorbikes are very primitive looking," said Barney. "Are they made by local artists in Senegal?"

"Not artists – children. I collected them over the years in North Africa. I was a free-lance photographer and I used to cover the Paris-Dakar Rally through the Sahara." He pointed to a tin car and Barney saw it was a crude likeness of a rally car complete with painted number and wheels made of wood. "The children in the African villages are fascinated by all these vehicles that appear each year as if by magic and race across the open desert. So they use whatever they can find to make toy versions and then stage their own races."

"They're not just models, then?"

"No, they push them with long sticks so they can run behind." Maurice picked up a glossy photography book and opened it to show pictures of the children running through the villages, pushing their ingenious copies of cars and motorcycles they had seen.

Barney wandered around the showcases looking more closely at all the toys these tribal kids had made out of bottle caps, bits of wire, flattened tin cans and woven or carved pieces of wood. Now they no longer seemed crude but imaginative and creative. He studied a pair of driver's goggles made of wire with tiny triangular metal sidepieces cut from an aluminum beer can. The lenses were made of fine green thread to simulate sunglasses. He went back to sit down and study the photos Maurice had taken. The book had been written by him several years ago.

"So maybe now you see why I don't wish to live in France anymore with all its waste and affluence and cheap Chinese imports," said Maurice, shaking his head. "Life is more real here. Africa is not Europe. Not yet."

"I've never seen such things, Maurice. This collection is wonderful – and valuable. What will you do with it – donate it to a museum?"

The Frenchman made a wry face. "I doubt any museum would be interested. Probably Lisette will just give it to the local kids when I die."

Looking at the model support vehicles reminded Barney of his mission here in Dakar. He explained to Maurice his plan to buy a 4x4 truck to get to Guinea and asked for his advice.

"*Ah oui,* I know *exactement* the place you must go. Everyone goes to this market to buy vehicles for travelling here in Africa. After the Dakar Rally finishes people sell off all their support vehicles and equipment and fly back to Europe and America."

"What kind of truck do you think I should buy?" asked Barney. "I can't afford anything new. It'll have to be an old one so I need something reliable that won't break down. A diesel of some kind. So far, all I've seen are French Peugeots and German Mercedes minibuses."

"There is only one vehicle suitable for the terrible roads of West Africa," said Maurice. "The Unimog is what everyone used on the rally for support vehicles. It can go anywhere and never get stuck. And you are in luck because the rally has moved."

"How do you mean – moved where?"

"For the last few years it has been changing routes because of the civil wars and danger in the desert route. So now all the support vehicles which the rally people used to buy here are no longer needed. You can buy lots of them cheap."

"Do you know where I can find one of these Unimogs?" asked Barney. It sounded to him like the perfect answer but there must be a catch. Probably they cost a fortune. He wondered whether he could trust the Frenchman or if he saw Barney as a way to make some easy money. Still, he had to trust somebody. Too bad Landon wasn't here to come with him to help choose one. But no harm in doing some research of his own in the meantime. Landon could always check out any likely prospects when he arrived. Where was he anyway?

Maurice conferred with Lisette and she brought out a tattered old address book that he thumbed through before making a phone call. When he returned to where Barney sat studying the photography book, he said, "I called one of my old rally mechanic friends and he gave me this address. You should find something interesting there."

"Can you show me what one of these Unimogs looks like in here?" asked Barney, holding out the book to him. Maurice flipped through the pages and pointed out two different pictures to him. He studied the square boxy utility vehicles with the huge tires and the body perched high above the ground.

"They look very old-fashioned," he said.

Maurice nodded agreement. "*Oui,* they do not change. That is the beauty of them. The same *camion* since the Second World War. So lots of spare parts all over Africa."

"Are they more popular than the Land Rover and the Jeep?"

"Those are only cars. If you want a 4x4 *camion* – a truck, then you need a Unimog. Every army in Europe and Africa uses them," said Maurice. "Next time you watch TV film of military troops moving around, look at the troop carriers – Unimogs."

Barney cheered up at this news. "So maybe old second-hand ones aren't so dear?"

"*Non, pas chèr,* you can find one here in Dakar very easy."

Easy.

Barney wondered about that. So far nothing he had done in Africa had been easy.

# CHAPTER 40

After Barney checked his email at the hotel Mamelle, he bought a street map and located the club where Landon was staying in central Dakar. He peered into the gloom of the empty bar with its tables and chairs stacked in one corner and an old black man mopping the floor in slow motion. For a moment Barney thought it might be Landon until the man turned to face him.

"Landon?" he said. The old man wagged his hand towards the rear and returned to his rhythmic swamping. Barney found a narrow staircase and climbed a flight of stairs. A door ajar revealed a bed with a reclining black figure whose head was hidden by the door. His right arm hung over the edge of the bed. The hand was missing.

Barney pushed the door open and entered. Landon lay asleep, an empty wine bottle cradled in his left arm. Barney considered leaving him to sleep it off but decided he might disappear on a bender so he leaned over and shook his shoulder.

"Landon – Landon! It's Barney. Wake up."

One eye opened, closed, then both opened and he focused on Barney's face. He attempted to sit up and Barney helped him swing his legs over the side of the bed. Landon gazed at the empty bottle in his hand then placed it gently on the floor.

"Rough stuff," he said at last.

"Landon, what are you doing in this place – why didn't you get a hotel?"

"Bass player in London gave me an address," he said. "Old friend of his owns the whole thing." He waved his empty sleeve in a vague gesture above his head. "Glad to see you, Barney. Been here three days now, waitin'."

"Looks like you've been busy." Barney picked up the empty bottle and put it on the bed table.

"I was fine the first two nights. Last night I met this lady…" he looked behind him at the bed as though he expected to see her still there. "We got talkin' about this 'n that." He stared at his stump. "She had a bad time in the civil war. Her husband and son both killed. I invited her up here so we might console each other."

"Drown your sorrows?"

"That, too," admitted Landon. "Mostly consolin'. Turns out she has family in Freetown as well as me."

"I guess you've been too busy to look for any vehicles," said Barney.

"Not true. My French isn't up to scratch but I asked around the club – got a few names and phone numbers for when you arrived." He leaned across Barney to pick up his jacket off the chair and his prosthetic harness and hand fell onto the floor.

"I see you brought it with you, Landon. Getting used to it at last?"

"I read somewhere you can get used to anythin' except the knout and the cat o' nine tails," he said, fumbling in the pockets of his jacket and producing a few scraps of paper. "Here," he handed them to Barney.

"What's the knout?"

"Dunno exactly. Some kinda medieval torture weapon."

"You have a melodramatic streak in you, Landon."

"Yeah. Losin' your right hand can bring that outtta you alright."

"I bet it has a great effect on the ladies."

Landon grinned at him at last. "You play the hand you're dealt." He put his left arm around Barney's shoulder and the two men sat companionably on the side of the bed.

"They sell coffee in this place?" asked Barney. "I got some news to tell you as well."

Landon nodded. "Downstairs. In the bar." He began strapping on his harness and Barney resisted helping him, knowing how proud the black man could be about his independence.

"You hear anythin' from your son yet, Barney?"

"Nothing. And nothing from Cassie, either. I need to email Alice and find out what's going on."

## CHAPTER 41

Landon and Barney stood staring at the collection of vehicles. They were at the place that the Frenchman, Valois, had told Barney a rally friend of his owned. A corrugated iron shack stood alone in the middle of the large lot but no one was inside.

"Shall we kick some tires?" asked Landon. The two of them moved towards an ex-army truck painted in standard camouflage colour. Its huge wheels meant the driver sat up high above the road and Barney wondered about its stability. Designed to carry troops, it had an open rear with a canvas roof and bench seats on both sides.

"If we took the seats out we could pack a lot of stuff in here, Landon."

"Yeah. But not too secure with just a canvas cover. We'd always worry about leavin' it anywhere. A closed box would be better – then we could lock it up."

"Let's look inside – see how complicated it is to drive," said Barney. He waited to see if Landon needed any help climbing up into the high cab compartment but he managed unaided and Barney went round to the passenger side to get in. The dashboard held only the most basic instruments and they peered at the speedometer to see how many miles it had done. Surprisingly few showed on the clock.

"These military vehicles are usually low mileage," explained Landon. "They only use them on manoeuvres and exercises so they don't go that far."

"There's a couple more of these Unimogs here," said Barney. "Let's take a look at them before we decide."

They checked out one painted a bright yellow with a dump truck style steel box and nearly bald tires.

"These tires must cost a fortune, Landon. Let's see if the other one has decent rubber."

"Yeah, I don't fancy changin' one of these monsters if we get a flat tire in the bush somewhere."

"Look at this one," said Barney. "This is more like what we want." They walked around another ex-army Unimog with good tires, an enclosed rear metal body with a side door and a small window, as well as rear opening doors. "What do you think it was – an ambulance?"

Landon opened the side door and looked in. Two metal tables were bolted to the inside walls. "It's an old radio communications truck. They've removed everythin' except these worktops."

Barney climbed up inside and gave Landon a hand up. "It's got full headroom and plenty of space to load everything into. We could even camp out in here – save on hotel rooms."

Landon thumped on the metal walls with his artificial hand. "Good and secure too. But it might be too hot for sleepin' in."

"This roof hatch opens to let the air in," said Barney, pushing the rusty cover upwards. We can sleep outside on air mattresses if it gets too hot."

"With all those big African snakes and scorpions? Not me."

"You only get scorpions in the desert, don't you? But we could put our mattresses up on the roof instead."

They climbed out and checked inside the front cab. Again the mileage seemed low but the cab had a deep layer of rubbish strewn on the floor and the dashboard.

"Somebody's just been back from a long trip is my guess," said Landon. "We need to check out the motor and drive it round a bit. Make sure the gearbox and four wheel drive works okay." He looked for the key to the ignition but it had been removed. "I guess it's time to find the boss man and start bargainin'. This could be the truck we want, Barney."

"What shall we offer for it – you have any idea, Landon?"

"Not a clue. Only one way to find out. We don't let on this is the one we want. Just ask about all of them and get a ballpark figure, then offer half what they're askin'. That's what my friend at the club said."

They climbed out and asked a man in a greasy mechanic's overall who to speak to. The mechanic pointed to a fat man talking hard to a young European couple beside an old dust-coated Land Rover. It looked like it had recently made the trek here across the Western Sahara. No attempt had been made to clean it up for sale. Presumably Africans didn't go by appearances, thought Barney, thinking of the obsessive way used car dealers in the UK washed and cleaned their potential vehicles for sale. They stood waiting for the sales pitch to end and the fat man to notice them.

He stopped speaking to the young couple and they continued poking around the Land Rover. "*Bonjour*. What you fellas lookin' for – this nice Land Rover? Just came in three days ago from Marrakech – no problems. Already got four, five people wants to buy –" He spoke passable English.

Landon held up his hand to halt the sales talk, shaking his head. "No thanks, man. We need a *camion.*" He pointed at the yellow Unimog. "Like that. How much you askin' for them."

"Everybody wants them Unimogs, my friend. But I can do you a special offer on that yellow one," said the fat man. He led the way over to the truck and opened the door. "Go ahead, climb in, see what you think."

Barney decided to let Landon do the talking and he nodded to him to go ahead.

"We already checked them out. You got three here, so maybe we can do you a favour and take one off your hands if the price is right," said Landon, kicking one of the giant tires.

"I don't need no favours," the black man grinned. "Plenty of customers here," he waved a hand at the people wandering around the vehicles.

"Not many buyers though, eh?" said Landon, pointing to the young couple who had moved on from the Land Rover to a nearby Jeep. "Maybe you askin' too much."

The fat dealer shook his head in denial. "You don't find nothin' cheaper in Dakar. That's why you come here. I am the best and the cheapest. Ever'body knows me. I been here for years, man."

Landon nodded. "First thing I want to tell you – we are serious cash buyers. No pissin' around with down payments or cheques or any of that crap. Show him how serious we are, Barney."

Playing the straight man, Barney reached in his pocket and brought out a large wad of *cefas* he had taken from the bank that morning on Landon's advice – 'let them see the cash'. He riffed through the notes and put them back in his pocket. The fat man smiled.

"So let's talk business," continued Landon. "Which of these three Unimogs is the best and the cheapest? We got a long way to travel and we don't want any breakdowns on the way."

"You goin' thru West Africa, you bound to break down, man. Some of them countries, the roads is only lines on the map. These Unimogs is the only trucks got a hope in hell of gettin' you through." The fat man led them from one to the other of the three trucks, mentioning figures which made Landon shake his head in mock surprise when he had finished his sales spiel.

"Man, what did I just finish tellin' you? We are serious buyers. Cash. Now. Ready to do a deal. Why you askin' me these crazy prices? These ex-army vehicles sell for a few hundred at auction sales everywhere and here you talkin' thousands. Stop jerkin' my chain and give me a sensible figure so we can do us a deal."

"I guess I can do a better price if you payin' me in cash," conceded the fat man, mentioning a figure twenty percent lower. "Which one you like?"

Landon, indicated the radio truck and replied with a number about two thirds what the fat man quoted. "But that depends how it runs. We need to test it first, okay?"

The fat man took some keys off a huge ring in his pocket. "You know how to drive one of these things?" He looked dubiously at Landon's artificial hand.

Landon nodded. "You just show me how the four wheel drive works, that's all."

He and the dealer climbed into the cab and started up the truck. It shifted back and forth a couple of times and the fat man hopped nimbly down so Barney could ride in the passenger seat. "Plenty of space in the yard to check it out. Just don't back into any of my vehicles, you hear?"

With a roar and a jerk, the truck lurched forward, Landon wrestling with the gears and Barney hanging onto the door handle.

"Boy, this steerin' is heavy. We are goin' to be stiff after a day of drivin' this thing." He wheeled the Unimog around the parking lot, shifting through the range of gears and in and out of the four wheel drive. "You want to try it now, Barney?" he asked, grinning at him.

Barney shook his head. "Not in here. It might get away on me and run right over one of these cars. What do you reckon, Landon?"

"This is the one for us. But we still need to do some more dickerin'. First of all, we ask for a full service. Then we get a mechanic to check it over, see it's okay before we hand over any money."

"Seems like a good price to me. Why don't we ask his mechanic to check it over and then close the deal?"

Landon laughed. "His mechanic? You think he's goin' to tell you anythin's wrong? I'll ask around the club – get someone we can trust and pay him a good fee to really check it out." He climbed down awkwardly and they went over to the corrugated iron shack to find the fat dealer.

Landon told him what he wanted and the dealer shook his head. "I sell these 'as is' – no guarantees. You want all that shit, services and stuff, you got to buy a new truck, man. You already have yourself a sweet deal."

"Come on, Barney. Time to move on, check out some of these others on the list. Lots more used trucks in this town. This man is not serious about doin' business. Wastin' our time." He took Barney's arm and steered him out the door of the tin shack.

The fat man followed. "Just a minute, man. Just a minute. God, you a hard man to do business with. Maybe I can see if my mechanic has time to change the oil and give it a quick check over. But I need to see some of that money first."

Landon shook his head. "You already seen it. And we want a full service, not just an oil change. I don't need your mechanic. I'll bring my own man tomorrow."

"I don't know," said the dealer, stalling. "I got to think it over. How do I know you gonna come back?"

"If this is as good a deal as you tell me and you really are the best and the cheapest, we'll be back," said Landon.

Barney took the large wad of currency from his pocket again. "Should we make a down payment now or wait till tomorrow?" he asked Landon, peeling some notes off the roll and watching the fat man's gaze.

"Put it away till tomorrow. The man knows we're serious buyers. What he doesn't understand is how to make a deal. Maybe by tomorrow he can make up his mind." He steered Barney out of the lot without looking back at the fat dealer standing by his tin shack.

# CHAPTER 42

Barney stood beside the sweating customs official on the quay at Dakar docks watching a freighter unload.

"How long before I can get my shipment off the boat?" asked Barney. A group of black men naked from the waist up, hoisted cargo nets out of the hold of the *Arnolfini,* using its donkey engine crane to lower them down onto the dock.

"Not much comin' off here," said the customs broker, shuffling through a sheaf of documents on his clipboard. "Maybe by tomorrow. What you say it is again?"

"Only children's school books – coming from the UK."

"Couple of crates or what?"

"More like a couple of pallet loads, I think," said Barney. He tried to remember the details from the email Alice had sent him yesterday but he hadn't printed it off in the internet café where he read it.

The squat pot-bellied man finished looking through his papers and removed his aviator sunglasses to squint at Barney in the dazzling light off the harbour.

"Nothin' here for anybody name of Roper." He held out his hand. "Show me the shippin' documents. Let me check them and see what they say."

"I haven't got any documents," said Barney. "Only an email that said they were on this freighter – the *Arnolfini*." He glanced up at the name on the bow of the Italian ship to reassure himself.

The customs broker looked incredulous. "What you mean you got no papers, man? You think I release shipments to anybody come down here and just ax' for somethin'?" He turned and strode back towards the old colonial brick customs building. "You come back with some proper documents before you ax' me again, mister," he said over his shoulder.

Barney hurried to catch up to him before he disappeared inside. "But I told you there aren't any papers, only an email notification. Will that do?"

"An' I told you I needs proper customs clearance shippin' documents – not some email anybody could make up." He stopped and removed his sunglasses again. "You any idea how much stuff gets stolen off these docks every day? I ain't losin' my job because some Englishman come here and tell me to release goods with no authorisation. You unnerstan' me?"

"I understand," nodded Barney trying to placate the irritated black official who stood glaring at him. "How do I get the right papers and what do I need?"

The man shrugged. "Tell them to send them to you from England. Why you didn't do this before the boat arrive, man? You know this gonna cost you storage every day it sit in that bonded customs warehouse."

"How long will that take?"

"I don't know. I ain't the post office. A week, maybe."

"But can you show me what I need to ask them for? If I could see the names of the forms it would help," pleaded Barney.

The little official gave his crumpled trousers a hitch up over his belly. He jerked his head towards the old brick building with the crumbling stone lettering that said 'Customs Shed,' high up on the wall facing the harbour.

"Come in my office and I see if I can find some completed forms."

Inside the gloomy room, he reached down a wire basket overflowing with papers and took off the top sheaf to spread out on the litter of other invoices on his desk.

"Here's what I needs before anythin' leave here. The people who sendin' you this shipment should have all these paperwork together, so you best get onto them quick 'less you interested in payin' storage. We charges by the day here."

"How much?" said Barney with a worried look. He had already given Landon most of his cash to pay for the Unimog. Why hadn't Alice paid for all this to be done back in London? He hoped he wouldn't end up with a large bill before he even started on his overland trip to his daughter in Guinea.

"Depend how big the shipment is. You say two pallets – could be any size," said the sweating broker from behind his cluttered desk. "An' you better arrange some transport for somethin' that size. It ain't goin' to fit in the back of no taxi."

Barney nodded, "We bought a *camion* especially for it, yesterday."

"Mmhmm. Well, don't go bringin' it down onto this dock here till you got them documents," he said, pointing to the forms. Barney hurriedly copied titles and numbers from them into his address book.

"But you still haven't told me whether my shipment is on this boat," said Barney. "Do you have some other manifests you haven't checked yet?"

The little official took a deep breath and held it. He glared at Barney. "Eeehh! Now you tryin' to tell me my job, mister? Best thing is, you leave right now and don't come back without no documents. Then we start lookin' to see if it arrive or not. I got no more to say to you till then." He dismissed Barney with a flap of his hand.

Barney left the old customs shed and wandered back onto the dock trying to decide what to do next. He began to wonder if Alice's books had been delayed. The official had looked through all his precious documents and said there was nothing for him. Could she have used another name? Cassie maybe? Or the charity – what was it called? *Les Amis de* something.

He toyed with going back to ask the aggressive black official to search under some other names but knew he'd be turned down flat with no documents to show him. He thought of another idea as he stood watching the men unload the ship.

They seemed to have removed the last slingful of cargo and were tidying up and sorting through the remaining pallets on the dock. An older man wearing a filthy tee shirt directed a crew of dockworkers loading boxes by hand. Barney took a twenty *cefa* note from his pocket and approached the foreman.

*"Excusez-moi, monsieur,"* he said, "Can you do me a favour? I'm looking to see if there is a pallet load of books here for me. The customs broker says it's not on his list but it might be under a different name." He held up the note to the man. "Could I just look at the names on these shipments to see if it arrived?"

The man took the money and nodded. He led Barney over to where the crew were at work and pointed to the labelling. "You ax' these men to shift them if you can't see the name, *comprenez?"* He returned to his wooden crate with a chair beside it, that served as his command post and Barney walked round the pallets reading the stencilled destinations and names. In less than five minutes he found first one of the pallets and then a second one both marked *Les Amis du CFA.* Pleased with his detective work, he made notes in his address book of all identifying details on the pallets, waved to the foreman and left the dockside.

He thought of confronting the customs official with this news but decided against it until he had some paperwork to show him. What he needed to do first was email Alice and ask about the missing documents. He set off to Landon's nightclub to use the internet in the café next door.

The club was down a side street not far off the *Place de l'Indépendence* and very central. Barney had moved there from his location on the outskirts of Dakar at Les Mamelles. He had asked Landon to see if he could get another room for him above the club. Although it was noisy at night, it was cheap and he wanted to save as much as he could for the trip overland to Guinea.

He hoped each day to hear from Cassie or Hunter but so far, neither had replied to his emails. In the internet café, he wrote to Alice and told her of the hassles with customs. If she sent him faxed signed copies of the relevant papers he could probably get the books released, he said. He told her about the Unimog and how useful Landon had been in getting them a good deal. He asked her if she had any news from Cassie or Hunter, then went to look for Landon.

In the bar, they told him he had gone with a mechanic to work on the truck. Landon's arrangement with the fat dealer included keeping it at his yard until they were ready to go. Barney found a local outdoor market and began looking for things they would need for the trip. After wandering about looking at everything from tools to plantains, he had bought only a cheap Chinese LED flashlight. What he needed was a list and he ought to wait for Landon, so they could compile it together.

Abandoning the market for today, he returned to the club and sat outside the bar with a beer. A woman in her fifties came out of the club and over to his table carrying a bottle of cola. She smiled at him and sat down.

"You mus' be Landon's friend. I hear all about you an' him go to Guinea soon, that right?" She spoke without any French accent and wore African clothes unlike the mainly western clothing favoured by many of the women in Dakar.

"Are you Lisabeth? Landon mentioned he met someone from Sierra Leone here," guessed Barney.

"What he tell you?" she frowned.

"Not much," he reassured her. "Only that you came from Freetown and lost your family in the civil war."

"I didn't lose them. I know what happen. They kill them right in front of me." She pushed up the loose sleeves of her patterned blouse to show him her arms. "This is what they do to me when I try to save my son." Long ugly scars in her ample brown flesh showed up a darker colour. "They was not much older than my boy but they all rape me and say they cut my hand off, I make any fuss about it." She pulled down her sleeves and took a swallow from her cola bottle.

"What did you do – I mean after?" asked Barney.

Lisabeth spread her hands in a gesture that might have meant despair or acceptance; he couldn't tell from her expressionless shiny black face. "Nothin' to do. They burn our village so everybody run off into the bush. After, I come back and bury my son an' my husban', then go to Freetown to my sister's house."

"How come you're living in Dakar now?"

"My sister an' me got a business in Freetown, so I come here to buy clothes take back to sell there. She run the shop an' I do the buyin' here."

"Landon said you knew his family," said Barney. "That must have been a surprise?"

Lisabeth laughed, showing a couple of missing teeth. "No surprise in Freetown, man. Everyone know someone related to you. I don't know his family direct but I know 'bout them." She sipped her cola.

"You ever been to Kissidougou?" asked Barney.

"That where your daughter at?" She nodded and said, "Lots of people run away to Guinea durin' the war. Plenty of refugee camps all round there. People lookin' for safe place for their children, they go to Guinea."

"That's what my daughter's doing," he said. "Working in a children's refugee camp. Mostly war orphans, she says. But the war's been over a long time, hasn't it?"

Lisabeth shook her head. "It keep breakin' out in different places, specially in the bush and in the east near *Cote d'Ivoire* and Guinea border. People too frightened to go back to their village. Them boy gangs runnin' around with guns and machetes, killin' people an' cuttin off their hands and foots."

"I don't understand. Why would they do that to women and children?" asked Barney.

"To teach them a lesson – so you don't tell no one where they are. An' sometime just for fun."

"Cut a child's hand off for fun?"

Lisabeth leaned forward in her chair and pulled back her voluminous sleeve again to show him her wrist. Just above it, a scar spread half way round her forearm. "See? That's where they starts to cut my hand off. They say, 'you want long sleeve or short sleeve?" She indicated her wrist and her upper arm. "I told them, 'you the tailor.'"

Barney stared at the scar. "Why did they stop? Not cut it off."

"They lookin' for food an' I told them I show them where we hide it in the bush, if they don't cut me no more."

"This doesn't happen now, does it?" he asked.

She nodded, "Still goin' on lots of places – away from the cities. Mostly boy gangs hidin' out in the bush an' attackin' the villages."

"What for?"

"Food, money. Stealin' the young girls to take back to their camps. Whatever they can find. Happen all the time, I read it in the paper."

"Can't the army stop them?"

"If they catch them, but people too scared to tell the soldiers where they are. They don't want them boys comin' back to chop off no more hands an' foots. If the soldiers gets too close, the gangs just move across the border into Guinea or Cote d'Ivoire. That way the soldiers can't follow them. After the army leave, they come back."

Barney looked at her. "Do you think these gangs might go to Kissidougou?"

"Not into the town, maybe but all around in the bush an' the villages," she said.

"I don't know where my daughter's refugee camp is exactly. It's near Kissidougou because she has to go there for supplies and the internet. She can use a computer in an NGO office to write home."

Lisabeth nodded. "Plenty NGOs everywhere but no jobs with them 'less you know somebody. What you call her?"

"Cassie. She's twenty-two last month," he said, remembering that he had not spoken to her since before her birthday and then only by email.

"How many children she have?" asked Lisabeth.

"You mean in the orphanage? I don't know for sure. Over thirty, I think."

Lisabeth laughed. "No, I means her own children."

"None," said Barney.

Lisabeth nodded. "She leave them all back in England with her momma, eh?"

"No, she hasn't got any children of her own – not here, or in England."

"She twenty-two and no children?" she said, her eyes widening. "How long she been in Kissidougou?"

"About ten months, I guess."

"Not long now," said Lisabeth. "She have a nice African baby soon." She laughed and slapped Barney on the arm as if to congratulate him. "How many gran'children you have already?"

"I haven't got any yet," he admitted.

"What! An old man like you an' you don't have no gran'children? How many other children you have?"

"Two more. One girl and one boy."

She shook her head. "You know what I hear 'bout England? They put all this bad stuff in the water. This man I met from Cameroon, he told me. He live there in London an' he won't drink the water. Only bottle water safe, he say."

Barney smiled. "Lots of people like to drink bottled water in the UK, but I think it's fine. Maybe he meant the fluoride when it's treated?"

"No, not fluoride. He tol' me all the birth control medicines the women uses go back in the recycle water. The water treatment don't have no affect, so all the Englishmen is becomin' sterile. Maybe that why you got no gran'children."

He laughed but saw she was serious, looking at him with concern. After a moment, he said, "It's true that the medical profession is worried that the male sperm count is dropping and they're not sure why. They think it might be stress."

"See? It's true what I tell you. That Cameroon man tol' me lots of young English people got no children and they 35 years old, some of them."

"No problems like that here?" he said.

"In Africa we got plenty children but not enough jobs." She finished her bottle of cola and rose to collect the glasses and cans from the table, then brought a cloth to wipe it down.

"You work here too, Lisabeth?"

"I helps out when they busy and the boss let me stay here when I visit sometimes, if he have any empty room."

"I see. You staying here now?" he asked.

She smiled her gap-toothed smile at him. "You mean with Landon? Maybe. You lookin' for company?"

"No, no, I just thought we could have a meal together one night – with Landon," he added.

"You want to eat here or go someplace else in Dakar?"

"If you know of somewhere good that's not too expensive," said Barney. "I have to be careful not to spend my trip savings before I even get started. I hear Dakar has lots of good music."

"I take you and Landon to a good place tonight if you want," she said. "We can eat Sierra Leone food and have some dancin' too."

Barney sat in the internet café next door to the club to check his email. He found a message from Alice and one from Hunter but still nothing from Cassie. His low-level uneasiness about his daughter increased, abetted in part by his conversation the day before with Lisabeth. He tried to put aside thoughts of marauding gangs of youths with machetes, fired up by home-brewed palm wine, amputating the limbs of women and young children. If Alice heard what Lisabeth told him, it would confirm her worst imaginings about Cassie. He determined not to make any mention of his own fears to her in his emails.

He opened Hunter's message first, eager to hear where they were.

*Hello Dad,*

*What a trip – we made it to the Cape Verdes a week ago but the boat is a mess. Poor old Betsy got caught in a gale and we lost the mast and ripped out some of the new rigging from the deck, so I guess that gives you some idea of the force of the storm. Thank god Lottie came with us or me and Clive might not have made it. He got hit by the falling mast and broke his collarbone so that left Lottie with only me to help.*

*I can tell you now, I have never been so scared in my life but she was amazing. She never panicked and knew exactly what to do - kept telling me worse things had happened on her Vendee Globe races. As if she thought horror stories would cheer me up. She knew how to rig a temporary mast from a spare jib boom and we limped into the*

*Cape Verdes a few days later and got Clive to the hospital. He's all strapped up in a harness now and still can't do anything physical but at least he can supervise the repairs to the Betsy. He's full of praise now for Lottie and no more cracks about women aboard boats.*

*We hope to leave tomorrow for Dakar and should be there in a few days with our new mast and Lottie in charge. I guess you're in Dakar by now waiting for us. Clive says for you to leave a contact address and message with the harbour master's office.*

*Hope you and Landon have found a good 4x4 to get us to Cassie's camp. Have you heard anything from her yet? She didn't leave any message for me here. Only Netta wrote to tell me she and Alice had shipped you the crates of books to take to Cassie's orphans. Hope there's going to be room for all our artificial limbs – we filled up Clive's cabin on the Betsy with them.*

*Lottie has promised Clive she'll help him sail as far as Freetown after we go upcountry.*

*He can wait in Dakar until she comes back from Kissidougou when we arrive. No wonder he dotes on her, she fusses over him and his broken collarbone and won't let him do anything except boss me around. She even trussed him all up with splints and stuff after the accident. Says she had to take a first aid course before she could go on the Vendee Globe boat race. I'm going to miss her when she goes back to Dakar but I'm looking forward to our overland trip to Guinea.*

*I didn't get any film of the storm because I was afraid my new video camera might get wet or damaged so I kept it sealed in a waterproof bag below deck the whole time. However, I did shoot a bit of the damage afterwards and some of the running repairs Lottie made to get us to the Cape Verdes. On top of everything else, she taught me how to swear in Czech, German, French and Polish. Very useful in the middle of a Force 10 gale.*

*Tell me about your trip overland to Dakar. We might stop in Nouadhibou if I can persuade Lottie, although she's determined to make up some of our lost time and will probably push the poor old Betsy non-stop.*

*See you soon (I hope)*

*Love, Hunter.*

Once again Barney wrote to Cassie to say that he now had an old 4x4 truck and her books would soon be loaded and waiting for Hunter's arrival. He asked if there were any change of plans and to let him know quickly before he left Dakar, as once on the road, internet contact might be difficult. He sent off the email and then opened Alice's message.

*Dear Barney,*

*Sorry about the cock-up with the documents for customs. Netta faxed them all to you today care of the harbour master's office so you can pick them up there now. I still have had no word from Cassie and hope you can get going to Guinea as soon as poss. Hunter sent me a quick note from the Cape Verde Islands to say they had some bad weather and had been delayed. Have you been in touch with him yet?*

*The truck you bought sounds perfect for the trip on those non-existent roads, so I hope you don't have any breakdowns along the way, or at least none that Landon can't fix.*

*Mrs Hollis had another stroke and never regained consciousness. Heck came back from Rome but not in time to see her before she died. Her solicitor read us her will and she left the house to Heck and me and everything else to Cassie's orphans, just as she told me she would. The only rider was that we couldn't sell the house for one year after her death. I think secretly she hoped it might bring us back together. She was a hopeless old romantic, rather like you.*

*I want to sell and move out – probably back to look after my parents but Heck wants to keep the house because he's done so much work to it. We've decided to separate and he will stay here, at least until the year is up and I'll start moving back into Highgate. There's tons of room and I can have my own space as well as keep an eye on George and Martha – not that they think they need it yet.*

*Heck and my father have been toiling away on some secret project for Cassie's orphans and won't tell anyone what it is, except Philip. Netta is convinced it's some old sailboat that Mrs Hollis' husband Arthur bought and they found it stored away under the railway arches in King's Cross. She thinks only a boat could turn three grown men into secretive little boys. Whatever it is, the three of them spend all their spare time down there and Mother and Netta get very annoyed at being shut out.*

*I don't care what it is. I doubt they'll ever get it to Cassie's orphans because I have this feeling she's not even in Kissidougou any more. I can't even contact Zinadine because I never had an email address for him, so now the only way to reach her is through the Amis du CFA and they just forward mail through their courier every couple of months.*

*I know you think I'm being my usual neurotic self but I don't care. There has to be a reason why Cassie has stopped writing and I just know something's gone wrong.*

*Please don't delay any more than you have to, Barney. I can't bear this not knowing much longer.*

*Take care and drive safely in Africa,*

*With love, Alice.*

Christ! He sat back in the plastic chair in the internet café to reflect on Alice's message. Could her intuition about their daughter be right? His feeling of unease ratcheted up another notch as he thought of all the possible scenarios to account for Cassie's silence. He longed to share his worries about Lisabeth's horror stories with Alice but dared not heighten her anxiety level any further. He could not recall a time when she had ever been this strange and fragile. It had always been Alice who was the strong one throughout their roller-coaster marriage and now the roles were reversed.

When Heck came on the scene, Barney had felt a huge sense of relief that Alice no longer needed him. He could be free at last to pursue his 3rd age explorations wherever they might lead him, without having to justify them to anyone but himself. Now his family seemed to have become vulnerable and he couldn't find any way to protect them.

He thought of this trip to Africa and what he had originally dreamed it would be – a voyaging into the unknown, full of anticipation, not worry. That was his over-riding sense of the trip now. First, worry about Cassie's disappearance, then Hunter nearly shipwrecked and Alice and Netta locked in a mortal struggle with their genetic inheritance.

He remembered the painter Delacroix's remark about man spending half his life finding something that has already been discovered and the other half digging the foundations of an edifice that never rises above the level of the ground. That summed up the way he felt about his own life at present. He tried to shrug it off and went to tell Landon about Clive and Hunter's expected arrival.

## CHAPTER 43

The chief in the village near the Guinean border with Sierra Leone had agreed to let Cassie use two empty thatched huts in the compound for her orphans as a temporary base. He told her the people had run off to the bush and might return anytime but she could stay until they came back. The chief had a small shop with a meagre supply of dried and canned food for sale and a huge sack of cheap lollipops. He gave one of these to each of the children when they first arrived, tired and frightened on the night of their escape.

Cassie wished she had listened to Zinadine on his last visit, when he told her about the reports he heard of a local armed gang that had attacked villages not far from the refugee camp at Kissidougou.

"This is not a safe place for you to be anymore, Cassie," he said, as they lay in her thatched hut that evening.

Emboldened by his arms around her, she shrugged off the danger. "They won't cross the border, will they? As long as we're in Guinea, we'll be protected. The army patrols check here every day, nearly."

Zinadine propped himself up on one elbow to look into her face in the dark. His other hand stroked her hair and she could only see the white of his eyes in his gleaming black face but she could hear the note of concern in his voice. "You could come back with me tomorrow and we'll find somewhere further away from the border – somewhere safe for the children, too."

"But I can't just leave them. It might take weeks to find another suitable refugee camp. Couldn't you look for a new place and then come back and help me move the children?" she said, drawing him down until he lay over her, his breath cool on her cheek.

"How can I do my work when I'm worrying about you all the time I'm not here, Cassie? This wasn't what we planned when we came here. I thought we would be a team – work together. I hate this being apart and only seeing you one or two days a month." He clasped her closer in his arms and the two of them let their bodies convey the longing they felt. Afterwards, he fell back on his side of the mattress and pulled her into the crook of his arm, the pale outline of her body just visible in the darkened hut.

She wanted to persuade him to stay but knew his training work meant constant travel around Guinea. She had not intended to become involved in refugee work; it struck her as so depressing and hopeless. But these orphaned children whom Grace gathered up and rescued were so vulnerable with their missing hands or feet, she couldn't leave once she knew them. What had originally been a temporary visit to the refugee camp with Raoul, the Cuban doctor from *Médecins Sans Frontière*, turned into an ongoing commitment for her. Zinadine sympathised but his interests lay elsewhere, in rebuilding infrastructure, schools and clinics, after the destruction of the decade long civil war.

"If we worked together – lived together, we could think about a family," he said. "Don't you want to have a child with me anymore, Cassie?"

"Oh Zinadine, you know I do. Just not now. I couldn't have a baby in these conditions. It's too risky." She tried to kiss him but he held back from her.

"That's what I'm trying to tell you. I want you to be with me all the time so I know you're alright."

"It wouldn't make any difference – we'd still be moving around constantly. I don't want a baby living in the back of a Land Rover."

"We could get a house somewhere," he said. "Be together, like we planned when we were students in Paris – remember?"

"How would that be any different? I'd be stuck in a house with a baby and you'd be away for weeks at a time. I'd still only see you once a month or so."

"Not if we had a house in Labé. I could be home most nights. It's only because you're far away down here in the bottom corner of the country that I hardly ever see you."

"I can't help it if your government put its refugee camps out of sight down here on the border, Zinadine," she said. "I think you just use it as an excuse not to visit more often," she teased. "You know where I am but I never know where you are. Very convenient."

"Then why do I spend every visit pleading with you to come back with me? Be serious, Cassie. You have to think about leaving here soon. I'm not trying to frighten you but I want you to realise how risky this camp has become. These boy gangs don't worry about borders – they make cross-border raids all the time and are gone long before the army patrols arrive."

He had left at first light the next morning, letting her sleep on and she woke disappointed that they had separated without reconciling their differences. Not that she could see how the problem could be resolved. As usual, she took her worries to Grace, the big Ghanaian nurse who made it her life's work to rescue these children and young people maimed and orphaned by the civil war.

She found her surrounded by a swarm of little ones vying for her attention. Grace had the ability to do all her multitude of nursing duties and at the same time nurture several children. The big black woman saw the look on Cassie's face and set down two of the youngsters, who climbed onto her ample lap the moment she sat anywhere. She stood up and opened her arms to envelope Cassie.

"I swear girl, I goin' to ban that Zinadine from visitin' here anymore. Everytime he leave you it take me a week to get you back to normal." She held Cassie at arm's length to examine her. "What he say to you this time, huh?"

The big woman's sympathy triggered the tears Cassie had been holding back and she sobbed in Grace's arms like a child. Grace stroked her hair but made no attempt to stop her tears, letting her get it all out. The two women, one heavy and black, the other slight and pale, rocked back and forth as they stood surrounded by curious children holding onto their legs. Some of the smaller ones began to cry in concert with Cassie and eventually she stopped to console them. She picked up a small girl in the standard blue and white shifts the orphans all wore.

"Oh Grace, it always ends the same. Zinadine wants me to go and work with him but I can't leave these children, I couldn't bear it." She nuzzled the tiny child who flung her arms round Cassie and buried her face in her neck.

Grace returned to her task of sorting through her small store of medications and shaking her head at the pitiful amounts remaining. "Maybe he right, Cassie. Ever'body think they indispensable, includin' me 'n you but we not. Always someone else ready to step into our shoes if we leaves."

"Do you really believe that, Grace? Who could ever replace you?" said Cassie, slipping her arm through the big woman's and squeezing her.

Grace let out her full-throated laugh. "Eeehh? Raoul find another new nurse by tomorrow if I was to leave. Ain't that so, Raoul?" she demanded, turning to the short, athletic young Cuban doctor who had come in to see her.

"Find who?" he asked, coming to the rickety table to examine Grace's medical supplies.

"This girl sayin' nobody could do my job but I tell her you get a new nurse tomorrow, if you want," she said, poking his chest for emphasis, "an' a lot younger 'n beautiful too." She laughed again.

"Never. Why would I do that? You're the only person keeps this whole place from collapsing around our heads." He turned to Cassie and spoke in a stage whisper. "Besides, I'm in love with her. I'm taking her back to La Habana when I leave."

Grace broke into a fit of giggles and the children grinned and giggled too in imitation of her.

"Can't you just see me in Havana with all those beautiful Cuban girls chasin' after Raoul here? I'd soon be skinny as you, Cassie, runnin' them all off."

"Can I come too, Auntie?" asked a solemn little boy who stood half-hidden in the folds of her voluminous flowered boubou. She hauled him up into her arms with one large hand.

"Don't you believe Doctor Raoul here, Anton. He just tellin' stories like he always does. Teasin' a poor old woman – gettin' her hopes up 'bout joinin' fashionable Havana society." She burst into more laughter at the image she had created. She put the boy down again and straightened up to look at Cassie. "Long as I don't start thinkin' I indispensable an' jus' do my job, same as you, then maybe Raoul here keep us around."

Raoul stepped up to her and stood on tiptoe to kiss the big nurse's cheek. "You wait and see, Grace. One night I'll come for you and we'll run off together to beautiful La Habana."

"I'll be waitin' for you," she said. "Meantime these children needs this medicine an' I don't figure they's enough here to go 'round. You want me to give them half dosage?"

Cassie left them arguing, to return to her hut and write up her journal. She had faithfully kept a record of all her time here at the amputee orphan's camp. Originally, she intended it as a way of communing with Zinadine but it had morphed into a more personal journal of her feelings and moods. She remembered Barney telling her once, that Virginia Woolf referred to it as taking her emotional temperature.

And three nights later, they had all fled. Zinadine's prediction had come true.

# CHAPTER 44

Cassie sat in her small hut, empty except for a camp bed and a small bamboo table with an oil lamp on it. She wrote copious notes, anxious not to leave out anything of their nightmare flight from the Kissidougou refugee camp with little but the clothes they stood up in, the frightened silent children and the few essentials Grace had managed to salvage with her typical methodical competence. Cassie had been too frightened to think of anything but a few personal belongings and rounding up the sleeping children.

She wrote rapidly in her attempt to catch up with all the days she had missed recording.

The gang of young men had arrived without warning just at dusk. She had heard reports from other villages as well as Zinadine's remark that an armed gang was in the area. They slid silently out of the bush and into the compound. The first she knew of them was when nine-year-old Ahmed stumped into her hut on his crutch. The little boy had lost his foot and lower leg to a landmine and his severed leg had been a suppurating wound when villagers took him to the clinic run by *Médecins Sans Frontières*. He was one of the first amputees

Cassie encountered when she came to the refugee camp and the child had appointed himself her guide and protector.

Now he told her in a hushed frightened voice that bad men with guns and machètes were outside, demanding food and money. Her first instinct was to grab the little boy and hide but the door of her hut opened straight onto the open area of the compound.

"Go and stay with the other children, Ahmed. Tell them not to come outside," she instructed him, pulling on a shapeless jacket over her bare shoulders.

"No, I want to stay with you," he said, taking her hand with his free one. "These are very bad man. Grace tell me to come and find you."

"Maybe they will go away again if we give them food. Please, Ahmed, I need you to watch the little ones and keep them inside." She urged him towards the door and followed him outside.

A group of young men stood around Grace and Raoul, speaking excitedly and waving their weapons in a threatening manner. Cassie hesitated, then tried to walk calmly over to join her colleagues. The youths barely noticed her at first as they shouted demands at Grace, who planted herself firmly in the midst of the agitated young men. Eight or nine of them pushed and jostled their way to the front, to take turns issuing threats and make menacing gestures with the long curved machetes. They spoke a mix of Krio English and Fula French and she realised they had probably come over the border from Sierra Leone. She pulled Raoul's sleeve.

"What are they saying, Raoul?"

"They want food and palm wine and money," he said. "But they say I must go with them across the border to a wounded man from their gang who was shot in the leg by the army patrol."

"Don't go, Raoul. They might not let you come back. Tell them to bring him here instead."

"Grace already told them that, Cassie. But they say the army patrol would catch them because they can't move fast enough with an injured man"

The gang leader, a young man with a semi-automatic rifle moved forward to grab Cassie roughly by the arm. He spoke in a loud voice over the clamour of the others, spittle forming in the corners of his mouth as he glared at her. She could make out nothing of what he said and turned to Grace.

"What's he want, Grace?" she said, trying to pull free from his grasp but he gripped her arm until she cried out in pain. The big woman placed her hand over the young man's and said something to him in the French patois. After a moment of glaring at one woman and then the other, he released his grip.

"He say you must come too so you can nurse this wounded man," she interpreted. "I told him you not a nurse, I am."

Raoul spoke to the leader and the group moved to the tables and benches in the centre of the compound. Grace went into one of the huts and told two or three of the village women who worked in the camp, to give the food they were preparing for the children to the men.

Raoul finally made them understand they didn't allow any of the palm wine the locals made into the camp and they would have to go to the nearby village for it. The leader sent one of his youths with a rifle to go with two of the refugee camp workers to bring some back to the camp. Raoul went into the clinic hut and collected his bag with some instruments and a small quantity of Grace's precious sulpha drugs to take with him.

Cassie followed him inside the clinic.

"Raoul, how do you know they won't kill you after you've treated this wounded man, so you won't tell the army where they are?" she said.

"They won't harm me, Cassie, don't worry," he said trying to appear calm although his hands were shaking as he put things in his medical satchel.

"How do you know? You saw how worked up they are. And if they get drinking that palm beer anything could happen to you." Her mind raced, seeking for solutions. "Couldn't we offer to collect this man at the border and bring him back here instead?"

He shook his head. "They don't trust us not to call the soldiers the moment they're gone, even though I promised not to say a word."

"You see? Don't go with them, Raoul. There must be some other way. Speak to Grace, see what she says."

"We've helped these gangs before, Cassie. They know about *Médecins Sans Frontières*. That's why they're here, because we treat their members when they get injured or sick. If they killed one of our doctors, they'd be refused help next time." He tried to smile at her but couldn't manage it.

"At least let me talk to Grace first, before you go. Don't agree to anything yet, okay?" He nodded and sat down on a low stool, clutching his satchel on his lap. With his thick round glasses and unruly black hair, he looked to her like a frightened schoolboy about to be punished. She slipped from the clinic and ran behind the other shelters to peer in the open rear part of the cooking hut. She beckoned to Grace who came outside and the two women moved into the near darkness at the back of the compound.

"Raoul's frightened, Grace. I don't think we should let him go with them. If they think he'll tell the soldiers they might shoot him, especially if they start drinking."

The big woman put her hands on both of Cassie's arms and looked into her face.

"I been thinkin' hard an' here's what we do. We tell them while they gone with Raoul –"

"Oh no, Grace!"

"Shush girl. Listen to me now. – After they goes with Raoul, we tells them we goin' to get them some money from people in Kissidougou. So then when they come back with him safe tomorrow, we give them the cash," she said. "How much you got left in them travellin' checks you told me about, Cassie?"

"Travellers' cheques? Not much – maybe 200 dollars."

Grace nodded, "Okay, we tells them you goin' to give them all that money and they be sure to bring our Raoul back safe in the mornin'. Then soon as he back safe, we leave this camp straight away with all the children."

"Leave? Where will we go, Grace?"

"I don't know yet, girl. I ain't figured that out. Only thing I know is, now they find us here, they gone keep comin' back. So we can't stop here no longer," she said. "We find somethin' else. Soon's they bring Raoul back, we gone. That's all I knows for sure right now."

"I hope you're right, Grace. Let's tell Raoul before they take him away."

She and Grace moved behind the huts back to the clinic where Raoul still sat clutching his satchel. He looked up, relieved when he saw them appear in the doorway.

"It's going to be alright, Raoul, Grace has worked out a plan to pay them money only when they bring you back safe in the morning," said Cassie, sitting with her arm round the young doctor's shoulder.

"You keep remindin' them they goin' to get lots of money when you comes back to us, you hear me, Raoul?"

He nodded. "Where will you get the money, Grace?"

"Cassie got them travellin' checks left – over 200 hundred dollars. She goin' in to Kissidougou first thing to get cash for when you get back. Everythin' be fine, you just do as they say – don't argue with them." The big woman pulled him to his feet and enfolded him in her arms like one of her orphans.

Cassie stood holding his medical satchel. "And tell them what you told me, Raoul. About how *Médecins sans Frontières* always help them, just like now." She too, hugged him and Grace put her arms round both young people.

Outside, the gang members sat drinking the local brew and shouting excitedly at the village women who served them the food. Two or three of them pulled some of the young women into the darkness to the rear of the compound. The women made no protest but submitted fearfully.

Grace spoke to one of the older women, telling her to keep the others inside until the men were gone. She and Raoul approached the group and spoke in a calm voice to explain the deal. Raoul stood nodding his head in agreement, as she talked in a mixture of Krio and Fula but he said nothing, only clutching his satchel.

The leader rose unsteadily to his feet and pointed his finger at Cassie who stood back by the clinic entrance. He motioned for one of his youths to fetch her but Grace put out her hand to stop him. She explained again about the money and said Cassie could not go with them, because she had to go and get the cash first thing in the morning.

The leader pushed past her and strode over to Cassie, dragging his rifle. She stood her ground as he approached, shouting at her and gestured for her to come with him. He tried to pull her back to the others but she resisted and broke free, running inside the clinic hut.

The young man stood wavering in the darkness away from the compound fire, until Grace and Raoul came over to tell him again to hurry and leave, so they could be back for the money in the morning. He turned to shout one last time into the darkened clinic entrance, before moving off to call the other gang members together. One or two came out of the darkness, doing up their clothing and waving machètes. Two of them led Raoul out of the compound and the rest followed, falling silent as they moved off into the night. The young Cuban doctor cast a last glance at Grace, as he was pushed out the gate.

The big woman waited until she was sure they had gone before she hurried into the clinic hut to find Cassie. She sat huddled on the low stool Raoul had been sitting on and Grace stroked her back and tried to reassure her.

"That Raoul is plenty smart, Cassie. He gone be fine, I promise you."

"What did that man say to me, Grace? Why was he so angry?" said Cassie, leaning her head against the big woman's heavy body as though to seek strength from her.

"Oh, he jus' boastin' to them boys how he be comin' back here. How he not scared of the soldiers – stuff like that. They always braggin' when they drinks that beer – how brave they is."

"But he shouted at me, Grace – what did he want?" she asked, fearing what the big nurse would say.

"Eeehh? I told you, girl. He jus' showin' off to them boys – they all drunk."

"Grace, tell me what he said. I want to know."

"He want you to go with them too, but I told him you got to get his money. He say okay then but he still want you, that's why he shoutin' an' pullin' at you," she said. "He said he takin' you with him tomorrow, after he get the money," she finished.

"Oh God, why didn't I go with Zinadine when he warned me. I'm so frightened, Grace. I saw what they did to those other women. What are we going to do?" She clutched the big woman's arm.

"We got to get ready for when they comes back, Cassie. Right now, we have to take all these children and leave here."

"Tonight? Where can we go?"

"To the Catholic church in Fanu," said Grace. "I knows the Father there an' he'll let us stay in his church tonight."

"Won't they find us, Grace? It's only the next village."

"Yes, but them boys all from Sierra Leone. They don't know these villages round here."

"You saw how frightened these women were. What if they told them where we went?"

Grace shook her head. "Ain't goin' to be nobody here when they gets back. I tell them all to go in the bush till it safe to come back."

"But we can't leave without Raoul, Grace – we have to wait."

"I'll be here with the money an' you go and stay with the children till I fetch him back. Now hurry, girl and get them children outside here straight away. Jus' get them dressed – leave everythin' behind. We got no time to pack any stuff 'cept my medicine." The big nurse pulled Cassie upright and propelled her out the door. "Jus' do like I say an' everythin' be fine. But hurry! Ask any of them women that haven't run away to help you. First thing in the mornin' you got to be in Kissidougou for that money, so get your own stuff now and then fetch the children."

Cassie paused outside the hut and clutched Grace's arm. "What will happen if I'm not here when that man comes back for me, Grace? They might take you instead. I'm coming back with you, too."

The big woman snorted. "Eeehh? You think that boy want an old woman like me? I give him the money an' he be gone. No, you stay with the children, like I say. Now go on. We can't waste no more time talkin' here," she said and turned back into the clinic hut to collect her scant horde of medical supplies.

Cassie moved in a daze, hauling the sleeping children from their cots and helping them dress. She told them to go out and wait for her by the fire in the compound, until she had collected them all. She had roused Ahmed first, who had not been asleep, only lying in his bed fully clothed under the blanket. His eyes were round with fear.

"That man say he's comin' back an' you best be ready," he reported.

"I know, Ahmed. That's why we're all leaving – right now, as soon as we can," she said. "I need you to help me get all the little ones dressed and out by the fire."

"Where we goin', Cassie? Those man waitin' for us in the bush."

"It's alright, Ahmed, they've gone over the border with Doctor Raoul to see a sick man. They won't be back until tomorrow morning." She handed him his crutch and pushed him towards the door but he resisted.

"They goin' to chop Doctor Raoul's hand off, Cassie?"

"No, they won't hurt him because he's helping them. Now hurry, Ahmed. I need your help."

The boy hopped nimbly out of the hut and Cassie worked steadily, waking and dressing the youngest orphans. She tried to keep thoughts of what might happen to Grace tomorrow when she faced the men alone. Ahmed's last remark spun round in her brain and she saw the leader taking his revenge out on her black friend with a machète. Her love for this big nurse, who had helped her through so many difficulties these past few months, overcame her fear.

She determined to stand by her and not leave her to face the gang alone. If it meant she had to go with them to prevent them maiming Grace, then she would do it. She would write a message for Grace to send to Zinadine and hope he could work out a way to rescue her. If she got out of this alive, she promised herself she would do what he wanted, live in Labé, and have their baby.

Her decision transformed her from feeling a helpless victim, to taking charge of her life even if the outcome remained unknown. She moved now with a firm purpose as the fear receded and she tackled the situation the way her black friend had taught her. The children, who at first began crying at the mood of pervading fear, sensed the change in Cassie and began to enjoy their midnight adventure, as she smiled and told them where they were going. They held hands in a long chain, in order not to separate in the dark and vied for position with either Grace at the front, or Cassie in the rear.

The column moved off with flashlight beams bobbing in the darkness. Ahmed held a small LED lamp in his free hand and ranged back and forth in the middle of the chain of small bodies, shining it in the tiny faces and reporting any crying child to Cassie. She sent the child she held forward with Ahmed, to replace the crying young one and bring it back to her.

Half way to the village, Grace halted the tiny column and moved back along it to take a head count. She finished up beside Cassie and shone her flashlight on her face.

"Minou is missin'. Did you see her when we left, Cassie?"

Cassie tried to recall whether she had seen the 13 year old or not. Minou had been a problem for them since she reached puberty, often disappearing in the evenings with one of the village boys. The two women looked at each other for a moment, realising the probable answer.

"We can't go back," said Grace, "not enough time and these little ones too exhausted to do this twice."

"I'll go and find her, Grace. You go on with the children," said Cassie, passing over the sleeping child she held.

The big nurse shook her head. "No, you'll get lost in the dark. Besides, I needs you here to catch stragglers."

Ahmed hopped into the light. "I know the way, Grace. I can show Cassie." He waved his little LED lamp, pointing it back down the path.

"You could wait here for us," said Cassie, "keep all the children around you till we get back."

"An' what if that girl off in the village somewhere with that boy? You might not find her till morning. No, we got to keep goin' Cassie. Get these children safe in that Catholic church."

Cassie shone her flashlight at Grace. "And if Minou comes back in the morning, when the gang returns – what happens to her then?"

"You wants me to risk all these children for one foolish girl? How many times we warn her to stay in the compound at night? I say no, we got to move now." Grace turned and strode back up to the head of the chain which had already begun to break up, as some of the older children drifted back to see why they had stopped. The big nurse chided them loudly, pushing them back into line and the column moved off again in the dark.

Ahmed limped along beside Cassie, shining his flashlight over the heads of the children in front of them.

"Cassie? I know where Minou is," he said.

"What? Why didn't you tell me before, Ahmed?"

The boy shrugged. "She with that boy, his momma work in the kitchen. I know where they live in the village."

She absorbed this piece of information and thought of telling Grace, but knew what her friend's answer would be. She tried not to imagine the scene, if the nubile young girl turned up in the camp in the morning when the gang returned. Could she risk leaving Ahmed in her place and going back without informing Grace? But how would she find her way at night? Or find the girl if she did get there?

"Ahmed? Are you sure you know the way back to camp?"

The boy nodded. "I can lead you right to their house, Cassie."

"I can't go, Ahmed. Do you understand?" She shone her flashlight on his face.

"You want me to go and find her?"

She nodded. "Could you do that, Ahmed? Bring her back to us in Fanu?" She kept the light on his face, watching him.

"Yes," he said, "I think so."

"Are you sure? You're not frightened?"

He looked up at her in the beam of light and nodded. "A little bit," he said.

"Do you know why I'm asking you to do this dangerous thing, Ahmed?"

"You don't want that bad man to catch you, Cassie," he nodded.

"No – oh god, Ahmed. Maybe you're right. I'm sorry, I shouldn't have asked you to go – it's not fair." She put her arm round the boy's shoulder and they walked along together at the tail of the column.

After a few moments, he broke free and turned round. "It's okay, Cassie. I'm not afraid now. I'll find Minou for you." He moved off, his LED lamp shining its thin bluish light back down the trail.

"Wait, Ahmed," she said but he was already gone. "Be careful," she called at the bobbing light and he waved it above his head in acknowledgment.

# CHAPTER 45

After Barney's experience with the officious customs man about releasing the school books from England, he was taking no chances. While waiting for Clive and Hunter to arrive in Dakar, he paid a visit to a Red Cross organiser that a friend in the UK knew. He explained to him that he was expecting his son to arrive any day, with a boatload of used artificial limbs for an orphanage in Guinea. He asked for help to clear the customs barriers, without paying huge bribes and having long delays.

The Frenchman offered to act as his agent and use his Red Cross influence to get the prostheses released quickly when *The Betsy* landed. He had an arrangement with the port officials for clearing Red Cross shipments and said he could pass it off as one of his.

Barney left him having a drink with the customs officer in the harbour master's office. He and Landon went down on the quay, to where *The Betsy* lay moored alongside a large wooden sailing scow. They clambered across the cargo boat and climbed down onto *The Betsy's* deck.

No one was in sight and Barney rapped on the roof of the main cabin. A minute later, the rear companionway cover slid back and the ash blond head of Lottie appeared, looking sleepy and dishevelled.

"Lottie – you made it!" he said. "We were beginning to get worried after Hunter's email from the Cape Verdes. Where are they?"

She emerged fully onto the deck and stood now nearly a whole head taller than him on her long tanned legs and bare feet. "Ah, Barnee!" she said, embracing him. "I could kiss you, I am so happy to see you here. I will kiss you," and she planted several kisses on his cheeks. "'Untair will be so glad you 'ave found us. And Clive, too. Poor Clive, he is still *invalide.*" She stepped back and put her head down the open companionway. "'Untair! Look who is here," she called. "We arrived so late last night, we just fell into bed. They are both still sleeping. "'Untair!" she called again, "Come and see – *vite!* Quick!"

Hunter's head stuck up through the hatchway, bleary-eyed with sleep and squinted into the morning sunlight. "Dad – you made it! Am I glad to see you." He stepped out on deck, still wearing only a pair of boxer shorts and the two men hugged and pounded each other's back. Barney held his son off and studied his tanned lithe body.

"I thought you might be in rough shape, after your storm escapade but you look fine – great, in fact." He hugged him again. "Not as good as Lottie – but good."

"Lottie always looks like she just stepped off a glossy magazine cover," said Hunter. "She makes me look like a bum most of the time."

The tall Czech girl slid her arms round him from behind and grinned over his shoulder at Barney. "If you 'ad seen me during the storm you would not agree, Barnee. For three days, I did not wash or even brush my teeth. I looked like a scarecrow with my hair sticking out like this." She demonstrated, holding out bunches of her blond hair from each side of her head. "But you 'ave not introduced me to your friend," she said, looking past Barney to Landon, who stood waiting for the family greetings to finish. He came forward now and held out his artificial right hand to her.

"Sorry, Landon. This is my son, Hunter and Lottie, his girlfriend and my future daughter-in-law, if I have my way."

Lottie held his hand for a moment, then leaned forward to embrace him and kiss his cheek. "I see you are already familiar with our cargo for Cassie, Landon. The children will be especially pleased to meet you, I think."

Landon held up his right hand in the air. "It would be nice to think it'll be of some use then, Lottie, instead of the usual embarrassment it is to most people."

"A new career as a role model," said Barney. "Makes a change from being a saxophone player. Landon's a jazz musician," he explained to Hunter.

"*Was* a jazz musician," corrected Landon, "now I'm a diesel mechanic and used truck dealer."

"So have you found a good 4x4 for us?" asked Hunter. "I hope it's big enough to hold all these limbs – they're bulky and awkward as hell to store. Practically filled up Clive's cabin."

"Where is he anyway – confined to his bunk?" asked Barney.

"No, he's just lazy. Got too used to Lottie spoon feeding him and decided to become a permanent invalid," said Hunter. "Come on below and we'll roust him out."

They all filed down the narrow companionway steps into the main cabin and Lottie rapped on a door at the stern end. "Clive! Visitors for you."

The door opened and Barney's old friend appeared, looking thin and haggard, with a shiny metal brace across his shoulders and a sling holding his right arm.

"Clive – you okay?" asked Barney stepping forward to embrace him but stopping in the act, uncertain.

"It's alright, I won't break," grinned Clive, standing stiffly upright and holding out his good arm to Barney. "This is all Lottie's handiwork. She patched me up, good as new, nearly." He held out his left hand to Landon who took it in his own left hand. "A fellow Mason, I see, giving the secret handshake."

Lottie whispered to Hunter and he bent over to raise a hatch cover in the cabin sole and lift out a bottle of champagne.

"Here we are, the very last bottle. Lottie made us save it for today," he said and held it up to them. "Kept nice and cool and snug wedged under the floor all through that storm. A 'drop of the old widow' as Dad would say." He set the bottle of *Veuve Cliquot* on the cabin table.

"I wanted to drink it before the storm, in case we all drowned," said Clive. "But Lottie convinced us we'd survive – and we did – just. Thanks to her."

The tall Czech girl reached down some glasses from a top cupboard and Hunter popped the cork, the way Barney had taught him as a boy.

"Here's to Lottie – the new patron saint of inept sailors," said Clive.

Landon looked at Barney, then accepted a glass from Lottie. "To Lottie and Cassie, wherever she is."

"You mean you still haven't heard from her, Dad?

"Not since leaving London. I was hoping you might have been in touch," said Barney.

Hunter shook his head. "No, the last news we had came from Alice when she forwarded the report from the *Amis du CFA* agent. That was back in Barbados before we left."

"So what do you plan to do now, Barney?" asked Clive, perching upright on a stool bolted to the cabin floor. Lottie passed him a glass of champagne and stood behind him, massaging his shoulder with her long tapering fingers.

"I'm not sure. But Landon and I have bought a 4x4 and loaded all Alice and Netta's books while we waited for you, so I suppose we should just continue." Barney looked at the others. "Unless anybody's got a better idea?"

"Can't we get in touch with Zinadine?" asked Hunter.

"I don't have an email address for him, do you?" said Barney.

Hunter shook his head and glanced at Lottie. "You know how we could reach him, Lottie?"

"I could ask Papa to track him down through his diplomatic contacts, I suppose," she said.

"That could take weeks," he said. "Let's just get going, now. I don't want to hang around here on the boat."

"What's the rush? It's taken us two months to get here," said Clive. "A couple more weeks won't make much difference. Besides, by then I'll have recovered enough to sail on down to Freetown."

"*Mais non*, Clive. That is foolish. You must have someone to go with you," said Lottie.

"Well, I suppose you could go with him," said Barney. "There's not enough room in the truck for four people plus all this stuff for Cassie."

"But I want to come too. 'Untair wants me to help with the documentary and besides I have not seen Cassie since Paris."

"What about Clive? Don't you want to finish the trip with him to Freetown and see the *Amistad*?" asked Hunter.

"But we planned this trip together, 'Untair. Now you say I cannot come?"

"You heard Dad, Lottie. There's no room in the truck."

She stood in front of them, eyes flashing, arms akimbo.

"So. I see. Now that I am no longer of use, you want to get rid of me, so you are free to meet all these African women." She turned on Barney. "This is what you teach your son, *n'est-ce pas?*"

"You can take my place, Lottie," said Landon. "I could help Clive sail to Freetown instead."

"But we need you," objected Barney. "You're the only one who knows how to fix the Unimog if it breaks down – unless Lottie is a diesel mechanic too," he smiled at her.

"Hah! Very funny. No, I am quite useless with motors, so you will of course not need me along." She turned to Landon. "I advise you to be very careful with these men, my friend. You see how they can use you and then discard you afterwards." She strode up the companionway steps to the deck.

"Lottie, wait!" Hunter went after her and the three men looked at each other in surprise.

"What was that all about, Clive?" said Barney. "I thought she was just joking at first."

"She's fiercely jealous with Hunter," said Clive. "And he adores her – never looked sideways at another woman the whole trip." He shrugged. "Who would suspect such a beautiful girl to be so insecure? It's Hunter who should be the jealous one."

"Well, they'll have to work something out," said Barney. "It's for sure there's no room for her with all this cargo. And Landon is the key to getting it to Cassie. I can barely steer the bloody Unimog, never mind repair it."

# CHAPTER 46

The Unimog lumbered along at a steady 40mph, laden with its joint cargo of books and prosthetic limbs. They had been forced to load all their rucksacks and camping gear on the roof rack under a tarp. The truck had a ladder welded to a rear door so they could climb up and down to gain access to the roof.

Throughout the day the three men rotated places to each familiarise themselves with driving the Unimog. But it wasn't until they left the main road from Dakar to head to the border of The Gambia that the roads started to deteriorate and their progress was slowed to a crawl by large potholes.

Landon showed them how to engage the 4-wheel drive and the Unimog demonstrated its prowess as an all-terrain vehicle, able to climb in and out of any hole. It frightened Barney, the way it plunged into and out of the deepest ruts and waterlogged holes despite the load it carried.

"This is nothing," said Landon. "Wait till we have to use the front and rear winches to get us out of trouble."

Hunter and Barney hung on to door handles and seat belts, as Landon wrestled the strange huge-wheeled machine along the pockmarked roads with a dexterity they could not match, even with two fully functioning hands. Barney was glad

Hunter had persuaded Lottie to go with Clive by boat to Freetown. She reluctantly agreed to wait until they had reached Cassie's refugee camp before coming to join them.

They sat at a remote crossing of The Gambia River waiting for the hand-powered ferry to arrive. It crouched on the far bank, while the lone operator took his time loading the assortment of cars, trucks and passengers with huge bundles onto the flat barge. Hunter took some footage with his camera as the ferry made the slow journey across the river. The ferryman turned a large winch handle, that dragged it by a cable passing under the bottom of the barge. Another passenger joined him and they talked and turned the crank together.

Nobody seemed in any rush and Barney thought the whole scene could have been lifted out of a painting by Constable, from another earlier era.

"These people look happy and content, Landon," he said. "Do you think this kind of lifestyle is going to suit you? Quite a change from what you're used to."

"If I want excitement I can always go into Freetown," said Landon. "It's only a half hour bus ride from my piece of property. But I think I'll be too busy building and growing vegetables to spend much time in town."

"I envy you your future," said Barney. "People have always dreamed of starting ideal communities. I know I have. But not many get around to doing it."

"My sister wants me to build a school. She says there's no place for the local children to go and they can't afford a bus into Freetown every day."

"You could teach them music, Landon."

"I suppose so. You don't need a school for that, though. Still, a school is a good start for a community. I thought of a more multi-purpose building – it could be a school in the daytime and a gathering place for music and dancing and eating together." He took out a small notebook and sketched a circular thatched building with open sides. "This was easy to build with local materials and it's right in the middle of the compound with small houses around it."

"Looks like you've been planning this for quite a while," said Barney. "Maybe I could stay and help you after I've been to Cassie's camp."

The ferry landed and unloaded its collection of people, bundles and vehicles. A slight European woman in jeans with her hair tied back off her tanned face, pushed a small motorbike up the bank from the ferry ramp. She mounted and tried to kick-start it but the bike refused to fire. Hunter went over to help her and she explained how to get it going. He too, tried and failed to start the little Japanese bike. He told her to get on and he ran behind, pushing it for a hundred yards. Still no luck. He shook his head in frustration and they wheeled it back towards Barney and Landon.

"Dad, this is Celia from VSO in England. Maybe you and Landon can get this thing to start for her."

She held out her hand to them in turn, smiling but making no comment on Landon's artificial hand. "Do you know anything about motorbikes?" She glanced up at the Unimog perched on its giant wheels. "Is this yours?"

Barney nodded and pointed to Landon. "He's the official mechanic on this expedition. All I can suggest is changing the sparkplug. It works for my lawnmower."

Celia frowned and he saw the wrinkles round her eyes and mouth. She could be nearly forty, he guessed and not the young woman she looked from a distance.

"God, I haven't got a spare one with me. I don't suppose you carry any, do you?"

Landon laughed, indicating the big Unimog. "Don't need them for this thing. It's a diesel."

She stared at him, uncomprehending.

"Diesels have fuel injectors, not spark plugs," he explained. "We might be able to clean up yours if that's all it is." He climbed up to the cab of the truck and returned with a handful of ring spanners. "One of these should do it."

The others watched as he removed the sparkplug and studied the tip of it, shaking his head. He showed it to Celia.

"Looks okay to me," she said. "Maybe it's something else?"

Landon pointed to the end of the plug. "The tip's broken off. It's useless. Probably fallen inside the cylinder head. Even if you had a spare plug, you couldn't replace it without taking out the broken piece."

"How do I do that?" she asked, looking in the sparkplug hole. "I can't see anything. Do we turn the bike upside down and shake it out?"

"You have to dismantle it. Quite a job unless you know what you're doing."

"And I haven't a clue," she said.

Hunter pointed to the ferry. "We're going on that ferry – the way you came, or we'd give you a lift."

"I don't recall seeing any garage on the road here," said Barney. "Do you know anybody around here who could fix it for you?"

"No. I'm supposed to be going to a village on this side of the river, to help a local midwife but it's out in the middle of the bush."

"Are you a nurse?" asked Hunter.

"A doctor," she said, pointing to her bag strapped to the back of the motorbike. "I was going to give a class to some of the local pregnant women for this midwife."

"Well, I expect she knew how to deliver babies before you came along," grinned Landon. "Why don't you come back with us to your base and get this bike fixed there? We can stick it up on the roof if you don't mind riding on Hunter's lap."

Celia looked at him. "Having the babies isn't the problem usually. It's what happens to them afterwards I'm concerned with. But I guess you're right, I don't have much choice."

"It's either my lap or push that thing all the way to where you're going," said Hunter, smiling at her.

"If you don't like the look of him, you could sit on my knee," said Barney. "But I warn you, they're pretty bony."

"Sorry, I didn't mean to sound ungrateful," said Celia. "Hunter's lap will do just fine. I was only thinking of those women the midwife has persuaded to come to her class. I don't often get a chance to pitch to more than one at a time."

Hunter climbed the ladder up to the roof and the others heaved up the little motorbike to him, to lash down on top of their camping gear. They all squeezed into the cab of the Unimog and rolled onto the waiting ferry. It listed alarmingly to one side under the weight and the ferryman shouted and waved his arms at Landon.

"What's he saying?" asked Barney.

"He wants us to get back off," said Celia. She stuck her head out the window from her perch on Hunter's knee and shouted above the noise of the engine. She drew her head back in like a turtle and turned to them. "He says we're too heavy to go with all the others. We have to wait and go on our own, next crossing."

"But we've already been waiting over an hour," said Landon. "Why can't the others get off instead?"

She called the ferryman over and he climbed up on the driver's side to speak to Landon. His short grizzled hair made him look about Barney's age but his arms bulged with muscles of a much younger man, from winching the ferry back and forth across the river. He spoke in a loud voice that was incomprehensible to them but his meaning was clear. They would have to get off before he would move his boat.

Landon eased the Unimog backwards through the crowded ferry deck, with its old *sept-place* cars piled high with bundles and plastic five-gallon cans of palm oil. Two or three more vehicles had driven on behind the truck and the drivers refused to budge. A long battle of wills took place between them and the ferryman, before they grudgingly backed off the overloaded barge to allow Landon to reverse out onto the ramp.

As he backed up the ramp past the waiting vehicles, the drivers shouted and swore at him for delaying them. The last man in particular, who had struggled to get his overloaded Peugeot on and then off again, shouted obscenities which Celia took exception to and screamed back at him. He gunned his engine and lurched down the ramp, belching black smoke from the old car. It managed to straddle the bank and the barge ramp before the rear end scraped the ground and it stalled. The driver climbed out to survey the problem, then glared back at them as they sat watching in the Unimog. Landon waved and grinned at him and Celia on her side made a rude gesture with her finger.

Incensed, the driver jumped back in his car, started it and revved the engine till the smell of burning rubber filled the air but the vehicle remained firmly wedged. The old ferryman came over to see the problem and began to berate the driver for holding him up. Several of the passengers in the man's vehicle tried pushing it forwards and then when that failed, tried to shove it back off the boat. Neither direction worked and at last, the ferryman indicated that he would move forward enough to let the car drop back off the steel boarding ramp, onto the concrete landing.

He winched the barge forward and the old estate car dropped suddenly nose-down into the water. The driver shouted for him to stop but the momentum carried the barge forward several yards. The car rolled gently deeper into the river as the handbrake failed to hold it back. It came to rest half submerged, when it bumped against the trailing ramp of the ferry. Everyone aboard peered down at the old car, as the driver struggled to escape by climbing out his side window. He waded back up the ramp with everyone laughing and enjoying the spectacle.

From the cab of the Unimog, they had a ringside seat, waiting to see what would happen next. The old ferryman and the now dripping wet driver stood shouting back and forth. It was obvious that if he moved the ferry again, the car would sink into the steeply shelving river. He pointed up the ramp at the Unimog and the driver turned to stare at what he pointed at. After more arguing by the old ferry operator, the dreadlocked driver walked up the ramp to Landon's side of the Unimog and looked up at him.

Landon said nothing but beamed at the subdued driver from high above him.

"Ferryman say you got to use that winch to pull me out," the stocky young man said with a defiant look.

Landon slowly shook his head, relishing the advantage he held over this angry man, who had abused him so freely. "Not my problem, man," he said. "He made me get off, so he can sort it out."

"But he move that boat and my car sink right into the river," the driver pleaded. "Come on, man, just hook that winch on and you pull me straight out."

Celia leaned across Barney to stare down at him. "I hope it sinks straight to the bottom and serve you right. Maybe you'll learn to speak properly to people in future," she said.

The man looked up through his dreadlocks, incredulous at her effrontery. "You crazy, woman? That car full of all those people belongin's." He pointed to the roof piled high with bundles.

"He's right," said Barney. "We should help them save their stuff at least."

"I know," said Hunter. "Tell him if he pays, we'll pull him out."

This seemed to mollify Celia and she sat back on Hunter's lap. "And he can apologise for what he said, too."

"Okay," said Landon. "Tell them either they let us on the ferry now or else they have to pay for a rescue."

Celia, who had been interpreting the man's comments, spoke to him direct, not raising her voice but in her most cool professional manner. She finished the ultimatum and sat back to wait.

The driver's eyes widened but he said nothing, then turned to go back down the ramp to consult with the old ferryman. They shouted and jabbed their fingers at each other but were interrupted by horns blaring from the opposite , as the long line of waiting drivers grew impatient. The old ferryman made his decision and spoke to several other drivers aboard. The dreadlocked man returned and nodded to Landon that the deal was on.

Barney and Landon operated the Unimog's front winch for the first time, attaching the heavy cable to the rear end of the old Peugeot. Before they pulled the car up the ramp, Celia stood with one foot on the cable and insisted on her apology from the surly young driver. He gave it with an angry look and she nodded, removed her foot and waved to Hunter in the cab. They signalled to him to start the winch and slowly it dragged the car back up the ramp, while everyone aboard the ferry cheered.

The old ferryman moved the barge back into position and several drivers backed their vehicles off, until the old man judged it was safe to load the Unimog on. Landon unhooked the cable after a log had been put in front of the old Peugeot's wheels. He drove the big lumbering truck into the centre of the ferry and some of the cars were allowed back on to surround it.

As the barge inched its way across the river at last, Barney spelled off the old man on the winch to smooth things over. Hunter did his best to prevent the still upset Celia from waving and taunting the dread-locked driver, who stood surrounded by his angry passengers, pointing at their sodden belongings.

Barney judged he and the old ferryman were about the same age and he speculated on how many years he had operated this barge, crossing back and forth every day all his life. He studied the old man's face, with his patchy beard and eyes creased by the sun. Despite the recent contretemps with the young driver, Barney reckoned it was a reasonably pleasant job, providing a useful service to the community, with plenty of opportunity to contemplate the ebb and flow of life. He wondered if the ferryman found time to do a bit of fishing when no traffic appeared.

If he had not been on this search for his daughter, he felt he might have stopped here for a while – long enough to get to know this old man; hear his views on life. The ferryman had conducted himself throughout the whole episode with the volatile young man, with a quiet dignity that impressed Barney. He smiled at him and tried to think of how to communicate his thoughts but as usual, the language barrier intervened and he contented himself with helping to turn the big winch handle.

He recalled that ferrymen cropped up as significant figures in most of the world's literature, acting as go-betweens from one world to another. Barney tried hard to imprint this experience on his mind to mull over at a later date. He remembered a story of the Buddha as he approached the end of his life, waiting by a river in a ferryman's hut for a while but even he too, had to move on.

Celia had invited them all to stay in her village compound and they met the old woman who owned three of the round thatched clay huts. The three men shared one of them, furnished simply with low cots and kapok mattresses. Barney looked up at the thatched roof and the poles and palm fronds forming a makeshift ceiling in the room. The floor was hard-packed clay and the door and window openings were made of bamboo poles lashed together.

He studied the construction of the building, as it was the first time he'd had an opportunity to see inside one. They had passed dozens of villages holding clusters of these thatched huts, always inside a walled compound. Mostly they were round shapes with conical roofs, as this one was but sometimes they were square. It looked like the main style of home in non-Arab West Africa, as he saw them all over Senegal and The Gambia.

Although the huts in this village compound had doors and windows made of wood or bamboo, many of the ones they passed had only openings and children and chickens ran in and out. He supposed that because the old woman took in travellers and NGO workers like Celia, she had pandered to their western habits of wanting doors and windows for privacy.

Violet, the old woman, cooked them an evening meal of jollof rice and potato leaf greens. Celia offered them some cans of orange soda she had in her hut. Barney was gradually getting used to drinking un-chilled beer and pop, as refrigeration was non-existent outside the main cities. The last cold drink he had tasted was in Dakar.

They all sat out in the compound at a long trestle table with a garish vinyl cover, while Violet served the food with enormous portions of rice. Her two grandsons ate with them and spoke good English, as they were students at a technical college in Freetown, home for a term break.

Hunter quizzed Celia on her work with the NGO.

"Are you with *Médecins sans Frontières*?" he asked.

"No, I'm with a VSO group working on a Red Cross project. It's dealing with AIDS clinics and birth control aimed primarily at women," she said. "But what I'm interested in doing, is educating women not to allow girls to be mutilated by female circumcision."

"Does it still happen much here in The Gambia?" asked Barney.

Violet clucked her tongue. "Happen all over Africa, not just here."

Celia nodded confirmation. "It's hard to persuade the women to change a custom they've known for generations," she said.

Hunter shuddered. "Do they really cut off the girl's clitoris?"

"Depends who's doing it," she said. "If they're lucky that's all that gets cut off. I've seen lots of cases where they've hacked off half their genitals."

"My god – who does it anyway?" he asked, "a local medicine man?"

She shook her head. "No. It's always the older women – often grandmothers or relatives of the girl."

"But how would they know how to do surgery like that?"

"It's more like butchery. They use a piece of broken glass or a knife usually," she said.

"And they do this on their own children and grandchildren?" asked Barney. He glanced at Violet. "Have you ever done this, Violet?"

She nodded. "I helps sometimes but I never done it myself."

Celia had untied her hair from the bun she employed while riding her motorbike. Now it framed her face and softened the lines round her eyes, making her look much younger. Barney wondered if she had a child of her own.

"Could you ever imagine doing that to a child of yours, Celia?" he asked.

She shook her long brown hair. "No. But I couldn't imagine allowing my adolescent son to be circumcised by a rabbi either, yet all the Jewish mothers allow their sons to be mutilated this way in western societies. So let's not be too hypocritical."

"It sounds a lot more dangerous what they do to girls here," said Hunter. "Why do they do it anyway? Is it supposed to be a rite of passage thing?"

"Yes, it happens when the girl begins to menstruate," said Celia. "They isolate them from the rest of the community and prepare them for the circumcision. It's incredibly painful and the girls are often terrified by the stories they've heard about it," she said. "Infection is common and they're traumatised for long periods afterwards."

Landon had said nothing during this conversation. He listened with interest to what Celia had been telling them. "Women don't talk about this to men but my sister in Freetown told me once, that she thought the reason was to prevent girls from straying from their husbands. She said if they could enjoy sex, they wouldn't remain faithful to their partners."

Violet nodded in agreement. "What happen to the family if the mother chasin' after other men? That's what the old women teach us," she said.

"Sounds like a tough situation to change, Celia. You having any success?" asked Barney.

"They listen to me and they remember what a horrific experience it was for them. I tell them most women in the west have not been mutilated but they don't leave their families. It's a slow process of convincing one woman at a time. I concentrate on the young mothers. The older women are hard to convince." She smiled at Violet and put her arm round her shoulder. "But I'm working on her."

Violet laughed and stroked Celia's hand. "This girl work hard for these women an' they respect her alright. Maybe they gonna change one day because of her," she said. "But she right enough, I'm too old to change."

"That's not true, Violet. You told me you didn't go to help with your sister Ama's grand-daughter last month."

The old woman nodded. "I told them I had to help you at the AIDS clinic, so they say okay this time."

"I guess it helps that you're a doctor," said Barney.

Celia smiled. "They don't see many women doctors out here, so it does help my argument a bit. But then I've fatally weakened it by not having any children or a husband, isn't that right, Violet?"

The old woman laughed aloud. "This girl workin' on me an' I workin' on her," she said. "But she havin' more luck than me. How many young men you chase away, Celia? Smart ones, too. Educated like my grandsons here."

"And they all want the same thing from me," said Celia, "and it isn't children."

"What is it?" asked Hunter. "A white girlfriend?"

She shook her head. "A free ticket out of here and a British passport."

Violet laughed again, "I think maybe she right. Some of them boys been educated in England an' they just wants to go back," she said. "I'm thinkin' I have to send her home to find a white husband an' bring him back here, but I worry she don't come back to us – he make her stay in England."

"I don't see any man making Celia do what she doesn't want to," said Hunter.

Violet squinted at him. "You already here, son. Maybe you can try."

"Yeah, maybe I will. We're off to a good start, Violet. She's been sitting on my lap all day and we got on just fine, didn't we Celia?" Hunter grinned at her.

"That's because his father was sitting right beside us, so he had to behave himself," she said. "Otherwise I would have just switched laps."

The old woman shook her head. "No, you don't want an old man like that," she pointed at Barney. "You needs a good strong young man to make babies."

Celia smiled at them unembarrassed, obviously used to Violet's match-making. "You can see what I'm up against, living here," she said. "If her grandsons weren't so young she'd be trying to marry me off to one of them." She teased the two boys, who had sat silent through this conversation and now grinned in acknowledgement that their grandmother had run the proposition by them on more than one occasion.

"All the same, she may be right," said Barney. "You're a great catch for any man, Celia. If I were 30 years younger…."

"Don't you start, Barney, I'm too tired just fending off Violet."

"You better lock your door tonight, Celia," said Landon. "You're surrounded by suitors of all ages." He winked at Violet and the old woman laughed delightedly.

In the darkened hut with only a candle to undress by, the three men climbed into their cots and Barney stared up at the flimsy ceiling. He could here rustling and scuttling noises and wondered at the source. He blew out the candle and drifted off to thoughts of bats, scorpions and snakes above his head.

Two hours later, a heavy thud landing on his legs woke him from a restless sleep. He let out a shout that woke Hunter and Landon, as he felt a scurrying over his body. He threw off the covers and leaped out of bed, bumping into his son as they searched for the candle.

"What is it, Dad – what happened?"

Landon shone his small flashlight on their startled faces. "I think it's a rat." He turned the beam on the floor and searched the room. The noise had woken Violet's two grandsons and they pushed the door open, holding a lantern.

"Rats!" shouted Barney, still unnerved by the sudden shock.

Hunter found the candle and lit it while the others peered under the beds. The beam from Landon's flashlight picked out a pair of shining beady eyes in one corner.

"There it is – under the chair!" he said and the two boys pounced, whacking at it with sticks they had brought in.

"Bush rat – don't let him out," they called. "Close the door."

But it was too late. The large bush rat raced over Barney's bare feet and out the door into the darkness of the compound. He let out another yelp and fell back onto his cot, as Celia appeared in the doorway wearing a boubou.

"What's all the noise in here?"

"Bush rat," said the boys, dodging out past her and holding up the lantern. "A big one."

"It fell out of the roof," said Barney, "landed right on top of me. I'm still shaking." He sat up on the edge of his bed, his heart racing.

Celia came over and sat beside him, taking his pulse. "Don't worry. It's probably more frightened than you."

"I doubt that," said Barney, breathing sterterously as he lay back on his cot.

"I'm frightened too, Celia," said Hunter. "Can I come and sleep with you?"

She laughed, "No you can't. I've got to get up early to get my motorbike fixed. Now just go back to sleep, all of you."

"I don't think I'll be getting much more sleep here," said Barney, sitting up and pulling on his shoes. "I'm going to sleep in the truck cab."

"Hope the boys catch him," said Landon, getting back into bed. "Bush rat is supposed to be good eatin'."

# CHAPTER 47

In the morning, Barney drove the Unimog on the road to Georgetown in The Gambia, trying to avoid the worst potholes. When Hunter took the wheel, he looked for the deepest ones and headed straight in to them, to see how the Unimog climbed in and out with ease. Landon, too, drove into them with confidence but didn't push the truck too hard. He had not been able to have the full service on it he wanted before they left Dakar and he had detected an ominous noise from the four-wheel drive at certain times.

"That Celia is one classy woman," he said. "I sure didn't want to leave this mornin'."

"Why didn't you offer to fix her motorbike for her, then?" said Barney.

"Yeah, I should have. But she wasn't interested in me. Plenty of old black men around here. It was Hunter she fancied."

"Too old for me. Besides, Lottie would pull that long red hair out if she caught us together," said Hunter.

"Don't worry," said Barney. "I won't mention she sat on your lap all day yesterday."

"And I won't tell her he wasn't in his bed when I woke up this mornin'," said Landon.

"I got up early to check Dad was okay in the truck. And then I went for a walk."

"Not much of a walk across the compound to Celia's hut," grinned Landon.

"I saw her light on, so I went over," admitted Hunter. "She's used to getting up early, she says. Part of her training."

"I guess they were discussin' birth control methods all that time, eh Barney?"

"If they weren't, I hope they were at least practising them."

Hunter wrestled the Unimog down into a mud hole and they all lurched forward, clutching at the dashboard.

"Take it easy, Hunter. We're only envious," said Landon. "First Lottie and then Celia. Two beautiful women after one young guy."

"As a matter of fact, she was telling me about all her amputees, after I told her what we had on the truck. She said Cassie would need a specialist to adapt these artificial limbs to fit her orphans," said Hunter. "Do you think she'll be able to find anyone like that out here in the bush, Dad?"

"Doubtful, unless she already has someone lined up – maybe through *Médecins sans Frontières*."

"Why do you think you haven't heard anythin' from her, Barney?" asked Landon. "She must know you're on your way by now."

"I have to admit I'm worried about her. When we still had no word by the time we left Dakar, it made me wonder how safe that refugee camp really is," he said. "It didn't help, hearing all those atrocity stories from your friend Lisabeth, either."

"Who's she?" asked Hunter.

"Landon's lady friend in Dakar, from Sierra Leone."

"But Cassie's in Guinea, not Sierra Leone, Dad. Why, what did she say, anyway?"

"Oh, she had a bad time durin' the civil war," replied Landon. "Lost her son and her husband – both in one attack by armed gangs."

"Kissidougou is right near the border and she said cross-border raids happen all the time," said Barney. "Alice is convinced Cassie's not even there anymore and that's why we haven't heard from her."

"Then why are we going there with all this stuff?" asked Hunter.

"Because if she's not there, we've got to find her. Wherever she's gone."

"Too bad we couldn't get hold of Zinadine before we left. It's for sure he knows where she is."

"We should be in Bassé Santa Su today," said Landon. "Maybe they'll have an internet café there."

"Don't speak too soon," said Hunter, braking the Unimog to a halt in the middle of the road. "Looks like a roadblock."

Ahead of them, a large two-wheeled cart had spilled its load of firewood and it lay across the road in a jumbled heap like matchsticks. One of the wheels had come off the cart and several people stood around. They had unloaded the rest of the split logs to remove the weight off the cart and had succeeded in propping it up high enough to fit the wheel back on. When they saw the truck, two of them came back to speak to Landon, assuming he would speak their dialect.

The two men kept gesturing under the Unimog and pointing at the main cargo hold behind the cab.

"I think they want to borrow our tools," said Barney. He and Hunter jumped down to unlock the steel box holding the collection of wrenches and spanners that had come with the truck, plus others Landon had gathered in Dakar. The woodcutters poked through them and found some to take back to work on the damaged cart wheel.

Barney watched how quickly they managed a makeshift repair using bits of wire, wood and hand tools. The rest of the people who provided the motive power, sat or squatted by the roadside until the wheel was lashed back onto the cart. Some of the women were fascinated by Landon's artificial hand, with its flexible thumb. When Hunter beckoned them to come back to the Unimog to see what was inside the truck, he caused a sensation. They stared at the piles of artificial limbs and called to the men doing the repairs to the cart.

Barney realised how impossible it would be to explain their mission and instead pointed to one or two young boys with the group. Making chopping motions with his hand at their arms and legs and mentioning 'hospital' several times, he pointed down the road saying "far, far, Kissidougou, Guinea." This triggered a loud discussion in his audience and much headshaking. Several of them motioned back down the road, in the direction of Sierra Leone.

"Looks like they want to divert us to a local hospital, Dad. Probably lots of amputees around here from the war." Hunter closed the door of the truck, while Landon retrieved his precious tools from the repairmen. They helped the wood-collectors reload the cart, with its immense top-heavy pile of split logs. But the women stood blocking the road and made circling motions with their hands, wanting the Unimog to turn around.

"Guinea – no, no!" they said, pointing back the way the truck had come.

"This could get ugly," said Landon. "Why the hell did you show them all those artificial limbs, Hunter? Now they want to hijack our load for Cassie."

"We don't have a lot of choice now, except to go with them," said Barney, nodding to two men who had climbed the ladder up onto the Unimog's roof, shouting and pointing off into the distance.

Landon reversed the truck round and prepared to follow the cart. It was only now Barney realised why so many people stood about. No horses or donkeys had been pulling it, only one man who stood between the shafts while all the rest – men, women and boys pushed the huge load.

"Maybe if we offer to pull the cart into town for them, they'll let us go," he said.

"It's worth a try," agreed Landon as he wheeled the Unimog around in front of the cart and they all got out to unwind the rear winch.

Barney beckoned for the two men on the roof to come down to help. When the women and boys saw the heavy cable with its big hook being unwound towards the cart they all cheered and shouted. Barney and Hunter helped the men attach it to the shafts and Landon winched it forward close behind the Unimog.

They were about to climb back into the cab, when a young boy of nine or ten was thrust forward to show them the way. The rest of the women climbed up on top of the cartload of wood and the men and boys scrambled up the ladder to perch on the roof. One man stood clinging onto the rungs of the metal ladder.

Shaking his head, Barney climbed into the cab beside Hunter who held the young boy on his knees. "Beats walking, I guess. Better keep it in low gear, Landon or you'll shake them all off."

"Or the wheel will fall off again," said Hunter.

The child said his name was Isaac and he directed them off the main road onto a dirt track through the bush. They emerged into a clearing with thatched huts on either side of the road and stopped outside one of the larger ones.

"Chief," said Isaac, pointing to an old man who sat on a low stool, watching three young women with long poles pounding mealie meal in a hollowed out stump. They turned to watch but kept up their rhythmic pounding of the grain. The chief made no move but several old women came out of other huts at the sound of everyone's arrival.

"Look," said Hunter, pointing at a trio of young teenaged boys, who approached them on makeshift crutches made of tree branches and rags for padding. "There's the reason we've been hijacked, Dad."

People scrambled down off the firewood cart and the roof of the Unimog, as Barney and Hunter unhooked the winch cable, surrounded by a swarm of naked and half-naked curious children. The two men who had originally approached them, now led them over to the old village chief where he sat in front of his hut. The three girls abandoned their long poles and joined the crowd around the strangers. Many of the women and girls were bare-breasted and Hunter grinned at Barney as he tried not to stare at them.

The two men spoke to the chief in Krio English, gesturing at Landon in the cab and the loaded cart behind the truck. One of them led a teenage boy on crutches in front of the chief and Barney.

"He say you have many arms and legs in the truck – like that man." The chief pointed at Landon, who waved his artificial hand as all eyes turned to him. The old man spoke an English Barney understood easily. "This man is my son and this boy is my grandson," he said, nodding towards the youth with the wooden crutch. A stump of leg extended below a pair of baggy shorts. His foot and lower leg had been amputated below the knee.

"We are only delivering these limbs to an orphanage in Guinea," explained Barney. "We are not doctors who know how to fit one for your grandson."

The chief spoke to his son who waved this information aside.

"My son says not important. He will help you fit one with all your tools," he said, nodding towards the Unimog.

Barney glanced at Hunter. "What do you think, Hunter?"

"We could have a look and see if there's anything that might fit him, I guess."

"This is your grandson?" asked the old man.

"My son," said Barney and the old chief nodded.

"How many wives you have?"

"He is my son from my first wife," said Barney. "I have a daughter and a step-daughter from my second wife. We are taking these artificial limbs to my daughter, who is working in an orphanage for amputee children in Kissidougou."

The old man rose and led the way over to the Unimog. Barney explained to Landon that the youth was the chief's grandson and they wanted him to have one of Cassie's limbs. Hunter unlocked the cargo door and a loud "Eeehh!" erupted from the gathered villagers at the sight of all the heap of hands and feet.

"You'd better try to find one," said Barney, "seeing as you packed all these on Clive's boat. Are they in any order?"

"Sort of," said Hunter. "All the hands and arms are on one side and the smallest are at the back. What size do you think he is, Dad?" He held up a leg with the harness of straps wrapped round it.

Barney spoke to the chief and the young teenager was boosted up to stand beside Hunter. Barney and Landon unwound the straps and held the limb against the boy.

"Too big, Hunter. See if you can find something a couple of sizes smaller," said Landon.

After foraging through the stacked limbs, Hunter pulled out several different sizes. "The rest are all too small, if these don't fit him," he said. He climbed down while Landon and Barney tried each limb in turn. None of them seemed quite right and they shook their heads at the village chief.

"Sorry, chief," said Barney. "But we don't have one to fit your grandson." He and Landon lifted the boy back down to ground level and gave him his crutch back. The chief's son who had been watching the whole operation closely, came forward and chose one of the legs they had tried. He nodded to the boy and two of the villagers lifted him up into the Unimog's cargo doorway. Everyone crowded round, as he unwrapped the harness straps and pushed his son's stump into the leather socket.

He stretched out the boy's sound leg and held them together. The limb was nearly two inches shorter. Peeling off his torn tee shirt, he stuffed it into the leg socket and pushed his son's stump down into it. Once again, he compared the two legs and now they were almost the same. Landon showed him how the harness supported the limb and they adjusted the straps around the boy's upper leg.

Barney looked over their shoulder. "What's going to keep the leg in the socket, Landon? He's filled it up with that tee shirt."

"It needs another leather strap to wrap right round the whole thing," said Landon. He pulled his belt out of his trousers and wound it twice around the stump and socket, but it was too loose. He handed it to the father and showed him where to make a new hole for the buckle. Using a hammer and a nail, the man punched another hole in Landon's belt and then wrapped it in place, buckling it tight. His son winced but said nothing and Barney and the father lifted the boy down to the ground, supporting him from both sides.

He stood uncertainly for a minute, testing his weight on the new foot.

Barney and the boy's father led him forward and the crowd of villagers melted back to let them pass. The young boy dragged his new foot at first, unused to the sensation but after circling round the truck once or twice he became more confident, kicking the leg out in front of him in an awkward gait.

The father said something to him and then nodded to Barney to let him go. The boy stood unsteadily, looked at his father, took a faltering step and fell to one side, his new foot stuck out in front of him.

"He's got no strength in that leg yet," said Landon. "He needs to practise walking with some support." He beckoned to two younger boys and they positioned themselves under his arms. The three of them took off again, wobbling up and down the dirt road. The village children ran after them and the men shouted encouragement. Women smiled and nodded, holding their hands up to their mouths as they watched.

Hunter brought his video camera from the Unimog cab to film the villagers' reactions and the children running round and round the trio of youths. His camera came to rest on the two other young men on homemade crutches, who stared at the chief's grandson.

The old chief insisted they should stay and eat, to celebrate his grandson's new-found mobility. While they waited for the women to prepare the meal, Hunter filmed the girls who had resumed pounding the grain with their long poles. They chanted a tune that matched the rhythm of their pounding and Barney stood watching, until one offered her pole to him to try. The other two girls giggled at his awkward flailing and inability to keep up with them. After five minutes, his arms ached from the attempt and he handed back the pole to the young woman.

He and Hunter joined Landon who was tinkering with the Unimog, lying underneath it while a clutch of tiny children dodged in and out under the huge wheels.

"Hunter thinks we should try to fit limbs for those other two boys, Landon. What do you say?"

Landon rolled out from beneath the transmission and stood up stiffly. "I thought we were takin' these to Cassie's war orphans? At this rate, we'll arrive with an empty truck."

"What difference does it make who gets them, though, as long as they get used?" said Barney. "These kids are victims too."

"If we sort out these two boys, the word will get round the nearby villages and we'll be here for a week messin' about as if we knew what we're doin', with you playin' Albert Schweitzer," said Landon. "I'm gonna turn the truck around, pretendin' I'm checkin' out that gearbox noise. When everybody's asleep tonight, we sneak away."

"Sneak away?" laughed Hunter. "This thing makes more noise than a tank."

"If we sleep under it like we usually do, we can shove our sleepin' bags in the cab and be under way before they know what's happenin'. It'll be pitch black, remember," said Landon.

"I hope you're right," said Barney. "But I'd still like to try to help those two kids. It doesn't seem fair to fix up the chief's grandson and leave them with nothing. Especially after they've seen that big pile of arms and legs. You saw the look on everybody's faces when Hunter showed them what we had inside."

"That's what I'm worried about. By mornin' we could have dozens of war amputees here." Landon turned to Hunter. "From now on, not a word to anyone what we're carryin' until we get to Kissidougou, okay?"

"Well, I'm with Dad on this. I say we fix these two young kids up anyway."

Landon shrugged. "Okay. Maybe you're right. We do it after supper and everyone's happy and won't suspect anythin' till it's too late. Once I get this truck goin', nothin's gonna stop us."

"What if they climb back onto the roof?" asked Barney. "Am I supposed to stand up there and repel boarders coming up the ladder?"

"Nothing we can do about that, Dad. The ladder's welded onto the side."

Landon unlocked the cargo door and nodded for Hunter to enter. "We'll worry about that at the time. Pass out some of those limbs to Doctor Schweitzer here, while I go and find those two lads." He headed over to the fire where some women stirred huge pots and mimed limping on a crutch. Several naked children ran off to find the boys. By the time he returned, Hunter had a selection of likely prostheses laid out on the ground for them to try.

The boys hung back at first, until Barney urged them to stand by Hunter to be measured for an approximate fit. Soon they began slipping their scarred stumps in and out of the appliances, looking for one their size. Some of the village men who had been standing around smoking, joined in the search . Barney stood back to watch how adept they were at working with simple tools.

Landon gathered up the unused limbs and slipped them back inside the cargo hold, locking the door. One of the legs fitted almost perfectly except it was an inch too long and the boy stood on it at an awkward angle. The other boy waited while the men shortened the leather harness straps to adapt the new leg for him.

They worked on, until young women carried over plates of food for them. Barney, Hunter and Landon sat by the fire, talking to the old village chief and eating the heaping mounds of swamp rice, with yams cooked to a mush.

"You do not need to go to Guinea," the chief said to Barney. "Plenty of people round here with only one hand or leg."

Barney tried again to explain. "I promised my daughter to bring these for all her war orphans. We can't spare any more after these boys are fixed up, chief."

"I have brothers in next village we can visit tomorrow," said the old man, ignoring Barney's reply. "They will show you many people need hands too."

Landon nudged Barney and nodded towards the men by the Unimog. While they ate, people had been drifting into the village and Barney saw three or four with missing limbs, keenly watching the two boys testing their new artificial legs.

Powerful local palm wine passed from hand to hand round the fire and the village men drank deeply. But for once, Landon took only a token swallow and Hunter and Barney followed suit. They feigned tiredness and explained they would sleep under the high-wheeled Unimog. Most of the villagers had drifted off and only a small handful of men sat round the fire, drinking with the cluster of new amputee arrivals. Barney crawled into his sleeping bag under the truck. He lay watching the people by the fire, who gestured towards the truck from time to time, talking in low voices.

"We should wait a couple of hours after they've all gone to sleep," he said. "All that palm wine ought to knock them out."

"I only had a bit and already I can feel it," yawned Hunter. "I may not stay awake."

"Don't worry, I don't plan on sleeping at all until we get well away from here," said Landon. "Just be ready to go when I give the signal."

They watched a group of men leave the fire and come over to look under the Unimog at the three of them feigning sleep and then moved off into the darkness. Barney could hear sounds of movement in the bush for some time afterwards and then only the odd screech from some night bird. He lay back listening to the even breathing of his son next to him, already asleep.

He wondered if Hunter's trust in a one-armed alcoholic and a 72-year-old father was misplaced. As always, when he found himself in a tight spot, Barney was assailed by doubts. Why was he doing this anyway? Did it make sense for a man to put himself in this position at his age? He thought of most of his friends back in Canada and England, living so-called 'normal' lives, sleeping in comfortable beds with comfortable wives.

His pursuit of life in the 3rd Age had often led him into risky situations he felt beyond his capabilities. How much longer should he go on chasing this chimera around the globe? Surely it was time for him to begin the last stage of his life, in quiet contemplation. Perhaps when he finished this project with Cassie, he could allow himself to go back to Canada and build the retreat centre he had planned for so long, on that island in British Columbia.

"Barney – ssst!" said Landon, only the enlarged whites of his eyes showing in the darkness. "Let's go. And don't use your flashlight."

They shook Hunter awake and all three crept out from under the truck dragging their sleeping bags and climbed into the high cab, easing the doors closed. The noise of the engine erupting into life, sounded loud enough to wake the whole village but nothing stirred. Landon shoved the old Unimog into gear and rumbled ahead with only parking lights on at first. Mingled shouts behind them rose above the noise of the engine and Hunter shouted.

"Look out!"

Landon braked and switched on the full beam of the headlights. In front of them, a great heap of firewood logs blocked the dirt road and the huge two-wheeled cart added to the barrier.

"Shit – we're trapped," he said, peering out the window at the loud cries coming nearer.

"Use the four wheel drive – go right over the wood pile," said Hunter. "Come on, Dad. Help me move the cart out of the way." He jumped down and Barney followed. They grabbed the shafts and heaved the empty two-wheeled wagon off to one side.

"Hurry up," yelled Landon, revving the engine. Hunter boosted Barney up into the cab and jumped in behind him.

"Go – go!"

Landon took one last look behind, then rammed the lever into gear and the Unimog ploughed straight into the pile of logs. The front end reared up and the huge wheels climbed the heap, sending logs rolling back under it. They clung to the dashboard as it rocked unevenly up and straddled the top of the pile. Pinpricks of LED lights flashed at either side of them. Thuds sounded above the din as stones and chunks of wood hit the sides of the truck body, followed by shouts and yells.

"They can't climb on the ladder up here, Landon, but they'll try when we come down the other side," said Barney, from their high perch atop the heap of logs. As if to prove it, several men now danced about below in front of the headlights, waving branches and firewood logs. With a roar, the Unimog crested the pile and Landon plunged it diagonally down the slope to miss the men in front.

"We're tipping over," shouted Barney, as he felt the truck lurch sickeningly to one side. Landon yanked the wheel hard around and headed straight towards the shouting men below. Hunter reached across and hit the air horn button, holding it down. The giant wheels danced down the heap and the men scattered to either side, as the Unimog hit the dirt road with the air horn blaring. Landon accelerated hard past the frightened faces.

In moments, they had outdistanced the running group of villagers and Landon switched out of four-wheel drive into a higher gear. The truck leapt ahead and they headed for the main road, where they had been diverted to the village the day before by the young boy.

"What's that noise?" asked Hunter. "It's coming from underneath."

They all listened as the Unimog thundered along the road, with Landon accelerating full throttle.

"It's the transmission," he said. "It's been getting worse for the last couple of days."

"Going over that heap of logs must've done it, " said Barney. "I hope it holds out till we get out of here."

"We're not far from the Guinea border now," said Hunter. "I looked it up on the map yesterday. We should be there by daylight."

"I'm not stopping until we put some distance between us and that bunch back there," said Landon. "I don't want to tackle any more roadblocks like that one."

"Thank god for the Unimog. I don't like to think what would have happened if they'd caught us," said Barney.

"Probably added us to the list of amputees," said Hunter, patting the dashboard, "if it wasn't for this old girl."

They rumbled on into the night and reached the border post while it was still dark. It consisted of an open-sided hut and a single bamboo pole lowered across the road. No one was about as the Unimog rolled up to the barrier. They sat idling for a few minutes, debating whether to wait here or try for another crossing further along the border.

"If we hang around, they might send a message to the police to hold us here," said Landon.

"Why don't we just head across country?" said Hunter. "There's no houses around. We could leave the road here and join it further along on the other side."

"I guess it's no problem with the Unimog. She's proved she's capable of tackling any kind of obstruction," said Barney. "We can always report in the first town in Guinea – say there was nobody here at the border post."

Landon backed off the road, put the truck in four-wheel drive and headed into the scrub bush, aiming to run parallel to the road. A clearing appeared in the headlights after a few hundred yards and he swerved across it to rejoin the road. He stopped the truck and switched off the engine.

"I need a piss after all that," he said and climbed down onto the roadway.

"Me too," said Barney.

"And me," Hunter opened the other door.

The three men stood in a row at the side of the road, pissing with relief.

"At least we made it to Guinea," said Barney. "Now all we have to do is find Cassie."

# CHAPTER 48

Alice sat at her father's desk in the old mansion flat in North London, composing an email to Barney. Her once lively manner had vanished and her face looked drawn and sallow, deep hollows in her cheeks. The news this morning had confirmed what she suspected all along about her youngest daughter. It added to her determination to go ahead with the operation. She had to keep her strength up for Cassie's sake and to bring her safe home somehow. If that meant having the second mastectomy, so be it.

Her deeper underlying fear for both of her daughters remained unresolved. No satisfactory solution had so far come to her mind. She spent most nights dwelling on how she could, or even whether she should tell them what lay in store for them, embedded deep in their genetic makeup, thanks to her.

Since her return to her parents' old garden flat in Highgate, she had wrestled with her dilemma. It coloured all her thinking and isolated her from everyone she cared about. Her mother and father accepted without comment, her explanation that she and Heck needed time apart to decide on their future. Her daughter Netta, whom she usually turned to, could not be told the real reason for her distress and Heck – poor Heck was baffled by her change of attitude toward him.

She had treated him badly, that much she admitted. But she knew she had no right to let him feel as if he were to blame.

So that left Barney.

*Dear Barney,*

*Why haven't I heard from you? There must be an internet café somewhere between Dakar and Kissidougou. Since you wrote to tell me the customs papers arrived and you had the crates of books, I've heard nothing. Until this morning.*

*The man from the Amis du CFA forwarded me a report from their field agent in Guinea. He said that because of cross-border attacks by guerrilla gangs, Cassie's refugee camp had to be disbanded. It happened so suddenly that all contact with them was cut off. They assume that the staff, volunteers and the orphans have all fled to different villages in the bush. They are trying to find out where they've gone but so far, nothing has been heard of them.*

*I cannot begin to tell you how frightened I am that something horrible has happened to Cassie and this report just confirms what I've feared would happen all along.*

*On top of this, I've made my decision to go ahead and have my other breast removed. I know it will spell the end of my relationship with Heck but I'm determined to stay alive until I find out what has happened to Cassie. She may need me when you bring her home and I want to be strong enough by then, to be able to help her deal with the consequences of my genetic bequest to her and Netta.*

*I don't know how I shall tell them but I know I must. I feel more than ever they must hear their fate together and not have to deal with the news alone as I have had to. With the sole exception of you, I have told no one about it for fear it would get back to Cassie and Netta second-hand. I know you think I'm a coward about many things but in this instance at least, I'm determined to be strong.*

*Please, please contact me as soon as you get this email and let me know where you are and how soon you will be in the Kissidougou area. I'm so glad Hunter is with you to help look for Cassie. Be careful, both of you, but hurry, Barney, hurry.*

*Much love, Alice.*

She clicked the send button on her laptop and sat back in her father's old wooden swivel chair, its arms worn satin smooth from age. Lately she and her mother seldom saw him except at mealtimes, as he worked on the mystery project with Heck. So far, despite her attempts to winkle it out of him, Martha had been unable to find out more than that it was 'something for the kids.'

George and Martha had adopted Cassie's war orphans as surrogates for the great-grandchildren neither of Alice's daughters had been able to produce. Netta's infertility had been a major factor in Alice's concern about telling her of her breast cancer gene. What if she had a grand-daughter and the gene got passed down yet another generation?

She went in search of her mother, in the big rooms of the old mansion flat she had known since childhood. Martha sat at an old Davenport writing desk, working on a memoir. Alice only discovered this by accident one day, when she asked her mother if she was keeping a diary. She had tried at different times, Martha said, but only ever recorded trivia, so she decided to attempt a memoir for her grandchildren.

Why not for her child? Alice had asked, but her mother said she was too close in time and she needed the distancing to be more objective in what she recorded. She had politely refused to let Alice read any of it – maybe after she died, she said.

"Dad still not back from King's Cross?"

Martha shook her head. "He and Heck are like two little boys, the hours they spend down there on that mystery project. He comes home some days with grease and oil on his clothes. I think whatever it is, it must have an engine."

"Has he said when it will be finished, Mother?"

"Pretty soon, I gather. He says Heck is a bit of a stickler for making sure everything is right, down to the last detail."

"Sounds like Heck alright. He was meticulous about sorting and cataloguing all Mrs Hollis's possessions at Tiberius Road."

"That house is so perfect, the way he's restored it, Alice. I don't know how you can bring yourself to sell it." Her mother rose to go into the kitchen and grasped the back of the chair to steady herself.

Alice stepped forward to take her arm. "Are you feeling okay, Mother?"

"I'm fine, dear. I just get these dizzy spells when I stand up too quickly. Old age, that's all."

Alice debated whether to tell her mother about the message from the *Amis du CFA* organiser this morning. She knew Martha would worry about her grand-daughter but she was so involved in the orphanage project, she felt it unfair to with-hold any news of Cassie, good or bad.

She made her mother sit down in the kitchen and poured them each a cup of coffee, then sat beside her to tell her the news from Cassie, or rather about her.

"I know it's not fair upsetting you when there's nothing we can do about it, Mother but I'm almost paralysed with fear. I can't think straight anymore. I've just emailed Barney to find out where he is. He and Hunter are my only hope. If they can't find her, I…." she trailed off and Martha put her arm round her only child.

"They will, darling, if anyone can. You know Barney when he decides to do something."

"That's what I'm counting on, Mother but I haven't heard anything from him since they left Dakar. God knows where they are now – lost in the African bush somewhere."

"Alice, don't. Cassie has told us often enough that once you're outside a city or major town, there's no internet and even if you do find one, they have no power to run it. We just have to wait. I'm sure we'll hear soon."

Alice stood up and paced round the old kitchen, picking things up off her mother's countertops and putting them back down in a different place.

"Does Dad say anything to you about Cassie? Is he worried, too?" she asked. Even at sixty-two, Alice often took her cue from her father's behaviour in times of distress, when she was unsure how to act.

"I'm sure he's concerned, Alice but he and Barney have a similar attitude to Cassie. They think she has a charmed life and nothing serious can happen to her," said Martha. "Of course, he hasn't heard this news from the CFA office."

"He seems so happy these days, I hate to tell him, Mother. Whatever he and Heck are working on, it's having a good effect on him."

"I suppose we can hold off for a few days and wait till we hear from Barney. What about Heck, dear – will you tell him? He might have some suggestion to make besides simply waiting. He's even more resourceful than Barney."

"I've been thinking about it for quite a while, Mother. I haven't spoken to him much these last few weeks, since he returned from Rome. He's very cross with me for leaving Tiberius Road and wanting to sell it."

"Maybe it's time to go and talk to him again, Alice. I remember once when your father and I separated for nearly a year and I went home to my parents, too. When we finally got back together, you were the result."

Alice smiled at her. She had heard this favourite story of her mother's many times before, during her roller-coaster marriage to Barney.

"I don't think you can look for a similar outcome this time, Mother. I'm a bit too old for that."

"Nonetheless, you can at least talk to him, dear. For Cassie's sake, if for no other reason."

"Alright, Mother. I suppose it's better than sitting here stewing over bad news."

On an impulse, that afternoon Alice took the Underground to King's Cross and headed down the back streets behind the railway station, to the row of old warehouses built under the railway arches. She had no idea which was the right one but she looked for Heck's tiny electric car. She spotted it parked outside one of the old ramshackle sets of wooden doors, that the station developers wanted to demolish. This whole area was barely recognisable to her, since the new high-speed Eurotrain terminal at St Pancras was built. The area was a mass of new glass, concrete facades and barricades. She threaded her way through a maze of temporary pedestrian walkways. The renovations crept up under the arches, transforming the old Victorian warehousing into European-style arcades, boutiques and bistros.

A massive padlock dangled unlocked, from the hasp on the wooden door. She pushed on it but it was fastened from the inside so she rattled it hard instead. A minute later, a bolt slid back on the inside and Heck stuck his head out the door.

"Alice!"

"Hello, Heck," she said. "I tracked you down." She pointed to the little green two-seater G-Wiz behind her.

"What are you doing here?"

"I came to talk to you. Aren't you going to ask me in?"

He looked doubtful, glancing back over his shoulder into the interior, then stood aside to let her in. The first thing she saw in the gloom of the old brick arch cavern, was her father sitting in a canvas deck chair with a mug of tea. The second thing she noticed was a full-size Victorian carousel, the gallopers gleaming under the bare light bulbs.

"A merry-go-round! Is this your big mystery project, Dad?"

George pushed himself up from his deck chair, his pale blue eyes peering at her over his steel-rimmed glasses.

"So you winkled out our hiding place, Alice," he said. "Oh well, we're almost finished. Just putting the final touches to it. What do you think?"

"It's enormous. How will you ever get this out to Africa, Heck?"

"Same way it got in here. It all comes to bits like Lego and then you re-assemble it," he said.

"The old circuses used to put them up and take them down, in every town they visited," said George.

"So is it working or just a giant climbing frame for the kids?"

"Of course, that's what we've been beavering away at all this time. Renovating the whole thing."

"Would you like a ride?" asked Heck. "Test drive it?"

"I haven't been on one of these things since Cassie was a child," said Alice.

"You can be our first customer," said George.

Alice looked at the gaily striped poles and the old calliope, which provided the music, in the middle of the carousel.

"Is it safe?"

"Sure. Go on, pick a horse," said Heck, switching on the old motor that powered the big fairground merry-go-round.

Alice climbed onto the platform and Heck boosted her onto a prancing galloper. "Hang onto this pole," he said, then nodded to George.

"Not too fast, Dad. I'm out of practice with these things," she called. Her father waved and pushed the long lever to engage the motor. The carousel moved forward in slow motion and Heck stepped off to stand by George. The two men stood admiring their handiwork as Alice sailed by, smiling nervously and clutching the shiny brass pole of her horse, as it glided up and down, forward and back.

The calliope churned out one of the tunes from its repertoire, as the horses moved in a stately canter. After a couple of revolutions, Heck called out to her as she passed.

"Faster, Alice?"

She nodded, removing one hand from the brass pole to wave briefly at them. George eased the throttle forward and the horses broke into a gallop, as the music speeded up to keep up with them. Feeling braver, Alice blew them a kiss as she sped by. Heck slowed the carousel motor down long enough to hop up on the step, then mounted the galloper next to her. As they floated past, George opened up the throttle again and they took off, first one horse surging forward then the other, as they passed and re-passed each other. Heck reached across and held out his hand to her and they galloped hand-in-hand round the old railway arch warehouse, the strings of lights under the canopy brightening up the gloom.

George waved at her as she rode past and she tried to conjure up a memory of this old man as her young father, putting her on the merry-go-round, at the Easter Fairs of her childhood on Hampstead Heath. He slowed the apparatus to a halt and Heck lifted her off her horse, holding her briefly before helping her down to ground level.

"Well, do you think those African kids are going to like it, Alice?" grinned George.

"They'll never let you turn it off," she said. "It's magical."

"I guess we're ready to unveil it to Martha and Netta then, before we dismantle it for shipping out to Cassie," said Heck.

Alice stood hugging her father, still caught up in her childhood reverie. "Wouldn't it be wonderful if we could all be there, to see those kids riding round and round," she said.

"Maybe we can," said Heck. "I've been thinking about who is going to re-assemble it out there and George and I know it inside out by now."

Her father nodded in agreement. "Instead of just shipping it, we could accompany it on the freighter. Heck was telling me how most of these boats have a few cabins for passengers." He looked at Alice. "D'you think your mother would like to have a last adventure by sea, before we get too old and decrepit? Perhaps I'll wait until she's had a ride on the gallopers first."

# CHAPTER 49

The little electric G-Wiz pulled up in front of the semi in Tiberius Road and Alice and Heck climbed out. She saw the changes high summer had brought to the garden and grounds as they walked around to the side door.

"You've done a beautiful job of the garden, Heck. I thought you might have let it go since I left," said Alice, trailing her hand along the espaliered fruit trees against the old brick garden wall.

"I did it for you, Alice. I couldn't quite believe you wouldn't change your mind about selling it, when you saw it in full bloom."

"That's what I've come here to talk to you about, Heck."

"Okay. Let's make some tea and we can sit out here while we talk." He led the way into the familiar old kitchen.

Alice followed and felt the same surge of delight she had experienced the first time they discovered the house. She wandered round the spacious room, opening and closing cabinet doors while Heck boiled the kettle. It was going to be a wrench giving all this up, no question and she steeled herself for the difficult words she had to say to this big rumpled man, who had become so much a part of her new life.

Heck made the tea and put it under a tea cosy on the table.

"Shall we make a tour while we're waiting for the tea to steep? We can decide where we want to start disposing of things,"he said.

They went into the living room and Alice looked around at all the familiar pieces left to them by Mrs Hollis. "I don't want to start in here, Heck. It's too hard."

Heck nodded, "Okay, maybe upstairs will be easier." He followed her up the curving elm staircase to the landing and she looked into each of the spare bedrooms in turn.

"I don't want to keep any of this stuff myself, Heck, but you always liked this old brass bedstead." She ran her hand over the dully shining brass rails.

"Where would I put it? I expect I'll just take a furnished flat until I decide where I want to live," he said, moving down the hall to the main bedroom. He stood aside to let her enter and they gazed at the old canopied four-poster that had entranced them both, the first day they discovered it. "Happy days," he said, perching on the side of the bed.

"And nights," said Alice, going round to sit on the opposite side. "Do you still sleep here, Heck?"

He shook his head. "Not since you left. Too many painful memories." He lay back and stared up at the folds of the embroidered canopy. "You used to say it was like being in a boat."

Alice leaned back against the pillows on her side and gazed out the window at the walled garden. Her fantasy garden, except now it was real and she was about to give it up. Along with her life with Heck, she reminded herself. Now was the time to tell him of her decision.

"Heck?" she turned towards him, formulating her speech. He looked at her, waiting, but no words came from her, only tears and he put his arm round her.

"Why do you do this to yourself, Alice? You were so happy here, once."

"I know," she said. "Everything's changed, Heck. It's over and it's not your fault, it's me."

"Nothing's changed for me. I still want you as much as ever, Alice." He drew her to him and lay stroking her back and she exhaled a long sigh.

"If only we could go back to the way things were. But we can't. I have to leave," she said, pulling him even closer.

For several minutes, they lay clinging together until Alice felt him stirring against her. "Do you really still want me, Heck?"

"You know I do, Alice. I've told you enough times that your operation hasn't changed the way I feel about you."

She pulled back to look at his face above her and smiled. "Prove it," she said.

He grinned back at her. "You mean it?"

She nodded and they set about each other like teenagers, rolling and gasping with pent-up longing. She pulled him on top of her and lay back to stare up at the canopy, as she had so many times before when they made love in this magical setting. This is your swansong, she told herself. Enjoy it.

And she did.

Afterwards they lay without speaking, watching the shadows lengthen over the garden below them. Heck held her in the hollow of his arm, his long fingers tracing slow circles round her remaining breast. Now she would tell him, then dress quickly and leave. A clean cleaving apart. Cool as a surgeon's knife. No mess, no fuss. Over and done.

"Heck?" she said, for the second time.

"Mmhmm?"

"I'm having my other breast removed next week. I've made the decision. I don't want to put it off any longer. My test showed positive for the BRCA1 gene and it's only a question of time unless I act now." She avoided looking at him while she spoke but turned to face him when he replied.

"BRC what? – what are you talking about?"

"BRCA1 – it's called the breast cancer gene. The only treatment is removal of my breast before the cancer reaches it." She spoke slowly, disengaging herself from his arm and sat up to reach for her clothes, strewn about the bed and the floor.

"You're having your other breast removed while it's still healthy?" he asked.

"That's not the worst of it," she said, putting on her padded bra. "It's hereditary. I've passed it on to Netta and Cassie."

"Good God!"

"Don't worry, I'm not expecting you to martyr yourself, Heck. I'll live with Martha and George and we can look after each other."

"Have you told them?" he asked.

"What good would that do? It doesn't change anything and it would only cause them unnecessary suffering, knowing their grand-daughters are fated."

"But your mother? Isn't she a carrier? I don't understand...."

"Presumably, but I certainly don't want her to think she's to blame."

"Jesus – where does it all end, Alice?"

Alice finished dressing and combed her hair at the long cheval mirror.

"Lately I've been thinking it's a good thing Netta is infertile. But Cassie…."

# CHAPTER 50

The noise from the Unimog's transmission grew louder and more ominous as they limped into Faranah, not far inside Guinea. Landon stopped at a roadside garage and Barney left them to search for an internet café to check for any news of Cassie. When he finally found one and read Alice's email, he was too stunned to think what to do next. If Cassie's orphanage had been disbanded what would they do with the supplies they had brought all this way? And more important, where had she gone? Would she still be in Kissidougou? Was she alright?

He walked back through the dusty lanes to the garage. Landon and a local mechanic lay prone beneath the truck. Hunter sat on the shady side, leaning against one of the huge wheels. Barney hunched down and relayed to his son the gist of what Alice had written.

"Jesus!" said Hunter. "That's all we need. This guy," he jerked his head to indicate the mechanic's feet protruding out from under the Unimog; "says there's a broken gear or something and he won't be able to fix it until we get a replacement part."

"Where are we going to find one around here?"

"Landon says we're not. We'll have to go to Freetown for it."

Barney slumped down in the dirt beside Hunter and leaned back against the big front tire. "That could take over a week to go there and back."

"More like two weeks, Dad. I've been reading the Lonely Planet and it says the roads in northern Sierra Leone are impossible unless you're in a 4x4. Or on a motorbike."

Landon crawled out from under the truck. "This is going to take a while dismantling the transmission to get the broken part out. I think we need to figure out how we can get to Freetown to order a replacement. I've been there several times to my sister's so maybe I should go." He wiped his left hand using an oily rag he held in the grip of his artificial right hand.

"Okay," said Barney. "I don't want to waste any time hanging around here, waiting for the truck to be fixed. I'm going to go on ahead and look for Cassie. Try to find out what happened and where she went."

"Hunter will have to stay to guard the truck while we're away," said Landon. "Otherwise it'll be stripped bare by the time we come back."

"No way. I'm going to look for Cassie with Dad. We need to find her and make sure she's okay."

"Well, somebody has to stay here," said Landon. "We can't all leave."

Barney peered under the truck at the mechanic. "It would be better if you stayed here to keep an eye on the repairs. At least you understand what's wrong, Landon. Hunter could go for the spare part and meantime, I'll search for Cassie."

"What if she's not in Kissidougou, Dad? I can travel a lot faster than you and track her down a lot quicker. Let Landon stay here in charge, while I go after Cassie and you travel to Freetown for the spare part. We can keep in touch with that internet place you found here."

Although Barney was anxious to go in search of his daughter, he knew Hunter stood a better chance of finding her. His son had knocked around Southeast Asia and was familiar with third world travelling.

The next morning Hunter and Barney left Landon under the Unimog and walked into town to find rides. Hunter squeezed into a battered *sept-place* heading south and left Barney to negotiate the trickier business of finding transport over the border into Sierra Leone. He soon discovered that the guidebook's warning about roads proved accurate. The only 4x4 capable of handling the rough tracks took two days to reach Kabala and had already gone the previous morning. It wouldn't return for at least three days.

The only option was to persuade one of the young local mototaxi bike riders to take him. It was a hard task, as most of them didn't want to cross the border and risk damaging their precious 125cc motorbikes on the washed-out roads. Finally, after wandering round the market area of Faranah asking every motorbike rider he could find, he met Armand, a somber man in his thirties, who agreed to take him across the border for an outrageous amount. They haggled a bit but the man told Barney the only reason he would agree to take the risk was for the money.

On the way out of town, Armand pulled over to point at a small two-room new building on the hillside above them.

"That is my school," he said. "I am a teacher."

"It looks empty," said Barney.

"An NGO from Denmark built it when the old school burned down in the war. But the government delayed teachers' pay month after month and then stopped." Armand's eyes flashed with anger and he kick-started the motorbike savagely. "So finally I had to leave and find a job to feed my family. I am a teacher but now I drive this mototaxi instead. It doesn't even belong to me. My brother-in-law lets me use it and I have to give him half what I earn."

They sped off along the rutted dirt road towards Sierra Leone. The roads to the border were unpaved but not impassable. After a long argument with three border officials who each demanded bribes, Barney managed to get his passport stamped. He rejoined Armand on the back of his little 125cc bike and they tackled what looked like a World War I battlefield, rather than a road.

Large trucks and 4x4s had churned up the track so that ruts became waist deep and Armand simply side-tracked, on footpaths around the worst parts. They wobbled across springy bridges one plank wide, over streams where local women and children filled large yellow plastic palm oil containers with water. All along the track, these bare-breasted women and girls carried the heavy jugs balanced on their heads. Even the small children had gallon cans to carry back to their villages.

Several times Armand stopped at the crest of a hill, to puzzle out how he should proceed. The track plunged down into holes deep enough to swallow a truck. They rode the ridges of the ruts at the risk of toppling down into these mud holes the size of bomb craters. The track had been churned up during the rainy season and now in the dry period, the mud had congealed into ridges resembling a moonscape.

Barney bounced around on the back of the motorbike until he could bear it no longer and pleaded with Armand to stop for a rest. But he would only allow a stop long enough to smoke his cigarette, before he insisted they continue. Hour after hour, they did battle with the ruts and cratered potholes, Barney's back tormenting him with jabbing pains.

At dusk, they arrived on the edge of the northern town of Kabala, where the track levelled out into some semblance of normal dirt road. The Lonely Planet guidebook mentioned the chief's guesthouse and Armand asked several locals, before he found it. The motorbike trip had taken nine hours. Barney could not remember a harder more nerve-wracking ride in all his travels through India, China and Tibet.

He slumped on the porch of the guesthouse, too tired to help Armand untie his rucksack.

"What will you do now, Armand? Have you somewhere to stay here?"

"No. I must get back tonight. My brother-in-law needs the motorbike for tomorrow." He sank down on the porch steps to take the rest of his money from Barney and stuffed it in his shirt pocket.

Barney stared at him in disbelief. "You're not going back to Faranah in the dark, are you?"

He nodded. "I must. I have a light, see?" He switched on the headlight of the motorbike, which threw a feeble beam of light on the porch.

"At least stay and have some food with me," said Barney. "Let me ask where the nearest restaurant is." He climbed with a stiff gait up the porch steps with his rucksack. A young student, one of the chief's grandsons, led him into a room with a mosquito-netted bed. The young man lit a lantern, as there was no electricity in the town. He spoke quite understandable English and led Barney and Armand to a nearby restaurant.

"This place is where all the NGO people eat," he said. "You will like it."

Armand wolfed down a plate of rice and chicken stew but Barney couldn't face anything except a beer and a plate of french fries. Armand refused a beer and drank an orange squash before hurrying out to his waiting motorbike. Barney stood watching him wobble off into the darkened dirt streets of the town, with its ragged rows of winking candles and lamps. He walked stiffly back to the guesthouse and crawled under the mosquito netting, to plunge into an exhausted ten-hour coma. He had seldom been this tired in his life. Could he maintain this level of hard travel all the way to Freetown, he wondered? He felt every one of his seventy-two years. Hunter had been right to insist on searching for Cassie, he thought, as he fell asleep.

In the morning, Barney looked in vain for an internet café but the only one he found, would have no power until the evening. He sat drinking a lukewarm bottle of pop at the NGO restaurant and half-listened to two white-shirted black men sitting nearby. Their white Land Rover with its tall two-way radio mast stood outside the door. They spoke to Barney and told him they were with a reforestation project, with headquarters in the town. He asked if they knew where he could find an internet café. One of them invited him to use his computer at their compound. But after all that, no word had yet come from Hunter, so he left to find the bush-taxi garage on the edge of town.

A young Australian woman in her twenties was setting up her tent in the guesthouse compound when he arrived back later. She told him she had come from Freetown and was heading to Guinea. Barney warned her what lay in store between here and Faranah. They agreed to eat together, at a bar-restaurant near the bush-taxi garage and walked up the dark lanes later that evening, when it had cooled down.

A morose-looking man served them in a distracted manner. The restaurant had several tables but they were the only customers. He had a bar along one wall and assured them he had cold beer. When he brought two cans to their table, they were the usual lukewarm temperature. Marcia, the Australian girl, shrugged her shoulders and pulled the ring tab off.

"This is Africa," she said. She told him what the transport was like between here and the capital. "When you get to Bo, there's a government bus that runs to Freetown but it leaves real early – like 4 am."

Mohammed, the sad-faced owner, cooked and served them a rice and fish stew. No one else appeared to be in the long restaurant bar.

"Do you run this all by yourself?" asked Barney as he paid for the meal.

Mohammed nodded, "This place belong to me and my wife but she die so now I am alone again." He looked to be only middle-aged.

"I'm sorry," said Barney. "How old was she?"

"Nineteen. She die havin' our baby. The baby die too," said Mohammed, wiping off the tablecloth. He straightened up, looking defeated.

"That's terrible." On impulse, Barney put his arms around the man and patted his back. "I'm very sorry, Mohammed."

As they walked back to the guesthouse, Marcia told him how many women died in childbirth in West Africa each year. The numbers shocked Barney. He remembered what the English doctor, Celia, working in The Gambia, had told them about the primitive way young girls were mutilated by circumcision practices.

"Not much of a life for Mohammed's young wife," he said, thinking of his own daughter, Cassie.

The road to Bo was paved in parts and the journey was possible by *sept-place* bush- taxi. After dark, Barney arrived in the city, notorious as the capital of the 'blood diamonds' industry. The unpaved streets were lit only by winking propane lamps from street vendors. Occasional bare light bulbs powered by noisy generators, flickered from the front of larger shops and hotels.

The hotel he chose from the guidebook had no electricity and only bucket showers and squat toilets. They were flushed by a pail of water, carried up to the room by a young girl of about thirteen. He found a café near the hotel, run by Lebanese and had one of the better meals he had experienced so far since entering black Africa. He wandered the darkened streets after eating and promptly got lost. He had to hire a young mototaxi youth to take him back to his hotel. The courtyard was full of white NGO Land Rovers, with their tall radio masts strapped to the front bumpers.

At breakfast, a tall black woman served him fried eggs in the barren roof dining room of the hotel. She brought him instant nescafé, although he had seen shops piled high with sacks of coffee beans the night before. The restaurant held only one heavy-set young man, wearing smart western clothes. He looked middle-eastern, not African. He ignored Barney and read a newspaper while he ate.

The waitress hovered round Barney's table and then sat down opposite him.

"What NGO are you with?" she asked.

"None. I'm just taking some supplies to my daughter. She works with war orphans – amputees."

"Eeehh! I use to teach these children but not anymore." She helped herself to some of Barney's coffee. "Every week more children come out of the bush to our school."

"Were they orphans, too?"

"Many, many orphans. Plenty with no right hand. Chopped off."

Barney listened to this tall black woman who said her name was Azalea, as she told him how her classes swelled to unmanageable numbers.

"Once I had eighty children. Eighty! How can I teach that many children? And only get paid half wages."

"So you are no longer a teacher?"

"I left my village and come to Bo," she said. "I make more money working here in this hotel than I can teaching."

"Do you see your family very often?"

"I send my daughter and her children money every month and I go back to my village once or twice a year."

"You have grandchildren?" asked Barney surprised. "How old are you?"

"Forty-eight," said Azalea. "I have plenty of grandchildren. How many you have?"

"None," admitted Barney.

It was Azalea's turn to look disbelieving. "An old man like you and no grandchildren? Why not?"

"I started late. I was over 35 when my first son was born. My children are still not ready to settle down, I guess."

"Thirty-five! I was a grandmother when I was thirty-five." Azalea changed tack. "Why you way over here in Africa, instead of at home with your family – an old man like you?"

"I told you. I'm looking for my daughter in Guinea. Her orphanage is near Kissidougou."

Azalea frowned at him. "You can't go to Guinea this way. The roads is closed for a long time now."

Barney grinned, "I just came from there – by mototaxi. Nearly killed me. It took me nine hours from Faranah to Kabala"

Azalea hooted with laughter and the stout young man glanced over at them. "You hear that?" she called to him. "This old man come through the bush from Faranah – by motorbike."

"I was only a passenger – I didn't drive," said Barney.

"He lookin' for his daughter in Guinea," she said. The man lowered his newspaper and Barney saw it was in some Arabic script.

"Why are you in Bo if she's in Guinea?" he asked in perfect English.

Barney explained about the breakdown and how his son was searching for Cassie, while he went to Freetown. The young man, who said his name was Suleiman, invited Barney to join him for some real Lebanese coffee, at his store in town. He appeared to know Azalea well and she pocketed his money without writing him a bill.

As they walked down the unpaved streets of this, the second largest city in Sierra Leone, Barney was jostled by throngs of street vendors. Young men in ragged tee-shirts pushed barrows loaded with huge sacks.

"Coffee beans," said Suleiman. "Undrinkable stuff. I have decent coffee – imported from Lebanon."

"Is that what you do?" asked Barney. "Import coffee?"

"No," said Suleiman, pointing up at a sign in front of them. It read 'Crescent Diamond Merchants.' Beneath the sign stood an enormous gleaming silver Hummer.

"Is that yours?" asked Barney and the stout young man nodded.

"One of them. I only use it when I go upcountry to our mines. I have a Mercedes here in Bo. Much more comfortable."

Inside the inner office in the store, one of Suleiman's workers appeared, with a tray holding a pot of strong Lebanese coffee and small cups. He set it down in front of Barney and poured some out. As they sat drinking, Suleiman explained the convoluted workings of the diamond business and how it was mainly run by the Lebanese. They paid the government a percentage and were given a free hand to operate in the country. Suleiman's grandfather owned the company and his father ran it, with Suleiman as the trainee learning the ropes.

"Do you keep any of the diamonds here?" asked Barney, pouring more of the powerful coffee.

For answer, the young man swivelled his heavy body round in his chair to open a small safe. He took out a cloth bag with a drawstring and casually poured out its contents onto a tray on his big mahogany desk. Barney was disappointed at how insignificant they looked, like tiny chips of dull broken glass.

"Not very shiny for diamonds, are they?"

"These are mainly industrial diamonds – unpolished," he said. "We don't do any cutting or polishing here. That's all done in Amsterdam. My father takes them there once a month."

"And you're in charge of the business here?" asked Barney. "It seems pretty quiet."

Suleiman poured the diamonds back into the bag and returned it to the safe. He drank off his coffee and leaned back in his chair.

"Bo's not so bad once you get used to it. My friends have lots of house parties and girls fly out from Lebanon or London to visit. I went to university in London. When I'm not visiting the mines, I go out with them – there's some good Lebanese restaurants around. Would you like to eat with us tonight?"

"I already tried one last night – best food I've had in Africa. But I have to get to Freetown and take the new transmission part back to Faranah. I'm very worried about my daughter since we heard the orphanage was disbanded," said Barney.

"How old is she?"

"Twenty-two," said Barney, handing him a small photo from his wallet.

"Same age as me," said Suleiman. "And she has been working with these war orphans, in the refugee camps in Guinea?"

"For nearly a year. I encouraged her to come to Africa but now I'm not so sure. That's why I want to find her and see she's okay."

Suleiman handed back the photo. "The guerrillas up north are disbanded fighters from the civil war. I have to deal with them all the time – armed boy gangs, out to get what they can. They cross back and forth over the borders between Cote d'Ivoire, Guinea and Sierra Leone, whenever the army chases them." He nodded at the photo Barney held. "She is in a dangerous place in Kissidougou – so near the border."

Barney put the photo back in his wallet. "My son is looking for her now. But I haven't heard from him yet."

"Nothing works in the north – no roads, electricity, internet, phones – everything destroyed in the war. This country could be rich but the government and police are corrupt so nothing gets rebuilt. Like Lebanon," said Suleiman.

Barney rose from the low leather couch to say goodbye.

"I must catch a bus to Freetown. You have made me even more worried, if what you say is true."

"All they want is food and money," said Suleiman, shaking his hand. "And liquor. In the villages, they steal the young girls, too. I don't understand. Why did you let her go to such a place?"

Barney shook his head. "That's what my wife said, too. I didn't realise the danger and she wanted to go. She's over eighteen so I couldn't stop her. But now I have to find this spare part and get back to my truck."

"When you come back to Bo, maybe I can help," said Suleiman. "I have many contacts up north. And in Freetown, too." He wrote on a card on his desk and handed it to Barney. "This man will be able to find your truck part if you show him this card. He handles all our equipment buying and importing."

"Thank you, Suleiman. I'll phone him as soon as I arrive."

Suleiman frowned. "Tomorrow is Saturday. Monthly cleanup day in Freetown. Be careful. Take a taxi and don't walk."

"Why not?"

"The police force everyone to clean the streets and gutters. A law the government passed, so they don't have to pay anyone. People get very angry at this dirty work – especially young men."

"Okay, thanks for the warning," said Barney. They left the cool inner office and went outside into the heat of midday.

"What is your daughter's name?" asked Suleiman.

"Cassie. Cassie Roper."

"Cassie." He hesitated, then said, "If you give me her photo I will copy it and ask some of my men to make enquiries, when I go north to the mines in a few days."

Barney handed him the photo and waited while the stout young Lebanese returned to his inner office. He watched young black men loading the enormous coffee sacks and bags of swamp rice onto their handcarts. He wondered why there where no draft animals – no horses, donkeys, oxen – only human power.

Suleiman reappeared, handed him back the photo and they shook hands once again. The young man heaved himself up into the passenger seat of the huge silver Hummer and his driver reversed out into the crowded filth-strewn street.

# CHAPTER 51

The first time that Barney had ridden in such comfort since he entered black Africa, occurred on the government bus from Bo to Freetown. One person per seat was unheard of before this. Each time the driver stopped at a town or village, the bus was mobbed by local vendors selling oranges, small bananas, sugar cane sticks and handfuls of hard boiled eggs. At one stop, he was negotiating with a woman for two eggs when a shout went up and the people scattered towards the thatched huts. An open truck full of uniformed police pulled up, who jumped down to give chase, whacking everybody in sight with long bamboo canes.

Everyone on the bus became very agitated and angry, shouting out the windows at the police. Barney watched a young man selling mobile phone cards, from a wooden booth the size of a telephone box. The man gathered up all his wares from the shelf and ducking down inside, pulled the hatch closed to wait out the attack.

"What's happening?" he asked a serious-looking black man sitting next to him.

"Cleaning Day. No business until cleaning is done. These people have refused and the police are punishing them," he said. A barricade had been set up across the road in protest and the police corralled several men to drag it to one side, while everyone shouted abuse at them.

The bus rolled on towards Freetown without further delays but the driver announced he would not go downtown because of Cleaning Day. He stopped somewhere in the outskirts of the capital and everyone got out. Barney and the serious-looking man shared a taxi, to take them to the beach area where Landon's sister lived. As he walked down the lane staring up at the houses, he missed his footing over an open ditch and fell forward, scraping his leg from ankle to knee.

He pulled his foot free of the oozing sewage and stared at the blood seeping through the slime and mud on his leg. A short fat woman appeared on the crumbling balcony above and called down to him. It was Landon's sister, Ama and she'd been expecting him for two days, since getting a message from her brother. She sent several children down to help Barney up the stairs and carry his bag. Another child brought a pail of water and Ama swabbed all the mess from his leg, which continued to bleed.

. He perched on the edge of the rusty bathtub and Ama squatted beside him. "That feel better now?" she asked, dabbing at his leg with a wet cloth.

"It hurts like hell. I think I should put some disinfectant on it," he said and searched through his bag for his first aid kit.

"Cleanin' Day but nobody touch that drain again. It always end up me havin' to do it," said Ama. "My gran'children play in that filthy water even though I say not to." She heaved her huge breasts back under cover as they slid out from the top of her vast boubou.

"I got to go out to my church meetin'," she said, rising, "otherwise I cook you some food."

"Don't worry about me, I'll go out later and find a café," said Barney. "I saw one as I came down your street."

"This street not safe after dark," said Ama. "You needs a flashlight to see."

"I'll be careful," promised Barney. He felt annoyed with himself for his accident, confirming to everyone that he was an old man who needed looking after. Ama shook her head doubtfully.

"Bijou can go with you – show you the way. I got to get dressed now."

While Barney slathered disinfectant cream on his leg and wrapped a large clean handkerchief around it to keep off the flies, the children hovered round him. He counted six of them, with a couple of others that may have been from the neighbours. Ama reappeared, dressed in her church finery and knotted headscarf, her wayward bosom firmly under control.

"I got time to walk up to the rest'rant with you if we leaves now," she said.

Barney limped along beside her as she sailed up the road. "Landon told me a lot about you, Ama. He's hoping you'll come to live with him at his place outside Freetown."

"An' I'll be glad to get out of this dangerous place," she nodded. "Not be worryin' about all my gran'children. I jus' hope he get here soon."

Ama left him at a small café bar at the top of her street. Loud rap music poured out of the open front of the café and a menu was scrawled above the bar. Barney ordered some chicken and rice and sat down outside at a long table with his bottle of beer. Several people chatted together in the loud emphatic way he had become familiar with in West Africa. A young black woman sat across from Barney, eating fried fish and drinking a beer. She smiled at him and they exchanged the usual traveller's remarks. She spoke a curious mix of French and Sierra Leone English patois. Her name was Fatmeh, she said and she worked for an NGO that rescued children who had been stolen and sold into servitude and slavery.

"Does that sort of thing still go on in Africa?" asked Barney.

Fatmeh assured him it did. "My son was stolen by these people two years ago. That's how I got into this work. The NGO help me trace him."

"And is he back with you now?"

"He's with my mother back in our village. Near Laba."

"Isn't that in Guinea?"

She nodded, "That's right. I am Guinea woman, not from Sierra Leone."

"Aren't you worried it might happen again?" asked Barney. The waitress brought him his food and asked if they wanted another beer. "Would you like another, Fatmeh?" She nodded and he ordered two more. While he ate, she told him her dilemma.

"My mother told me those people come back to our village lookin' for more children. She said they promisin' good homes and a real school and pay money each month."

"What do they want the children for?"

"They say only to help in rich people's houses but once they buy these children the family never see them again. I been away from my village for eighteen months, savin' money to go back home and look after my son – teach parents all about these evil people."

"When are you going home – soon?" asked Barney.

"I'm set to go last month, till someone stole my purse," said Fatmeh. "I lose all my bus fare to Laba, my cell phone, my ID. Everythin'." She wiped her mouth with her hand. "Now I got to start all over."

"Didn't you go to the police?"

Her eyes widened in anger. "Eeehh! Police - they won't do anythin'. All they after is bribe. I say I not payin' any bribes and they tell me to go away. They say they might arres' me because I don't have my papers. Illegal immigrant."

"Have you been to the Guinean embassy? Maybe they can help you," said Barney.

She shook her head, her long plait of glistening black hair swinging. "They tell me I need a *lettre passeé* but first I must have a statement from the police, sayin' my documents stolen." Her large brown eyes filled. "I jus' want to go home and look after my son."

"How old is he?"

"Nine. My mother says he gettin' too big for her to manage. She says I need to come home and keep him out of trouble."

"I have to go down to the harbour tomorrow to find my friend's boat," said Barney, "maybe I can ask him to help. He's been here for awhile now and probably knows his way around."

"I can meet you here tomorrow after work. Thank you for helpin' my son." She clasped his hand and he patted hers, unsure what help he could offer.

Next morning Ama insisted on finding the right kind of taxi for Barney. "You don't take them private ones – charge you the earth."

His driver picked up and dropped off several others along the way towards the harbour. The traffic clogged the unpaved streets and drivers honked and shouted at each other, detouring down narrow lanes to avoid the blockages. As they neared the port, he spotted many of the old wooden colonial houses. They were all in dilapidated condition but he could see how elegant they once must have been.

At the docks, he stared out at the boats, trying to spot *The Betsy*. A tall, two-masted old schooner lay anchored in the harbour and he realised it must be the '*Amistad*' that had so inspired Clive. *The Betsy* was moored near the schooner and he could make out someone moving around on deck. He shouted a few times but the wind was onshore and the person paid no attention.

A burly man, wearing only oily shorts, poled his battered tin boat past and Barney called him over. He pointed to *The Betsy* and the man swung his boat expertly round at the dock, motioning Barney to jump in. In ten minutes, they pulled alongside Clive's old yacht. He had gone below, so Barney paid the man and climbed aboard, calling.

"Clive! – you there?"

"Barney? What the hell are you doing here?" Clive's head stuck up through the hatchway. "Come on down, I've just made some coffee."

"Not instant, I hope," Barney hugged his old friend and felt the angular metal brace beneath Clive's loose shirt. "You still wearing that harness?"

Clive stood unnaturally straight, held by the brace for his broken collarbone. "Yeah, the doc here said I should keep it on for a while longer."

They drank Clive's local grown coffee with its harsh strong flavour and Barney gave him a run-down on their trip and why he had to come to Freetown. He took the small broken gear from his rucksack and unwrapped it to show Clive. "You think I can get one of these here?"

"Possible, I suppose, but more likely they'll have to fly it in from Dakar. I don't know much about four-wheel drives, only marine diesels. Nice and simple – forward and back, that's it. Tell me more about Cassie. Have you heard – is she safe?"

Barney shook his head glumly. "No news since I left Faranah. Hunter's trying to pick up her trail and went on ahead, while I came here for the broken spare part. Landon's sleeping in the Unimog and standing guard till I get back." He dug out the card Suleiman had given him. "I got this contact to start with."

"Let's go into town and order your new gear. I know an internet place that usually has power from their own generator. You can check to see if Hunter's emailed you."

"There's one other thing," said Barney. "I met this young Guinean woman last night..."

"Jesus, Barney – don't tell me. You arrive in town and get mixed up with a woman on your first night."

"It's not like that, Clive. She's in trouble and asked me to help. The police are giving her a hard time and I said you might be able to suggest something."

"Me? Don't pass her on to me. I got enough problems of my own – stuck here with a broken neck and can't sail my boat anywhere since Lottie left me."

"Lottie's gone? Where?"

"She flew back to Dakar. Apparently, she knows lots of people there in the music business. She got bored sitting around here with an old invalid, so I told her to go."

Barney outlined Fatmeh's story briefly to Clive and her problems getting her papers replaced, because of police obstruction. Clive thought the best plan was for both of them to accompany her to the police station and get the necessary document for the Guinean embassy.

"They're always looking for bribes," he said. You pay and after that it should be simple enough."

"I hope you're right. She claims they've been pissing her about for over a month, threatening to jail her as an illegal immigrant."

"Hmmnn. How old did you say she was?" asked Clive.

"I don't know – she's got a nine year old boy. Twenty-five maybe."

"Is she small or big and strong?"

"What? Neither. She's tall and slim. Why?"

"Good. That's better than fat. She can move about faster." Clive paced up and down the cabin. "I've got an idea that might suit all of us. Want to hear it?"

Barney nodded, "Shoot."

"Okay. Suppose this girl – what'd you say her name was – Fatima?"

"Fatmeh."

"Fatmeh. Right. Suppose Fatmeh takes Lottie's place on board and helps me sail *The Betsy* out of here and up to Conakry in Guinea. We help her find a bush-taxi to Laba, then sail back here to collect your spare part."

"What about the police and her documents?"

"Forget it. They could mess you about for weeks. We bypass them. Once we're in Conakry, it's obvious she's Guinean – she speaks the local French dialect. We explain she lost her ID and pay for a new one. What d'you think?"

"It might work, I guess," said Barney. "I'm seeing her tonight after work. I can bring her down to meet you on the boat."

They went ashore in Clive's dinghy and spent the rest of the day prowling round garages, showing the damaged gear and meeting only shaking heads. By five in the afternoon, they still had found nothing. Suleiman's contact could not be reached. Barney left to meet with Fatmeh but Clive said he had one or two more contacts to check and would buy some fish to cook for them all onboard, later.

That night they ate fish stew and jollof rice, a Guinean dish that Fatmeh insisted on preparing for them. After dinner, they sat on deck drinking beer and hatching their plan to spirit her out of the country, without the police and customs finding out. Clive had had some partial success locating the spare part. A mechanic he met, knew of a crashed army Unimog they could possibly cannibalise but it would take him a few days to do it.

"Meantime, we can sail to Conakry, drop Fatmeh off and return to Freetown, to a great spot I visited by local bus – Lakka Beach. I can anchor off there and recuperate on *The Betsy* till you get back from delivering Cassie's arms and legs. By that time," said Clive, "I should be out of this harness and me and you can sail back to Canada. How does that sound?"

"Maybe you both come with me to my village and meet my son Nabil," said Fatmeh. "My mother be very happy to meet you."

"What will people in your village say when you turn up with two old white men?" asked Barney. "They might get the wrong idea."

Fatmeh laughed her infectious throaty laugh. She was in a happy mood for once and her usual sad demeanour had vanished. "Eeehh! They will say I am very lucky."

Two nights later, the man with the old tin boat ferried Fatmeh out after dark to *The Betsy*. Clive and Barney had cleared with the harbour master to leave at dawn. They smuggled Fatmeh below.

"You'll have to share the forward cabin with Barney," said Clive. "I have to lie flat on my back with this thing and those bunks are too narrow for me. Also I warn you, he snores like a hog."

Fatmeh's eyes filled with tears. "I don't care. He can snore all he likes. If not for him I would never see my son, Nabil." She threw her arms round Barney's neck and he patted her back reassuringly.

"This was all Clive's idea, Fatmeh. It's his boat."

She turned to Clive and embraced him too.

"Now let's all get some sleep," Clive said. "We want to be gone before dawn and not have any last minute inspections."

Barney lay awake in the dark, aware of the sleeping form of Fatmeh, a foot away from him on the other bunk. The thought of a dawn raid made him nervous and he turned from one side to the other. A cool hand reached across and stroked his back. He turned over and her hand slid down over his pot belly and touched him lightly. To his surprise, he felt himself become rigid and erect with anticipation. A moment later, she slipped onto his bunk, her slim narrow form easily fitting beside him.

"Fatmeh, you don't have to do this," he said with reluctance.

"I want to, Barney," she answered, continuing to stroke him.

"Oh god," he sighed, giving in to the surge of desire inflamed by her touch. He lifted her on top of him and she smoothly slid him inside her, pressing her firm body against him. He lay almost unbelieving, his hands roving over her soft velvet skin, the long glistening skein of hair, wondering if it were real. His hand touched the short tight curls surrounding her cleft and she squeezed him with her thigh muscles. He tried to spin out the moments, not wanting it to end, stopping her movements when it became unbearable but at length he came, clutching her frantically and almost crying with delight.

She lay on top of him, drawing his hand away when he wanted to bring her to orgasm. His mind flew back to the stories the Englishwoman, Celia, told of the circumcision rituals of young black girls. He wanted to ask her if she had this happen to her.

"Fatmeh, when you were a young girl, did they…" he searched for the right word. "Did they – cut you, down here?" He touched the wiry curls lightly.

She nodded her head on his chest, saying nothing. He could think of no suitable reply and stared at the cabin roof, where the hatch let in the light from the stars in the clear African night. He stroked her firm velvet skin, feeling his erection de-tumesce and slip slowly out of her body.

A thought he had been suppressing all during their coupling rose unbidden - AIDS. Everywhere he went in West

Africa, billboards warned in graphic terms of the danger of this disease, now reaching epidemic proportions throughout the continent. How could he have been so irresponsible, he wondered? What if she were HIV positive? Would she even know? He lay holding her, calmly stroking her body while some part of his brain wrestled with the consequences of his lapse of judgment.

It was too late now. The deed was done. He only half-regretted it and wondered if it had been worth the risk. How many men his age would have succumbed in his circumstances? It surprised him that he was still capable, it had been so long since he had been with a woman. He drifted off into a troubled sleep, Fatmeh still resting on his chest.

The trip to Conakry and back to Lakka Beach near Freetown took a little over a week. Ashore, Barney put Fatmeh in a bush-taxi to Laba, promising that he and Clive would try to visit her and her son before he left West Africa. She had melted into the busy port traffic in Conakry to wait for him, while he and Clive cleared customs. After he had made sure she was safely on her way home, Barney spent a fruitless two hours searching for a VD clinic, to get himself tested for possible HIV infection. Nobody could direct him to one, so he returned to the boat. Although Clive suggested staying in Guinea for a few days, Barney told him he had to get back and find the elusive spare part for the Unimog.

Lakka Beach, a few miles outside of Freetown was all that Clive had described. They anchored offshore among the local fishing boats and came ashore to eat at one of the outdoor barbeque cafés, dotted along the blinding white beach. A group of three Italians sat under one of the thatched parasols, eating shellfish and barracuda kebabs and drinking beer.

They were from a nearby clinic run by *Médecins sans Frontières* and said they had been there for nearly three years. Their clinic boasted a small operating theatre with immunizing facilities for the local people.

Barney and Clive ate a pile of fish kebabs before taking the local bush-taxi into Freetown. At one of the villages, Barney recognised the name the apprentice called out and dragged Clive off the minibus.

"Ama told me this is where Landon's compound is," said Barney. "I'd better have a look before I go back to Faranah, so I can report to him."

They asked around and a small girl led them down a side lane in the village to a thick bamboo-hedged compound. Inside, a very old woman bent over a raised area, hoeing potatoes. She told them her son looked after the place for Landon and lived in one of the half dozen thatched huts dotted around the compound. She proudly pointed to a large circular woven thatched roof building in the middle of the property and said her son had built it for Landon.

"Schoolroom," she said.

It was totally open on all sides and stood on braced poles dug into the hard-packed ground. The son had gone to Freetown, so Barney took a few pictures and they left to look for Suleiman's contact downtown. This time they were in luck. The man had heard from Suleiman and sent one of his staff to locate the spare gear. He had a delivery going to Bo and told Barney he could have a ride in their vehicle, if he came back tomorrow morning.

On the way back to the boat, Clive went ahead and Barney visited the Italian doctors' clinic. He hadn't told Clive and didn't want to – he couldn't face the ridicule he felt sure Clive would dish out for his stupidity.

One of the young doctors listened without comment to his story and then offered to test him for HIV. He could process the test in their own small lab. Barney waited with rising anxiety while the doctor went off to the lab. He returned a half hour later with the result.

"Nothing," he said. "Negative."

Barney breathed in several deep breaths, feeling the relief spread through him.

"Of course, we cannot be sure until we do a follow-up test in a month's time," said the young Italian doctor, who looked to Barney to be about eighteen. "If that also shows negative, then you're probably clear."

"A month," said Barney slumping down again in his chair. "But I have to leave for Guinea tomorrow. I don't know exactly when I'll be back here."

The young Italian shrugged. "No problem. You can have the test done anywhere in West Africa – there are plenty of AIDS clinics all over."

Barney thanked him and returned to *The Betsy*, to absorb this disturbing piece of information. He would just have to sweat out this next month in a state of permanent anxiety. And if at the end it proved to test HIV positive – what then?

He spent a restless night in the narrow bunk he had so recently been sharing with Fatmeh, agonising over his future.

Where were all his Buddhist principles now, he asked himself, in a mire of self-pity.

# CHAPTER 52

Hunter sat in the small airless room in the internet café trying to find the words which would convey the urgency of his situation without unduly alarming his father and step-mother. He had been in Africa for nearly three weeks, searching for his sister. He found her old refugee camp easily but it took over a week to follow the trail she and the orphan refugees had taken, moving from one village to another, seeking a safe haven. He had been too stunned at first to do much serious filming, appalled at the horrific injuries the children had suffered.

It seemed to him too inhuman simply to record their pain without first engaging with them somehow. He came upon some off-duty western aid workers on a nearby NGO agriculture project, kicking a football about and persuaded them to lend it to him for a while. Back in the children's camp, he coaxed a listless group of small orphans to join him in a game of kick about. He gradually gained their confidence, setting up opportunities for them to score goals between the tin can posts and clowning around in attempts to make them laugh. Soon they were seeking him out and leading him by the hand to play ball with them each afternoon.

In the mornings, he followed Cassie about documenting her work in the refugee camp and often putting his video camera aside to help her with the children. He was alarmed at how thin and drawn she looked and secretly worried what Alice would think when she saw his footage.

Cassie had become expert in first-aid and field dressings and he filmed her calming and soothing these traumatised children, speaking her few words and phrases of their local dialect she had picked up in the camp. At first, he assumed she was so thin because of the strain of overwork but when he came upon her vomiting in the open latrines behind the tents, he began to worry that she had contracted some kind of virus or infection.

"It's nothing, Hunter," she assured him. "Just some low-level flu bug – it comes and goes. I've had it for ages and it never amounts to anything."

"Have you told Raoul?"

"No, really it's not worth bothering him with – he's got far too much to deal with here as it is."

He didn't pursue it until a few days later, she wasn't at her usual post and he went looking for her. He found her in her sleeping tent with a fever and incoherent. Raoul, the Cuban doctor with *Médecins sans Frontière* was in the camp and he rushed off to find him. He sat writing up his notes in a tent full of kids lying on camp beds. Hunter tried to explain what had happened but couldn't find the right words and urged him to see her straight away.

The doctor began gathering some things from his bag. He spent over half an hour examining Cassie, taking blood and urine samples, questioning her while Hunter waited outside. He came out eventually to explain in halting English what he suspected. Cassie had lost a lot of fluid and was very dehydrated from the vomiting and diarrhoea, which it transpired she had evidently picked up in the camp some time ago. She had some form of gastroenteritis and although he couldn't be sure until he had the test results, probably a liver infection too – most likely hepatitis – it was endemic in the refugee camps, he said.

"How long will the tests take?" asked Hunter.

"We have no lab here in the camp. I will have to send them to Kissidougou."

"Can I do anything meanwhile?"

"I will give you some rehydrating salts and you can try to get as much fluid into her as you can. Keep her cool and bathe her face and arms. I will ask Grace to look in on her when she finishes with the morning clinic."

"Should I try to feed her anything?"

"No, only liquids for now." He shoved back the tent flap and left.

Hunter spent the next few days learning how to nurse his step-sister. Grace, the big black nurse showed him how to care for her and looked in on them whenever she had a chance. The tests came back and confirmed what the Cuban had suspected. He started Cassie on a course of antibiotics but Hunter could see no improvement in her condition.

She had periods of lucidness when she recognized him and would talk animatedly about the camp and her life here with Zinadine, before lapsing back into bouts of fever and vomiting. At times, fluid poured from both ends of her and he fled to Grace and the Cuban doctor for help. Raoul stood over Cassie's cot and shook his head.

"I think you must move her. She is not responding to the basic drugs we have here. Probably more tests will be needed – we cannot do them anywhere around here."

Hunter found a contact number in Cassie's belongings for Zinadine, who was off in northern Guinea. He caught a lift into the nearest town and phoned Zinadine's office to leave a message. Someone said they would contact Zinadine that evening and tell him what had happened to Cassie. Hunter made them promise to explain she must be moved out of the camp urgently. He walked the three kilometres back to the refugee camp, where a young amputee called Ahmed waited for him. He seemed to have appointed himself Cassie's protector.

Eighteen hours later, Zinadine arrived in a long-wheelbase Land Rover. The rear seat had been removed and a stretcher bed was in the back.

"Hunter! What happened?" The two of them shook hands and then embraced. They had not seen each other since Hunter's release from prison in London a year ago. Hunter found the Cuban doctor and Raoul briefly outlined to Zinadine in French what treatment Cassie had received. He wrote a letter for him to pass to the hospital in Laba.

Cassie was in one of her lucid spells when Zinadine went in to see her. They spent a quarter of an hour alone, before he finally emerged to help Hunter fetch the stretcher from the Land Rover. Grace supervised the transfer of Cassie to the stretcher and then to the back of the vehicle, where she squatted beside her on a pile of cushions and blankets.

Hunter packed his rucksack and video camera and went to say goodbye to Raoul, the Cuban doctor and thank him for his help.

"We shall miss Cassie – especially the children. *Bonne chance.*"

Hunter rode in front with Zinadine, who drove as fast as he dared over the pot-holed road. He swore in frustration each time they were held up by street markets in towns and slow moving vehicles in the country. They stopped only for hurried drinks and snacks and to refuel the Land Rover from jerry cans strapped to the roof rack. The big nurse plied Cassie with rehydrating fluids she had brought from her closely guarded hoard. It was dark when they arrived in Laba and Zinadine had to ask repeatedly for directions to the hospital.

By the time Cassie was ensconced in a small room on her own and had been seen by the resident staff doctor, it was nearly midnight. They had taken more samples and would do more tests in the morning. There was nothing to do except wait now, so Hunter found a cheap hotel near the hospital. He slept as though drugged and woke late the following morning. Zinadine was staying with a friend and was already at the hospital when Hunter arrived.

"I've spoken to two of the doctors here and they both say the same thing," he told Hunter. "Cassie would be better off back in England or France. They are doing some tests but so far they agree with Raoul, that she has some complicating problem that they are unlikely to identify here. What do you think, Hunter, shall we take her back to London?"

"Is she well enough to travel right away?"

"They want to observe her for twenty-four hours and then they'll decide but they said we could go ahead and make arrangements," said Zinadine. "If you try to get in touch with your parents, I'll see when we can get a flight out of here."

"Will you come back with her, Zinadine?"

"Of course. I've already arranged for my project manager to send out someone to take over my duties while I'm away."

"Cassie told me you were practically a one-man operation and that's why she hardly saw you anymore."

"Nobody's irreplaceable, Hunter. By the time she's back on her feet again, she'll be sick of the sight of me." Zinadine grinned at Hunter and the two men allowed themselves the luxury of looking ahead to when Cassie might be back to normal. They separated to get on with their tasks and agreed to meet back at Cassie's bedside later in the day.

During this waiting period, Grace told Hunter and Zinadine what had happened, after they fled the refugee camp near Kissidougou.

"That girl save my life – an' Raoul too, sure enough," she said. "I tol' her to stay with the children, coz I knew what them boy gangs do with young girls like her. But she insist she comin' back with me to pay the ransom for Raoul."

"Where did she get the money?" asked Hunter.

"She still had some of them travellin' cheques so she cash them and bring two hundred dollars herself. She wouldn't let me go alone. That gang leader might take the money and then not let Raoul go if she not there." Grace wiped her eyes with her large hands. "I told her not to come but she don't listen."

Zinadine stared at Hunter. "She told me nothing about this."

Grace nodded. "That's right. She don't like to talk about it to nobody – not even me and that girl like a child to me."

Apparently what the big nurse feared might happen, occurred. The gang leader had arrived at the deserted camp the next morning with a tired and frightened Raoul, to demand the money. He released Raoul when Cassie gave him the money, then took her with him at gunpoint back over the border to their camp.

For three days she nursed the wounded man and tried to fend off the gang members, saying she was with the gang leader. Each night he would come to her in the darkness, was all that she ever told Grace. The big nurse said nothing of this to Zinadine but privately told Hunter of his sister's ordeal.

The army patrols were getting nearer each day and when the gang decided to move camp on the fourth day, they could only move slowly, carrying the wounded man. A patrol ambushed them and they all fled, dropping the invalid and leaving him with Cassie. The army took her to the Guinea border and handed her over to the police. She never heard what happened to the wounded man but Grace had no doubt the army patrol had executed him after Cassie left.

Zinadine held his head in his hands. Hunter sat stunned at this news.

Two days later, they were in Dakar, staying at the home of one of Zinadine's friends from university. He had found an empty aid cargo plane, returning to the coast for another load and bribed the pilot to take them with him. Grace was reluctant to hand over her charge but Zinadine promised to follow her instructions to the letter. She coached him and Hunter in her transit care. She returned to the temporary refugee camp and her troupe of amputee orphans.

In Dakar, a Senegalese doctor pronounced Cassie fit enough for the onward journey after a few days rest. Zinadine again went off with all their passports, to book a flight to

London. Hunter found an internet café and warned his parents of their impending arrival in two or three days. He tried to prepare them for the shock of seeing their youngest child so ill, without frightening them unduly. The last he had heard from Barney, was that he had found a spare gear for the Unimog. He was returning to Faranah where Landon waited with the 4x4. He hoped his email would catch him before he started back.

At least Alice was in London and so was his step-sister, Netta. He decided to ask Netta if she would meet them when they arrived and arrange for Cassie to be admitted to hospital by their family doctor. Zinadine would send her the flight details as soon as he had found a plane. He emailed Alice they would be in London soon and she could be at the hospital when they arrived. She could get the details from Netta.

He and Zinadine decided to look after Cassie between them and not try to admit her to hospital in Dakar. Hospitals were dangerous places and she would probably pick up some further bug in her weakened condition. His friend's house was clean, with a roof terrace overlooking the sea. They rigged up an awning over Cassie's cot on the roof and took turns sitting with her, while they waited for their departure flight.

She was over the worst of the bouts of fever now. They coaxed her to eat small portions of a soup prepared by the ancient grandmother of Zinadine's friend. Although Cassie tired easily, she wanted to attempt sitting up for part of each day in preparation for the plane journey to London. Zinadine had booked a wheelchair to meet them at the airport for when they left and again when they arrived in London.

"What a shame to be here in Dakar and not be able to enjoy it," said Cassie.

"It'll still be here when you get back," answered Zinadine. "We'll hit every club in town, I promise."

Cassie smiled wanly. "The way I feel now, I don't think I could ever dance again. Maybe mother was right and I just don't have the stamina for life in Africa."

"We'll see, we'll see," he said but a worried expression crossed his normally smiling face.

"There'll be an awful lot of disappointed kids if you decided not to come back," said Hunter. "Besides, I've only started my film."

The Senegalese doctor came for a last visit on the morning of their departure and wrote them a note for the flight crew, declaring her fit to travel. They wheeled her on to the plane and the flight attendant settled her between them, in one of the three-passenger bulkhead window seats. By folding up the armrests, it was possible for Cassie to lie down if she felt unwell. They could take turns standing or sitting in an empty seat nearby. She dozed most of the way, leaning her head first on Zinadine's shoulder and then on Hunter's, as the airplane ploughed up the coast of Africa, over the Canaries to England.

# CHAPTER 53

A worried Netta, clutching her fiancé Philip's arm, met them as they cleared customs at Heathrow, pushing a dazed Cassie in the wheelchair through the arrivals hall. The two sisters clung to each other awkwardly, with Netta hanging over the wheelchair.

Cassie smiled but said little, contenting herself with holding Netta's hand, as Zinadine wheeled her over to a row of seats, away from the passengers pouring out of customs.

"Doctor Neilson has ordered an ambulance to take you to the Royal Free Hospital," said Netta, "but only one person is allowed to ride with you, Cassie. I've persuaded Mother to meet you there. Would you like me to come with you? Hunter and Zinadine can go with Philip in our car. The ambulance men are waiting right outside."

Philip touched her elbow. "Let Cassie choose, Netta."

"Of course, of course – sorry, I only –"

"Would you mind if Zinadine rode with me, Netta? We need to rehearse what we're going to tell Mother." She gripped Zinadine's hand and smiled at him. He tried to return her smile but looked a bit nervous at the prospect of meeting Alice again.

Hunter laughed. "Zinadine's a little gun-shy at the thought of seeing Alice. He's afraid she's going to tear him off a strip."

"No she won't – we'll stick together," said Cassie and she raised their joined hands to the others.

"Good, that's settled. Hunter can ride with us and give me all the news," said Netta, linking her arm through her step-brother's. She led the way to the waiting ambulance and the others followed with the wheelchair and the luggage.

On the ride back into the city, Philip drove and Netta and Hunter sat in the back seat, while she quizzed him on a hundred details of their trip and what the doctors had really said about Cassie's illness.

"How bad is it, Hunter? – just between us."

He shrugged, "Nobody really knows. From what I can gather it's a combination of things – some serious, some not so serious and some they just don't know. That's why they wanted her to come home so she can see a specialist in tropical diseases."

"Thank god for the NHS," said Philip.

"At least you're alright, Hunter," said Netta, squeezing his arm. "You are, aren't you? You look a bit thin –"

"The food in the refugee camps is pretty basic – I had to force myself to eat it – most of the time it was just mealy meal. Not exactly appetizing."

At the Royal Free Hospital, Cassie was spirited away for a series of diagnostic tests, leaving Zinadine to struggle with the admissions people. Doctor Nielson, the family GP, had smoothed the way by leaving a letter for the medical staff, stating he would be in to see her later that evening after his surgery hours. Netta had warned Alice to phone first to be sure they would let her visit. She had been told no visitors until all tests, x-rays and scans had been completed.

When Alice finally managed to get permission to see her daughter, she found her in a separate room off one of the women's wards. She had been isolated until the results of the tests were known. Cassie and Zinadine sat on the bed holding hands like two small children. He quickly slid off the bed to make room for Alice to embrace her. She dropped her bag and coat, gathered up her daughter and rocked her in her arms, the two women hugging silently for several moments.

Alice released her sufficiently to study the ravages of the mystery disease on her child. In the simple hospital shift, Cassie looked painfully thin, her hair hanging limp about her face. Alice studied her carefully, stroking her head and arms, then turned to look at Zinadine.

"Zinadine, you promised me. You said you would take care of her and now you bring her back like this. Look at her – she's like a stick insect."

Zinadine shook his head and lifted his arms in a despairing gesture, unable to meet Alice's eyes.

"It's not his fault, mother. He didn't want me to go to the refugee camp but I went anyway."

"I warned her of the risk, Mrs. Roper, but she refused to listen to me," he said unhappily.

"You should have stopped her all the same," said Alice, giving full vent to her pent-up anger. "Especially when you knew the danger. I shall never trust you again with her."

"Mother please," said Cassie, pushing herself free from Alice's clasp. "Don't blame Zinadine – I told you already he tried to stop me."

"Well he obviously didn't try hard enough – and now look at you. God knows what ghastly bugs you've picked up…."

The door suddenly opened as Netta burst into the room followed by Hunter and Philip.

"Mother! You're not upsetting her, are you? I could hear you out in the corridor." She elbowed her way past Alice and threw her arms protectively round Cassie. The two sisters clung together and Alice retreated to a chair by the bed.

"I'm sorry, but I was so upset when I saw her – and I'm so angry with Zinadine for letting this happen...."

"She won't listen to me, Netta. I've told her it was my decision – nothing to do with Zinadine –"

"Shh, shh – alright Cassie, I understand – you mustn't upset yourself. You know what Mother's like – she worries about you all the time and then takes it out on the rest of us. Pay no attention, Zinadine, she'll apologise for her behaviour when she calms down."

"No, please, I understand completely," said Zinadine, embarrassed. "She's quite right – I blame myself for what has happened to Cassie. I should have insisted, but...." He broke off, looking miserable.

"There, you see?" demanded Alice. "I knew he could have stopped her – "

"You're wrong – he couldn't," said Cassie leaning forward to address her mother. "I'm not a child to be ordered about...."

"Okay – let's stop right there," said Hunter coming up on the other side of the bed. "Unless we all want to get slung out of here by the nurses, before we can even see Cassie. She's here now and that's all that matters." He looked at the unhappy face of Zinadine, "And if it wasn't for Zinadine, she'd still be in a first-aid tent in Guinea. As soon as he knew she was ill, he pulled out all the stops to get her home – left his job, everything – and I for one am very grateful." He crossed the room and embraced him. Philip too, shook his hand and Netta gave him a warm kiss, then looked pointedly at her mother.

After a moment's hesitation, Alice got to her feet and crossed to stand in front of the tall young man. She took both his hands in hers.

"Netta's right, I'm as much to blame as anyone – I should never have allowed her to go in the first place. Thank you for all you've done to bring her home. Will you forgive my outburst?"

"I think we both know how pointless it is to try to change Cassie's mind when she's made it up," he said. "But I still feel very badly about breaking my promise to you to look after her."

He and Alice embraced warmly and everyone smiled with relief.

"Good," said Cassie. "I hope we're all agreed that I brought this all on myself for not listening to my elders and betters. The only one who hasn't been blamed is Dad and he was the one who encouraged me to go in the first place."

"Lucky for him he's not here," said Philip. "Where is he anyway?"

"The last I heard he was on a beach outside Freetown," said Hunter. "He probably didn't get my email yet."

"That's so typical of Barney," said Alice. "Make a mess and leave the rest of us to clear it up."

"Mother, that's not fair. He can hardly be blamed for Cassie getting sick," said Netta.

"Why not? If he hadn't encouraged her to go she might still be in Paris, working at the UN."

"Dad is the only one who didn't treat me like a child. Just because I'm the baby of the family, you all act like I'm a mental defective, incapable of making up my own mind," said Cassie, sinking back on the bed. "I wish he was here now." She began to cry and the others looked sheepishly at each other. Alice took a step towards her but Netta held her arm and nodded to Zinadine, who crossed to the bed. Cassie flung her arms around his neck and sobbed loudly.

"Let's all go and have some tea, shall we?" said Philip. "Give them a bit of breathing space."

Everyone trooped out of the room, taking a reluctant Alice by the arm. Philip led the way to the hospital coffee shop where they sat and discussed strategy.

"It's obvious we're too much for her all at once," said Netta. "Shall we work out a rota for visiting – one or two each day?"

"But I want to come every day," protested Alice.

They agreed that Cassie would want to see Zinadine every day, until he had to return to Guinea. Hunter said he was happy to hear of her progress second hand for a few days, as he had been with her night and day for the past month. Alice and Netta rotated alternate days. The battery of tests would take a week to complete and then whatever treatment Cassie needed would have to follow that.

In the days that followed there was still no word from Barney, although they bombarded him with emails.

# CHAPTER 54

When Barney returned to Lakka Beach near Freetown he found the email from Hunter waiting for him. Although his son had tried to play down how ill Cassie was, he had been unable to hide his worries for her and how important it was to get her back to the UK for diagnosis and treatment. He urged his father to hurry and join him so they could arrange her return. Meantime, Hunter said he would also try to raise Zinadine who was working somewhere in northern Guinea.

The news from his son drove his nagging concerns about his own possible AIDS infection to the back of his mind. Clutching the new spare part, he said goodbye to Clive and left early the next day, on the proffered ride to Bo from Suleiman's agent in Freetown. They arrived in Bo late in the day and the driver dropped Barney off at the young Lebanese diamond merchant's store downtown.

He pumped Suleiman's hand. "I can't tell you how much I appreciated your help in getting the spare gear for my truck. I'd probably still be hunting for it if your agent hadn't got involved."

The heavy-set young man looked pleased to see him. "What will you do now? I mean about your daughter?"

"First I have to get back to Faranah so my friend can repair the truck," said Barney. "But I've heard more bad news from my son, when he found Cassie. She's very ill and the local doctor told him she needed to get back to London for treatment as soon as possible.

Suleiman looked concerned. "A refugee camp is no place for a sick European. They have only minimum sanitation – she could easily get much worse. You must go direct and not wait for your truck to be fixed."

Barney nodded, "Yes, I've been thinking the same thing all the way from Freetown today. I've decided to just drop the new spare off with my friend and then go on ahead to be with my daughter."

Suleiman came round his desk to take Barney's arm. "Come with me. I have a suggestion." He led him into the outer office and spoke in the local dialect to one of his workmen. The man stopped his book-keeping and left the office. Suleiman took Barney outside and pointed to the gleaming silver Hummer, that still stood in the same spot under the diamond merchant's sign. "I have sent Azil to find one of my drivers," he said. "He should be back with him in half an hour or so. This man knows the roads to Faranah well. He will take you there. But first let us eat some Lebanese food before you go. It is a difficult journey – even in a Hummer."

"I couldn't possibly afford to pay you for the use of your 4x4 and driver," said Barney. "But I appreciate the offer very much. I'll get some food from a street stall and find a bush-taxi right away. I hope you won't think I'm being rude but I don't want to delay any longer, Suleiman. I'm very worried about Cassie."

"I have not asked you for any money and I expect none," said Suleiman. "I too, am concerned about your daughter and wish to help, that is all. Come, there is a small Lebanese café across the street that belongs to my cousin. We can wait there for my driver. You must eat," he urged, stressing the importance this activity held for him.

In the café, Suleiman ordered a selection of hot and cold dishes and Barney found he had a powerful appetite. He had eaten only bananas and a mango the entire journey from Freetown. He accepted Suleiman's offer of help, knowing it could shorten the time until he saw Cassie. Telling the stout young merchant about her illness only increased his worry.

"When I went to Kenema a few days ago, I asked about your daughter and gave photocopies of her picture to several of my contacts," said Suleiman, dividing portions of the tapas-style dishes between Barney's plate and his own. "No one had heard anything, until yesterday I had a message saying a white girl had been rescued by the army, near the border some time ago. They took her to the Guinea border and handed her over to the police." He shrugged and continued eating. "It may have been another tourist backpacker. Black people say all white people look the same to them." He smiled and wiped his mouth on a large white napkin. "I think my driver is here now."

They rose and Barney tried to pay the bill but the proprietor waved it aside. Across the street, a stocky muscular African stood beside the Hummer, waiting for them.

"This is Hassani," said Suleiman. "He works for me and knows the back-country, so you will make good time with him driving. I hope you find Cassie soon and that I may have the pleasure of meeting her one day."

Barney and the driver loaded his rucksack into the huge long wheelbase vehicle, adding two sleeping bags Hassani produced from the outer office. Barney shook hands again with the stout young Lebanese and thanked him again for his generosity.

"I have told Hassani to stay with you, for as long as it is necessary to get your daughter to safety. Salaam alaikum."

The silver monster 4x4 backed out into the early dusk and roared out of the rundown city towards the north.

The next twenty-four hours passed in a blur for Barney as he dozed and jounced over the cratered roads and tracks leading to Guinea. The farther north they travelled, the worse the road became and the huge Hummer whined and growled in and out of mud holes and over increasingly impassable terrain. Hassani handled the heavy 4x4 without comment, knowing which holes to tackle head-on and which to skirt round, through the thick bush.

When he could no longer bear the stress of watching Hassani plunge the big machine into the rutted potholes, Barney crawled into the rear of the vehicle. He stretched out on the unfolded sleeping bags. They stopped for brief periods of rest in small villages, where Hassani procured bowls of swamp rice and greens, washed down by warm bottles of orange squash and cola.

The border post was closed again when they reached it in late evening. Without pausing, Hassani swerved off into the bush on a detour he had made many times before. The big 4x4 swept into Faranah after dark and Barney tried to recall where he and Hunter had left the Unimog over two weeks ago. The monosyllabic driver cruised his behemoth around the main dirt roads leading into Faranah. Barney suddenly spotted the roadside garage, with the Unimog nosed off under a baobab tree beside it.

Landon appeared from behind the garage, at the sound of the Hummer pulling up beside their truck. He and Barney pounded each other's backs like long-lost brothers.

"When I got that email from Hunter sayin' how sick Cassie was I didn't know what to do," said Landon. "I wanted to leave this thing here and go look for him myself."

Barney introduced him to Hassani and briefly explained why he had arrived in such an expensive vehicle. He produced the precious spare part and handed it over to Landon.

"How soon do you think we can be back on the road?"

"Two days maximum," said Landon, unwrapping the grease-coated gear. "The mechanic who helped me dismantle it, is away on a job and won't be back until tomorrow afternoon. But I can at least get started in the mornin'."

"How would you feel if I left you to get on with it and go ahead with Hassani in the morning, Landon?" asked Barney. "I've got the use of this Hummer until I get Cassie to a hospital and I don't want to waste the opportunity. Otherwise, I'd stay and help you. Not that I've got a clue how these four-wheel drive trains go together."

Landon laid down the spare part on a stool. "What's the point in us takin' all these arms and legs to Cassie's refugee camp, if no one's there, Barney? I been thinkin' a lot about this since you left. Most of these amputee kids are refugees, right?"

"From Sierra Leone," said Barney. "They came to Guinea for safety, Cassie said."

"But now it's not so safe anymore," said Landon. "I've talked to a lot of people here and they say these boy gangs are attackin' villages and refugee camps on night raids, all along the border south of Kissidougou. The army patrols have lost control of the area again."

"Suleiman told me the same thing," said Barney. "He says it's too dangerous for Cassie and her war orphans in that area."

"Yeah. So anyway, I been plannin' and thinkin' about my school compound outside Freetown. Why couldn't we take all these children there?"

"I went there with Clive a few days ago. Your sister Ama told me where it was," said Barney. "I had no idea you'd done so much already."

Landon grinned. "Not that much when you consider how many years I been messin' about with this idea. And it all stops dead when I'm not there to organise the work," he said. "Still, there's enough shelter there for these kids and it beats livin' in the bush. At least they'll be safe."

"So you wouldn't mind if I go off with Hassani and get Cassie out of there? We can organise sending the kids to Freetown after you unload the Unimog of all these artificial limbs at your compound."

"I'll stay here and fix the truck and wait to hear from you, Barney," said Landon. "If you don't get in touch by the time it's repaired, I'll take off for Freetown. Just concentrate on findin' Cassie for now."

Landon led Hassani and Barney through the darkened streets to a bar he had found, where an African drummer was teaching him to play the djembe. They ate some swamp rice and hard-boiled eggs and listened to the musicians. Hassani left them drinking beer and walked back to sleep in the big Hummer. Barney listened to Landon talk of his plans for the school and the war orphans. He'd had plenty of free time to work out the details for his dream project, waiting for Barney to return with the new gear.

"You remember how we talked back in England about me bringin' Elinor's boys out to Freetown when I got settled here, Barney?" he said. "Well, I emailed Russell and he says my ex-wife, Natasha and him are sharin' the boys. She looks after them through the week and Russell has them on the farm at the weekends. He claims he only agreed to do it for the free labour."

"Russell's not so bad," said Barney. "The women all give him a hard time but he's done lots of things for the hospice over the years. He just likes to pretend he's a lone wolf."

"Yeah. Anyway, I offered to have them at my compound for a few months if he and Maddy paid their fare out to Freetown," said Landon.

Barney waited while Landon played a set on the djembe drums with his musician friends. He insisted he had to get some sleep, so he and Hassani could leave early in the morning. As they ambled back to the Unimog in the dark, Barney got up the courage to ask Landon if he and his woman friend from Dakar, did more than just sleep together.

"You mean did I get my leg over with Lisabeth?" laughed Landon. "Sure I did. She's one sexy lady. I told you she knew my sister in Freetown, remember?"

"Weren't you worried about the AIDS thing?" asked Barney.

"I don't take any chances with that stuff. Everywhere you look you see warnin's," said Landon.

"So you practised safe sex?" pursued Barney.

Landon laughed again. "Practise. That's what we did all right. Practise."

"I see."

"You plannin' on gettin' in a little practice yourself, Barney?"

"No, just curious."

"Use it or lose it. That's what they say."

"Mmmnn."

Barney woke to the roar of the Hummer's engine and Hassani passing him a cup of the bitter local coffee. Landon poked his head out from his sleeping bag under the Unimog and waved goodbye as they pulled out onto the dusty dirt road to Kissidougou. They made good time, as the roads were in much better shape than in Sierra Leone.

He followed Hunter's directions and by the afternoon had reached the small village in the bush outside Kissidougou. Hassani stopped the Hummer in the middle of the village street where children of all ages, many on wooden crutches, instantly surrounded it. A tall black woman emerged from one of the thatched round huts and shooed them out of the way. They made a path for her to the mud-covered Hummer.

Before he could speak, she had opened the door and helped Barney out. The next moment he was smothered in a moist embrace, his face pushed into her large bosom.

"I been waitin' for you, Mister Roper," she said. "I knew you be here soon. Jus' like Hunter say. I'm Grace an' I'm in charge of all these children." She heaved a thin little boy up on her hip while she talked. "This a fine machine, bigger than Zinadine's."

"Zinadine – is he here?" asked Barney.

"Come inside an' we can talk. Bring your friend," she said nodding towards Hassani, who had a crowd of curious faces round him. He spoke to the children in their Sierra Leone dialect as they led him inside one of the huts. Grace took Barney into another one and introduced him to Raoul, the Cuban doctor with *Médecins sans Frontiéres*.

"Where's Hunter?" asked Barney, looking around the bare walls of the mud hut. "And Cassie – isn't she here?"

The big woman shook her head. "They gone over a week ago. Hunter send Zinadine a message and a day later that boy show up here in a big white Land Rover."

"I tried everything I could but Cassie just got weaker and weaker. We have very few medical supplies here, *monsieur,* only the basics," explained Raoul. "I advised them not to wait any longer."

"But where have they gone?"

"Zinadine has many contacts with the NGOs working here in Guinea. He knew of a cargo plane returning empty to Dakar and they drove up north to catch a lift. From there I think Hunter planned to fly your daughter back to London," said Raoul.

Grace pulled an envelope from a cardboard box on the table that held a small stock of medicines. "Hunter leave this letter for you. Cassie don't go until he write it. She one stubborn girl, your daughter. She get that from you, maybe?"

"Maybe," said Barney, opening the grubby envelope.

*Dear Dad,*

*I'm sorry we didn't wait for you but both Raoul and Grace thought we should get Cassie to a hospital as fast as possible. She is quite weak and can't seem to keep anything down that Grace has tried to feed her. Zinadine borrowed a Land Rover from an NGO friend and organised a lift to the coast on an empty plane going to Dakar for aid supplies but we had to leave right away to catch it.*

*If the doctors in Dakar say she is well enough to travel home, I'll book a flight to London from there.*

*I hope you got the spare part okay and fixed the Unimog. I sent Landon an email the same time as you, telling him Cassie was ill. By the time you get this note we'll probably all be in England. When I get to Dakar, I'll email Netta and Alice to expect us home.*

*Cassie told me to say that she has a favour to ask you. We know that you and Landon are going to Freetown after delivering the supplies to Grace and Raoul. The problem is this camp is only a temporary place and the village chief wants them to find somewhere else.*

*Cassie says will you help Grace and Raoul move the children in the truck to a safer place somewhere further from the border? Raoul thinks his organisation could find them someplace in the north, away from the trouble. She has asked Zinadine to promise to come back right away to help out but he won't consider it until she is in hospital and out of danger.*

*I will see Lottie in Dakar and ask her to help as well.*

*Cassie is determined to come back quickly – she says she wants to see all her orphans wearing their new artificial limbs and learning to read all the books you brought.*

*I know email is impossible around Kissidougou but keep checking yours whenever you get a chance and I'll keep you posted.*

*Grace has managed to keep all the children together throughout this whole disruption. She's totally devoted to them. I call her Amazing Grace. And Raoul will be delighted to get hold of all those new arms and legs for the amputees. He came out from Cuba as a specialist in prosthetics and has been frustrated by the lack of supplies. I'm sure with your handyman skills you and Landon will be able to help him fit all the kids with new limbs.*

*But first, as Cassie says, they must find somewhere safe.*

*I know you'll do your best for her and for them, Dad.*

*Much love,*

*Hunter and Cassie.*

Barney showed the letter to Raoul and Grace in turn. Raoul read it in silence, nodding in affirmation of Hunter's remarks about the prostheses. Barney had to explain that they were still on the Unimog with Landon, back in Faranah. Grace read slowly, mouthing the words and exclaiming 'Eeehh!' from time to time. She laughed aloud at one point.

"That what he call me, right enough. 'Amazin' Grace.' I tell him Cassie is the amazin' one." She clutched Barney's arm. "That girl of yours has kept me goin' when I feel I can't go no more. And now here she say she comin' back to help me again."

Barney listened to both of them describe their current plight and realised they had no clear plan, except to find somewhere away from the marauding boy gangs. Most of the local women who had been working with the children had run away in fear of further attacks.

He outlined Landon's proposal and asked them what they thought of it. Grace was thrilled at the thought of being back in her adopted country and knew it was safe around

Freetown. Barney asked Raoul if he knew of the Italian clinic run by *Médecins sans Frontières* outside the capital. The young doctor had heard of it but had not visited the coast yet. Both of them jumped at the possibility of a permanent base.

"How many orphans do you have, Grace?" asked Barney.

"Twenty-six," she said. "I had twenty-seven but one girl run off with a boy from the village near the refugee camp."

Barney made a quick calculation. "We could squeeze ten in the Hummer but the truck is full of books and artificial limbs. That means three trips to Freetown. And one of you would have to stay here with the rest of the children."

"I'm not leavin' till every last one of them goes," said Grace. "You take Raoul with you first trip. An' he can start workin' on those new limbs 'stead of mopin' about here an' botherin' me."

Raoul grinned at the prospect and hugged the big nurse. "When you get to Freetown we are going out to celebrate, Grace. Just like I promised Cassie." He grabbed her by the waist and danced her round the bare hut.

"I be waitin' for you," she laughed. "That is one promise you goin' to keep."

Barney explained that he must return the Hummer to the diamond merchant in Bo. They could take a bus from there to Freetown and Landon could follow in the truck. He was anxious to get back to Faranah and catch Landon before he set out on his own. If Hassani led the way, the journey could be quicker with less chance of another breakdown, in one of the gaping potholes pockmarking the route.

Grace had an objection to the plan. "Who goin' to look after these children in Freetown when you gets there? Raoul gonna need some help."

"Landon's sister has already agreed to live there with her five grandchildren," said Barney. "She can be in charge until you arrive, Grace."

It was left to Grace to choose which of the orphans to send in the first batch and they clamoured for a seat in the Hummer with Hassani. She chose several of the older children to look after the little ones. With many loud wails and tears, those left behind ran after the dirt-caked vehicle, as Hassani drove slowly out of the village. Barney and Raoul sat in the back, surrounded by excited children clutching small parcels of treasured belongings.

Landon had finished the repairs to the Unimog when they arrived in Faranah. At Barney's suggestion, he opened the door to the cargo bay for Raoul to have a quick look. The excited young doctor wanted to go through the stock of artificial limbs right there and then. But Barney insisted they push on to Bo and return the Hummer to Suleiman. Raoul insisted on taking two or three of the prostheses into the cab and rode with Landon while he studied the possibilities. Every time they stopped for a rest break on the journey, he made Landon dig out another batch for inspection.

The children treated the trip as an adventure and loved taking turns riding in the front of the huge 4x4 with Hassani, as he wrestled the Hummer over the rutted track. They were all sleeping in jumbled heaps on top of each other and Barney, when Hassani wheeled into Bo early in the morning.

Suleiman sent the tireless Hassani off to feed the children and clean the filthy vehicle. He took Barney across the street again to the Lebanese cousin's café for breakfast. Landon and

Raoul went off in search of leather straps and buckles to adapt the harnesses.

"So where is your daughter?" was the first question of the heavy-set Lebanese, as he ordered coffee and pastries. "Did you send her back to England?"

Over breakfast, Barney briefly filled in Suleiman on the incidents surrounding Cassie's departure and his present situation with Raoul and the amputee orphans. He thanked him for the use of his giant 4x4 and driver and asked if it would be possible to continue to Freetown before returning it.

"How many more children are still in Guinea?" asked Suleiman, beckoning to the waiter to bring more pastries.

"Sixteen, plus Grace – the nurse."

"That will mean two more trips in your truck," said the young merchant. "In one week's time I must make my visit to the mines and will need the Hummer. Do you think you can go to Freetown and back twice in that time?"

"I don't know," said Barney. "What do you think?"

"Probably not. But you could do it from here if you went back straight away. I will ask Hassani if he can do it. From here to Freetown is not difficult with the regular bus."

"Suleiman, you're like your illustrious namesake – magnificent. 'Suleiman the Magnificent.' I can't thank you enough. If my daughter were here she would shower you with gratitude."

The stout young man's usual lugubrious countenance broke into a grin at Barney's flowery tribute. "Although my father and grandfather would not admit it, the diamond business is guilty of causing many of these atrocities. For my part, you are welcome to use the Hummer and Hassani to rescue the other orphans – but only for one more week. My father will be back from Amsterdam to collect the diamonds so I cannot be late. Will you give me your word?"

Barney pumped his hand and assured him they would have the big Hummer back on time, if he could borrow Hassani, the demon driver.

"Hassani will need someone to look after the next batch of children if the nurse won't leave until the final trip," said Suleiman. "I will ask Azalea from the Hotel Corona, if she will go with him. She used to be a school teacher."

Barney left the café to tell Landon and Raoul and arrange the bus trip to the capital. Because the Unimog only lumbered along and Landon didn't want to risk going too fast for fear of another breakdown, he and Barney left Raoul with the children at the bus garage in Bo. Hassani and Azalea drove off in the gleaming clean Hummer, with a scribbled note to Grace from Barney, to collect the next group of ten amputees.

# CHAPTER 55

At Lakka Beach near Freetown, Ama stood arms akimbo as the old ex-army Unimog entered Landon's compound. She tussled with her unruly bosoms to keep them in check, as Barney and her brother climbed down from the high cab. Landon had tried to prepare her for his changed appearance and missing right hand but the shock registered on her face. She stared dumbstruck at his scarred features for a few moments, before gathering her older brother into her ample embrace.

Barney stood aside, to let them struggle with their reunion unobserved. He wandered round the compound, looking into the set of traditional round thatched huts Landon and his friends and relatives had built over the last few years. Only the old woman he remembered from his first visit and her grown son, lived in the compound to maintain it and grow fruit and vegetables. They used only a small portion of the land Landon had set aside for food and he foresaw a lot of work involved, in bringing the weed-infested plot into use to feed all Cassie's orphans.

Ama and Landon came arm-in-arm to seek him out.

"We goin' to need lots of help with thirty-one children here to look after," she said. "I hope you plannin' to stay for awhile, Barney."

"There's only ten to start off with," said Landon. "They should be here by now."

"Plus my five grandchildren," said Ama. "The Congo Cross minibus go past in half an hour. I guess that leave us plenty of time to get ready." She shook with laughter and one of her ponderous breasts rolled out from her loose boubou.

"All the older ones can sleep in the main school building for now," said Landon. "At least it has a roof if it rains."

"No rain comin' here for a long time yet," said Ama, "but we gonna need somethin' for all of them to sleep on."

"What about Raoul's clinic?" asked Barney. "Shall we unload all the artificial limbs into one of these huts for now?"

"I'll pile the boxes of books in a corner of the schoolroom and cover them with our sleeping tarpaulin." Landon paced about the large open-sided thatched building, eyeing his domain. Ama went off to tend to a large pot of swamp rice, on the open fire pit in the centre of the compound.

"I thought Clive might be here by now too," said Barney. "I think I'll walk down to Lakka Beach to find him."

Ama sent one of her granddaughters with him, to make sure he didn't get lost and the nine-year old skipped along ahead of him. They approached the clinic run by the *Médecins sans Frontières* doctors and Barney silently calculated how much of the month remained, before he would know his fate. It had been less than ten days since his HIV test so he had another 21 days to go. The mad rush of the last week and a half had almost banished the thought of the next test but it lurked in the corners of his mind, coming out to torment him at unguarded moments.

"What would I do differently, if I knew right now?" he asked himself. He could think of nothing more pressing than completing the task his daughter had set him – but after that? Perhaps the time was approaching to begin the period of reflection, the final stage in the Indian four ages of life. He would have to wait and see.

Ahead of him, the distinct ample profile of *The Betsy,* swam in the midday shimmering heat haze over the beach. He could make out a man swimming beside the boat and assumed it must be Clive. He gave Usha, his young guide, a coin to buy a soft drink from the beach café where he and Clive had eaten before he left. He shouted and waved his arms at the water's edge and Clive glanced ashore, then returned his wave. He hauled himself into his dinghy and Barney realised his friend no longer wore the brace and harness across his shoulders. A few minutes later, the dinghy bobbed ashore and Clive stepped out to greet him.

"You feel strong enough to help me unload the Unimog?" asked Barney, embracing his old friend.

"I'm getting fit again by doing lots of swimming," Clive said, hauling the little white dinghy high up above the tide line on the sand that burned their feet. "How's Cassie – did you see her?"

"No. Zinadine and Hunter took her off to Dakar and then London. I'm hoping there's an email waiting for me when I go into Freetown later." He called to Usha, who sat in the shade of a coconut palm drinking her bottle of warm pop. The three of them strolled back to the compound into pandemonium. Raoul and the first lot of children had arrived. They were engaged in some elaborate game of hide and seek with Landon, shrieking and hopping about, while Ama dished up her rice and vegetable stew. Raoul rooted about inside the back of the Unimog, hauling out all the artificial limbs and harness and laying them on the ground according to size.

"What do you think, Raoul? Will there be enough to fit out all these kids?" asked Barney.

"I can't be sure until they all arrive," he said, "and I can match them up. Looks like we have *beaucoup de* legs anyway."

They worked all afternoon storing the books and limbs and emptying the Unimog for its return trip to Bo, for the next contingent of war orphans. Landon said he didn't need to go, as the roads were good enough for Barney to drive. Raoul was determined to begin fitting his first child. The stocky Cuban said he would concentrate on the legs, so that all the children could first learn to walk unaided. He had chosen a quiet girl of about twelve who sat on the ground near him, staring at the growing heap of arms and legs.

Barney planned to leave early next morning for Bo and took the local packed minibus into Freetown to find an internet café. He tried three places before he discovered one with a generator working. There were several messages in amongst the junk mail. He opened Alice's first.

*Dear Barney,*

*I don't know whether to curse you or bless you. Cassie is home or rather in the Royal Free Hospital and seems to be responding to the treatment now that they've diagnosed what it is – something intestinal with an unpronounceable name.*

*She arrived looking like a scarecrow and is still painfully thin but she manages to keep her food down now so that is progress. I tore a strip off Zinadine for allowing this to happen and I would've done the same to you if you'd been here. But I'm just grateful to you both for bringing her back home.*

*The doctor is letting her home to recuperate and already Cassie is talking about returning to Africa. She says if she went back by boat, the sea air would cure her in no time. She even asked the doctor and he agreed. I can't believe it. I just want to padlock her in the house for the next six months but I know it's no use. Zinadine plans to fly back as soon as she comes out of hospital. Hunter says it's my fault for being so hard on him. Cassie has made them both promise to go back and help you and Landon move all the children to a safe new base.*

*When I tried to get Heck to persuade her to stay, he said we could all go out on the freighter he's shipping the merry-go-round on. He and Dad already told Cassie what they've been restoring all this time and I have to admit it's marvellous – the children will love it I'm sure.*

*So it looks like everyone is planning a sea voyage shortly to come and see Landon's school and meet all the war orphans and amputees. Mother and Netta and I have a vested interest in seeing the three young girls we've fostered – have you met them yet? Their names are Zena, Elizabeth and Adina. We leave Tilbury docks next week and it takes twenty-one days to Freetown on the Firenze. I just hope you'll be ready for us. I'm very nervous about going to Africa but try not to let it show in front of Cassie. She is a changed person and I know that she fully intends to live in Africa with Zinadine. So if I want to see anything of her and any grandchildren in the future I'll have to get over my fears.*

*I suppose I ought to thank you for Heck and I trying one more time. I'm still not convinced he could love me with no breasts but he says it will make no difference. We'll see. At any rate, we're putting up a united front for Cassie, as I can't bring myself to tell her and Netta the truth yet. Maybe on the voyage.*

*Which brings me to you – us. I feel at last ready to deal with our divorce and have filed the papers for the decree nisi. I know this is what you want and it seems dog in the manger of me to refuse.*

*We'll be on the high seas soon so prepare for an invasion.*

*With love, Alice.*

Barney let out a sigh of relief reading about Cassie's recovery. He agreed with Alice that she shouldn't return so soon but knew how powerfully her life in Africa with Zinadine drew her back. Three weeks at sea should do her good anyway. He opened the other email from Hunter, saying he and Zinadine would be back as soon as Cassie left hospital in a few days. He had seen Lottie briefly in Dakar and she promised to join him back in Freetown.

He sent Cassie an email, assuming Zinadine or Netta would be passing on her messages.

*Dear Cassie,*

*Just heard from Hunter and your mother that you are on the mend – you had us all worried there for a while. When I met Grace and Raoul and saw what you were all doing with the orphan amputees I knew you had found something worth doing. I'm proud to be a small part of it. Landon and I are in the midst of shuttling the children and Grace from Kissidougou to Lakka Beach near Freetown to his family compound where he's building a school. It will be safe there and Raoul is already busy fitting the amputees with the new arms and legs Hunter and Clive and Lottie brought over on 'The Betsy'.*

*Grace is still in Guinea with the remaining children but we hope to have her out within a week, as we got some unexpected help from an admirer of yours – a Lebanese diamond merchant in Bo called*

*Suleiman the Magnificent - or that's what we call him. The roads in the north of Sierra Leone are murder and only big 4x4s like our Unimog and Suleiman's huge Hummer can get through. I'm off in the morning to collect another ten children.*

*It will be a race against time to finish the thatched huts before you get here, so they'll all have somewhere to call home at last.*

*Looking forward to seeing you soon.*

*All my love, Dadxxx*

The next two weeks passed in a hectic round of shuttling back and forth to Bo and Faranah. The indefatigable Hassani ferried all the children and last of all Grace, to Bo where Barney collected them in batches. He brought them the rest of the way, with Azalea keeping watch over the excited but nervous children. By the time he finished ferrying them to Lakka Beach, Landon and Clive and a handful of Ama's relatives, had built more thatched huts in the compound.

Lottie arrived the same day as Hunter and Zinadine. Clive asked some of the sailors from the *Amistad* he had become friendly with, to join the work party. Lottie disappeared into Freetown one day with Hunter and announced on their return that she had persuaded the Cultural Minister to come and officially open the centre. They had agreed a date for three days after the *Firenze* docked in Freetown with Cassie and Alice and the others.

# CHAPTER 56

Grace, Ama and Azalea had their hands full, restraining the assembled children from escaping onto the dock and running up the ramps to the *Firenze's* decks. Hunter moved about filming the arrival from all angles for his documentary on Cassie's orphans. Two or three other passengers lined the rails along with Cassie's group. She stood leaning over the side to scan the waiting cluster of black and white faces. A lone figure broke free and raced up the gangway. Everyone cheered as Zinadine wrapped his arms round a glowing Cassie and bore her down to the group behind the barrier. She was followed by Alice and Heck, George and Martha and lastly by her sister Netta, alone. Yet again, her partner Philip had to attend an Anglo-Saxon conference, where he was delivering a paper on the Venerable Bede.

Lottie abandoned her role as Hunter's sound assistant, to plunge into the crush and squeeze Cassie, towering over her old friend by a foot. They had not seen each other since their heady days at the Sorbonne over a year and a half ago. Cassie pried herself loose, only to be engulfed by Grace. The black nurse wept and laughed at their reunion, while the children tugged urgently at Cassie for recognition. Barney greeted all the others and waited for an opening to catch his daughter's eye. She spotted him at last and waved him over.

"Dad!"

They embraced and she clung to him, his youngest child again. "I think I'm going to cry," he said.

"I haven't stopped since we landed, Dad. I'm so happy to be back and have you all here."

"Let me look at you," he said wiping his eyes and holding her at arms' length. "You don't look like a stick insect at all. You look wonderful. Your mother's been exaggerating again."

Cassie laughed and reached for Zinadine's hand as he stood behind her. "Gran and mother have been force-feeding me five meals a day the whole trip. I must have put on a stone in weight since we left."

The whole group surged about on the dock, with knots of children breaking off to clamber over the strange painted slingfuls of carnival horses, being unloaded from the mixed cargo hold of the little Italian freighter. Heck and George hovered around like nervous mother hens, as their precious jigsaw pieces of the old fairground merry-go-round piled up on the crowded dock.

Landon, with Clive and a team of young sailors from the *Amistad,* loaded the cargo onto the Unimog, to begin ferrying it to his compound.

Lottie stood between Cassie and Zinadine to make her announcement. "I 'ave persuaded the Minister of Culture to open the new centre," she said. "He said he would like it to coincide with the new government's official restoration of electric power the day after tomorrow. He will make sure the press photographers are there when he throws the switch. They are promising electricity for six hours to the whole of the Freetown area."

"Day after tomorrow?" said Heck. "We'd better get this stuff moving if we're going to have it all bolted together and running by then."

"Don't look at me," said Landon. "I'm up to my eyeballs with unfinished work at the compound."

"I guess it's me and Clive," said Barney. "Unless you can prize Raoul loose from his new limb fittings."

"Absolutely not," said Lottie. "The whole point of this event is to get the government behind the project. We must 'ave as many of the children fitted as possible by the opening."

"I suppose I could ring Suleiman the Magnificent," said Barney. "See if he would lend us Hassani to help."

Landon grinned. "If you get Cassie to ask him, I'm sure he'd agree." He turned to her. "You have a secret admirer, Cassie. He keeps your picture pinned up over his desk."

Alice broke into the group, clutching the hand of a young girl of twelve, who stood unsteadily on her newly acquired artificial leg. "Adina and the other children want to show us the new school and where we're going to sleep," said Alice. "We need a guide to show us the way, Barney."

Over an hour later, a cavalcade of battered *sept-place* taxis pulled into Landon's compound. Ama, Grace and Azalea took over, leading Cassie and Zinadine round the transformed property, surrounded by an excited troupe of hopping, shouting children. They tugged at the young couple, pulling them into the new thatched huts to show them where they now lived. Hunter roamed about alone, shooting footage of their arrival for his film. Lottie had disappeared. Landon plunged into a string of last minute jobs he wanted to finish before the opening.

Netta, Martha and Alice took the three amputees they had fostered, Adina, Elizabeth and Zena and walked the half-kilometre to Lakka Beach for a swim in the ocean.

Throughout the day, a steady trickle of old trucks delivered the jumble of merry-go-round sections to an empty corner of the compound where George and Heck struggled to disentangle them. Barney drove the Unimog back and forth Clive stayed on the docks to supervise the unloading and make sure nothing vanished in transit.

Raoul had enlisted the help of two of the Italian doctors from the *Médecins sans Frontières* clinic, to fit the artificial legs first. He planned to have all the amputees walking by the opening with not a crutch in sight, he told Cassie. She and Grace fell seamlessly back into their former routines. Landon helped them set up their temporary clinic in one of the round thatched huts. He even provided a padlock for Grace to put on the cupboard for her cache of medicines.

By evening, everything from the docks lay strewn around the compound and Heck and George had begun the task of assembling the old Victorian carousel. Landon strung up some lanterns on poles, so they could work into the night and Ama and Azalea cooked cauldrons of swamp rice and vegetable stew, to feed the groups of visiting adults and children who kept appearing in the compound.

The next day, with twenty-four hours to go until the official opening, Barney woke to the noise of hammering and loud voices. Clive and Heck were arguing with George over the plans for the huge fairground machine.

Mid-morning, a familiar silver Hummer drove into the compound, with Hassani at the wheel and two more of Suleiman's workmen with him. Cassie's phone call had worked.

Hassani greeted Barney silently and then joined Heck, Clive and George amid the piles of half-assembled machinery, with his two workers. Barney left them to puzzle over the plans and went to find his daughter. She and Grace sat in the big open-sided schoolroom, opening boxes of books from the pallet loads he and Landon had carted all the way from Dakar in the Unimog.

Martha and Alice sorted books into stacks for the rough shelving Landon had provided. Netta sat on the floor with her foster-child, Zena, surrounded by a handful of the younger orphans, reading from one of the storybooks.

"Can you spare an hour to go for a walk, Cassie?" asked Barney.

Grace looked up at him. "I jus' get this girl back an' you tryin' to take her away. I already sent Zinadine packin.'"

"Can we go after lunch, Dad? I need to get this mountain of books sorted for the opening tomorrow."

Leaving the women, he made his way out of the compound. He headed towards Congo Cross and then when he was sure no one saw him go, he changed direction and made his way to the clinic run by the Italian doctors. Inside, he sought out the young man who had provided the AIDS test over a month ago. He explained why he was back and the youthful doctor nodded.

"I can do the test – *nessun problema,*" he said. "But the lab technician is away. You will have to wait a day or two for the results."

Barney grimaced. "My friend and I are leaving late tomorrow – sailing for Canada."

The young man shrugged. "You will 'ave to delay, perhaps."

# CHAPTER 57

Barney took the AIDS test, then left the clinic distracted, unable to figure out his next move. Now that his future would be decided in the next two days, he could no longer avoid thinking about it. If the test result showed him to be HIV positive, what would he do?

He could stay on here and make a life with Cassie, Zinadine and Landon, helping out with the orphanage and school, he supposed. At some point the truth would have to come out and he didn't relish trying to justify his behaviour to his daughter. But perhaps she could accept it. Daughters were notoriously forgiving. Nonetheless, he didn't look forward to it.

His time in Africa was over. He felt he had now to move on. His children had only a peripheral need of him and he hadn't entirely finished his 3rd Age explorations. He recalled Ram Dass saying that 'ageing has another agenda.'

What he wanted to do was go back to Vancouver and take his boat, the *Sea Mist,* over to build the retreat centre on Vosges, in the Gulf Islands. It would be a working retreat project for defining 3rd Age roles for over-sixties – a real community, based on ageing and change. But would he last long enough to complete it? Or even have the energy to carry it out? He couldn't decide but he knew he had to make the attempt.

Besides, he told himself, he might not have the HIV virus at all. He knew his propensity for opting for the doom and gloom scenarios – Alice had told him that often enough. So then, another reason for going ahead with his dream, regardless. He remembered Sartre's dictum, that one should always act *as if* life had meaning.

He returned to the compound to collect Cassie and the two of them slipped off to walk down the sandy track to Lakka Beach. They sat under one of the bamboo beach umbrellas, gazing out at Clive's old boat. *The Betsy* tugged gently at its anchor in the clear green waves lapping the dazzling white beach.

Cassie finished recounting her experiences with the boy gang and its leader. "Things happened that I haven't told Zinadine about, Dad. It would only cause unnecessary suffering – for both of us. Isn't that what you said the Buddha taught – don't cause unnecessary suffering? When I thought I was going to die, I used to say to myself, how would Dad handle it and that helped me not to panic."

"I never thought I was much good as a role model for you, compared to your mother," said Barney.

"I didn't see it in male/female terms – more like what's important and what's irrelevant – the way you taught us."

"Don't sweat the small stuff, you mean? Your mother says I love to pontificate – says I can never resist the opportunity to point the moral."

Cassie stirred the white sand with her bare feet like a small child. "That's only a tiny part of it. What I mean is, how you believed in me and gave me the backbone to take chances. I'm timid and shy by nature but I felt stronger knowing you supported me, in whatever I did. Netta said you did the same for her, when she went searching for her real father."

Barney smiled ruefully. "Too bad I couldn't do the same thing for Hunter. Your mother says I cut him loose too soon and he lost his way."

"Hunter had to find his own way back – or forward. I guess boys have it tougher than girls in some ways. Zinadine is nothing like the rest of his family."

"He knows how to make you happy. He's learned that much anyway, Cassie. It's enough to be going on with, I think."

"Mother doesn't think so. I haven't told her yet that I'm pregnant but I wanted you to know. I want to make sure you have a good reason to come back here soon."

Barney felt a sudden urge to ask if she was sure it was Zinadine's and not the boy gang leader's. Instead he hugged her and said, "My first grandchild – I hope she's like her mother."

"Don't wish that on her, Dad – all the mistakes and bad choices I've made."

"Did your mother tell you her decision on the voyage out?"

Cassie nodded, "She told both Netta and I together. Netta says she's going to adopt, as she can't conceive anyway." She studied the sand trickling between her toes, not looking at him. "I'm hoping it will be a boy."

"Will you tell Zinadine – about the genetic thing?"

" Maybe – one day. Not yet."

They returned along the beach past the ruined grandeur of the abandoned colonial mansions, collapsing into the sand dunes. They cut across the tidal pools and back up to the rutted dirt road to Landon's compound. Cassie was swept up into the final rush to organise the school for the opening the next day.

Barney made his way to the corner of the compound where Heck and Clive and Hassani's team sweated over the fairground equipment. It looked a hopeless jumble to him and he sat down beside George, who pored over the plans.

"Doesn't look like this is going to happen in time for the grand opening, George," he said.

George pushed back his straw hat with a grease-smeared hand.

"We've still got over twelve hours, Barney. Hassani and his workers are amazing. You'd think they put these things together every week. Heck reckons they must be used to patching stuff up and working with old-fashioned equipment."

"Will I just be in the way, George, or can I do anything to help?"

George nodded towards a stack of boxes all carefully labelled, piled under a nearby palm tree. "Remember that old train set you and I built for Hunter and Netta? Heck helped me pack it up to bring along for the kids here. We've got no time to re-assemble it now – unless you want to do it. Maybe Hunter will remember how it goes together."

They worked on into the cool of the evening, with the children getting more and more excited as the huge old merry-go-round began to take shape. By morning of the big day, it stood gleaming and shimmering in the sunlight. The women came to admire their handiwork, exclaiming and offering extravagant praise to the tired workmen. Even the silent Hassani allowed himself a smile of satisfaction. The children stroked the bright-painted manes of the gallopers, each selecting their own favourite.

Alice voiced the question everyone was thinking. "But will it work, Heck?"

"We'll have to wait and see when the government switches on the power," he said.

"What time will that be?" asked Cassie.

"Lottie said they told her six pm," said Hunter.

"Where is she, anyway?" asked Barney.

"Gone to pick someone up from the airport," said Clive. "Probably some official she's invited to the opening."

The day passed in a mass of last-minute preparations. Hunter and Barney unpacked the train set in the middle of the open schoolroom floor. Grace and the children strung home-made decorations everywhere about the compound, from the open-sided school building to the clinic, huts and main entrance. Even the Unimog got its share.

Ama, tucking her unruly bosom into her floppy boubou, came to find Barney. She wanted him to go down to meet the fishermen on Lakka Beach and bring her back some barracuda for her fish stew specialty.

"Go ahead, Dad," said Hunter. "I've got Ahmed to help me. Raoul's fitted him with his new leg."

"I'll go with you, Barney," said Alice. "I need a break from Mother and Netta's relentless book sorting."

They carried large woven straw baskets to bring back the fish in and Barney showed her the way along the shore, past the old ruined mansions toppling into the sea near Lakka

Beach. The fishermen hadn't yet landed their catch and the local women stood about in groups, waiting for the high-prowed wooden dugouts as they jockeyed for position. Barney and Alice sat back under the palm trees that leaned drunkenly over the beach. They watched the pirogues prowling back and forth, before one suddenly turned to ride a big wave up onto the beach.

The heavy wooden fishing boats needed many hands to manoeuvre up the shore and everyone pitched in, making use of successive waves to inch the boats crabwise up from the water's edge. As each pirogue came ashore the others cruised offshore, waiting their turn to land.

"That's what you call a community effort," said Barney, watching fascinated by these choreographed landings.

Alice leaned back against a palm tree trunk, shading her eyes with her hand. "Maybe next time around you'll come back as an African fisherman, Barney."

"And you – what will you become, Alice?"

"Nothing so ambitious," she said. "Maybe something from the plant kingdom," she stroked the trunk of the tree. " A nice palm on a desert island somewhere, with no people."

"That's not your style at all. I see you as something showy – a flame-red bougainvillea, maybe."

She smiled at him and patted his arm. "I'm going to miss you when you go back to Canada, Barney."

"I doubt that – now that you and Heck are over the worst. In a way I wish I was going to North Africa with you, instead of Vancouver."

"'Over the Top on Hannibal's Elephant' – that's what Heck's going to call his next book," she said.

"Sounds like a blockbuster to me. I want a signed copy."

She rummaged in her straw basket. "I've got something even better for you – signed by me," she said, handing him a folded document.

"The *decree absolute,*" he said, opening it.

"Just what you always wanted, Barney."

"Not always."

"No. Perhaps not. Anyway, you're a free agent at last. You can pursue your 3rd age exploring unencumbered, now."

"I think this next stage is going to be more reflective than active, Alice. This African venture has worn me out."

"And did you gain lots of insights travelling round the fabled Dark Continent?"

"Lots of experiences – I'm still waiting for the insights," he said.

"Perhaps they'll come in your reflective stage – sitting in your island retreat in B.C. Or on the way back on *The Betsy* with Clive." She nodded towards Clive's old yacht, riding easily on the glittering waves beyond the prowling fishermen's dugouts.

"Are you happy to leave Cassie here in Freetown with Zinadine?" he asked.

Alice sighed. "Resigned, I suppose. I can't deny Zinadine is devoted to her."

"Will you come back after your Moroccan trip to spend time with them here?"

Alice nodded. "And you?"

"Perhaps I'll wait until I have a grandchild to visit."

They made their way down to the fishing boats and collected two huge barracuda for Ama, before heading back to the compound. As they approached the gates, a large black

Mercedes pulled up beside them and a long white arm waved out the window. Lottie leaned out and called "*Regardez*!" Beyond her, the round beaming face of Suleiman appeared at the wheel of the big car. She indicated the back seat and Barney half-expected to see the Cultural Minister. Instead he looked at the grinning faces of two teenage boys.

"Mason! – and Gareth," said Barney. "My god – how did you get here?"

"Lottie and Russell arranged it with Landon," explained Gareth, his face glowing almost as red as his hair from the heat.

"Landon said we could stay as long as we liked," added Mason, the younger one.

"I think Russell was glad to have us go since Maddy died last month," said Gareth.

Barney absorbed this news, as the big black car drove on into the compound. The two boys piled out and pounced on the waiting Landon.

Maddy dead. He knew he should have expected it – she had warned him she didn't have much longer. He felt suddenly empty and bereft. This tall brave woman, with her brightly coloured turbans covering her bald head had meant more to him than he realised at the time. And now she was gone, with no formal goodbyes. Was this how it would happen with him, he wondered? Gone, with only a passing comment before the rest of the world moved on?

# CHAPTER 58

The government minister arrived in a white Land Cruiser but no fanfare or cavalcade of vehicles, usual with African leaders. The next two hours saw more and more people pour into the compound and then the feasting began with Ama triumphant, presiding over her team of helpers. Scatterings of children tested out their new-found mobility on Raoul's improvised limbs.

Cassie, Zinadine and the minister led the tour of inspection of the school, clinic and compound, ending up at the silent waiting carousel. Heck and George took over, explaining the intricacies of the calliope while kids claimed their steeds, anticipating the power that would bring the gallopers to life. Hunter had recruited Mason and Gareth to help assemble the train set, also waiting for the electricity.

With still an hour to go until dusk and the switching-on ceremony, Barney slipped off once again to the *Médecins sans Frontières* clinic. It was closed, with only an old African caretaker sitting quietly outside in the fading light.

"No doctor here?" he asked the old man.

"Mebbe tonight – mebbe tomorrow," said the old caretaker. "You want me to take a message?"

Barney's spirits slumped as his fate was delayed once more. He and Clive had already planned to slip off with the outgoing tide at dawn – would he have to go without knowing the outcome of the AIDS test? It could take them several weeks at sea to reach Barbados – weeks that he might be taking some kind of medication, if he was HIV positive. He scrawled his name on a scrap of paper followed by the one word 'Results?' and left it with the old man, then dawdled back to the compound in the gathering darkness.

A sudden shout greeted him as the compound sprang into light. The cultural minister had thrown the power switch and tiny lights sprinkled the darkness. In the corner where the shout had come from, the old fairground organ calliope wheezed into life. Barney watched as the gallopers moved into slow motion, gliding up and down and forward. The adults cheered from the sidelines as the children clung to the necks of their horses, with a mix of fear and delight. Hunter dodged in and out, abandoning the train set to film the squealing children.

For the next two hours George and Heck started, stopped and reloaded the merry-go-round. An endless string of impatient children of all ages from the local community waited, as priority went to the amputees, being boosted up onto the gallopers. Some of the smaller children, overcome with the unexpected excitement, cried and clung to Grace and Cassie. Barney saw Netta comforting two small boys and went over to speak to George. He nodded, went to join Martha and Clive took over the controls.

The huge roundabout slowed to a stop and now the adults took the places of the children on the gallopers. Grace, Raoul and Netta with her foster-child Zena, climbed into the swan boats and motioned for all the orphans to join them on the seats. Clive pushed the ornate clutch lever forward and the heavy fairground machine eased into slow motion.

Barney stood by himself, watching everyone smiling in anticipation, memories of childhood rides showing on their gleaming faces. The calliope churned out its wheezing repertoire as the painted gallopers posted past him.

Cassie and Zinadine, Martha and George, Landon and Azalea, Hunter and Lottie, Heck and Alice, Gareth and Mason, all waved to him as they flashed by, faster and faster. He stood mesmerised as the music rose and fell in time with the surging ranks of horses, bearing everyone he loved past him, until the faces merged into a blur and he realised tears were running down his cheeks. He turned to stumble into the darkness of the compound and walked back out the front gate.

In the sudden African night, he didn't at first recognise the old caretaker from the Italian doctors' clinic, approaching him up the sandy track. The old African peered at him, then held out his hand, holding a folded slip of paper. He said nothing, only nodded in the grave manner of the older people Barney had met throughout his journey here and walked back the way he came.

Barney stood in the middle of the road staring at the piece of paper for a long time before he unfolded it. There were only two words written in a scrawl. He walked back towards the flickering lights at the compound gate to read his future.

*HIV Negative.*

He was clear. Free.

For several moments he stood, gulping long deep meditation breaths, before moving out of the darkness back towards the light.

**THE END**

**A SINGLE STEP** is the third book in **THE 3RD AGE TRILOGY.**

The other two books are **IN HOT PURSUIT,** the first volume, set in Vancouver and London; and the second book, **THE BLUE-EYED BOY**, set in Vancouver, China, Tibet and Nepal.

They chart the travels and search of Barney and his wife Alice as they explore, each in their own way, living in the 3rd age of life, when family ties, work and career obligations are behind them but only the unknown lies ahead.

If you would like to read more about the whole trilogy, you can find free sample chapters of each book and details about ordering at the website: **www.3rdageworld.com**

**A SINGLE STEP** is the third book in **THE 3RD AGE TRILOGY.**

The other two books are **IN HOT PURSUIT,** the first volume, set in Vancouver and London; and the second book, **THE BLUE-EYED BOY**, set in Vancouver, China, Tibet and Nepal.

They chart the travels and search of Barney and his wife Alice as they explore, each in their own way, living in the 3rd age of life, when family ties, work and career obligations are behind them but only the unknown lies ahead.

If you would like to read more about the whole trilogy, you can find free sample chapters of each book and details about ordering at the website: **www.3rdageworld.com**

CPSIA information can be obtained at www.ICGtesting.com
232237LV00003B/3/P
9 780981 389530